Greene County Killer

A Jesse Watson Mystery

Ann Mullen

Afton Ridge Publishing
P.O. 162
Stanardsville, Virginia 22973

ISBN 13: 978-0-9725327-7-8

This book was printed in the United States—
Land of the free, home of the brave.

Book designed by Ann Mullen

Library of Congress Control Number:
2007910417

First Edition

Also by Ann Mullen

What You See

South River Incident

A Crying Shame

Middle River Murders

This book is dedicated to

ELSIE JOYNER & JOYCE HAYES

A lot can happen in four days...

CHAPTER 1

THE CHRISTMAS HOLIDAYS WERE in full swing, and we were planning a big get-together at our house for Christmas Eve. We had plenty to celebrate. Billy and I were married on Christmas Eve a year ago, and since then we've had a son, Ethan, now just four months old, and we adopted a little girl named Maisy who will have her first birthday in January. How she came to live with us is a story all in itself.

My sister, Claire, is finally divorced from Carl the jerk and is getting married in the spring to her fiancé, Randy Morgan. Randy's the son of Abigail and Pete Morgan, two wonderful folks who live next door to her in Washington, D.C. Abby's sister, Isabel, also lives with them. You put those two women together and you have yourself a real handful. I met the Morgan family a few months back during one of my snooping excursions.

Billy's sister, Beth, and her husband, Adam are expecting their first child in the early part of the summer and the whole clan is waiting for the happy day.

Mom survived an attack by a revenge seeking serial killer out to get everyone near and dear to our new friend, Daisy Clark. Daisy was a member of an elite social club in Stanardsville, but the group is now defunct thanks to the death of a couple of its members who were hunted down and murdered by said killer. That was another scary time in our lives.

Fortunately, everyone in the family is still alive—and considering the many diverse and dangerous occupations in this family—that leaves something to be said.

Hello. My name is Jesse Watson. Welcome to my world.

I moved to the beautiful mountains of Virginia a few years ago with my folks, and my life changed forever. Unfortunately, on a sadder note, my dad died shortly after we moved to Stanardsville. It took Mom a long time to come to terms with his death, but eventually her grieving became less and less, and then she met Eddie. Eddie is a nice guy and hopefully, Mom will now have a companion for the future.

I dated Cole James, a Greene County deputy, but after a couple of months, that relationship went south. Then I married his best friend (and the guy I was working for), Billy Blackhawk—Cherokee Indian/private investigator. It turns out that Billy is the man of my dreams. He's not exactly the kind of man I was expecting to end up with, but I'm sure glad I did. He's sixteen years older than me and he's been around the block. Sometimes he's too smart for his britches, but that keeps me grounded. I can't imagine my life without him. Because of him and Cole, who are doing their best to rebuild their friendship, I got my P.I. license, and now work with Billy hunting down bad guys and snooping on little old ladies.

Billy and I live in the house he built when he was married to his first wife, Ruth. I don't mind that, because the way I figure it, she's the one who gave up a wonderful man, and I'm the one who was lucky enough to snag him. Since I moved in, we've added several rooms to the two story house and I have made it my own.

The Blackhawk Compound, as Billy's family refers to it, is huge. Located on the outskirts of Charlottesville, deep in Albemarle County, the land was divided into sections so that all of the Blackhawk children could build a house on it and live close to their parents. Chief Standing Deer Sam and his wife, Sarah, raised four boys and two girls, and it turns out that all of the brothers still live on the compound. A long time ago, they helped build nice houses for their two sisters, but it turned out that neither one of the sisters liked the seclusion, so they eventually moved to the city.

Bear Mountain Road leads into the Blackhawk Compound, and the private road keeps unwanted visitors out most of the time, but not today.

Today, our private world was invaded.

As tradition has it, the Blackhawk men would go out a week or two before Christmas and kill a deer. They would skin it and then prepare it to be frozen so that it would be ready for the Christmas dinner. This year, Billy and his brothers had killed two deer and were patting each other on the back as they skinned it in the garage. Cole was also there, and Chief Sam was present to supervise the operation.

Billy called me to the garage to see what they were doing. He was so proud.

Of course, this almost made me sick to think of, let alone watch. I was expecting to lose my dinner if I stayed any longer. They all laughed at me when I said something about Bambi's mother.

"It tastes just like beef," the chief said.

"You eat steak, don't you?" Jonathan asked.

"Yes, but that's different."

"How so?"

"Ah…"

"Come on, admit it, Jesse," Cole said. "You've had deer before, and you liked it. Your mother is the one we had to convince to eat it."

"Yeah, she's kind of funny about eating one of God's creatures, as she calls them." I had to laugh at myself for being so silly about the whole Bambi thing. "Deer meat is good."

"It's great," Daniel said. "If it is prepared right it can be a real delight, a feast for all."

"You got that right," Robert added. "I own a restaurant. I know."

"Thanks for bringing me out here, Billy," I said. "But I think I've seen enough." I looked at the remains of the two deer hanging upside down with those sad eyes, and that was it for me. "I'm leaving. Don't let me stop you guys from doing your thing." I turned and headed out of the garage.

Billy stepped in front of me, kissed me on the cheek, and winked.

"We're just about finished. All we have left to do is clean up. I love you, `ge ya."

"I love you, too… *u-we-ji-a-ska-`ya*."

"Hey, that was pretty good," Chief Sam said. He smiled. "Your Cherokee is getting better. I knew we'd make a good squaw out of you eventually."

The guys chuckled.

I walked away, waving to the men as I tromped through the snow that
had fallen the day before. Winter was setting in, and as usual, snow covered the ground. It wasn't snowing now, but according to the weather
report, it would be soon. It does that here—snows one day and then snows
again the next day. And before you know it, ten or twelve inches have
accumulated.

Billy closed the door behind me, but I could still hear their laughter. I
felt right at home with these guys, even my ex-boyfriend, Cole.

I was reminiscing as I walked up the steps to the front porch. I cinched
my coat against the cold, turned, and then stood there looking out into the
distance.

The driveway was filled with cars and the garage was filled with a
bunch of crazy men. Soon the house would be filled with both our fami-
lies celebrating Christmas, and the merriment would be so heart warming.
I loved family gatherings. Life couldn't get much better, I thought to myself.

Light snow began to fall, and I had to smile at the fact that I had just
thought about the possibility of another round of the white stuff. You see,
I love the snow. It makes things seem so homey and picturesque. We had a
couple of inches on the ground already, but hadn't had any major snowfall
so far. Usually, by Christmas it would've snowed several times, but not
this year. This year, I think Mother Nature was saving it all up for one big
blizzard. I was waiting for that time to come.

When I left to go to the garage with Billy, Mom and Billy's mother,
Sarah, were inside doting over Ethan and Maisy, while they discussed
important matters such as my sister's upcoming wedding and the soon-to-
be new addition to the family. Athena and Thor were curled up by the
fireplace, as usual, and Spice Cat lay on the mantel just waiting for a
chance to get into something—or tease the two dogs.

Oh, the family pets got along just fine, but sometimes they needed a little extra attention, so they would lie in wait and then when you least expect it, they would jump up and tear through the house like a bunch of wild animals.

I expected it was about that time, so I prepared myself for the assault. I turned and grabbed the doorknob, but instead of heading into a war zone inside, I was shaken by a rumble outside.

An explosion off in the distance shook the porch beneath my feet and lit up the sky. I stumbled and had to grab onto the railing for support. I felt as if I was on a ship in rough seas. The vibration didn't last long and once I steadied myself, I looked up to see a sky full of red flames above the trees. A plume of black and grey smoke followed. The explosion was almost deafening, and it had come from the direction of Jonathan's house!

"Oh, my God!" I screamed as I ducked down. "What's happening?" I grabbed the door, shoved it open, and then ran inside.

The dogs were howling and running around in circles, while Spice Cat jumped on every piece of furniture in the house, meowing.

Mom and Sarah met me at the door, each holding one of the kids. "What was that?" Mom screeched.

"Are my guys all right?" Sarah wanted to know.

"I don't know what happened," I said as I looked around. "Is everyone okay in here?"

"We're fine," Mom said. "What about Billy and..."

"Stay here," I demanded. "I'll go check on them."

I had barely gotten the words out of my mouth when Billy burst through the front door. He looked around to see if everyone was okay.

"We're fine," I said to him. "Billy, what was that?"

"I don't know, but I'm sure going to find out. I want all of you, and that includes you, Jesse, to stay in the house while we see what happened."

"But..."

Billy turned to me and put his hands on my shoulders. "I want you to stay here and look after everyone. Lock the door and don't open it to anyone until I get back. This is serious, Jesse."

"What do you think happened? Is someone after Jonathan... or us? Is there something you haven't told me?"

I knew Billy pretty well by now, and I knew that sometimes he would keep things from me to protect me. Only at the last minute and only if he had to, would he tell me what was going on. That drove me crazy, but I had come to live with his ways because he was usually right.

"What's going on?" I demanded. "I know you're hiding something from me. I can tell by the look on your face. Now what is it?"

"We think someone just blew up Jonathan's house, but we're not sure. We're going over to check it out."

"I thought that came from Jonathan's house!" I said as I looked at Mom and then Sarah.

They stood silently, hugging the children.

The dogs had settled down and Spice Cat had gone back to his place on the mantel as if nothing had happened. Animals are strange creatures.

"Shouldn't we call the fire department, son?"

"Cole already did, Mom," Billy replied. "He was on his cell phone the minute the explosion occurred."

A car horn blared outside.

"I have to leave. Now I want you ladies to stay here, and I'll call you as soon as we find out anything." He looked at me and said, "Take care of them."

"I will," I said, almost in tears. "Be careful, Billy."

He kissed the kids, Mom, and Sarah, and then hugged me before he turned and walked out the door.

We heard the slamming of car doors and engines racing. Once the men were gone, the three of us stood in one spot dumbfounded, trying to figure out what to do next.

I was scared and I knew this wasn't going to be good. If that was Jonathan's house that had just gone up in flames, we were all in for a hard night. I looked at Mom and Sarah and said, "Let's go to the family room and try to calm down. We can watch television. Billy will take care of everything."

"I can't believe you're not running after him," Mom said. She looked at me as if she was trying to figure out what was wrong with me. "You want to go watch T.V. at a time like this?"

"What else can I do? Billy told me to stay here."

"When did that ever stop you before?" Sarah chimed in. "Get your gun and go be with your husband. I know you want to. You're partners. That's what partners do. They stick together. We can take care of ourselves."

"But…"

"Don't worry about what Billy will say," Mom added. "You can handle him. You always do. Besides, he might need you. Like Sarah said, you're not just his wife, you're his business partner. I think the name on the office door says Blackhawk & Blackhawk, doesn't it?"

"I can't believe that the two of you are encouraging me to do this. You know Billy will have a fit."

"He'll get over it," Sarah said, agreeing with Mom.

I hesitated, and then said, "I really want to go, but I promised Billy I would stay here, so I'd better stay here. We'll wait a little while and if we don't hear anything, then maybe I'll go over there."

"You sure have settled down," Mom said, grinning. "I told you that having children would change your life. See what I mean?"

"You were right, Minnie," I replied, calling her by her given name — a practice I used when I wanted to distract her. "You always are… just like my husband."

Sarah laughed at the two of us.

"You know better than to call me by my first name!" Mom chided me. "How many times have I told you not to do that?"

"Aw, Mom," I said as I reached over to hug her. "You know I love you."

Her attitude got a little puffy as she turned to Sarah and said, "I hope your children don't treat you like mine do."

"Of course, they do. You know how kids are. One minute they're just as sweet as they can be, and the next, they think they know everything. One thing is certain; they always keep you on your toes."

"I couldn't agree more."

They turned and headed toward the back of the house to the family room. Sarah stopped in mid-stride, turned, and asked, "Are you coming, Jesse?"

"Yes, I am, but only if y'all promise to behave yourselves and stop talking about how your children drive you nuts. None of us are like that." I snickered nervously.

My stomach was tied in knots, but I was doing what I could to make the best of what was sure to be a horrific situation. Why would someone blow up Jonathan's house? I thought about the type of people he comes in contact with and then realized the many enemies he could have. Jonathan is a bounty hunter—that says it all.

Then I had another thought. Maybe the heater exploded. Yeah, maybe that's what happened. Perhaps the pilot light went out and… I was just trying to rationalize the situation, but discovered that since I didn't know what the situation was, there was no rationalizing that would do me any good. I just had to wait to see what had happened.

One long, long hour passed without a word. We could hear the sirens in the background. Several times we went to the front door to look out.

Ethan and Maisy were down for the night, so we tried to make small talk while we waited. But small talk is nothing but useless chatter. I wanted information. I was frantic and had reached the end of the line. I had to do something.

Mom and Sarah all but pushed me out the door when I said, "Okay, I've waited long enough. I'm going over there. Where's my gun?"

CHAPTER 2

W E TIPTOED PAST THE CHILDREN'S ROOM as the three of us headed toward the front door. I made a quick stop by my bedroom, went in and retrieved my gun and handbag. Mom and Sarah chatted anxiously as they stood by the bedroom door waiting for me.

Once at the front door, I grabbed my coat from the coat hanger and was poised, ready to brave the cold and whatever else waited outside. Hopefully, nothing bad had happened. That's what I kept telling myself.

I put on my coat and was just about ready to go outside when a set of car headlights came up the driveway. I quickly took off my coat and hung it back on the rack.

Mom and Sarah also saw the headlights and looked at me with that look in their eyes.

"Hurry up and look busy before Billy gets here," Mom said. "We don't want him to know…"

"I'm already ahead of you, Mom." I ran to my bedroom to stash my purse and then rejoined them.

Mom, Sarah, and I went to the kitchen and were going to pretend to be doing something other than what we were going to do when a knock at the door startled us.

"Who's that?" Mom asked.

"I don't know," I answered.

"Billy wouldn't knock at his own house," Sarah added.

We stared at each other before I finally stepped foreword to go answer the door. I reached over, pulled the curtain back, and then peeked through the front window. I let out a sigh of relief.

"It's just Geneva," I said.

"What's she doing here?" Sarah asked. "I thought they were on vacation. They're supposed to be in South Carolina."

"She's here now," I replied as I grabbed the doorknob.

Geneva is Sarah's sister and when we were in the process of adopting Maisy, she showed up at our front doorstep with her estranged husband, Eli, wanting to be a part of the child's life. Not only did she accomplish that, but Sarah and Chief Sam sold them a piece of land on the compound, and Billy and his brothers helped build them a house. So now they are back in the fold.

It seems that Geneva and Eli had long ago parted ways, but were brought back together once their son and his wife died. Actually, Vicki Cherry was raped and murdered, and then Brian Cherry killed himself. But before Brian killed himself, he asked Billy to take care of his child. Brian was Billy's cousin and family, and nothing was more important than family to Billy.

Billy had learned that the hard way. His ex-wife Ruth left him because he spent more time on the job trying to make a living than he did with her and their two boys. He swore that would never happen again. It was too late to fix their marriage, but he made a point of being there for his boys as they grew up. Will just graduated from the University of Virginia and is doing an internship at the hospital, and John has one more year to go at Virginia Tech. Billy is so proud. We're hoping that the boys will join us for our Christmas celebration.

I opened the door and greeted Geneva. A gust of cold air rushed in.

"Whew! It's cold out there," she said as she shook off the snow.

"Where's Eli?" Sarah asked as she peeked around Geneva, looking for him. "Didn't he come over with you?"

"Oh, he's at home in bed," she replied. "The trip wore him out. That's what he said, but I know the truth. He likes to travel, but he hates to go visit my friends. He thinks they're pretentious. He says there's not an honest one in the bunch, but that's not true. They've been my friends since childhood, and I see no reason to give them up just because he doesn't like them."

"Come on in and take off your coat before you freeze," I said and then looked over at Mom. "Why don't you make a fresh pot of coffee?" I looked back at Geneva. "How about a nice piece of pie? Mom makes the best..."

"Hold on a minute!" Geneva exclaimed. "What's going on at Jonathan's? I tried to go over and see what was happening, but they have it barricaded. The cops are everywhere. Jonathan isn't hurt, is he? I heard an explosion, but I wasn't sure where it came from until I saw the flames. They were shooting way up into the sky. I tried to wake Eli and get him to go see, but he wouldn't get up. He didn't even hear the explosion. He could sleep through anything. He told me to forget about it. He said nothing was wrong, but I knew better. You don't have a blast like that and have nothing to be wrong. Where is Jonathan?"

"Thank goodness he was here when the explosion occurred," Sarah replied. "I'd hate to think what would've happened if he'd been at home."

I could see the look of fear in her eyes. The thought had never crossed my mind that Jonathan could be dead right now. My stomach churned.

"That's it! I'm going over there. It's been over an hour and nobody has even called. Why don't you ladies sit down and have some coffee and pie? I'm going to check on the kids and then I'm leaving."

"You go now," Sarah said. "We'll check on the kids."

"Yeah, we'll check on the kids," Geneva said. "I had a wonderful time visiting with my friends, but I missed my granddaughter. I'm so glad to be back at home, and I'm dying to see Maisy."

Dying is not a word you use in the company of three women who have been sitting around waiting to hear news about a catastrophe. I ran back to my bedroom, grabbed my purse, and headed to the front door. I pulled my coat off the rack and grabbed the doorknob.

"Do you have your cell phone?" Mom asked.

"No, I forgot about it."

Sarah walked over to the table in the living room, picked it up out of the charger, and then brought it to me. "Be sure to call us the minute you find out anything."

"I will," I said as I buttoned my coat.

"Don't get into trouble," Mom added. "I don't want to have to come bail you out of jail."

I gave Mom the eye.

"You do have a tendency to open your mouth at the most inopportune time and it gets you into trouble. If the police won't let you pass, just come back home. Don't do anything irrational."

"Har... har."

"I mean it, Jesse. I don't want you to get shot."

"I'm not going to get shot, Mom. Don't be silly. I'm family. They'll let me through. I'll tell them who I am, and they'll wave me right on by."

"Don't bet on it," Geneva said. "They wouldn't let me pass."

Mom grinned. "You don't know my daughter. She doesn't take no for an answer."

"That's for sure," Sarah agreed. "She'll get in. I'd bet on it. I've yet to see anyone get in her way... not even a cop. I've seen how she handles them. Detective Trainum adores her. He's a hardened cop; I could tell from some of the stories he told, but Jesse had him eating out of her hands."

"That's because he knows my daughter has a good heart."

"Okay. I'm out of here. Lock the door behind me. We don't know what the situation is, so to be on the safe side, we're not taking any chances. Considering what seems to happen to this family, nothing would surprise me."

"Everything's going to be fine," Mom said, trying to reassure everyone.

"I'm sure," I said. I figured that later I might wind up eating those words, but for now I was going to try to keep only good thoughts in my head. With that said, I took my leave. I heard the deadbolt click behind me. As soon as I stepped out onto the front porch I smelled the acrid air. The pungent odor burned my nostrils as I grabbed the collar of my coat and pulled it over my nose. Nothing was going to stop me from my mission, not even that funky smell. I could just imagine what the guys must be going through if they were breathing in that caustic odor. I hoped that Billy had his handkerchief with him. That's all I could think about as I made my way to my Toyota 4Runner.

A while back I had gotten rid of my red Jeep. I loved that automobile, but too many bad things had happened to me in it. So one day Billy brought home a brand new Toyota 4Runner for me. It was black as night, and I couldn't have been happier.

Billy was always doing things to make me happy. It was his way. He said he would never neglect his wife again like he did with Ruth, and he has stuck by his words. Sometimes he would bring me flowers for no reason, and he always had a smile on his face. How could you not cherish a man like that?

I just turned thirty-four in September, and Billy will be fifty-one come next June. It took me forever to get him to tell me when his birthday was, but I finally pried it out of him. Even though he's several years older than I am, I still think he's the sexiest man alive. I love him. What can I say? He's Cherokee and has the dark skin and long hair you'd expect to see on an Indian. He's tall and muscular, just like his three brothers. From the back you can hardly tell them apart. Now Chief Sam is a different story. I think he's shrunk with age. I had to laugh at that thought.

I made my way to where my Toyota was parked and climbed inside. It was cold, but it didn't take long to heat up. Seconds later, I was backing up and heading down the long driveway. I was nervous and didn't know what to expect, but I was determined not to be deterred. I would get through and find out what had happened. Nobody was going to stop me.

I made a right turn at the end of the driveway, and it wasn't long before I reached Jonathan's driveway on the left side of the road. I stopped in the middle of the road and looked around. There was no one there. The road was open. Ah, ha! I thought. This is going to be a piece of cake. I turned into the driveway and was coming around the bend where the road curves and was immediately confronted by two Charlottesville Police cars. Up the road a ways was an Albemarle County Sheriff's car. A Channel 29

News car and a van with a huge antenna on top were parked alongside the driveway.

Through the trees, I could see the flashing lights of the fire truck and other emergency vehicles.

A police officer held up his hand while another one came up to my car. "I'm sorry, ma'am, but you're going to have to turn around. You can't go in there unless you're emergency personnel. The smoke is still thick and it's not safe."

Before I could respond, a newsman with a microphone and a guy with a camera stepped up beside the officer. The guy with the microphone shoved it into my car window and began asking questions as the light from the camera glared in my eyes.

"Who are you?" the guy with the microphone asked. "Are you related to the owner? Do you know anyone who would have a grudge against Jonathan Blackhawk? Being a bounty hunter, I'm sure he's made a lot of enemies in his line of work. Do you know who would do this?" He fired questions, one after another at me, but didn't give me time to answer any of them.

The police officer got between them and me, and then politely asked the men to step back.

The two men complied.

"I'm Jesse Watson-Blackhawk and this is my brother-in-law's place. I live right up the road."

"Oh, you must be Billy's wife," the officer said. "We were told to keep an eye out for you. Captain Waverly said you'd be coming."

"What made your captain think that I would show up? He doesn't know me that well."

"I don't know anything about your relationship with our captain, but here you are."

"I can see that I'm going to have to have a talk with him. Is my husband all right? What about the rest of the guys? What happened? Did Jonathan's house burn down?" I sounded just like the reporter.

The officer didn't respond. He walked off and became engaged in a conversation with someone on his shoulder walkie-talkie.

"Are you going to let me pass?" I yelled to him.

"I'm afraid not, Mrs. Blackhawk," the second officer walked over and said. "It's a real mess back there and it's not safe." He pointed in the direction of Jonathan's house.

"How bad is it?"

"Let's just say that the fire department's got their hands full."

"I promise…"

"No way," the officer said. "You're going to have to leave."

"Okay, now I'm really ticked off," I mumbled. "I don't have to leave. I can sit right here."

"If you want to pull off to the side, we can't stop you. But we have to keep the road clear for fire and rescue personnel. You're going to have to move your vehicle, or I'm afraid that I'm going to have to arrest you."

"You know that if you don't let me through, I'm just going to pretend to leave and then park my car down the road and walk through the woods. That could be dangerous. It's snowing, it's dark, and I could get hurt — and it would be your fault. Are you willing to take the blame for my being injured?"

The other policeman chuckled.

"What's he laughing about? I don't think it's a bit funny," I yelled as I stuck my head out the window.

I began to muster up a few tears. I was slightly irked at the cop and his captain. I had to get past these guys. Now it had become a quest. I don't like it when someone tries to tell me what I can and cannot do. I'll show them.

"We were told that you would probably show up and try to get by, and that you would even cry to get your way."

The tears that I had been holding onto and was about ready to let spill out, dried up.

Aggravated, I pushed the button to roll up my window and put my gearshift in reverse. I backed the rest of the way down the driveway and out onto Bear Mountain Road… without running into a ditch.

Backing up is me at my worst. Nine times out of ten, I'll run off the road or into a pothole. I don't know what the problem is, but I just can't seem to get a grip on that part of car control. Maybe I should get aggravated more often.

I could've parked on the side of the driveway, but that would mean that the cops would be watching my every move, so I came up with a better plan. Once I got onto Bear Mountain Road, I pulled over and parked. I reached into my purse, dug out my cell phone, and then punched in the numbered key for Billy's cell phone. I was angry that Billy hadn't called. He knew we would be worried. How bad could it be? As I sat on the side of the road and listened to the phone ringing on Billy's end, an ambulance came rushing out of Jonathan's driveway with its lights flashing and siren blaring. Then another ambulance came rushing out right after.

"Oh, God," I said out loud. My heart started racing and I broke out in a cold sweat. What's happening? Who's hurt? My mind was out of control. Then I started to pray.

"Please Lord, don't let that be Billy… or Jonathan… or…"

Jonathan's Humvee came barreling out onto the road right behind the ambulance. He got so close to the emergency vehicle that it looked as if he was touching its bumper. A second later, Robert's Dodge pickup was bringing up the rear.

I waited for Billy's truck to follow… but it was nowhere to be seen.

The fake tears I had been saving up to use on the officers turned into real ones and started to flow like the South River after a heavy rain.

Where's my Billy? Why isn't his truck coming out?

He wasn't answering his cell phone. I broke the connection and then tried Jonathan's number. It rang several times before anyone answered.

"I can't talk right now, Jesse."

"How did you know it was me?"

"Dad told me before he handed me the phone."

"Then give the phone back to the chief, so I can talk to him."

There was a brief pause and then the chief answered. "Hello, Jesse." His tone was somber.

I could tell that he was in distress. The only time I'd ever heard him speak in a quiet voice like that was when something bad had happened, like the time Jonathan got shot by the same woman who had kidnapped my mother and tried to kill her.

Naomi Kent killed two members of the Stanardsville Social Club, an innocent bystander, and then tried to kill Daisy's husband, Gabe, and my mother. Her intentions were to kill everyone close to Daisy Clark and then finally kill Daisy. She was also, in an indirect way, responsible for the death of Kansas Moon, Daisy's brother. Jonathan just happened to be someone who got in her way, and he took a bullet for it. Fortunately, he made it through all right, and so did Gabe and my mother. Mom was saved by Sheriff Hudson and my dog, Athena. Athena ran off and when the sheriff, on a final check of the premises, found her outside Kansas Moon's house barking up a storm, he knew his search was over. I will always be indebted to him for rescuing my mother, and it goes without saying that Athena has P.I. potential. She and my other dog, Thor, make a good team.

The chief was very upset about his son and terribly disturbed by what happened to my mother. He told me that she's family and even offered his services as a spiritual healer. Sarah concurred. Occasionally, Mom will talk with him about religion. She's a Southern Baptist and devoted to her religion, but at the same time, she's very open-minded.

"Just tell me the truth, Chief Sam. Who's hurt?"

As if to gather up the nerve to tell me, he spoke slowly and distinctly, his Cherokee accent coming through. "The first ambulance carries an injured firefighter. The other one carries my sons, Daniel and Billy."

"Are they alive?" was all I could get out.

I had a sharp pain in my chest that rose up to my throat. My breathing became labored, and my head was on the verge of exploding. Either I was having a terrible anxiety attack or this was the real thing. The big one! I was having a heart attack. I just knew that I was going to die sitting right here in my car.

I gasped as I dropped the phone and dug in my purse for my bottle of little yellow pills. It was the only thing I could think of to do to keep from losing my mind. Like an addict getting ready for a fix, I unscrewed the cap, shook out one of them into the palm of my hand, and then popped it into my mouth, dry-swallowing it. I almost gagged trying to get the pill down. I looked over in the seat and saw a half-empty bottle of water left over from God-knows-when. I snatched up the bottle, unscrewed the cap, and then guzzled what was left. The water had small slivers of ice still left in it, probably left over from when it had started to freeze while sitting in an unheated car.

I picked the phone up from my lap and tried to chill out as I spoke. "Are Billy and Daniel going to be all right?"

"Billy was overcome by smoke and Daniel took a nasty fall. Hopefully, they will be okay. Both were being given oxygen. Daniel passed out, but Billy was still conscious when they put them in the ambulance."

"Should I go get Sarah and meet you at the hospital?"

"Yes, I think that would be a good idea," he replied. "Tell her the boys are going to be fine."

"Are they?" I was trying to get the chief to tell me what he really thought so I would know what to expect. I needed to put my mind at ease. But as always, he was tight-lipped and assumed the best.

"I hope so, but I do not know. We will know more before the sun comes up. This, I am sure." He paused for a minute and then continued. "Jesse, I am counting on you. You must not let me down. Please keep my wife calm. I worry about her."

I sat up straight and heeded his words. "You can count on me, Chief Sam." I closed up the cell phone and put the car in gear. I had to get home fast and then get us to the hospital in one piece.

It was snowing heavily by now and I could hardly see through the flakes, but at least I had regained my courage and control of my emotions. Now all I had to do was deal with that little yellow pill I had just taken. Normally, I'm not a pill-popper, but this wasn't a normal time.

I had stopped nursing Ethan at the beginning of December because something always got in the way, and then I'd have to run out of the house for one reason or another. I didn't think it was fair to him, and I was pleased that I got to nurse him for the few months that I had. Thank goodness for that, because tonight I popped that pill without thinking twice about it. I had to get a grip on my anxiety. People would be depending on me. I had to remain calm for the sake of my family.

CHAPTER 3

THE DRIVE UP TO MY FRONT PORCH seemed to take forever. The falling snow made visibility almost impossible, and the road was becoming treacherous. Our driveway was frozen and slick. I could just imagine what it was going to be like out on the main roads. Even an SUV can't stand up to icy roads. I knew something bad was going to come out of all of this. I could feel it. I especially had that eerie feeling the minute I stepped into the house.

Instead of barking wildly and acting like a bunch of loony animals, Athena and Thor met me with sad faces. They both sat together shivering as if they were cold, and the only sound they made was an occasional whimper.

I knew they weren't cold, and that they only acted like this when they sensed impending doom. We've been there before and they have never let me down. Dogs have a way of telling when things go awry... at least, mine did.

The butterflies in my stomach started flapping their wings faster.

"What are you doing home so soon?" Mom asked. "Did you find out anything? Where's Billy?"

"She didn't get past the cops," Geneva said, almost sarcastically.

I ignored her remark.

"I'm sorry I didn't call, but it was hectic over there," I replied. "Geneva's right. The cops wouldn't let me pass."

"I'm shocked," Mom said. "You didn't force your way in?"

"You didn't cry?" Sarah asked. "Crying always works for you. You said so yourself."

"Not this time. I could've raised a stink, or snuck through the woods, but I didn't. Instead, I backed out of the driveway and pulled off to the side of the road."

I walked to the kitchen and ran myself a glass of water from the tap. I stood by the sink and contemplated on how I was going to tell them about Billy and Daniel. From the feeling I got from Chief Sam, things were not good. I didn't bother to take off my coat.

"Let me fix you a cup of coffee," Sarah said, and went about doing so.

"Stop, Sarah. We don't have time for that. We need to get to the hospital. Billy and Daniel were overcome by smoke."

Mom immediately went into overdrive.

"I'll pack up a diaper bag." She walked over to the refrigerator and pulled out a bottle of formula for Ethan and then went to the cabinet for another can of the ready made mixture. "I knew something was wrong when you didn't take off your coat."

"Leave the kids with me," Geneva said as she walked over toward me. "I'll take care of them while the three of you go to the hospital."

Not on your life, lady. I was getting used to Geneva, but I still didn't trust her. Who would stay away from their grandchild just because the child's mother didn't like you? Not me. I didn't like that situation right from the get-go. I knew there was something else going on, but who was I to question? I kept my mouth shut when she showed up at our house a few months ago wanting to see Maisy, but I always kept it in the back of my mind that something smelled funny. I would give her time. After a while, everyone shows their true colors. So far, she hadn't done anything to make me believe that she had anything other than good intentions, but being the skeptic that I am...

Mom looked at me and saw that all too familiar look in my eyes. She obviously didn't trust the woman anymore than I did. That's my mother. She never says a bad word about anyone, but she'll think it. She has an uncanny way of seeing right through people. Most can't fool her. I know. I've tried many times, but she can always tell when I'm fibbing. I don't lie—I just stretch the truth.

"That's okay, Geneva. I'll stay," Mom said. "Jesse worries about me. She doesn't want me out in the snow or rain, or anytime the weather is bad. I know she's going to tell me to stay home, so instead of arguing at a time like this, I'm going to go ahead and do what she wants me to do. Am I right, Jesse?"

Mom was good at making up excuses that didn't hurt.

"You know me well. I surely don't want to drag the kids out on a night like this, and I'd feel better having someone who can spend the night. I don't know how long this is going to take. And the weather is pretty rough out there. The snow is really coming down."

"If you don't want me to watch your kids, why don't you just say so?" Geneva didn't sound ugly; she just wanted a truthful answer.

"Okay," I turned and said. "I know you're Sarah's sister, but I barely know you. Why would I trust my children with someone I don't know?"

"You have a point," she replied. "It takes time."

Guilt trip.

I rebounded.

"If you'd like to stay here with Mom, I'm sure she could use the company."

"Yes, I'd like that," Mom replied, backing me up. "We can watch television while we wait." Mom glanced over at Geneva and then back to me. "You will call the minute you hear something, won't you? You know I can't sleep when I'm worried."

"Yes, Mom. I'll call as soon as I find out how they are."

"Let me get my coat," Sarah said.

She walked over to the door, retrieved her coat, and then slipped into it. She pulled a scarf from one of the pockets and wrapped it around her neck. She reached over to the table by the door and grabbed her handbag. She stood waiting for me.

I put the glass in the sink and turned to leave. I hesitated for a second, and then spoke to Geneva.

"I don't mean to sound hateful, but I have a lot on my mind."

Geneva put her hand on my back and said, "It's all right, Jesse. After a while you'll come to see that I mean you no harm. I have no intentions of snatching Maisy and fleeing the state."

Stunned, I looked at her in disbelief.

"I'm nobody's fool. I know you don't trust me, but you will in time. You'll see that I only have Maisy's interest at heart. I love the child, and I know you do, too. All I want is for us to be a family, but I know that takes time. So far, I think I have plenty of that, but you never…"

I gave her a little hug just to let her know that I appreciated what she said, but then I turned and fled. I left her standing there still talking as I opened the door and walked outside. Knowing my mother as I do, she'd stand there and listen until Geneva got it all out, then she'd figure out a distraction.

Sarah and I jumped in my 4Runner and buckled up.

"This is going to be a rough ride," I said as I started the car.

"Not as rough as the one you just wiggled out of, I think."

I looked over at Sarah and said, "I'm sorry. I know she's your sister, but…"

"You don't trust her."

"That's right, I don't. But I'm willing to give her the benefit of the doubt. I've tried not to make snap judgments, but it's hard."

"And I think you've done well."

"You do?"

"Yes, I do." She reached over and patted me on the shoulder. "I know what it's like to have to earn trust. Remember, when I married the chief, I was the only white woman in the bunch. It took a long time before the rest of the family accepted me."

"I thought they all loved you. That's what the chief told me."

"He has a way of stretching the truth. The truth is, his mother, Noreen, used to make grunting noises the whole time she was around me. It's only now that she gives me the respect that I deserve."

"What made her change her mind about you?"

"I told her that she could think what she wanted to about me, but if she didn't show me respect in front of my family, she would die a lonely old lady without her son and grandchildren around for comfort, and that I'd tell anyone who would listen about how rude she was to me. She and I both knew her husband would have a fit if I told folks about her behavior."

"I guess it worked. She comes to all the family functions."

"It doesn't hurt that Joseph makes her behave."

"He's a nice man. He reminds me so much of Chief Sam."

"They are a lot alike."

"I'll try to be more tolerant, but I find it hard to believe she didn't insist upon seeing her only grandchild—the only one she has. I would've never let Vicki stand in my way. If that was really what the problem was. I don't know. I wasn't there."

"I was, and I can tell you that Vicki hated my sister from the moment they met. It was obvious. At the wedding, Geneva made a simple comment about losing her only son, like some mothers might do, and Vicki hit the roof. She accused Geneva of smothering Brian, and then said a few other harsh things. I'm so glad that Brian was in another room and didn't hear the ugliness. Vicki was a controlling woman. Don't get me wrong; I liked her, but she had a meanness about her that she saved just for my sister. I don't know where it came from, but to me it was apparent that she either got her way, or made life miserable for everyone around if she didn't. I tried to stay out of it. I held my tongue."

"You have never been one to raise your voice or be hateful to anyone. You and my mother are so much alike. I'm glad I have you for a mother-in-law. Actually, I don't even think of you as that. I consider you to be my second mom."

"I thought your Aunt Edie was your second mom."

"Oh, yeah. That's right." I smiled. "You can never have too many moms." I thought about Aunt Edie for a second. "I sure do miss her."

"You should give her a call."

"I already did. I invited her for Christmas, but Uncle Bill is too ill to travel."

"Is it his blood pressure again?"

"Actually, it has never stopped being about his blood pressure, but now he has other problems. She said they would try to make it for New Year's Eve. I told her about the fireworks display that you and the chief put on. She's looking forward to it."

"I will pray for your uncle."

"Please do. I worry about him. He doesn't let much slow him down, except when it comes to his health. He doesn't have much control over that. I pray for him all the time."

"Your mother's right about you. You have such a kind heart. I recognized that in you when we first met."

"Oh, you mean the time Billy dragged me to your vet clinic to have buckshot dug out of my shoulder. Boy, now that was a real trip. Here, I had just met him and already I allowed him to get me into all kinds of stuff."

"We took care of you."

"You sure did. I took a liking to both of you instantly."

"Do you mean me and the chief, or me and Billy?"

"All of the above."

"I thought so. I was hoping so, anyway. I saw something special in you. I knew there was chemistry there between you and Billy that you didn't recognize. I told the chief. He said he saw it, too. He said you would make a fine squaw for his son."

"Tsk... Tsk. So many secrets."

"We have a tendency to keep our feelings and thoughts to ourselves."

"I've noticed."

"Unlike you—a woman who wears her heart on her sleeve."

"Is that what you think?"

"Oh, yes. But that's the lovely thing about you. You're not a fake, and you speak your mind. I'm sure your mother wishes you wouldn't at times, but on the other hand, I know she gets a kick out of your fearless zest for life, and how you jump in with both feet. She's proud of you. She says that you're just like your dad. Every time she looks at you, she sees Mack."

"She told you that?"

"Yes."

"My dad was a wonderful man. I miss him so." My throat closed up and a tear spilled down my cheek. "I wish he was still here with us. He would've loved to see me so happy... married with children... and all."

"I'm sorry. I didn't mean to make you cry."

"It's not you," I said, fishing for a tissue in the console glove box.

"Here, let me get it. You need to watch the road. We don't want to end up in an ambulance being rushed to the hospital."

As soon as the words were out of her mouth, the two of us started crying. She handed me a tissue.

"Okay, no crying," I said as I dried my eyes. "I won't be able to see how to drive."

All of a sudden, Sarah let out a howl that startled me. She was wild and shaking terribly as she ranted. She shook her head and then put her hands to her ears.

Quickly, I found a driveway to pull into.

"What..."

She clinched her fist and beat on the dashboard. "I'm so tired of having one of my boys get hurt. I'm sick of running to the hospital and watching the doctors pull one of them back from the jaws of death. I'm sick of it, I tell you. Just sick of it!"

Sarah was having a major meltdown. I'd just got finished telling her how controlled she was and now she was anything but. I had to help her get though this if we were to proceed.

She cried for a few minutes and when the spell passed, she looked at me through sad eyes and said, "I have a bad feeling and it's tearing me apart."

"I have the same feeling, but I'm trying not to think bad thoughts. I don't know what to do about it, so I'm just going to tell myself that Billy and Daniel are going to be all right. They're Blackhawk boys, for Pete's sake! They can handle anything."

"You're absolutely right. What was I thinking?" She dried her tears and then stuffed the sodden tissue in her purse. "I'm ready to go."

I waited for the cars to pass and then pulled back out onto the road.

We rode in silence for a few miles before our fears surfaced again.

"Did you get to see anything while you were at Jonathan's?"

"No, I never made it any further than the first bend. All I could see was the smoke in the background. The cops weren't going to let me pass, so I backed down the driveway and pulled off to the side of the road."

Sarah let out a little laugh. "I can just see you now. I bet you were fit to be tied."

"I was frustrated... and fit to be tied. I only left because I wanted to get out of their sight. I knew I could come up with an idea if I had a chance to think it over. But I never got the time. A minute later, I looked in my rearview mirror and saw the ambulance... and then another. I couldn't reach Billy on his cell phone, and when I didn't see his truck behind the ambulances with Jonathan's Humvee and Robert's pickup, I knew something was wrong. I called Jonathan's cell phone and talked with the chief."

"What did he say?"

"He was quiet." I glanced over at Sarah for a second.

She looked up at me and said, "That's not good."

"My thoughts exactly. I couldn't get much out of him, except that Daniel and Billy were being taken to the hospital because of smoke inhalation. Daniel took a fall."

"That's really, really not good."

"I know. It reminded me of the time Jonathan got shot."

"Oh, yeah! He was hot as a firecracker, but his silence was more worrisome than his anger. I was afraid that he was going to have a stroke... seriously."

"He said they were going to be fine, but you know me. I'm a worrier."

"Me, too."

After another fifteen minutes of white-knuckle driving, I finally pulled into the parking garage across from the University of Virginia Hospital. At least, the pavement in the garage wasn't covered with snow, but getting across the crosswalk would be a different story. I had on a pair of tennis shoes, and when I got out of the SUV, I looked down at Sarah's feet and laughed.

"What is it?"

"I have on tennis shoes and you have on a pair of slip-on loafers. We'll be lucky to make it across the street without falling on our butts."

"I thought about my shoes when I got in the car. I wore these inside my boots, but I was in such a hurry, I forgot the boots. Fortunately, these shoes are made out of leather. I guess we'll just have to do the best we can."

"I guess so. Here, take my hand."

"I thought young folks didn't let your mama hold your hand."

"Not me, sugar. I ain't proud. Come on. Hold onto me. If one of us goes down—we both go down."

"Then we'd better hold onto each other, because at my age, if I fall, I can promise you that something's going to get broken."

The two of us shared a laugh as we held hands and crossed the street in the blowing snow. It's good that we did, because it would be the last laugh we'd share for some time.

We shook off the flakes as we walked into the emergency room. The entrance was slippery, but once we got inside it wasn't quite as bad. We stood and looked around for the chief or Jonathan, but didn't see anyone. All I wanted was to see Billy coming around the corner with a big grin on his face, but that didn't happen either.

We walked up to the admitting desk and inquired about Billy and Daniel Blackhawk. The lady behind the desk looked at her computer, punched in a few keys, and then asked us to have a seat. She said someone would be with us shortly.

"Can't you tell us anything? You must know something by now."

"I want to see my sons," Sarah said loudly.

I looked at the woman's nametag and said, "Heidi, isn't there anything you can tell us? Billy's my husband, and both men are her sons. We're frantic."

"I'm sorry," she replied. "I wish I could, but I don't have that information, yet. I'll let the doctor know you're here. That's the best I can do for now. Please have a seat and someone will be with you soon."

"Okay, we'll sit over here," I said, pointing to the center of the room. "Please call us as soon as we can see Billy and Daniel."

"Yes, ma'am. I will."

"Let's go sit down." I grabbed Sarah's hand and led her to a chair.

"I don't want to sit down and wait," Sarah said.

"I know. Give me a minute. Wait until she gets busy and then we'll go find out what's going on ourselves. From the looks of things it won't be long. This place is hopping."

A group of people came in and walked up to the front desk, and as soon as Heidi got busy with them, I grabbed Sarah's hand and off we went down the corridor. "We're going to find our guys and no one's going to stop us!" I looked this way and that, but didn't see Billy. "Where can they be?"

"I don't, but they have to be here somewhere. Maybe we should wait in the lobby like that girl said."

"That's not happening. I want to find my husband. I have to, or I'll go nuts with worry."

We came to a large double door that had the words NO ADMITTANCE on it.

"Where does that lead to?"

"I don't know, but I'm going to find out." I put both of my hands on one of the doors and pushed, but nothing happened. The door wouldn't budge. "Isn't this just dandy? The doors won't open from this side. Come on. Let's go this way." I pointed to the next hall over.

We walked down a different corridor. As soon as we got to the end of it and turned the corner, we saw Chief Sam standing in the hallway. His head was hung down, and Jonathan had his hand on his father's shoulder. Both men looked sooty as if they had tried to fight the fire themselves. They were talking to Dr. Bryant, the same doctor who had given us the news about my dad the day he died.

I looked at Sarah and then the two of us took off, hand in hand.

The minute the chief looked up, I knew a tragedy had struck. It was written all over his face. When we reached him, he put his arm around Sarah and said, "Daniel is dead."

CHAPTER 4

I WAS JUST ABOUT TO ASK ABOUT BILLY when Sarah let out a wail that could've been heard all the way out in the parking lot. Tears streamed down her cheeks as she went into a much worse tirade than she had earlier in the car. She was inconsolable and looked as if she was about to collapse. There was no fixing this disaster.

"I want to see my son," she cried. "He's not dead. I know he's not dead! I want to see him! Let me see my son!" She pushed past the chief and headed for the double doors.

I was too shaken to speak. I couldn't move... and I was concerned that Sarah was going to have a heart attack. This kind of news is hard to take for anyone.

Jonathan reached her before she got through the doors that now stood open, and wrapped his arms around her, trying to give her comfort.

"Mom, he's gone. There's nothing we can do for him. It was his time."

"I don't believe that bull!" she cried as she pulled back. "People don't have a certain time they're going to die. If they did, why would they call it an accident? If it was his *time to die* then I want to talk to God about it! Daniel is too young to die. He has his whole life ahead of him! He has a family!" She stopped for a second and looked around. "Oh, my God! What about his family? What about little Greg? What's he going to do without his father? No, this can't be happening!"

Sarah turned her anger toward Dr. Bryant. She grabbed his shirt and started screaming at him. "Why didn't you save my son? Why did you let him die? What kind of doctor are you? Where's Billy? Is my Billy dead, too?"

"I'm sorry, Mrs. Blackhawk," Dr. Bryant said, not trying to pull away from her. He'd obviously dealt with hysterical family members many times. "We did all that we could for Daniel. His injuries from the fall were too extensive."

"What fall?" Sarah screamed. She turned to Chief Sam. "What's he talking about?"

"Daniel fell through the floor," Jonathan said. "We should've never..."

"It is not your fault, son," Chief Sam said. "It was an accident. My boys should've never gone in the house to begin with, but it's too late now to change things."

"Billy's going to make it," Dr. Bryant said as he looked at me and nodded reassuringly. "He's suffering from smoke inhalation, but he's going to be all right."

His last words were a welcomed relief to my ears. Billy was going to live! I almost fell to the floor when I heard that, but I kept it together for Sarah's sake. I couldn't jump up and down and sing praises, because Sarah was dealing with the grief of losing a son.

I couldn't hear what Dr. Bryant whispered to the chief, but I figured that he had plans to sedate Sarah. She needed it. He motioned to an intern who had been standing behind him, and then I heard the word Valium. A minute or two later, the intern returned with a syringe and a gurney. Dr. Bryant managed to get Sarah to sit on the gurney while he administered the shot.

Then I thought about the pill I had taken earlier. That's probably why I didn't go ballistic when I heard about Daniel's fate. During Sarah's outburst, I stood quietly off to the side. I was in shock and consumed with grief. I cried silently as not to be a bother to anyone. I was in my own little world. I was crushed by Daniel's sudden death, but once Dr. Bryant said that Billy was going to be all right, I let out a sigh of relief.

Jonathan walked over and put his huge arm around my tiny shoulder and said, "Come on, I'll take you to see Billy."

"Thank God, he's alive!" I said, relieved.

I looked over at Sarah, who was now sitting on the gurney and being held by Chief Sam. The look in her eyes broke my heart. She had the same look my mother had when she found out that Dad had died... empty, forlorn, and consumed with pain. I reached out to her, my tears unrestrained. "I'm so sorry," I cried as I walked over to her and hugged her. "I hate this. I'm so tired of worrying about our family. Does it ever get any better?"

"This is the way life is," the chief said. "We live. We die." He wrapped his arms around the two of us, and then Jonathan followed suit. The four of us stood by the gurney and cried.

We cried until there was nothing left. Our tears dried up, and we tried to pull ourselves together and deal with our tragedy. We had lost one of our own, but we would make it through.

Finally, I looked up at Jonathan and asked, "Will you take me to see Billy now? I don't think I can make it on my own. I'm a little weak at the knees."

"Sure," he whispered. "Put your arm around my waist and hold onto me."

I did as he told me to.

"Oops, sorry about the soot," he said, offering his apologies.

"I don't care about that. A little soot ain't going to hurt me, pal. I'm just glad that you're alive."

"I am, too."

Sarah crawled down off the gurney and was a little wobbly from the shot, but she wasn't about to let us go without her. She said so.

"I'm going, too. I want to see Billy. I want to make sure that he's all right like the doctor says."

Dr. Bryant, who had been patiently standing by, turned and led the way. Behind the double doors, patients lined the walls and were separated by curtains. We passed several who, at the sight of them, made me gag. Their bloody cuts and broken bones were a sight to behold.

"Are you going to be all right?" Dr. Bryant asked.

"I think I'm going to be sick."

He motioned to the intern, who in turn, quickly led me to a bathroom.

I closed the door behind me and tried to throw up. Unfortunately, that wasn't in the cards. All I did was dry-heave. I grabbed a paper towel, ran it under cold water, and after squeezing the excess water out, I wiped my face. The cold paper towel felt good. I stood and stared at myself in the mirror, and the first thing that came to mind was the night Billy and I made love right after Ethan was born—which was a no-no so soon after giving birth. For a second I thought I might be pregnant, but realized that wasn't possible. I had already had my six-week check up a long time ago and a period since then, so I was out of the woods. No, this was just a case of nerves and drugs. I never should have taken that pill on an empty stomach. It had been hours since dinner. I needed some food on my stomach, but that was going to have to wait. Then I looked in the mirror again and smiled at the thought that I would still have a husband to give me more babies if I wanted them. I had to go see Billy. I threw the paper towel in the trash and left the bathroom.

Jonathan was waiting in the hall for me.

"I'm going to make it," I said. "Thanks for waiting. I guess Sarah and the chief have gone to see Billy."

"Yeah, Mom couldn't wait. She's a mess. This is going to be hard on her."

"Losing a child is hard on anybody. She needs to be with Billy. Maybe seeing that he's alive and going to be okay will be a comfort."

I put my arm around Jonathan's waist and the two of us walked down the aisle. I tried not to look at the other patients, but it was hard. There was so much blood and suffering. It tore me apart.

"I guess your house is a goner, huh?" I asked Jonathan, trying not to think about my surroundings.

"Oh, yeah. It's done for. There's nothing left but a brick chimney and a pile of rubble. Someone set fire to my house, and then an explosion took out the garage, the sheds, and even burned the leaves off every tree for at least a five-hundred foot circle around the house."

"What kind of blast could do something like that?"

"Dynamite. C4."

"Are you kidding?"

"No, I'm not."

"Who would do such a thing?"

"I found this." Jonathan reached into his pants pocket and pulled out a small piece of metal.

I looked at it closely and asked, "What is that? It looks like a broach of some sort, like a woman would wear on the collar of a suit jacket. I've seen Mom wear something similar."

"It's the Purple Heart."

"That's the medal one gets when they've been wounded in battle. My dad got one for his injuries sustained in the line of duty. Hey, could this one be yours? I'm sure you earned a few medals. Where did you find it?"

"No," was all he said. We reached Billy's bed, so our conversation ended. "We'll discuss this later," Jonathan said as he motioned with a wave of his arm in Billy's direction. "He's over here."

I stopped listening to Jonathan the minute I saw Billy. I burst into tears at the sight of him. He was still covered with soot, had tubes in his nose, and an I.V. drip was connected to the top part of his hand—the only visible part of his body that had been cleaned. He had a few small patches that looked like burns on his arms.

I walked over, took his hand in mine, and then kissed it. "I… I…" I tried to speak, but couldn't.

"You don't have to say anything, `ge ya," he said and then went into a coughing spasm.

"Nurse!" I screamed.

An intern appeared from around the curtain.

Billy coughed a couple times and then took a deep breath. The coughing stopped.

"He's going to be coughing a lot," the intern said. "But that'll let up after a while. It'll take time, but for now, if he doesn't cough up blood, and he doesn't have any problem breathing, he's okay."

I was still holding onto Billy's hand as I cried.

Sarah was sitting in the only chair in the small alcove of the room and appeared calmer than earlier. The shot the doctor gave her must be working. The chief stood beside her with his hand on her shoulder, his concern for her undeniable. He watched as she patted the top part of Billy's arm and then ran her hand through his hair trying to smooth it over like a mother would do to a child when giving comfort.

I stood beside his bed. I was exhausted. My energy was drained, and I figured that had something to do with the pill that I had downed earlier. I didn't say anything, but I kept holding onto Billy's hand—as if I were to let it go, he would go, too. I leaned over, kissed him on the cheek, and whispered into his ear, "I'm so sorry about Daniel."

"What about Daniel?" he asked, and then had another coughing fit. "Where is he?"

Stunned, I looked up at everyone.

There was a hush in the room.

"We haven't had time to tell him," Chief Sam whispered. "We just found out and this is the first time we've been allowed in to see Billy."

Billy's coughing stopped, but his face was still red. He was very angry. He's a Cherokee like the rest of his brothers and sisters, and when he got angry, his olive skin took on the color of a dark crimson.

"Where's my brother? Is he hurt?" Billy looked around the room at our faces. "Is Daniel dead?"

Softly, Jonathan uttered the one word, "Yes."

Billy was outraged. He sat straight up in bed and let out a howl unsurpassed by anything I had ever heard. It sounded like the growl of a lone wolf about ready to attack. "I will kill the one responsible for my brother's death. He will die a thousand deaths." His scream resonated throughout the emergency room, and for a split second, silence filled the air.

"Shh," I said, putting my finger to my lips. "You'll have the cops in here, and then they'll take you off to jail for making threats. You know how they are. They take one little word out of context, and then they haul you off to the slammer."

Billy lay back down on the bed and closed his eyes. A tear ran down the side of his face. I wiped it away with my fingertips and kissed his face where the tear had been. It broke my heart to see him hurt like this.

"The cops are already here," Jonathan said. "They're everywhere and they're going to be in our faces for a long time. They want to find out who did this almost as much as we do. You can't go set fire to a person's house and not have it all over the news, especially when there's such a big explosion."

No one said a word... or asked any questions about what might have caused the explosion. They knew Jonathan well.

"Someone has to be held accountable," Jonathan continued. "And when someone dies as a result, it's twice as bad."

"Yes, it is," the chief said. "It is bad. We will find this person and we will make him suffer. He will suffer as we have... as we will for years to come."

"I agree," Sarah added. "The person who killed my son must die."

I was shocked. Sarah was normally the sane one in the Blackhawk bunch when it came to letting the police do their jobs... but not this time. This time it was evident that she wanted revenge. She wanted someone to pay for this terrible atrocity that had been done to her family. She wanted blood. We all did.

"Where's Robert?" Billy asked as he opened his eyes.

I had forgotten about Robert. He wasn't around when we met up with Jonathan and the chief, and once we found out about Daniel, he had slipped my mind.

"He left the same time Cole did. Cole got a call from his mother. It seems she took a spill and needed his help. Robert went to find Greg. He didn't want him to hear about this on the news or over the phone, so he went to tell him in person. He's going to bring him here. He said he would make the rest of the calls once he got up with Greg."

"That's right," Billy said. "He's got all those ex-wives that have to be told."

"And don't forget the rest of the kids. You know this is going to be hard on them," the chief added. "We will have to give them comfort."

I was listening to everyone talk about Daniel when I realized that I hadn't called my mother. "Oh, God! I have to go call my mother and tell her what happened, Billy," I said. "She'll go nuts with worry. I'll be right back."

"We don't want Minnie to be put in a padded cell. Go, `ge ya. I'll be here when you get back. But make it quick. I'm not staying in this hospital for long." Billy tried to smile, but his pain was too deep. His hurt would never go away—this I knew for sure. He coughed again.

"Stop, before you hack up a lung."

He actually smiled this time, without coughing. "You are such a silly `ge ya."

"And you are a stubborn warrior." I looked around at everyone. "See what I'm going to have to put up with in Ethan? He's just like his father. I dread the day the two of them start running around chasing after bad guys... and you know they will. Lord, I'll lose my mind."

"And where will you be when that happens?" the chief asked.

"Right behind them, I guess... me and Maisy... the whole crew together. We'll be one big happy family of private detectives. I can see it now."

I kissed Billy again and then left him alone with his family. I was sure they would discuss what they were going to do about avenging Daniel's death since it was declared that they would. For the time being, I didn't want to know. It was all I could do to absorb the situation and come to terms with losing someone I love... again. The anger inside of me concerned me. I felt as if I could kill the person responsible, and I didn't want to think that way—not today, anyway. I walked down the corridor, out into the lobby, and then out the front doors. I stood under the covered roof over the sidewalk and pulled the cell phone from my coat pocket. Sarah and I had left our handbags in the car, but not before I stuffed my phone and keys in my coat. I punched in the numbered key for my house, and waited.

Mom answered the phone on the third ring. "Hello, Jesse," she said. "Don't beat around the bush. Tell me straight out. What happened? How is everyone? Where are you?"

"Somebody set Jonathan's house on fire and then there was an explosion of some kind. The place was burned down to the ground."

"Knowing Jonathan, he probably had dynamite in his basement. That's probably why there was an explosion. He's a real character!"

"True. He also said something about C4, but that's not important right now."

"What else, Jesse?"

"Billy's in the hospital suffering from smoke inhalation, but he's going to make it. He has a few burns, but nothing serious."

"And…"

"Daniel is dead."

"Oh, no…" she said, sadly. A moment passed before she spoke again. "I'm so sorry, honey. I knew something was wrong when you didn't call. It's been over two hours since you left. It's almost midnight. I was so worried. I've had two cups of coffee so I could stay awake, and now I'm as jittery as a June bug."

"I'm sorry, Mom. But I didn't want to call until I knew everything."

"How's everyone holding up?"

"Not too well. I'm worried. Sarah said she wanted to kill the person who's responsible for Daniel's death. I've never heard her speak like that. She's usually the quietest one, but now she's on the warpath."

"I hope you didn't say that to her, about being on the warpath."

"Of course, I didn't. I was just thinking out loud, but I am worried."

"She has every right to be angry. Her son is dead. I'd feel the same way. Lord help me, I don't know what I'd do if I was in her shoes."

"How's everyone there?"

"Geneva fell asleep in the recliner, and Ethan woke up about forty minutes ago, so I gave him a bottle. Now he's fast asleep again. Maisy's still asleep, but then again, she usually sleeps through the night. The dogs are standing guard, and I don't know where the cat ran off to."

"I need to get back to Billy."

"You go ahead, honey. I'll take care of everything here. Don't worry about us. We'll be fine. I know it's late, but I'm going to call your sister and brother. They need to know. If something happens and Billy gets worse, I want you to call me. No matter what time it is."

"Don't worry about him. He's going to be okay. The doctor says he'll make a full recovery. My concern is what's going to happen when the

Blackhawks get together later. You know they're going to go after whoever did this."

"Can you blame them?"

"No, I don't blame them, but I am surprised to hear you say that."

"You've got to stop thinking of me as an old fuddy-duddy. I've learned
a few things about the real world."

"Since you moved to the mountains."

"Yes, since I moved to the mountains and met the Blackhawk family."

"You just can't help but love them, huh?"

"And learn from them."

"Yes, we both have certainly learned a lot about life from them."

"The fire department and the police are still over at Jonathan's house,
or what used to be his house. Geneva went over there, but they wouldn't
let her in." Mom laughed. 'She's a character."

"Yes, she is. Look, Mom, I need to go. I'll be home as soon as I can."

"Take care of yourself, Jesse."

"I will, Ma."

I said good-bye, closed up the cell phone, and slipped it back into my
coat pocket. My hands were so cold that I had to rub them together to keep
them warm. It felt as if the temperature had dropped ten degrees since I
was outside last. I turned to go back into the hospital, but when I looked
up, I saw Robert and Greg heading my way.

Greg came up to me and put his arms around my shoulders. "My
father is dead," he cried.

"I know," I said, tears welling up. "I'm so sorry, Greg. I loved Daniel.
He was a good man. This isn't right. We'll catch whoever did this. I promise you." We hugged for a while before he stepped back. Although Greg
was now eighteen, he was still a kid at heart when it came to his folks. I
think most are.

"Do they have any idea who set the fire?"

"I don't know, Greg. I haven't had a chance to talk with Billy or anyone else about it, but I'm confident we'll catch the one responsible."

"We'll make him pay when we do. They better put him in jail, because he won't be safe on the outside."

"I know you feel that way now, but we can't take the law into our own hands. That's what cops are for."

"You really believe that?"

"I don't know what I believe, to be honest. If Billy would've died, I probably would feel the same way you do. I'd be ready to shed some blood. I'd be out there after someone's scalp."

"I rest my case."

I slid my arm around his shoulder, and the two of us started walking toward the hospital entrance.

Robert followed.

"How's Grandma and Grandpa holding up?"

"Who?"

He looked at me and laughed. "Chief Sam and Sarah."

"Oh, wow! I haven't heard them called that in a long time."

"That's because we don't see each other that much. You and Billy are always on the go and I have a life, too. But we need to rectify that."

"We sure do, Greg. We get so busy with our own lives that we don't see our loved ones as much as we should. It's a shame. Don't worry; I'll make sure we don't let time pass without our seeing each other more. When something like this happens, you realize how quickly life can be snatched away."

"I'm glad that Billy's okay. I don't think I could've stood to lose two people I love at the same time. It'd be too much to bear. Mom's really upset about Dad. Even though they were divorced, they still loved each other. I asked her once why they weren't together if they still loved each other, and she said Dad had that wandering eye. He loved women. You know how that goes. I have friends just like that. They can't commit to one woman, so they wind up being alone. Now, me—I know how to commit. That's why I have the same girlfriend I've had for the last three months."

"That long, huh?" I stopped, turned, and looked at Robert and then asked, "Have you reached any of the others?"

"I called Greg's mother, Reba, and she said she would call Joan and Barbara. She also said that she would see to it that the other four children were told before they heard it on the news."

We walked in the hospital and headed down the hall. When we reached the corridor to the emergency entrance, Robert stopped.

"This is where we part. I'm taking Greg to see his father."

"Okay," I replied, not knowing what to say. I was surprised at first and then realized that I also wanted to see my dad when he died in the hospital. I wanted a chance to say good-bye. I kissed Greg on the cheek and said, "Be tough, Greg. It's not going to be easy. Trust me, I know."

Robert and Greg disappeared down the hallway as I turned and walked through the double doors.

As soon as I got through the door, I could hear a ruckus going on down at the far end of the huge room... down where Billy was. "Oh, me. What's he doing now?" I said out loud.

A guy sitting on one of the gurneys to my right said, "That guy down there wants to leave the hospital. He kept talking about killing someone. The doctor just gave him a shot."

"Yeah," the girl with him said. "The guy was getting rowdy... loud, you know. I thought for sure they were going to have to call the cops."

I hurried down the aisle to Billy's bed, slipped in beside him and said, "I hear you're causing trouble." He was getting groggy, but it didn't stop him from speaking his peace.

"This is just the beginning. Somebody's going to die for killing my brother."

CHAPTER 5

HOSPITALS HAVE ALWAYS MADE ME NERVOUS. Every time I turn around it seems as if I'm paying this one or the one across town a visit for one reason or another. I guess it comes with the territory of being a private investigator… or bounty hunter. The only safe occupation in this family was that of being the owner of a restaurant, veterinary clinic, or a car dealership… until today. Today, being the owner of a car dealership couldn't keep Daniel alive. But then, it wasn't the job that had killed him. A match had been the culprit.

"When are they going to release him," I asked, looking over at Sarah and Chief Sam.

"Jonathan's talking with the doctor about it now," Sarah replied. "I think they want to keep him overnight, but Billy says he's leaving."

"I'm getting out of here," Billy said as he raised his head. "*Tso-s-da-nv-tli u-yo-hu-sv! A-gi-hna-lv, uhna-lv-hi!*"

"I don't understand, Billy. What are you trying to say?"

"His brother is dead and he's mad… mad as a dog," Chief Sam said. "We need to get him out of here."

"But what about the doctor? What did he say?"

"He was going to release Billy until he started yelling. Dr. Bryant had to give him a shot to calm him down and now he says he doesn't want to release him while he's under heavy sedation."

"He has every reason to be mad. I'd be angry too if…"

Billy sat up in bed and pulled the oxygen tubes out of his nose. He took a deep breath and exhaled. He didn't cough this time. He looked up at the chief and then down at his hand. The chief reached over, turned off the I.V. drip, and then removed it from the top of Billy's hand. A speckle of blood remained where the tube had been removed.

"Can you stand on your own?" the chief asked.

Billy slowly let his legs drop off the side of the bed and then stood up. He placed his hand on the wall for support, and stood there for a bit.

"I'm ready to go," he replied.

"Where's your coat?" I asked, looking around the room. "You can't go outside without a coat. You'll catch a cold. It's freezing."

"That is the least of my worries."

Jonathan and Dr. Bryant appeared.

Dr. Bryant had a surprised look on his face. "I know I can't stop you from leaving, but I'm advising you to stay overnight. I know that you're not going to listen to me, so the only thing I'm going to say is — if you start coughing up blood, you'd better get back here as soon as possible."

"I understand, John."

"Expect to be coughing up some pretty nasty looking mucus. Your lungs will…"

"I know. I know," Billy agreed. "I'm going to be in pain and breathing will be difficult for a few days. Doc, no pain could be as bad as losing my brother. I have to get out there and find out what…" Billy went into a coughing spasm. He sat down on the bed until it passed.

"See, it's only going to get worse if you don't take care of yourself."

"I'll take care of him," I said.

"Okay," Dr. Bryant said. "Read and sign this form." He handed the clipboard to Billy.

Billy took it and signed the form without bothering to read it.

No one said a word.

"Let's get out of here. I have work to do."

"Let me get a wheelchair…"

Billy looked at Dr. Bryant and said, "Don't bother. I don't need it."

Dr. Bryant looked at me and said, "Don't let him drive."

"I won't. You can count on that. Where's his coat?"

"Check with the nurse's station." He looked at Billy. "I want you to take care of yourself. You have no idea how bad this can get if you don't."

"I will be all right. There's a killer out there, and I have to find him." Billy patted the doctor on the shoulder, turned and started walking away.

The rest of us followed. We stopped at the nurse's station and picked up Billy's coat. After he slipped into his jacket, we all walked down the hall out to the lobby. There we met up with Robert and Greg.

"How you doing, brother?"

"I'm going to make it," Billy replied. He looked over at Greg. "I'm sorry about your dad, buddy."

"Yeah, me too."

"I'm going to stay here and wait for the rest of the family," Robert said. "There are arrangements to make."

"We're staying, too," Sarah said. "We want to see Daniel before…" She started to cry again.

I hugged her and said, "Jonathan and I will take Billy home. Call me on my cell phone if you need anything. Okay?"

"Thanks, Jesse," Chief Sam replied. "We will be fine. Just make sure you take care of Billy."

Jonathan handed his car keys to the chief and said, "You might need these."

We hugged each other, and then Billy, Jonathan, and I walked out of the hospital. It was a terribly sad moment for all of us—one that would stay in our memories forever.

"I'll go get the 4Runner while you and Jonathan wait here."

"I can walk."

"I know you can, but it's cold and it's snowing out here. Will you just let me have my way this time? Okay?"

"This time? `Ge ya, you always get your way."

"I see your sense of humor is still intact. Keep an eye on him, Jonathan.

I'll be right back with the car. Just give me a minute."

"What about you? It's a dangerous world out there."

"I have my mace," I said, assuring them that I would be safe.

I didn't have my mace, but I knew Billy would never let me go alone if he didn't think I had some kind of protection. He knew I didn't have a gun, because I wouldn't carry one into a hospital, so I lied about the mace. I stepped out through the hospital doors and braved the weather. The snow was still coming down. I wondered about Jonathan's house. I didn't think the snow would amount to much if the ground was still warm. Perhaps we could find some clue as to who the guilty party was. And what was the deal with the medal that Jonathan showed me? I crossed the street and went up the steps to the second landing. Just as I rounded the corner, a small man stepped out from the shadows and confronted me. He was dressed in black and had a ski mask pulled over his face. All I could see was his eyes, nose and mouth. His voice was squeaky as if he had just reached puberty. He smelled of smoke.

I was frightened out of my wits. I was so close to my car, I could almost touch it, but the man was between it and me.

He stepped forward and said, "Nobody was supposed to die, but it's too late now to cry over spilt milk. It's not over, yet lady. You can tell your friend that I'm going to make everyone of those lying jerks pay."

Although the man wasn't much bigger than me, I knew if it came to hand-to-hand combat, I didn't stand a chance. I tried to reason with him.

"Daniel Blackhawk is dead, so someone did die. What do you mean you're going to make them pay? Who are you talking about?"

"You tell your bounty hunter friend that everyone will pay. He'll know what I mean. If he doesn't know now, he will soon. I'm sorry that his brother died. All I meant to do was burn down his house, so he could see what it's like to lose something he cared about. And if the bounty hunter had died in the fire, well, what can I say? He deserves to die. Now that I think about it, I wish he had. I'd feel so much better." He turned to leave.

"Wait. What are you talking about?" I stepped forward.

"Lady, don't get in my way." He pulled out a gun. "Don't make me use this."

I was stalling, trying to get more information out of him. I didn't know what to do, but I had to come up with something fast. This guy obviously had a beef with a few people, and it sounded as if he planned to act on his anger... again. He might not have meant to kill anyone, but now that someone had died, he had nothing to lose. Others might die now that he was up to his eyeballs in murder.

Had he been out here the whole time waiting for me? Had he been lurking around where we lived? He sure knew who he was after, and he wasn't about to let me get in his way. I was about ready to drop-kick him in the groin and then knock the gun out of his hand when all of a sudden someone blew their car horn. The horn startled the man. He shoved the gun back into his pocket and ran off.

I didn't bother sticking around to find out where he had run to. I grabbed my keys, pushed the button to unlock the car, and then jumped in. I hit the door locks and tried to stick the key in the ignition. My hands were shaking so badly that it took me a few seconds to get the key in the ignition and get the car started, but when I did, I put the gearshift into reverse and backed out of the parking spot. I put the car in drive and took off. I kept my eyes open for the man just in case he jumped out at me again. This time I'd have a defense. I reached in the back and dug my purse off the floorboard. I pulled my gun out of the purse and laid it in my lap. I drove slowly as not to raise suspicions. I didn't want to be cited for driving recklessly in a hospital parking lot... with a gun sitting in my lap. When I reached the exit, I slipped the gun down the side of my seat. I didn't think the woman who took the parking money would appreciate my having a gun. But the money taker wasn't there. I guess at this time of night they didn't charge for parking. I didn't know and I didn't care. All I wanted to do was get out of there. My hands were still shaking when I pulled up to the hospital entrance.

"What took you so long?" Billy asked as he opened the car door.

I reached in the back and pulled out Sarah's purse and handed it to Billy.

"Give this to Jonathan and have him take it to your mother before we leave. She might need it."

Billy passed the purse to Jonathan and chuckled. Jonathan walked away shaking his head.

"What's the matter with him?"

"You give a guy like Jonathan a purse, and you have to ask?"

"Oh," I laughed. "I guess I should know better. I could've taken it to her."

"He'll get over it."

A few minutes later, Jonathan returned. He crawled into the back seat.

"I'm sorry, Jonathan. I should've taken the purse to your mother. I didn't think."

"Don't worry about it, Jesse. Mom got a good laugh out of it."

"I'm sorry."

"Don't be. She needed to laugh."

"Yeah, I don't think she'll be laughing much for a while."

"None of us will."

"Are we leaving? We have a killer to catch." Billy asked.

"Ah…"

"What's wrong with you, Jesse?" Billy reached over and put his hand on mine. "You're shaking. Are you that cold? Do we need to turn the heater up?"

"I think I just met the killer."

"What?" Billy asked.

"Are you serious?" Jonathan asked, leaning forward. "You met the guy who burned down my house?"

"I knew it!" Billy ranted. "I should've never let you go to that parking garage by yourself! Women should never be out by themselves at night. It's too dangerous!"

"I don't believe you just said that, Billy Blackhawk! I can take care of myself," I said as I pulled out onto the road and into the blinding snow.

"What did the guy look like? How do you know he's the one?"

"He was small, about my height, and was wearing a toboggan type ski mask. He was dressed in black. He's the one. I'm sure of it. He said he was. He must've been hanging around the hospital, because he knew about Daniel. He said that no one was supposed to die. All he wanted to do was burn down Jonathan's house. And now that someone died as the result of his actions, he doesn't care anymore. He was trying to make you pay, Jonathan."

"Me? What did I do?"

"We didn't get into the reasons why, but I got the feeling he wasn't going to quit what he was doing. I really don't think it would've mattered to him if you had gotten killed. The fire was just an avenue for him to vent his anger. Now that someone has died because of his actions, there's no reason for him to stop. He's up the creek no matter what. And… he has others he's going after. He said he was going to make those lying jerks pay. Do you know who he's talking about?"

"I do have a few enemies. In this kind of work, you make a lot of people mad."

I stopped at the light on Rt. 29. The snow was making it hard to see, but at least the traffic was slow. It was ten minutes to one.

"Are we going home or to Jonathan's house? Not that it makes any difference. I know you two won't quit until you've come up with something. I just need to know which driveway to pull into."

"We will go home and drop you off," Billy said. "I need to get my truck."

"I don't think so, Tonto. Remember, I'm the other half of Blackhawk and Blackhawk."

"You got that from your mother. She's always saying that."

"I know. She's wonderful, isn't she?"

"I do love her," Billy replied. "And she has a point."

"Let's go to my house so you can get your truck, and I want to have another look around before the evidence is washed away. Lu Ann should be there by now."

"You called Lu Ann?"

"I sure did. You don't think the Charlottesville Police or the Albemarle County Sheriff's Office are going to come up with anything, do you? I couldn't take any chances. Besides, she's the best there is."

"Who's Lu Ann?" I asked.

"Lu Ann Knots is a profiler. She's the one to call if you want to know anything about a criminal's behavior," Jonathan replied.

"They used to date," Billy added, smiling. "They were hot and heavy for a long time, but then she got tired of his ways and dumped him."

"That's not true," Jonathan snapped. "Our parting was mutual. She wanted to settle down and have children, but I wasn't ready."

"Are you ready now?" I asked, cynically.

"I could be."

"I'm stunned," Billy said. "I didn't think anyone could get you to settle down."

"I'm getting older and it wouldn't hurt to have a little structure in my life. Mom said it was about time, and she might be right. There are two problems though. She has her career, and I don't have a home... anymore."

I felt a choking feeling in my throat as a tear rose. It slipped out before I had a chance to stop it.

"That's so sad, Jonathan," I cried. "I'm so sorry about your house. I'm even more sorry about Daniel. At least, you can rebuild your house."

"That's true," Jonathan agreed. "But I can't bring my brother back."

"No, but you can find the guy who did this and see that he gets punished."

"You can count on it. He will be punished."

"Severely!" Billy promised. "He'll regret the day he ever crossed a Blackhawk."

I turned onto Bear Mountain Road, pulled over to the side, and then put the car in park.

"What are you stopping for, Jesse?"

"Let's lay it all out on the table," I demanded. "Just what are we going to do when we catch this guy? I keep getting these vibes, and I don't know what to think. Are you going to hand him over to the police, or are we talking about elimination here? Do you want to capture the guy and torture him until he dies? Now what is it? I mean, I need to know where we stand."

Billy and Jonathan looked at each other, but didn't speak.

That said it all.

We sat there in the dark for a few minutes, until I finally said, "Okay. I can see that you haven't made up your minds, but that doesn't matter. I'm in. What do you want me to do?"

"Picture the guy, Jesse. Is there anything about him that stood out? Anything at all?"

I closed my eyes and tried to picture the scene in the garage. A shiver ran up my spine as I thought about that exact moment. It wasn't one I wanted to relive, but I had to for Daniel's sake. Someone had to be held accountable for his death. The person who caused his death had to be brought to justice.

It was clear to me that the Cherokee way of justice might not necessarily be my way of justice, but I was going to refrain from forming an opinion until the time presented itself. When I had to make a choice, I knew I'd make the right one. I have a good heart and a sense for what's right and what's wrong. I would stand by my man and his family. They are honorable people. They wouldn't commit murder, but they would get revenge. I'm sure. I wanted to be a part of their revenge.

"Jesse, are you listening?" Billy asked.

"Yes. Sorry. I was thinking about something. I need an answer to my question from you and Jonathan."

There was another long silence.

"I think we've been down this road before. Don't ask your question unless you are prepared to hear the answer," Jonathan said. "It might not be the one you want to hear. Think about it for a second."

Billy reached over, put his arm around my neck, and pulled me close to him. He kissed me aggressively on the lips.

"Wow! That was hot!" I said as I pulled back. "Literally. Are you running a fever?" I reached up and touched his forehead. "You're burning up! Here, take one of these."

I grabbed my purse, reached in and pulled out a bottle of pills. It was the wrong bottle. I threw it back into my purse and dug down for a different one. I pulled out two separate bottles — a bottle of aspirin and a bottle of Tylenol.

"Let's see, should you take aspirin or Tylenol?"

"Give him the Tylenol. Aspirin is for aches and pains."

"That's correct. You shouldn't take aspirin for a fever... only Tylenol."

"Here, just give me the pills."

Billy took the bottle of Tylenol, shook out three pills, and threw them into his mouth. He chewed up the pills and then swallowed them.

I was shocked. "I'm surprised that you didn't choke. They're so dry, and you took three!" I exclaimed. "That's too many!"

"I'm a big boy. I need more than most people."

"Then here, chew this." I handed him a stick of gum. "Your breath smells like a chimney. The kiss was nice, but the breath has to go. It wouldn't hurt for you to take a shower either."

Billy and Jonathan chuckled at me again as Billy took the gum from the wrapper and stuck it into his mouth.

"Are you happy now?" He leaned over and kissed me again.

"Very much so. Jonathan, get out of the car."

After that comment, all three of us broke out into laughter.

"Jesse, you're such a refreshing breath of fresh air. No wonder my brother loves you so much. Dump him and marry me! I'm a much better catch than he is!"

"I can't. I love him. Besides, I thought you were going to hook up with *L-u A-n-n*." I dragged out the syllables of her name.

"You never know," Jonathan admitted. "I just might. She could be the one. I've always had a thing for her, but you know how that goes."

"Wow! That would be a surprise." I had to smile.

"No more putting it off," Jonathan said, the tone in his voice becoming serious. "This situation is different than the countless others we've been involved in. This is family."

Jonathan and Billy looked at each other.

"Here's the answer to your question, `ge ya. We're going to do the same thing you said you'd do if anyone ever hurt your mother," Billy stated. "If I catch him, I'll shoot him dead in the street."

"And I wouldn't think twice about it," Jonathan added. "Like I said, this is family."

CHAPTER 6

T HE DRIVEWAY TO JONATHAN'S PLACE was empty. The police that were
stationed there earlier were gone, and so were the press. But after
the drive on the winding road came to an end and Jonathan's burned-out
place came into view thanks to the headlights of the vehicles on the scene,
we saw a fire vehicle, one police cruiser, and another unknown vehicle.
Two men walked about with flashlights. I pulled over to the side so that
the exit would be clear.

"Whose SUV is that?" I asked as we got out of the car. "Could that be
L-u A-n-n?"

A black Suburban with dark tinted windows was parked off to the
right. A dome light inside the SUV was on.

"Yes, that's her," Jonathan replied, walking toward the remains of his
home.

"What a mess," I said, looking around.

The air had a harsh, burnt smell.

A policeman walked over to us and held out his hand to Jonathan. The
two men greeted each other. "Sorry about your brother, old buddy," he
said. "We're going to catch whoever did this. I promise you." He looked
around and sighed. "What an explosion. If this had happened in the city,

we'd have one heck of a problem. This could've gotten out of control. Fortunately, the fire department contained the fire quickly. I'd hate to think what would've happened if it had been summer. We'd have a wildfire for sure."

I recognized the policeman right away—it was Captain Waverly.

"How're you doing?" he asked as he shook Billy's hand. "I was real sorry to hear about Daniel. He was a good man. We're going to catch the person who did this."

"Thank you," Billy replied, his sorrow evident.

"Hello, Mrs. Blackhawk," the captain said. "I hope you're not mad about earlier. My guys told me they sent you away. Frankly, I was a little surprised you didn't slug one of them."

"I thought about it, but jail isn't my idea of a good time."

The captain laughed. "I see that your wit is still in rare form."

"As always," I agreed and then got serious. "Can we have a look around, or will we be disturbing evidence?"

"Go ahead and help yourself," Captain Waverly replied. "We're finished here. The Fire Marshal is having one last look around and then we're leaving. I'm sure he will want to talk with each one of you at some point." The captain looked at Jonathan. "Lu Ann Knots is over there in her car. I don't know if she's finished with the scene or not, but I can sure tell you that she's finished with us. My guys almost arrested her, until she showed them her credentials. I didn't know she was coming. Are the two of you still dating?"

"No, we're not."

"Whew! She's a spitfire! I don't want her mad at me." He laughed and then looked back at me. "She's almost as bad as you are!"

"You know I'm a nice person, captain," I said sheepishly. "I ask a lot of questions, but I don't cause any trouble."

"No, you don't. That's true. Am I going to have to lecture you about staying out of police business on this one?"

"This is my business, Captain Waverly. This incident involves a family member, so I have every right to stick my nose in." I turned and walked away, leaving him standing there with his mouth agape.

I scanned the scene before getting too close to what was left of the structure. Shards of glass, metal, and other debris littered the ground. Jonathan's house was now one big pile of rubble. One lone brick chimney remained where there used to be a fireplace. Occasional puffs of smoke rose as I tread through the snow-covered ashes. The surrounding trees were scorched. Only tree trunks remained standing as far as the eye could see, some burnt so badly that the bark was gone. What was once a metal shed now lay bent and tangled into a hunk of twisted, melted steel. The concrete foundation was all that was visible of the wood shed that once stood next to it.

"There's not much left," I said as Billy walked up to me. "It's sad. I've never been to a scene like this. I don't even know what to look for."

"Yes, it is sad," Billy agreed. "We're not going to be able to tell anything in the dark. We need to come back in the morning when it's light so we can pick through the ashes. I just hope we don't get a lot of snow tonight, because that could hinder our investigation. If the snow settles in, it might be a while before we come up with anything."

All of a sudden, and as if on cue, the snow stopped.

I looked over in Jonathan's direction. He was talking with the lady in the SUV. "I guess Jonathan will have to stay with us for a while. He needs a place to live until he rebuilds his house. He can use the room upstairs across from Mom's."

"I will talk with him."

Jonathan walked over and introduced the woman. "This is Lu Ann Knots," he said to me, and then looked back at Lu Ann. "And this is Jesse Watson Blackhawk."

"It's very nice to meet you," I said as I held out my hand.

She extended her hand and replied, "Nice to meet you, too. I'm sorry the conditions aren't more favorable." Her handshake was firm, but not hurtful. "I read about you in the papers a few months ago. Your mother was almost killed. I hope she's recovered from her ordeal." Not waiting for an answer, she looked over at Billy and said, "I'm sorry for your loss. Daniel was in the wrong place at the wrong time."

"Thank you, Lu Ann," Billy responded, softly. "We will hurt for a long time. The pain will be hard. That's for certain."

"I'm sure you will," she agreed. "I'm positive that I will be able to analyze the arsonist's behavior and give you enough clues so that you can catch him before he does this again."

Lu Ann appeared to be close to my age, or possibly a few years older. Her blond hair was cut short to her face, and she was a tall, muscular woman. I could tell from her broad shoulders that she probably exercised on a regular basis. At first glance, I understood why Jonathan had been attracted to her. She was just right for him. She was almost his height, lean and probably could hold her own against any man. She's one of those women you meet who exude physical strength. I wouldn't want to meet her alone in a dark alley... and have her be mad at me. I'd never survive.

"I'm finished for now," Lu Ann said. "I'll be back in the morning."

"Fluvanna is a long way to drive this late at night," Jonathan said. "I'm sure we can find you a place to sleep if you want to avoid the drive. Mom and Dad would love to see you again. You know how they feel about you. It might actually make them forget about this horrible mess for two minutes."

"You're more than welcome to stay with us," I added. "We have plenty of room."

Billy softly elbowed me in the side.

"That's very nice of you, Jesse. Thanks for the offer, but my fiancé will be waiting for me. I can handle the drive." She turned back to Jonathan. "I'll make it a point to see your folks tomorrow and express my condolences. I'll call you. Is your cell phone number still the same?"

"Yes... yes, it is," Jonathan stammered. He was obviously stunned by the announcement of her engagement.

She said good-bye, walked over and got in her SUV. She tooted the horn as she headed out. We watched her taillights disappear into the darkness.

"She has a fiancé, huh? I guess you're a day late and a dollar short. Sorry, Jonathan. I think she would've been perfect for you. Next time you find someone you're attracted to and think there might be a future there, don't wait so long to snag her. Women won't wait forever. You have to jump in with both feet… ready or not. What have you got to lose? Now it's too late."

"Don't count me out just yet, Jesse."

"Wow, she's so big. Her size alone is intimidating. I bet she can kick some butt. That's probably why you like her. She can keep up with you. "

Jonathan grunted.

Captain Waverly walked over and said, "I'm going to put up a strip of crime scene tape across the driveway, not that it's going to do much good. Anyone who can pull off something like this surely won't hesitate to let a little piece of tape stop him from entering the property again if he wants to. It isn't as if he has any respect for the law."

"Do you have any idea who did this?" I asked.

"At the moment, we have a few in mind."

"A few? You mean more than one? Oh, my," I gasped. "Do you think he might come back? Could others in our family be in danger?"

"Anything's possible," Captain Waverly said. "I'd lock it up tight if I was you. We got an arsonist on the loose. They're scary and unpredictable, and I'm willing to bet he has more targets. We need to find him soon."

"You called him an arsonist. So you think he's done this before?" I asked.

"Anyone who deliberately sets a fire is an arsonist," he said. "And I don't want to speculate on his past this early. Let's just say I don't think we've seen the last of him."

"Captain Waverly…" I started to say.

"We're going to call it a night, captain," Billy butted in. "We'll get out of your way so you can put up the tape. Come on, Jesse. I need a shower and a meal."

"Wait a minute," Captain Waverly said as he held up his hand. "Mrs. Blackhawk has something to say and I want to hear it."

I looked at Billy and saw that look in his eyes. It was a look I'd seen many times. I was just about ready to hand over the information about the man in the garage to captain Waverly, but Billy didn't want me to. We have a code—when one of us gives the other the eye, it's time to zip it up.

"I've told you to call me Jesse. I think we know each other…"

"Forget it," the captain said. "I know when I'm being sandbagged. I'll be in touch."

"I'm sure you will," Billy mumbled under his breath.

"Where can we reach you, Jonathan? The Fire Marshal will want to talk with you, and I have a few more questions."

"Call me on my cell phone," Jonathan said as he proceeded to rattle off the number. "You can reach me at that number anytime regardless of where I am."

"Okay. I'll see you folks later," Captain Waverly said. "Again, I'm sorry for your loss." He turned and walked off in the direction of the Fire Marshal. The two of them shared a few words and then got into their respective vehicles… and waited.

"We'd better leave," Billy said. "They're waiting on us."

"What was that all about? Why didn't you want me to tell him about the guy in the parking garage?" I asked as we walked to the 4Runner.

"Because we'd be out here all night, or worse yet, he'd want us to come into the station. I'm not going there. I'm beat. I want to go home, take a shower, and maybe have a bite to eat. Then I'm going to crawl into bed and snuggle up next to my beautiful wife." Billy hugged me gently.

"That sounds good to me," I said. "Are you coming home with us, Jonathan? We always have room for one more. Right, Billy?"

"You bet. I need a place to stay, and someone has to drive Billy's truck home. Come on, brother. Let's get out of here. I've had enough for one day."

"Me, too. Let's go." Billy reached into his coat pocket and pulled out his keys. He tossed them to Jonathan.

"I'm sorry about Lu Ann," I said as I opened the car door. "She seemed so perfect for you."

"He who hesitates loses," Jonathan said as he walked over to Billy's truck.

"Don't you mean, *he who hesitates is lost?*"

"Not in this case."

"I see your point." I jumped in the car and started it. I backed up in the yard, turned around, and headed down the long, winding driveway. The snow on the ground had turned into a slushy quagmire. The SUV fishtailed twice before we got to the end of the driveway. "I'll need to wear my boots tomorrow," I said. "My poor feet are freezing. By the way, why did you poke me back there when I offered to let Lu Ann stay at our house?"

"I don't want to get involved with what's going on with the two of them. I've been there before."

"I see."

I pulled up in front of our house and shut off the engine. All the lights in the house were off, which was unusual. I made it a point to always leave a light on in the living room. I picked up that habit from my mother.

Jonathan pulled up behind us and shut off the truck. When we didn't get out of the SUV, he walked over and crawled in the back seat.

"What are we waiting for?" he asked.

"Billy and I were still discussing what we plan to do tomorrow."

"Tomorrow you will need to stay home and watch over our family," Billy said.

"We're not having this discussion again, Billy. I'm going to be with you on this. Mom can run the house. She has a gun."

"Your mother has a gun?" Jonathan asked, not quite surprised.

"Have you ever seen her house?"

"You know I have—many times."

"My dad had a bunch of guns. At her house in Dogwood Valley, she keeps a handgun—a .38 Special hidden on a shelf in her bedroom closet downstairs, and upstairs she has a shotgun safely hidden in a cubbyhole. She's prepared for anything. She keeps a shotgun and a rifle on a rack above her dresser in her bedroom at our house. And she knows how to use every one of those guns. My wonderful husband taught her."

"I am a good warrior," Billy said, nodding his head back and forth in agreement with himself. "I teach squaw well. I will teach her many more things in this lifetime."

"Yeah," Jonathan said, chuckling. "You let her hear you call her a squaw and she'll hurt you. That woman scares me sometimes. I'm serious. She's just like our mother. All she has to do is give you one of her looks and you'll wish you'd been beat. Those looks. Man, I'm telling you. Women say more with their eyes than they ever could with their mouths."

"You didn't know Lu Ann was engaged, huh?"

"It was a surprise."

"You thought she was going to wait for you."

"Yes, frankly, I did. We don't get to see each other that much because of our jobs, but I thought we had something. Usually, I get a name and then I go out and bring in the bail jumper. She analyzes the characteristics of a criminal. She does a workup on his behavior and helps the police find the bad guy using her profile. Our jobs don't usually intertwine."

"I didn't see a ring. A woman has to have a ring to make it official."

"Lu Ann never wears jewelry on the job. She had a guy rip out an earring once, and ever since then she's given up on the jewelry. She said it hurt so badly, she almost cried. I'm sure the ring will appear sometime."

We sat there in silence for a while, and finally Jonathan asked, "What's going on here? Why haven't we gone inside?"

"It's dark inside. We never turn off all the lights."

"It sure looks suspicious to me," Billy said. He reached under his coat. "Oh, crap, my gun is in Jonathan's car. He took it when they put me in the ambulance."

"That's okay," Jonathan said. "I have mine." He reached under his jacket and pulled out a Glock 9MM handgun—the weapon of choice by almost anyone involved in any kind of police work, whether it be bounty hunter or private investigator.

"You didn't take that gun with you into the hospital, did you?" I asked. "Can't they arrest you for that? It's like taking a gun to school. They won't let you do that either."

"I have a permit to carry my gun anywhere. My job requires me to carry a gun at all times. It comes with the territory. I never know when I'm going to run into an irate guy I hauled into custody. They usually stay mad for a long time."

I reached over and pulled my gun out of my purse and handed it to Billy. "If I had to choose, I'd rather you have the gun instead of me. Just in case there's nothing wrong, please don't scare my mother to death."

"Why don't we call her first," Jonathan suggested.

"We'll wake the kids."

A brief silence ensued.

I pulled my cell phone from my coat pocket and dialed the house. Mom picked up right after the first ring. "Jesse, is that you?" She sounded as if she had been asleep.

"Why are all the lights off?"

"Because everyone is asleep."

"I always leave a light on. We thought something might be wrong."

"Geneva can't sleep if there are any lights on. She says she has thin eyelids."

I burst out laughing. "She what?"

"I know. I thought it was silly, too, but I let her have her way."

"We're coming in. Don't be afraid."

"Where are you?"

"In the front yard. We've been sitting here a while trying to make up our minds whether or not to bust through the front door."

"I'll put on a pot of decaf."

"No…"

She hung up the phone.

I closed up the cell phone and said, "Mom's putting on a pot of coffee, so after you guys get a shower I'm sure that she'll have a meal ready for you."

"I don't think I'd mind it a bit. Since you mention it, I am hungry."

"Me, too," Billy agreed. "My stomach's been growling, and I could sure use a cup of hot, steaming coffee."

We tucked our guns away, got out of the car and walked up the porch steps to the front door. Mom greeted us with sleepy eyes. She was dressed in her bathrobe. "You'll have to excuse the way I'm dressed, but it is three in the morning."

"It has been a long day," Billy admitted. He took off his coat and threw it across the room. The coat landed at the bottom of the staircase.

Mom and I were shocked at his behavior. She quietly closed the door behind us and then walked over to Billy. She put her arms around his waist and then patted him on the back. She tried to comfort him.

He stood rigid as if he were in another world.

Jonathan didn't say a word, nor did he act surprised.

"We'll get though this, Billy. We'll help each other deal with the pain. You helped pull me through when Mack died, so I'll be here to help you. I know the pain. It's too much to endure alone. You'll have your family by your side the whole time. We share your grief."

His tense body seemed to relax a little.

I had never seen Billy act this way, but then again, he had never lost a brother. His grief was overwhelming.

I walked over and picked up his coat. "This needs to go in the wash. It smells like smoke."

"No," Billy said. "It will be washed after I find his killer. Hang it in the laundry room."

I walked out of the living room to the laundry room and hung the coat on the rack by the door. When I walked back to the living room, everyone was in the kitchen. I smelled fresh coffee brewing.

That was my mother's answer to the problems of the world—coffee or hot chocolate. She was always there with one or the other. It was her way of trying to make you feel better.

I walked into the kitchen and looked around. "Where are the dogs? Where's Spice Cat?"

"Athena and Thor are guarding the door to the kids' room. Ever since you left they've been right there and haven't moved, except to let me pass when Ethan woke up. They sure are protective of the children. I don't know where Spice Cat is. I haven't seen him since the explosion, but I'm sure he's around somewhere."

I walked around the corner and looked down the hall. Athena and Thor were lying by Ethan and Maisy's room. I called to them, but they didn't move. They knew something was up and weren't about to leave the kids. If they have that much concern in them, then maybe I should pay attention. I walked back to the kitchen and almost tripped over Spice Cat.

"I see you've come out of the woodwork," Mom said to him. "I was wondering when you'd finally show up. Are you hungry?" She opened the cabinet door, scooped up a cup of cat food, and then filled the bowl on the floor.

I looked over at Billy and Jonathan. The three of us looked at Mom and laughed.

She ignored our stares. "Y'all might want to go take a shower before the sun comes up. The smell isn't the most pleasant. I'll have coffee and something to eat when you're finished."

Without saying a word, the three of us turned and headed down the hallway.

"Go through my clothes and find something to wear," Billy said to Jonathan. "I want to check on the little ones."

"Let me have a look, too."

We looked in on the kids. They were still fast asleep. Athena walked over and sat beside Maisy's crib, staring up at anyone who came near, while Thor did the same by Ethan's crib.

"Take a break guys. Nobody's going to hurt these kids, least of all one of us. Go somewhere and take a nap," I demanded.

They both stretched out and laid down where they were. They wouldn't move.

"Okay, if that's the way you want it. But I better not catch either one of you in their cribs. You'll be dog meat!"

Athena sat up and barked at me.

"Be quiet," I whispered. "I didn't mean it. You know how much I love you guys."

Ethan stirred, but went back to sleep. Maisy never made a sound. We backed out of the children's room and stood in the hallway.

"Pick out a room upstairs and make it your own," I said to Jonathan. "Just don't choose my mother's. I think you know which one is her room."

"Yes, I do," he replied. "She has guns on the wall over her dresser and a picture of Jesus hanging next to them. That's a little ironic. Oh, how does she like the private bath we put in for her a few months back?"

"Very much. She speaks fondly of it often." We both smiled.

Billy helped Jonathan rustle up enough clothes to see him through a few days, until he could buy more, and then they hit the showers.

I waited for five minutes, giving Billy time to enjoy some of the hot water before I stepped into the shower with him. He smiled and said, "I'm so lucky to have you as my wife. Where have you been all my life?"

"Waiting to find you."

We kissed and caressed each other's body. I wanted more, but Billy insisted that we wait. He was concerned that our shower would take too long and Mom would know what we were doing.

"You are such a kind man," I said as I dried off his back. "No wonder I love you so much. You're always thinking of others. I especially adore the fact that you think so highly of my mom. It means a lot to me."

"I know it does."

We got dried off and dressed in lounging pants and a T-shirt. When we reached the kitchen, Mom had a place set for each of us. Jonathan was already at the table chowing down on scrambled eggs and grits, a cup of hot coffee by his plate.

"I didn't realize how hungry I was until I smelled this food," Jonathan said. "My compliments to you, Mrs. Watson. You know how to soothe the savage beast. Food does it every time."

"I told you to call me, Minnie."

"Okay, Minnie…"

We ate and tried to engage in small talk, avoiding the hard subject. Mom had insisted that we eat and then go to bed. It was almost four o'clock. We could talk in the morning. We complied.

When Billy and I finally hit the sack, I was exhausted. I fell asleep in his arms. I hadn't been asleep for very long when I was awakened by a dream. I was being chased around an old metal fifty-five gallon drum by a teenage boy wielding a knife. We were in the back of a tractor trailer, the bed covered with hay. I kept tripping over the hay. The last time I fell down, the boy raised the knife and then plunged it deep into my chest. Blood spurted everywhere. That's when I woke up, sat up in bed and screamed. Sweat poured from my body.

"It was a kid!" I yelled. "It wasn't a man at all. It was a kid!"

CHAPTER 7

B ILLY MUMBLED SOMETHING AND THEN rolled back over. He was deep
in sleep. Normally, he would've jumped up and comforted me, but
after what he'd gone through in the past several hours, his body and mind
were burned-out. He needed to go to that place we all go to when life gets
too hard—the land of pleasant dreams.

The land of pleasant dreams is a place where we can find comfort,
solve everyday problems and then awake feeling refreshed. At least, hopefully, most of us have a place like that we visit occasionally when we
sleep. And then, there's that other place—the dark side.

The dark side of dreams is where evil lurks and our worst fears are
imagined. The most horrible thing that can possibly happen in life will
happen in that place. Demons lurk there, and death is only a short footstep
away. I know. I've been to that place many times. Tonight, I had a long,
ugly visit.

I saw the young kid's face. It was as plain as day, and I knew that if I
ever saw that face again, I would recognize it. I just couldn't tell if it was
a boy or a girl. I assumed it was a boy, because I just couldn't imagine a
girl coming up with such a horrendous idea as burning down a person's
house. Someone could've died in the fire. A girl wouldn't do that, would

she? I let my mind drift, and then I realized that I had to reset my thinking. I've read newspaper articles many times where a female was involved in something awful. They can kill, maim and torture with the best of them. So, maybe the person who torched Jonathan's house was female. Maybe… but I just had such a hard time believing it.

It was that voice…

I looked over at the clock on the nightstand by the bed. It registered 7:15. It was time to get up. I crawled out of bed and went to the bathroom to wash my face and come to life. I heard Ethan's tiny cry. I walked out of the bathroom and headed to the nursery across the hall.

Athena and Thor were standing at attention at the children's door. If I had waited a minute later, they would've started their barking ritual. They always did. If the children let out a peep and someone didn't jump up and run to them, the dogs would howl and wouldn't stop until they were sure that someone came to the rescue. The children must be fed!

Mom met me in the hallway with a fresh bottle for both Ethan and Maisy. She handed me one of the bottles and then went to changing Maisy's diaper.

Although Maisy was almost a year old, she still took a bottle. I didn't know when they were supposed to give up the bottle, but if it was time, I'm sure Mom would've said something. I usually yielded to her advice. She had raised three kids, and none of us had died from being underfed or sucking on a bottle too long.

"How's my babies doing this morning?" I asked as I walked over and started changing Ethan's diaper. He looked so content.

"I'm doing fine," Billy said as he walked up and stood behind me, looking over my shoulder. He had already gotten dressed for the day.

"How's my little warrior?" he asked as he reached down and touched Ethan.

"I tried to wake you a few minutes ago, but you were in dreamland."

"Actually, I wasn't visiting that wonderful place at all," he replied. "Everything was black, and then I had a vision. The sound of a baby's cry woke me."

"What kind of vision?" Mom asked as she walked in the room. "Was it a dream about the babies, or was it one of those real visions I hear the chief talk about?"

"It was a real vision," Billy whispered. "I saw the person who killed my brother. I saw the face as plain as day, and then it was gone. It will come back. I will meet that face again in the real world. I have faith."

As soon as the words were out of his mouth, an ominous feeling settled over the room. I felt a lump rise in my throat. I stifled the urge to cry.

I didn't want to start out the day on a dark note, but I could see there was going to be many dark days to come. I thought about Christmas and our planned celebration. I guess we would need to put that on hold. I would also wait to tell Billy about my dream.

"Let's save this until after the children are fed. It's going to be a sad time in our lives, and I'd like to have this one moment of serenity with my children."

"Yes," Billy said. "We should not discuss such sad matters around the children. It can wait."

"Why don't you sit down and feed your son?" I asked, handing Ethan to him. "It will help you to feel better."

"That sounds like a good idea to me," he said and then looked at Ethan. "What do you think, son? Would you like your old dad to feed you?"

Ethan let out a cry.

Billy immediately stuck the bottle in his mouth and said, "I guess that was a yes!"

Mom and I let out a little giggle.

"They sure do let you know when they're hungry," Mom said. "I remember when my kids were little. That seems like a lifetime ago."

"It was, Mom."

"I agree," Geneva said as she stood in the doorway. She looked unkempt and in need of refreshing her makeup. "Kids have a way about them, whether it's in their cries or grunts, to let you know what they want."

Athena and Thor circled and then sat down in the doorway, refusing to let her pass.

"Move," I commanded the dogs. They got up and moved to each side of the door. If they could've given me a dirty look, they would have.

"That's okay," Geneva said. "I need to be getting home. I'm surprised that Eli hasn't called here already. He probably woke up and wondered where I was. His memory isn't what it used to be."

The phone rang.

Geneva smiled and said, "I'll get that. It's probably him right now." She turned and left to answer the phone.

With the children fed and ready to start the day, we went to the kitchen. I placed Ethan in his baby lounger that Billy had built just for the purpose of having a safe place for Ethan to sit among the adults. Maisy had her own high chair next to the table. We sat down at the table while Mom busied herself in the kitchen. When she stayed with us, she ran the kitchen. That was fine with me. Cooking wasn't my forte.

Geneva was still talking on the wall phone.

Ah, the wall phone. I remember you well. I had planned on getting rid of that old dinosaur, but after Mom's wall phone helped save her life, I wasn't about to give it up. But that's another story.

Geneva hung up the phone and turned to us. "That was Eli. He said to tell you how sorry he was and that he'd stop by later today. I'm going home and fix him something to eat. It's like a ritual with us. I fix his breakfast and he cooks dinner."

"That sounds good to me. I hate to cook," I said. "I'm terrible at it."

Mom and Billy laughed.

Jonathan walked into the kitchen and said, "And that's the truth."

"How do you know?" I asked.

Jonathan rolled his eyes and said, "I've eaten some of your cooking. You do well when everything is instant. It's the complicated dishes like potato salad that gives you a hard time."

I looked over at Billy and said, "You told him?"

"I think I might have mentioned the first time I taught you how to make potato salad. The incident is still quite fresh in my memory. I was surprised that you couldn't cook, considering your mother is such a fine one."

"That was so funny," Mom agreed. "You should've been there, Geneva.

You would've fallen over laughing. I still laugh when I think about Jesse and that potato salad."

"That's enough," I said. "I know I'm not a good cook. I never claimed to be."

"I'm sorry, honey. Did we hurt your feelings?" Mom asked.

"Yes, you did. I'll probably be scarred for the rest of my life."

That statement cracked up everyone. They all laughed. At least, they were laughing and not crying. I had contributed something that would help them start their day out on a happy note. There were going to be so many sad days ahead of us. I hated to think about it.

"I have to go," Geneva said as she walked to the door.

Billy got up from the table and followed her. He opened the door and peeked out.

"There's six inches of snow on the ground, Geneva. Would you like for me to drive you home?"

"No, that's okay, Billy. I can handle a little snow. I lived in Maine for over five years. If you can drive in the snow there, you can drive in anything." She waved good-bye as she walked out the door.

Billy walked her to her car, making sure she didn't fall. When he returned, he walked over and sat down at the kitchen table.

The smell of bacon filled the air. We sat around the table and ate as we discussed our plans for the day. Billy and Jonathan talked around Daniel's death and tried their best to deal with the situation without being maudlin.

"I'll call Mom after breakfast," Billy said. "We need to go over there to discuss what's going to happen in the upcoming days." He looked at me.

"I'll stay here and take care of the kids. You need to be with your folks. You can let me know what the arrangements are when you get back," I replied. "That way Mom can take a break and go home for a while if she wants to."

Mom lives in Dogwood Valley in the little town of Stanardsville an hour away, but she doesn't spend much time there. She stays at our house more often than not. I once suggested she sell the house, but she wouldn't hear of it. She wasn't about to give up her independence. She felt that as long as she had a place of her own, she'd always be in control of her life. I agreed, and let it go. Besides, having her own place allowed her to get away from everyone and have a little peace and quiet. She could also spend time with Eddie, the new man in her life. I told her to invite Eddie to dinner more often, but we've only had him over a few times. I think Mom feels guilty about seeing him. I've told her more than once to get over it. We just want her to be happy. She's slowly coming around.

"I'll go home and check on everything, but I'll be coming right back. You'll need me now more than ever. The next few days are going to be really hard."

"That's true," Jonathan said. "I called Mom on my cell phone last night, and she's having a bad time. She cried the whole time I tried to talk to her."

"I know how she feels," Mom said. "When Mack died, I felt lost." She reached over and placed her hand on Jonathan's, and then reached over and grabbed Billy's. "If it hadn't been for this guy insisting that I start my life again, I'd probably be in the loony bin. I was a mess. Billy came over one day and asked me to help him at work. He said he desperately needed someone to run the office while he and Jesse chased down bad guys. I knew that was a ruse, but I did what he asked of me, and I'm so glad I did. It saved my life. I was so depressed. Jesse can tell you. Neither one of us got out of bed for days... until Billy came over and told us to get moving. We did, and we made it through. He's a wonderful son-in-law."

Billy smiled.

"See, I got you to smile," Mom said. "My job is done."

A terrible smell floated through the air. I looked over at Ethan and then back at Mom.

"Not yet," I said, laughing.

"Jesse, you're something else," Mom said. She got up to go get Ethan.

"Mom, I'm kidding. You don't have to do that. Billy will."

Everyone laughed again.

I smiled, got up from the table, and then walked over and picked up Ethan. I tried to hold my breath, but that was a useless feat against the foul odor coming from such a small child.

"Come on, stinky fellow. We have business to take care of. Billy, would you join us?"

"I can't wait," he replied as he got up from the table and walked with us out of the room."

"Would you keep an eye on Maisy?" I asked Mom.

"Sure, honey. You know I will."

The phone rang just as we walked out of the room.

Once we reached Ethan's room, Billy turned to me and asked, "What's on your mind? I know you didn't get me to come in here with you so that I could watch you change our son's diaper. You have something to tell me that you didn't want to say in front of your mother, or you would've…"

"I had a dream last night… or this morning. I guess it was this morning since we didn't go to bed until after four."

I lay Ethan on the changing table and changed his diaper.

"What was the dream about?"

"That doesn't matter, but the point is, I think the man who accosted me in the parking garage last night wasn't a man at all. He was a boy, possibly a teenager."

I picked up Ethan and held him close, loving the feel of his soft baby skin and the now pleasant smell of a freshly diapered infant.

"That's interesting. Why didn't you want to tell me this in front of your mother?"

"She has this thing about young kids… teenagers especially. She believes that if people were better parents, kids wouldn't turn out so bad. She's probably right. That's why I didn't want to bring this up in front of her. I'm positive it was a teenager, or a young adult. From his size and the tone of his voice, I'd say he wasn't much older than sixteen, maybe seventeen. That's pretty young to start burning down houses. And speaking of that, Jonathan said something about C4 and dynamite. Is that why his house not only burned, but also exploded?"

"There could have been other materials that would have caused an explosion. I don't know what he had in his basement, but it was enough to cause a big boom. That's for sure. We'd have to ask Jonathan."

I thought to myself for a second. "Ah, that's why we didn't hang around the crime scene for long. Jonathan had explosive material stored in his house. Could it be that he didn't want the cops to find out?"

"The fire inspector will discover what was in the house, but Jonathan says not to worry. He has it covered."

We stared at each other for a minute. "I don't think I want to discuss this further right now."

"That's a good idea. For now, the less you know about the contents of Jonathan's house when it was torched, the better."

"What about the vision you had?"

"Oh, of my brother's killer… yeah, it might well be a young adult. I have a feeling the dream you had has something to do with my vision. There is definitely more to come. He isn't finished. I saw others die."

"That's scary."

When we returned with a freshly diapered Ethan, Mom was talking to someone on the phone.

"Who's she talking to?" I asked Jonathan who now was sitting over by Maisy's highchair.

He looked up at me and said, "She was getting fussy because everyone left her alone. She wanted some attention." He stroked Maisy's tiny arm. "Oh, your mom's talking to Claire, and from the way the conversation's going, I think Claire's coming here."

"I figured she would."

Mom hung up the phone, walked back over to the table and sat down. "Claire said the children will be out of school for the Christmas holidays after tomorrow. She said she'd be here for the funeral."

We didn't say anything.

"I'm going to stay here with the kids while Billy and Jonathan go to see Sarah and the chief," I said.

"I'll go check on things at the house and be back in time to fix supper," Mom added.

"Don't worry about supper," Billy said. "I'll get Robert to have his restaurant employees bring over some food. I'm sure he's already thought about it, but in case he hasn't, I'll tell him to send food to our folks' house and then bring some here."

"I don't mind cooking. I want to do something to help. "

"I know you don't mind, but maybe you could just be here and help with the kids."

"You never know when we'll have to run out after some bad guy," I added.

For once, Billy agreed with my statement.

"We do have a bad guy to catch." He looked over at Jonathan. "We need to put a stop to his madness before hc kills someone else."

Jonathan reached into his pocket, pulled out something, and then handed it to Billy.

"I found this last night in the driveway. Someone's sending me a message." Jonathan had showed the medal to me at the hospital and said that it was a Purple Heart, but we didn't get a chance to discuss it further.

"It's a Purple Heart, or what's left of it. The ribbon's missing."

Billy looked at the medal and said, "Is there any way to identify the recipient?"

"I'm afraid not. Shoot, nowadays you can go online and buy one of these medals for $36.00."

"I bet you got a lot of medals in your line of work," I said.

"Medals are for those who are in the public eye. My whole career was based on secrecy and being able to go unnoticed by others. SF operates in small groups and is highly trained to endure what others couldn't. We do the job that can't be done. The highest honor for us is the Green Beret. That's the goal of an Army Ranger."

"Do you have one?"

"Haven't you seen the picture Mom has of me in the family room?"

"Gosh, I don't remember."

"Check it out some time. I was hoping that one of these days I'd have a son who would let his daddy take a picture of him in it. You know—a kind of father and son thing. I could take a picture of him wearing my Green Beret and then sit the picture next to mine. Hey, wouldn't it be a hoot if he joined the Rangers? But I guess that's not going to happen. I think I'm destined to be single."

"Don't be so sure," I said. "You never know what the future holds."

"How true," Billy added.

"Mack has a Purple Heart," Mom said. "It's at home in a velvet case. I haven't looked at it in a long time. He was wounded in action. That's what that medal stands for. A man receives one for wounds sustained in battle. Mack had a scar on his leg caused by shrapnel. It almost put him out of commission."

"I remember you talking about that," I said. "I also remember the scar. It was bad."

"He recovered and could still perform his duties," Mom continued. "He used to talk about it all the time, and he never failed to show me his scar every time he talked about it. I guess he thought I had forgotten the story. He would go on and on."

"He did like to tell his war stories," I agreed.

I got up to clear the table. I scraped the plates and then put them in the dishwasher. I turned to Jonathan and asked, "What do you think happened to your house? You said something about explosives earlier."

Billy looked over at me with a frown on his face, as if he didn't want to go there. But it was too late. I had already opened the can of worms.

"I can't say for sure. I think someone torched my house and some of the stuff I had in the basement exploded."

He was evading my question. I knew it was time to let it go, but I couldn't help wonder what he was doing with something so dangerous in his house. I didn't know, but I was sure that I'd eventually find out.

"Are you saying that you had dangerous material in your basement? Where would someone get that kind of stuff?" Mom asked.

Jonathan didn't have a chance to say anything.

Mom continued with her trip down memory lane.

"I remember hearing Mack talk about explosives. He told me that working with them was a short-term career. I asked him what he meant and he said that eventually one goes off that's not supposed to. I said I thought that was crazy. Why would someone want that job if it was so dangerous? He said there was a person for every job. If there was a job to be done, there was always someone to do it."

"That was a smart analogy on his part, and how true it is. Explosives are dangerous, but there's always someone to handle them—like he said—a job for everyone. Being an Army Ranger isn't for everybody. For me, it was the only thing. I wanted to be one the first time I saw that movie about the Green Berets. I knew that was going to be me some day. Now I serve in the Reserves."

"I thought you were a bounty hunter," Mom said, looking confused.

"I am, but I can be something else. When it came time to re-up, I decided to take a break and do something else. But I didn't want to give up my career completely, so I joined the Army Reserves. Once an Army Ranger, always an Army Ranger. That's what we say, and it's the truth."

"I can see what you mean. Look at Jesse. She used to be a single secretary, and now she carries a gun and goes out at night stalking bad people. That's a contrast to her previous career."

"What career? I earned a wage and that's about all. I barely had a life. But look at me now! I have a family and a challenging career. My job helps people in need of answers that they can't get anywhere else. When they need help because the police have done all they can do, those folks come to us. We find the answers for them—most of the time."

"I dread thinking about the danger ahead when you all go after Daniel's killer. It's going to be different this time. It won't just be a job. You'll be out for blood... and rightfully so... I guess."

I was a little surprised at her understanding of the situation. She was well aware of what could happen when this guy was found, but didn't try to dissuade anyone. In the end, I was sure she would try to show us the way of the Bible and inject some of God's word.

"We're always out for blood," I said, jokingly. "Don't worry, Mom. Billy and Jonathan won't scalp him, but the chief might."

"I wouldn't blame him," she said. "I don't condone murder, but I could have an open mind when it comes to an eye-for-an-eye."

"I'm shocked, Minnie," Jonathan said. "Now here I thought you were a Christian woman."

"I am, but that doesn't mean I'm blind. I know neither one of you have it in you to murder someone, but self-defense is another matter. That's the way it usually turns out, so I'm not going to worry myself. If I do, I might have to start taking some of Jesse's pills."

Bill and Jonathan looked at me.

"What pills?" I joked. "I ain't got no stinking pills."

"Could you be called back into service?" Mom asked Jonathan, changing the subject.

"Yes, I could at any time."

"I was just wondering if you guys finished up in the garage," Mom inquired. "You were skinning a deer."

Billy slapped his forehead and said, "I forgot all about that." He looked at Jonathan. "Don't worry. We were putting the last of the deer meat in that old refrigerator out there when the blast occurred. The meat's safe, but we didn't get to clean up."

"I'm surprised that a bear hasn't come along and done that for us."

I looked over at Mom. She looked back at me. "I sure hope not," I said. "When a bear finds a source of food, you never get rid of it."

"Ain't no stinking bears running around now," Billy said, mocking me. "They're in hibernation. We'll check it out before we leave."

"Check it out, or clean it up?"

"Both."

"If we have clean up detail, we need to get moving," Jonathan said.

"Listen, guys. Why don't I go clean up the garage? You don't want to go over to your folks' house smelling like blood."

"You don't know what you're in for, Jesse," Billy said. "You gagged at the sight of the deer hanging up. How are you going to be able to mop up blood? The garage's heated. It probably smells rank right about now."

"I have an idea," Mom suggested. "Why don't we call that clean up crew who cleaned up the blood from my kitchen floor? I know you remember them."

"That's a great idea," I said. "Where's the phone book?"

"Do you know how much they charge?" Billy asked. "It's outrageous."

"I'm sure they charge by the job size. This shouldn't cost very much. It's not as if someone was killed and blood splattered all over the place." I looked up and saw the agony in Mom's eyes. "I'm so sorry, Mom. I didn't mean it like that. I'm sorry to bring those memories back. Please forgive me. I'm just glad I was there with you. Lord knows what the outcome would've been if you had been alone. I fret about that day often. Now that I think about it, maybe I should go home with you."

"And drag the babies out in this mess?" Mom said. "No, you don't need to go with me. And don't worry about what you said. I've come to terms with what happened. I had to save myself and my child."

"Yes, but I didn't need to bring it up again and remind you of that horrible time. I'm sure the visions are still vivid in your mind. I'm so sorry."

"I don't think I'll ever forget that scene, but I try to put it behind me." Mom walked over and hugged me. "Let it go, Jesse. I'm trying to."

"All right," Billy said, changing the subject. "Go ahead and call them, but be sure to get an estimate first. Then make sure they dispose of what's left of the carcasses."

"That's gross. I'm not getting an estimate. I'm calling them and have them do the job. You two get going."

Billy and Jonathan got up and headed to the front door.

A second later, Athena and Thor, who had been sitting guard by the fireplace, sprang into action. They started barking, and then Spice Cat came out from the middle of nowhere again and jumped up on the kitchen table.

"Spice Cat, have you lost your mind?" Mom asked as she went over, picked up the cat, and then sat him down on the floor. "Now I'll have to scrub that table. She went to the sink, washed her hands, and then grabbed a dishtowel.

The phone rang, and for some odd reason, all of us stopped and stared at it.

After three rings, I walked over and picked up the receiver. Hesitantly, I said hello.

"Hello, Jesse. This is Cole. Is Billy there?"

"Yes... yes, he is. Just a minute." I handed the phone to Billy and said, "It's for you. It's Cole."

"Hello," Billy said. "Thanks... thanks so much. We're fine." He listened without speaking for a few minutes, and then continued. "Are you kidding? Sure, I'll tell him. We're on our way over to Mom and Dad's house. Why don't you give us a call later? Maybe when you get a chance, you can drop by and we can compare notes." Billy hung up the phone and turned around to look at us.

"It seems that our firebug has struck again. Around three in the morning someone set fire to a house on Rt. 33 in Ruckersville. Unfortunately, this time the residents were home. Two people were killed. One of them was the sister of a Greene County deputy."

CHAPTER 8

W HEN CHIEF SAM AND SARAH DIVIDED UP their property for their children, they planned it so that the road would end at their house. There were four sections of land on the left and four sections on the right of Bear Mountain Road for their six children, leaving two extra parcels (in case someone like Geneva came along and needed a place to live). The rest of the expansive acreage was at the end of the road where the chief and Sarah's huge house sat. It was a fine house, too. I remember the first time I stepped foot in it. It was so overwhelming. Their Cherokee heritage was quite prevalent. Even though Sarah was not Cherokee, she loved being surrounded by her husband's treasures, beliefs, and his past.

One day I decided that I would add to our home as much as I could to keep my husband's culture highlighted. So far, I have done my best. I shopped at the Noon Whistle Pottery in Stanardsville and bought many fine pieces of pottery. I purchased several dream catchers from a store in Charlottesville and hung them throughout the house, and then I took a ride with Mom and Claire over to Graves Mountain Lodge in Syria and stocked up on homemade jams and jellies. That seemed like a lifetime ago. So many changes have occurred since then, but the best of it all was the day I married Billy. All of these thoughts were going through my head as I walked down the hall to check on the kids.

Mom helped me put the kids down for a nap before she left, and so for the first time in a long time, I had time on my hands. I felt lost. My life had been so busy that when I finally had some time to myself, I didn't know what to do. I paced back and forth, the dogs trailing me. Even the cat was restless. I walked to the back of the house and sat down in a chair in the family room. Spice followed me and then jumped up on my lap. He purred and drooled.

"You silly cat," I said to him as I rubbed his head. "I guess I just don't give you enough attention, do I? That's okay. Carrie and Benny will be here soon and then you'll have someone to play with. They love you to pieces." I propped my feet up on the ottoman and reached over for the remote control. I clicked on the television.

Live footage of the carnage at Jonathan's place was played out all over the screen, followed by the fire at the house in Ruckersville. The two incidents were being linked, and the reporter stated that the police were looking for a serial arsonist—one who was also a killer. The fires occurred approximately three to four hours apart. The Blackhawk name was mentioned several times during the broadcast, but the names of the two dead people from the fire in Ruckersville were being withheld. Speculations were made by the reporter that the two dead people were Jeremy and Lynn Myers. Lynn Myers was the sister of Greene County deputy, Ronnie Crumpler.

That name sounded familiar. Then it occurred to me. The small country market down the road a few miles from our house was Crumpler's Market. I wondered if there was any relationship. I would have to check to see if there was. I had met the store owner some time ago after I moved into Billy's house. He was such a nice man. I hated to hear that this might be his daughter. I would stop in and see him the next time I got out. I could always use a gallon of milk.

I was filled with sadness. I turned off the television and got up to go to the laundry room. I thought that maybe there were some dirty clothes that needed to be washed, but I should've known better. The hamper was empty. I looked up at Billy's coat hanging on the rack. I grabbed it, put it to my nose, and sniffed. I don't know why I did that, but it made me feel better. The jacket smelled of smoke and Billy's cologne. I ignored the smell of smoke.

The phone rang just as I was about to hang up the coat. I dropped it on the washing machine and ran to the kitchen to answer it. I was lonely, but not lonely enough to have the kids awakened by the phone. It would just make them cranky.

"Hello," I said, noticing that the Caller ID readout listed the office number.

"Hello, Mrs. Blackhawk. This is Sue Ellen from the office. Is Mr. Blackhawk home? I need to speak with him."

Several months ago, Billy hired a pleasant and very competent secretary named Sue Ellen Posey to run the office. It was time. I was pregnant and Mom was done with office work.

Of course, Billy let me make the decision about who to hire since he didn't want me to get jealous of his choice. Not that I'm the jealous type... anymore. The only person I'd ever really been jealous of was my sister, Claire, because she seemed to have it all. Then I met Billy and realized I had wasted too many years wanting what she had. Go figure.

"I'm sorry, Sue Ellen, but Billy's not here. He went to see his mom and dad."

"The phone has rung non-stop all morning. The press wants an interview. I've put them off as long as I can, but now they're showing up at the office. I finally locked the front door. I'm in Mr. Blackhawk's office now."

"I tell you what, Sue Ellen. Lock up and go home. Let the answering machine pick up. Call in and check the machine about every hour or so to see if a real client has called and then your day is done."

"Thank you, Mrs. Blackhawk. Normally, things like this don't get to me, but this time it's different."

"I know exactly how you feel. And Sue Ellen, please call me, Jesse."

"Thank you, Mrs. Blackhawk... I mean, Jesse. I'm sorry that I had to call you about this. And I'm terribly sorry about Daniel Blackhawk. I know you and Mr. Blackhawk must be so sad. Losing his brother is awful."

"Billy... you can call him Billy."

"I'm just so used to calling him Mr. Blackhawk. I think I should keep it professional. I'm afraid I might slip in front of a client and that wouldn't look good."

"I guess you're right. But please, call me Jesse. I'm not your boss." She laughed.

"I'm married, too, Jesse. I know who the boss is."

"Hey, do you know the man who owns Crumpler's Market? Is he related to that deputy? You know the one whose sister was killed in that fire in Ruckersville?"

"Oh, wasn't that so sad? Yes, it was his daughter. Her husband was the one who was accused of having an affair with the wife of the guy who jumped bail and was finally hauled in by Jonathan Blackhawk. Then the man hung himself in jail. It turns out that the guy was innocent after all. He was arrested for beating his wife, but it turns out that the other guy was the one who did it. It was awful."

I didn't say anything. It seemed to be too much information for me to take in at one time. Later, I would sort it out, but for now, the facts added up to only one thing: These two cases were related.

"Jesse, are you still there?"

"Yes, Sue Ellen, I am. Thanks for calling. I'll tell Billy about what's been going on at the office. Go home and get some rest. You deserve it."

"Thanks," she said. "I'll be back in the office first thing in the morning. Have a good day."

I said good-bye and then hung up the phone. The minute I placed the receiver in the cradle, it rang again.

"Hello," I answered.

"Hello, this is Lu Ann Knots. Is this Jesse?"

"Yes, it is. What can I do for you, Lu Ann?"

"I've been trying to reach Jonathan, but his cell phone is turned off. Do you, by any chance, know where he is? I need to talk with him."

"He's over at his folks' house."

"Could you give me their number?"

"I don't think it's a good idea to call over there. They're planning their son's funeral. I'll be glad to pass along a message."

"Oh, you're right. I understand that he's staying at your house. Would you mind if I stop by and wait for him. I have some important news that just can't wait."

"Sure, you can. Come on by. How long do you think it will take you to get here? I only ask because the children are napping and I don't want you to ring the doorbell."

"I'm in Stanardsville at the moment, so I would say about an hour. Is that all right?"

"That's fine. I'll see you then."

"Thanks, Jesse. I'll be there shortly."

I hung up the phone and stood there for a little while just in case it was going to ring again. Finally, after deciding it wasn't going to ring again, I turned and walked down the hallway. As soon as I got to the nursery door, the phone rang. I spun around and ran back to the kitchen. I snatched up the phone and said, "What?"

"Are you all right?" Billy asked.

"I'm sorry," I replied. "This is the third phone call in the last fifteen minutes. I didn't want the children to wake up, yet. You know how they get when they don't get a full nap."

"Who called? Was it anyone important?"

"Yes, it was. Sue Ellen called and said the phone has been ringing off the hook. The press wants an interview. I told her to go home and let the answering machine pick up. I could tell that she was in a tizzy. She needed a break."

"That's fine. Did you tell her to check the messages every hour or so?"

"Yes, I did. We had a very informative chat. Did you know that Lynn Myers is Ronnie Crumpler's sister?"

"Yes. And her husband was the one who was having an affair with the wife of the guy Jonathan went after for jumping bail. It all seems to be connected."

"How did you know this?"

"I'm a private detective. I know everything." Billy chuckled. "How did you find out?"

"Sue Ellen mentioned it, and I put the pieces together."

"So, who else called?"

"*L-u A-n-n* called for Jonathan. She has something important to tell him. She wanted the number at your folks' house, but I told her it wouldn't be a good time to call over there. She's coming over here. She should be here in an hour."

"We're coming home in a few minutes."

"Is everything okay over there?"

"It could be better. We'll talk about it when I get home."

"I'll see you when you get here."

"I love you, Jesse."

"Same here," I said and then hung up the phone. I walked over to the desk in the living room and picked up the portable phone. This time, if someone called, I wouldn't have to run to answer the phone.

I figured it was time to get dressed. I went to the bedroom and pulled out a pair of jeans and a fresh T-shirt and slipped into them. I stood in front of the full length mirror and looked at myself for a second. Compared to Lu Ann, I looked like a child. How can one woman be so toned? Amazon woman was the first thing to come to mind. That's okay... I don't need to be massive to get what I want. Am I jealous of this woman? Maybe my feelings had something to do with the fact that she knew the phone number here at our house. How did she know Billy's phone number? Let it go... I told myself. There's no need in getting jealous. Billy loves me... not her. Oh, Lord. Here we go again. No, I won't let my insecurities take over!

I went to the bathroom and brushed my teeth and then combed my hair. I told myself that I would take the time to get my hair cut, even if it was only a little bit. My long hair had become a nuisance. It always got in the way when I was holding one of the kids. Although, Billy did like it long. Perhaps I wouldn't get it cut, but it sure needed a dye job. It was no longer red. It was a mousy brown.

I heard the front door open and close.

I walked out of the bathroom through the bedroom to the living room and looked around. There was no one there. I got scared. I couldn't think

straight and couldn't remember what I did with my handbag, so I ran to
the bedroom and pulled open the top dresser drawer where I kept my .38
caliber handgun. I checked to make sure it was loaded—I knew it was—
but I checked anyway. Then I held up the gun in front of me and walked
back into the living room. I looked around. Why hadn't the dogs barked?
I walked down the hallway and looked in on the children. They were still
fast asleep with both dogs on the floor by their cribs. If the dogs didn't
bark, then there was no reason to be scared. I lowered the gun and walked
from room to room. I checked all the doors to make sure they were still
locked. They were.

"What is wrong with me?" I asked out loud.

I heard a creak on the stairs behind me. I turned, raised my handgun,
and prepared for the worst.

"Whoa, girl. Hold it a minute."

"Jonathan! Have you lost your mind? I could've shot you."

Billy walked through the front door, dusted the snow from his boots
and then looked up. "What's going on here? Jesse, put the gun down."

My hands were shaking and I couldn't seem to move. Billy walked
over to me and slowly took the gun from me.

Jonathan didn't move an inch.

My body trembled. I felt sick. I couldn't speak.

"It's all right," Billy said as he put his arms around me. "Everybody's
on edge. We just don't want anyone to get shot."

"I'm sorry," I said, looking up at Jonathan. "I heard the door open, but
nobody was here. Then you came creeping down the steps. Why didn't
you call out?"

"Rest assured that I will next time. I like living."

I guess the look on my face had given me away, because Jonathan
walked down the stairs, came over to me and gave me a big bear hug.

"Don't fret. Everything is okay, Jesse. I should've called out, or at
least knocked on the door before walking in on you. I'm sorry. It won't
happen again. Next time, I'll announce myself. That way you won't have
to shoot me."

"Oh, Lord," I cried. "I'll never live this one down."

"Sure, you will," Billy said, smiling. "But you can bet that nobody will come through that door again without knocking. Hey, I think I'll knock next time, too."

"It's not funny. Is it, Jonathan?"

"It's funny now, but it sure wasn't funny when I was staring down the barrel of that gun. There's nothing like a .38 to the gut."

Billy and Jonathan smiled at each other.

"You wouldn't be laughing if the gun had gone off."

"You got that right."

"I need a drink."

"Speaking of which," Billy said. "What's this about a bottle of pills you have?"

"They're drugs," I replied, sarcastically. "I've been downing them ever since I met you. I have an addiction." I looked at Billy and could tell that he thought I was serious. "I'm only kidding. I got those pills a long time ago for my anxiety. I don't usually take them, but I took one when I found out that you were in one of those ambulances. I thought you were going to die."

"Are those the same pills you gave your mother that time?"

"Yes, they are."

"Aren't they awfully old? Are they still any good?"

"I don't know, but it sure worked for me last night."

"Oh, me. My brother has C4 in his basement and my wife takes drugs. What am I going to do with the two of you?"

"So, you did have C4 in your basement?" I said to Jonathan. "Isn't it against the law to possess explosive material like that?"

"It's a long story," Jonathan replied. "It wasn't supposed to be there. It wouldn't have been if... Like I said, it's a long story. And it wasn't the C4 that caused that huge explosion. I didn't have but a teeny, tiny amount of the stuff. However... the other materials in the basement are another thing."

"You'll have plenty of time to explain that to the ATF," Billy said. "They're going to be all over you about it."

"You let me worry about the ATF. They don't know their head from a hole in the ground. I'll take care of this mess."

"You say that now," Billy said. "They'll be leading you away in handcuffs, and you'll be telling them how dumb they are."

"It's not going to happen. They're not going to give me any grief."

"How can you be so certain... unless..."

"Let's not discuss it now."

A car pulled up in the driveway. I heard the crunch of the tires in the snow. I walked over and peeked out the window. "It's the black Suburban. *L-u A-n-n* is here." I looked over at Jonathan and smiled. "She called and said she had something important to tell you. She probably wants to ask you to marry her. She never did love this guy she's engaged to, and all you have to do is say you'll marry her, and then everything will be fine."

"You're a real jokester, Jesse. She gave up on me a long time ago. If she still cared about me, she would've never gotten engaged. Nope, my time has come and gone. She's done with me. She's probably come here to scold me about the volatile chemicals I had in my basement."

I opened the door before she had a chance to ring the doorbell. "Welcome, Lu Ann. Jonathan just arrived." I motioned for her to enter. "May I take your coat?"

"Sure," she replied. She walked in and said hello to Billy and then looked at Jonathan. "Hello, Jonathan."

"Hello, Lu Ann. It's nice to see you again. Jesse said you had something important to tell me. Have you worked up a profile on the arsonist, yet?"

"That can wait," she said. "I have something else I want to talk about first."

"Billy and I were about to... ah... do something." I looked at Billy. "Come on. Let's give them some privacy." I looked at Lu Ann and said, "Actually, if you want to you can go back to the family room and close the door."

"No, that won't be necessary. If I'm going to make a fool out of myself, I might as well do it in front of everyone." She walked up closer to Jonathan and said, "I've been in love with you for so long, I can't remember when I wasn't. I want you to marry me and I want us to have babies—

preferably a son who won't follow in his father's footsteps and store a chunk of C4 and other dangerous materials in his basement. Say the word, and my engagement is off. Otherwise, I'll tell you what else I came here to tell you, and you won't see me again. I can't continue living…"

Jonathan grabbed her up in his arms and kissed her passionately.

Billy and I stood there with our mouths open. Seeing the two of them together reminded me of the first time Billy kissed me. It was so romantic.

"Ah…" I murmured. "That's so sweet."

When their kiss was finished, Jonathan looked at her without hesitation and said, "Will you marry me?"

"Yes, I will," Lu Ann answered.

"When would you like to get married? I'm ready anytime you are."

"It'll have to wait until you get back from your next mission."

"What next mission?"

"The one I promised Lester you'd go on. You know what you have to do, don't you?"

"When did you talk to him?"

"First thing this morning. I called him at home and got him out of bed. He wasn't too happy."

"What's going on here?" I asked, sticking my nose in.

"That's classified," Lu Ann replied, explaining nothing further.

"That's good enough for me," I said. I didn't understand what was going down, but if it had anything to do with keeping Jonathan out of trouble with the ATF and out of jail, it was fine by me.

"Last night when you said you were engaged, I knew you weren't in love with the guy," Jonathan said to Lu Ann. "If you had been, you would've worn the ring just so I would see it on your finger. No, I thought something was up, and I was right."

"You hoped something was up," Lu Ann said, mocking him.

"How did you know I would ask you to marry me?"

"You're still in love with me. It was written all over your face. That's when I realized I was still in love with you."

CHAPTER 9

J ONATHAN AND LU ANN PUT the discussion of their upcoming wedding plans on hold, now that it had been decided that there would be a wedding to plan. There were more pressing issues at hand. We gathered in the kitchen to talk about those issues over a cup of coffee.

"What did you all decide about Daniel's funeral?" I asked.

"Daniel will be buried in the family cemetery, of course," Billy said. "We'll have a graveside service and then a celebration of his life afterwards at Mom and Dad's house. Beth will take care of his obituary and then she's going to call all our relatives. The service will be day after tomorrow on Saturday."

"Okay," I said. "I'll make sure that I call Claire and Jack today and tell them. They're the only family on my side who are close with the Blackhawk family. The rest are distant relatives that even I hardly see... except for Aunt Edie and Uncle Bill. Uncle Bill isn't well, so they won't be here for Christmas." I paused and then looked up from my cup of coffee to Billy. "I guess we need to cancel the Christmas party. We can have a small dinner just for us. I'm sure your mom..."

"Oh, no, Jesse. Mom wants us to go ahead with our plans. She'd be disappointed if we called it off. She said that even though this would be a sad Christmas because she'll have a missing son, she can't allow the family to forget about the good times. We must celebrate the future. Daniel would want us to carry on. He was such a big partier, and he loved the women. That's what got him in trouble with his former wives."

"He just couldn't keep his eyes off the young ladies," Jonathan added. The two brothers looked at each other and shared a warm moment.

"Yeah, he sure did have a thing for pretty women. He used to tell me that I'd better watch out. He had his eyes on Jesse."

I smiled. I could see where this was going, and it was a trip that needed to be taken. When you lose a loved one, it's important that you have another loved one to talk with about it. Billy and Jonathan needed to share their memories, and I wanted to be a part of that sharing.

"He flirted with me all the time, but I never took him seriously. He'd do it right in front of Billy." I looked over at Jonathan and Lu Ann and then smiled. "I saw how he acted around women, and they loved him."

It was almost eleven o'clock. The kids would soon be getting up from their nap. I knew the minute Athena and Thor sashayed into the kitchen and lay down by my feet that the time was near. I could count on them to be vigilant. They were like clockwork. Any second, I would hear a cry echo up the hallway right to my ears. Other times, their wild barking would alert me to anything and everything that was going on outside the house whether it was an intruder or a leaf falling to the ground. They also are a good judge of character. They act rabid when they're around someone they mistrust or just plain don't like. I've seen them snarl and bare their teeth as if they were going to eat someone for dinner. When I was pregnant with Ethan, I walked to the end of the driveway with the two of them once and that was the last time. They almost attacked the mailman right in his car. Later, it turned out that the guy was a child molester. He got arrested a few weeks after our encounter. A few months back, a crazy woman abducted Mom and when Athena took off into the woods, I didn't pay much attention to her absence. If I had, we would've found Mom sooner. So now, when Athena and Thor talk—I listen. And Spice Cat—he's a real character. He hisses at evil people. I've seen that, too. Most of the time, he just lies around and makes himself right at home... anywhere he wants to.

"He was being himself, Jesse. He wouldn't mess with one of our women, but he'd make us think twice when we were in the wrong. He'd tell us to go buy flowers or candy and say we were sorry... and to stop being so pigheaded."

"He told me the same thing about one of my old girlfriends. He said that if I didn't want her anymore, he did. It woke me up."

"What did you do?" I asked. "Did you crawl back on your hands and knees?" I chuckled.

"Jonathan doesn't crawl back to any woman," Lu Ann said. "I have first-hand knowledge. He gives up and walks away." She grinned at Jonathan.

"That was the old me," he said. "This time I have seen the error of my ways and want to make amends. If that means I have to marry you to keep you, then so be it. I guess I'll just have to bite the bullet."

"I don't believe you said that!" I exclaimed. "You turd!"

Lu Ann reached across the table, put her hand on mine and said, "Don't believe a word he says, Jesse. He's spent the last two years pining over me, and he's finally come to realize that he has to get off his duff, or lose me forever. Isn't that the truth, Mr. Turd?"

The two of us laughed until we had tears in our eyes. That's all it took for us to become friends—two women sharing a good laugh over a man.

"What could be better?" Lu Ann asked. "If you can't laugh at your guy..."

"Or better yet, we can laugh at them, but nobody else better!"

"Are we missing something?" Billy asked, looking over at Jonathan.

Lu Ann and I were still laughing.

Billy and Jonathan made an attempt to ignore us by continuing their conversation. "I think he did it to keep us on our toes," Billy said.

"And it worked, most of the time."

One of the children started to cry.

"I guess that's for me," I said as I got up from the table. "Lu Ann, would you like to come meet our children, or would you rather sit here and listen to men being men, telling their lies?"

"I can do without the lies." She smiled and then looked over at Jonathan and said, "I've had enough to last a lifetime. I'm ready for some good old honesty, and a husband who will be my slave."

The two of us laughed and chatted as we walked down the hall to the nursery.

"Ah, how beautiful your children are," Lu Ann said when she walked into the room and looked down into their cribs. "And what a lovely room. I love the murals on the wall. Nursery rhyme characters are the best. My sister did her nursery very similar to this."

"So, you have a sister?" I asked as I changed Ethan's diaper. Maisy stood up in her crib and waited her turn. I leaned over and gave her a kiss on the forehead. "Hang in there, sweetie. You're next."

"Yes, I have two sisters—Lily and Maggie," Lu Ann replied. "Lily went out with Daniel a couple of times, but that didn't go anywhere. His wife, Barbara, had just left him and he was on the rebound."

"I guess there's still plenty to learn about the Blackhawks."

"Is there anything I can do to help?"

"Can you change a diaper?"

"I sure can. I have a niece who is six months old, so I've had plenty of experience."

Lu Ann looked around to see where everything was, and then went to work. She was holding Maisy in her arms waiting for me when I picked up Ethan.

"Where to now?" she asked.

"We're off to the kitchen," I said with a smile. "Love, clean diapers, food and a bottle—that's all they ask of us."

"Until they get older."

"Yes, that's true. Next thing you know, they'll want to borrow the car. I dread the day."

We walked back to the kitchen just in time to hear a car pull up in the driveway and the telephone ring. Jonathan got up from the table and went to answer the door while Billy got up to answer the phone.

The phone call was brief. I looked at Billy and asked, "Who was that?"

"It was your mom. She said she was on her way back. Everything at the house was fine."

"That was quick."

"She can't stay away from us for long," he added. "She wanted Eddie to follow her back. I told her it was okay."

"That's fine with me if you're sure you don't mind."

"I think it's a good idea. She likes him, and he's good for her."

I could tell this was going to be a very busy day. It wasn't even lunch time yet, but I was already tired. I didn't get to sleep until almost four, and when I did, it was a restless sleep. Then I was up at seven. My concentration was slack at best. My thoughts kept going back to the man/boy I encountered in the hospital parking garage. He was standing there telling me that he was sorry, and then he goes out and does it again. Except, this time, his actions killed two people. The question that haunted me was, why me? Why did he seek me out?

"Come on in," Jonathan said. "We've been waiting for you."

"How is everyone doing?" Cole asked, looking around. He smiled at me and nodded to Lu Ann. He shook hands with Jonathan and then walked over to Billy. "I'm so sorry about Daniel. Captain Waverly says they have the usual suspects, but nothing definitive. We're comparing the crime scene in Ruckersville to the one here to see if there are any similarities."

"What have you found out so far?" Billy asked. "When Jonathan and I talked to Captain Waverly this morning he said they were certain that an accelerant was used. He said it was gasoline. That's a sure sign of an amateur."

I looked over at Billy just as he glanced up at me. He had been to the crime scene this morning, but hadn't said a word about it. I guess he had more important things on his mind. I would've wanted to go with him, but I had to stay home with the kids. Mom needed some time to herself. I know it was selfish of me, but I kept hoping that she would hurry up and get back. I wanted to be a part of this investigation.

The only way for me to have complete freedom and relieve Mom of the demands of taking care of my children was to hire a nanny. This thought had been in the back of my head for a couple of weeks, but I'd been afraid to broach it. I didn't want to hurt Mom's feeling, but I didn't want to continue getting her to baby sit. No... she needed the time to have a life of her own. When I got up the nerve, I'd talk to her about it.

"From what they've pieced together so far, they think the person who set fire to Jonathan's house might have gained access through an entrance door, poured gasoline all over the floors and left a trail to the woods. Then he struck a match to the trail. I guess he never expected the house to be a storage hold for explosives." Cole looked at Jonathan. "What did you have in your basement? Never mind. I'm sure it will come out in the report."

Lu Ann walked over to Jonathan. She was still holding Maisy in her arms. "He obviously ran like a jack rabbit, because they didn't find a body in the woods. If they had, they wouldn't be thinking that the guy who did this was also responsible for the fire in Ruckersville. What we have is a plain old-fashioned arsonist. A person who uses something as volatile as gasoline likes to set fires. He enjoys the blaze, but isn't smart enough to use something less dangerous. If he keeps this up, he'll most likely be killed by one of his fires."

"We can't wait for that to happen," Cole said. "Three people are dead."

"Would you like a cup of coffee?" I asked Cole as I walked over and put Ethan in his lounger.

"That would be nice," he replied as he sat down at the kitchen table.

I looked at Lu Ann and said," You can put Maisy in her highchair if you want to. I'll fix her some juice in her Tommy Tippy cup, and then fix a bottle for Ethan."

"I don't mind holding her, but I guess she can't drink from a cup if I do," Lu Ann said. "She doesn't get a bottle?"

"Sometimes she gets one in the morning, but usually she just gets one at night before she goes to bed."

Lu Ann walked over and put Maisy in her highchair. Athena and Thor were on her heels, keeping their eyes on her every step. Once Maisy was in her chair, the two dogs lay down.

"Your dogs sure are protective," Lu Ann said. "My sister's dog is the same way."

"Yes, they are." I looked around. "I don't see the cat anywhere. Sometimes he hides when we have visitors."

"About the fire in Ruckersville," Cole continued. "The guy poured gasoline around the foundation of the house and up on the porch. The he doused the shed and both cars in the driveway. The place went up in flames instantly. We think the folks inside were asleep and by the time they tried to escape it was too late. The fire department found both bodies on the floor in the hallway. We're waiting for an autopsy to determine the cause of death."

I poured a cup of coffee for Cole, walked over to where he was sitting, and put the cup down in front of him.

"Thanks, Jesse," he said. "Where's your mother?"

"She went home to check on things. She needed a break. She'll be back any minute."

"She spends most her time here, doesn't she?"

"Yes, she loves being around the kids."

Cole and I have a history together, but we both have put that behind us. We're on friendly terms and our relationship is no longer one of romance and lust.

"How is your mother?" I asked Cole. "I heard that you were called away from the hospital last night."

"Oh, you know Mom," he replied and then looked around the room. "She's always got something going on." He didn't elaborate.

I looked out of the kitchen window and saw the snow coming down.

"It's snowing again," I said to anyone who might be listening.

"It's that time of year," Cole said. He looked around at everyone who, up until now, had very little to say. "What's going on here? There's too much small talk and not enough questions being bantered about."

"We really haven't had a chance to discuss the details of what's happened," Billy said. "We just got back from Mom and Dad's house, Lu Ann showed up, and now you're here. What do you want to talk about?"

"Do you have any thoughts on who might have set the fire?" Cole asked. "Lu Ann, what's your take on the matter? You're the profiler. If Jonathan called you in on this, he had a good reason. These guys usually do their own work, but now they've got you here. What's up?"

"I have very little experience with arsonists," Jonathan said. "I figured I needed outside help. I want my brother's killer caught, and I'm not going to leave it in the hands of the Charlottesville Police Department, the Albemarle Police Department, or the Albemarle County Sheriff's Office. I want results now—not six months from now."

"The CPD, APD, and the Albemarle County Sheriff's Office are competent, and I'm sure they're going to catch the guy who did this," Cole said, taking up for the force. "We've worked hand-in-hand with them and I can tell you that they're a good group of officers. They work their butts off solving crimes and putting the bad guys away. Each county works together and they're relentless."

"The truth is," Lu Ann added. "Jonathan wanted my help on this, and he also wanted to ask me to marry him, so here I am."

Cole smiled at Jonathan. "Well, what was her answer?"

"What do you think? You know she can't resist my charm."

"It's getting deep in here," I said, looking over at Lu Ann. "Men—I swear. What will we do with them? Their heads are so big."

"We're getting married after we find the guy who set the fire that caused Daniel's death," Lu Ann said. "That's priority one. Everything else can wait. We'll invite you to the wedding."

"You can bet I won't miss this event for the world," Cole said. "I can't believe that you reeled him in."

"He's not a fish," Lu Ann said, laughing. "He's a catch, I agree, but I didn't lure him in."

"All right, that's enough!" Cole demanded. "What are you all hiding?"

"Where do we start?" Billy asked. "What do you want to know?"

"Don't think that our Sheriff's Office hasn't talked extensively with the CPD. Because of our relationship, Sheriff Hudson and Captain Waverly agreed that I should come over here and find out what you wouldn't let Jesse tell the captain last night. He knows you're under a lot of stress and the pain from losing your brother must be unbearable, but if she knows something, we need to know what it is."

Everyone looked at me.

"Tell him about the guy in the garage," Billy said. He looked back over at Cole. "I wouldn't let her say anything last night because we were tired and dealing with the loss of Daniel. I had just been released from the hospital and didn't want to spend three hours at the precinct." He coughed to prove a point.

"But if you have information that could help this case, wouldn't it be to your benefit to pass it along as soon as possible?"

"Yes, it would," Billy replied. "But my brother is dead. The killer isn't going anywhere and a few hours wouldn't make much difference. We'll spend the rest of our days hunting down this guy if we have to, but right now, this family is hurting."

"I realize that, Billy. I'm sorry if I seem heartless, but we need to know what you know if we're going to catch this guy. You know how critical time is. It could make all the difference in the world as to whether or not we catch this guy."

"Wait a minute," I said. "This has been hard on all of us. You'll have to forgive us for being a little out of it."

"You guys are never out of it. If anything, you're right on top of everything—no matter what."

"We've never lost a brother before," Jonathan angrily added. "Our brother is dead, so give us a break!"

"I'm trying to help, but if you tie my hands, I'm not much use to you."

"Stop it!" I said. "Let's work together on this and maybe we can put the culprit behind bars before the next millennium." I looked over at Lu Ann. "I think it might help if we got your input. You're the professional here. Tell us your take on the guy and I'll tell you what I know, which I can assure you isn't much. It might just be a prank."

"What do you mean?" Cole asked. "What happened?"

"I want to hear from Lu Ann before I say anything."

"Okay. I can go along with that. Lu Ann…"

"I talked with Captain Waverly and the Fire Marshall. I also talked with the firemen and the policemen on the scene. I did a physical examination of the crime scene, and I took pictures."

"What's your initial assessment?"

"The person who did this was not knowledgeable in explosives. He set a fire that could've easily killed him. This was personal—very personal. This is someone Jonathan knows or has come in contact with professionally—maybe someone who Jonathan's hunted down and brought in, and now the guy wants payback. Or it could've been a relative of someone who has been hunted down by Jonathan. Either way, this was of a personal nature done by someone with limited knowledge of fires. I think it was done on the spur of the moment. The guy found an open window of opportunity and used it."

"And I don't think the guy who burned down Jonathan's house had any idea of the destruction it was going to cause," I added. "He didn't mean for Daniel to die. It was an accident. He just wanted to burn Jonathan's house down to make him pay for something. I don't know what that something is, but now that someone has died, he has nothing to lose. He said something about making everyone pay. I got the impression he wasn't going to quit until he got satisfaction."

"You sound as if you've met the man," Cole said, astonished. "Have you?" He looked around at everyone as if he had just accidentally stumbled across a rattlesnake in the woodpile. "What's the deal here?"

"Jesse had an encounter with a man in the hospital parking lot that lay claim to the fire, or at least insinuated that he had set it as part of his plan for revenge. He claimed that he never meant to harm anyone. I guess he wanted to burn Jonathan's house down hoping to make him suffer financially."

"And I don't think it's a man, unless he's a mighty small man with a squeaky voice," I said. "I think it's a young person—possibly a teenager with a grievance against Jonathan and some others he thinks have done him an injustice. I don't think he knew what he was doing when he torched Jonathan's house. I'm sure he didn't plan to set off such a big explosion. He reeked of smoke. He seemed nervous. Wouldn't you be freaked if you found out that your actions had killed someone by accident? I'd be frantic. What started out as a simple payback turned into murder, and now it's too late to say you're sorry. Torching a house is a lot different than killing someone."

"Can you identify the man... ah... kid?" Lu Ann asked me. She looked at Cole. "It makes sense to me. From what I've concluded, I think it could've been done by a young person. An adult would've used a more sophisticated method."

"The kid was my height and was close to my weight. He was dressed in black and had a ski mask pulled down over his head. All I could see were his eyes, nose, and mouth."

"That's not much to go on, but it's a start." Cole said. He stood up and started pacing the floor. "I can't believe you've held this back from the police. Do you have any idea what this could mean for you? You could go to jail."

"How many times have you said that to me?"

"That's because you're always getting into something."

"No, I won't go to jail," I said. "You can make this work out to our advantage, or I'll swear that I don't know what you're talking about."

Cole was stunned by my cockiness, and I think everyone else in the room was, too. Nobody said anything for a moment.

"Just tell the sheriff that Jesse thought the guy was a wacko, and that she didn't believe him when he confessed to setting the fire," Lu Ann added.

"That's not going to work. Sheriff Hudson knows me better than that," I said. "He knows I'm not some silly woman who could be fooled so easily. I'm smart, and I know when someone's trying to pull my leg. That statement will go over like a lead balloon. You'll insult his intelligence if you try to pull that one over on him."

"I'll figure out something," Cole said. "Is there anything else you can think of? You haven't left out any other details, have you?"

"He set the fire and now he's lurking around. How else would he know that Daniel died? He confronted me in the parking garage and then went to Ruckersville and set another fire. He has to be stopped."

"The fires could be connected, but is this kid the one who set both fires?" Cole said. "He could have an accomplice."

"That's true," Jonathan agreed. "Both fires were set in the same manner. They both used gasoline, a rookie's means. Could we be dealing with kids? Gang members?"

"I don't think so," I said. "This kid didn't seem like a gang member."

"How can you tell?" Lu Ann Asked. "Have you had any dealings with gang members? Let me tell you one thing—they're ruthless."

"No, I haven't," I replied. "I do know that gang members have no conscience. They attack without provocation and then stand back and laugh at their deeds. You're right; they enjoy inflicting pain on others. This guy was sorry that Daniel died. I really don't think he meant for anyone to get hurt. He said he wanted Jonathan to suffer, but not like this."

"Could you pick out this guy in a line up?"

"I doubt it. I didn't get to see his face."

"Would you give it a try if I arranged a line up?"

"Sure, I'll do what I can, but I think it's a waste of time. I can't do it right now. I have to wait for Mom to come back so she can watch the kids."

Lu Ann started to say something, but stopped when she looked at me. Women have a way of reading each other, too... just like men do. I knew she was going to offer to watch the children, but she could tell from the look on my face that I was using my mother as an excuse.

"Okay," Cole said. "I'll head on back to Stanardsville and have a talk with Sheriff Hudson. If he agrees, we'll make arrangements for you to do this in Charlottesville at the precinct. How's that?"

"I just hope you're not wasting your time and mine."

"You'll probably be hearing from Captain Waverly shortly."

"I'm not going anywhere."

Cole turned and headed for the door. He stopped, looked back at us and said, "Again, I'm real sorry about Daniel. We'll catch the person who did this. I promise."

A minute later, he was gone.

The four of us sat back down at the kitchen table and had a frank talk about the possibility that a young kid had pulled off this horrible crime. Billy and Jonathan wanted revenge for Daniel's death and no matter what I said, they were determined to have it. They were certain that someone from Jonathan's past was the one responsible, not a young kid.

However you looked at it—the outcome wasn't going to be pretty.

CHAPTER 10

T HE SNOW WAS STEADILY COMING DOWN, leaving a clean, fresh blanket on the ground. It looked as if we were in for another one of our famous mountain blizzards. After spending the last three winters here, I've come to realize that this was par for the course. We were destined to have at least one heavy snowfall at some point in time.

Jonathan and Lu Ann had left to go over to his place and sift through the ashes before the snow got too deep, while Billy and I waited for Mom to return. We were in the nursery on diaper duty, having a discussion about his visit to the crime scene.

"I wanted to go with you when you went back," I said.

"I'm sorry. It was a last minute decision. We decided to go over and have a look around before we went up to Mom's house."

"What did it feel like being there again?"

"Strange," Billy said. "I can still see Daniel falling through the floor. It was awful. One minute he was there and the next he was gone. Jonathan said he broke his neck when he fell. It was just one of those weird moments that life throws at you."

"I know what that's like. When we moved to Stanardsville, I was so happy. I met Cole and my life started to change. I was no longer lonely.

Then I came home one day and my dad was dead. How can you be so happy and then so sad all at one time? It's not fair."

"This, I cannot explain."

"Then we found each other." I leaned toward Billy and kissed him on the cheek as I finished putting a clean outfit on Maisy. "Now I have a wonderful husband, two beautiful kids, and a mother who loves to stay with me almost as much as I love having her here. Daniel's death will be hard to deal with, but we'll get through it. We'll find the person who did this."

"I worry about Greg. He was very close to his father."

"It'll be hard, but he'll make it through. They say kids are resilient. They bounce back quickly. I'm not so sure about that, but however you look at it, we'll be here for him. I'm just glad he has a girlfriend."

"Yes, having a girlfriend will help. He'll have someone to comfort him. I think he's in love."

"I think you're right."

"There's nothing like having someone to love."

"I agree," I said, grinning. "Is he going to stay at his father's house?"

"Yes," Billy replied. "When Jonathan and I arrived at Mom and Dad's, he was there. They were discussing the future."

"I bet that was difficult."

"Very much so, but Greg is strong. He is a Blackhawk. He will carry on. He will make his own way now."

"He's certainly old enough to live by himself. He's eighteen—that's legal age."

"The chief said Daniel left a will, and it states that Greg gets the house and the car dealership. The rest of his assets will be divided equally among his other children."

"I guess the ex-wives don't get anything." I chuckled a little. "At least, by law they're not entitled to anything unless it's in the will. Isn't that right?"

"Daniel loved his women. They will all share in his fortune."

"I'm impressed," I said, surprised. "Usually when a marriage ends, so does the civility."

"Their marriages might have ended, but not their relationships."

"That's a good thing. I'm sure it made it much easier on the children."

"Daniel never claimed to be anything but what he was—a man who loved women. He wanted to make them happy, but the problem was that they couldn't handle his inability to stay committed. He remained devoted to all three of his wives."

"They must've really loved him."

"Oh, they did. All of them. But sometimes that's not enough. They moved on, but continued to respect him for his devotion to his children. In a divorce that's what matters the most—the children."

"You are such a smart man."

"Yes, I am," Billy smiled at me and then changed the subject. "If you want to satisfy your curiosity, why don't you run on over to Jonathan's place—I guess that's what we'll have to call it until he builds a new house."

"For him and Lu Ann."

"Ah, you're not making fun of her name anymore."

"No, it would be disrespectful."

"Now that you've gotten to know her and you like her."

"Yes."

We headed back to the kitchen, the one place where we seem to spend most of our time now that we have small children, and continued our discussion.

"Were you serious about my going over to Jonathan's?"

"Sure. I know you have something burning in you. You need to go feed that hunger."

I had to laugh. "You think I'm burning, huh?"

"I think you might come up with something, stumble onto a clue."

"I just have to see the place for myself. I might find something others have missed. You never know."

"You're the one who always throws something into the ring, and it's usually worth paying attention to."

"Will you be okay alone with two kids, a couple of lazy dogs, and a mysterious cat?"

I looked over by the fireplace in the living room and saw Athena and

Thor cuddled up. Thor rolled over and then Spice Cat stood up and stretched. He had been napping in between the two dogs.

"Oops, my mistake. The cat isn't so mysterious after all. He was just hiding. Speaking of animals—how are the horses? I haven't had time to even walk out to the stable to check on them."

"They're fine. The chief has been taking care of them. He loves Dusty and Rusty. He mentioned this morning that he had hired someone to take care of the animals for a while. He has his hands full with Mom. Jenny and Beth are over there trying to help out. They're going to the funeral home with Mom and Dad to make final preparations for Daniel's service. But Mom's such a wreck. Dad says her health isn't too good. He's very concerned."

"He mentioned that to me earlier. What *is* her problem? Do you know?"

"Dad had a talk with Dr. Bryant and from what he told him, the doctor thinks Mom might have developed adult onset diabetes. He urged Dad to get her to come in, but Mom refuses. She says she's too busy right now."

"Say no more. I'll get her to go to the doctor, if I have to carry her myself. My Uncle Bill has the same thing—along with a few other health issues—and now he's in a bad way. And… he's been going to a doctor for a long time. You can't let an illness like this go untreated. If he had, he'd be dead by now."

"I appreciate that, Jesse. Maybe you can get her to go to the doctor after the funeral."

"You can bet on it."

"Go change and put on something warm," Billy demanded. "It's getting nasty out there. I want you to carry your…"

"I know what to carry," I said as I kissed Maisy and then put her in the playpen close to the table. She immediately started playing with her toys.

"A gun, a cell phone, and my wits. If that's not sufficient, I'll stick my Buck Knife in my boot." I turned, bent down, and kissed Ethan on the forehead as Billy fed him his bottle. "He's such a little angel." I kissed Billy on the lips. "You're so sexy. When I get back, we need to do something about this appetite I've been suppressing."

"I'll fix a roast."

I reached over and touched his face. "I see you're not hot like you were last night. I guess you weren't running a fever. I was worried."

"Don't worry about me, `ge ya. I am fine."

I went to the bedroom and changed into something more practical for the cold weather I would encounter. I slipped into a pair of Levi's, a T-shirt, and a turtleneck sweater. I chose a pair of socks that were thick and came up to my knees. Inside one of the socks I slipped the knife. I went through my top dresser drawer and found the .38 and .357 that I had placed there earlier.

Since the kids came along, I quit hiding my .38 under the bed and the .357 in my purse. It was too easy for them to get to. So now, two guns were kept in the dresser and a third, my new 9MM was the one I kept in my purse—on top of my dresser and out of reach. I made sure of it each time I sat my purse down. I try to learn from my mistakes.

A while back, I accidentally left my purse with a gun in it on the floor by the sofa while Claire's two children were here. That time the error saved our lives. But luck can sometimes turn to tragedy, so now when I put my purse down, I make sure it's out of the reach of inquiring little minds and busy fingers. The purse goes on top of my dresser—no exceptions.

I checked my oversized handbag to make sure the 9MM was still there and then pulled the .357 from the dresser drawer. I grabbed my knee high snow boots from the closet, slipped them on, and then stuffed the .357 in the left one. I was ready for anything. I felt fully dressed—weapons and all.

I kept thinking about how wonderful my husband was to let me go running off in the approaching snowstorm while he sat at home tending to the kids. He probably just needed a little solitude to reminisce about his brother. Don't we all when a loved one dies?

I walked into the living room and sized up the situation.

"I see the animals are cozy by the fire, and it looks as if you have everything under control. Do I need to bring in more firewood before I leave?"

"I got it covered. You better hurry up before your mother gets back.

You know how she is when she thinks you're going to get into something."

"Like I said earlier, I'm always getting into something. That's my job. I just feel like I need to go over there and have a look around for myself. I'm pretty good at what I do. You taught me well. Hopefully, I might come up with something others might have missed."

Billy looked up at me and grinned. "You do have a way about you. I trust those feelings you get."

"There's usually something to them, isn't there?" I slipped on my heavy winter coat and then grabbed the doorknob. "Later, we need to go see you mother. At least, I do. I haven't seen her today and I want to. She needs her family."

"I will be here when you get back."

Billy seemed quiet, almost subdued, but I knew I would probably feel the same way if something happened to my brother or sister. I know I'd lose my mind if anything happened to my mother. I blew a kiss in his direction and then walked out the front door.

An eerie feeling came over me as I walked down the porch steps. I pulled my gloves out of my coat pocket and slipped my hands in them. A cold blast of air hit me in the face as I walked over to the side yard and opened the door of the 4Runner. I climbed inside, laid my purse in the other seat, and then saw the keys lying on the console.

"That wasn't smart," I said to myself. "I must be losing my mind."

I stuck the keys in the ignition and started the car. As I backed out into the driveway, a strange feeling that I wasn't alone came over me. I looked around, but didn't see anyone. I shook my head.

"Now I know I'm freaking out. I'm imagining things. I've been watching too much late night television. I'm going to have to stay away from those scary movies."

I drove down the driveway until I came to the end. I looked both ways, and then turned right onto Bear Mountain Road. When I got close to Jonathan's driveway on the left, two Greene County Police cruisers, the Greene County Sheriff's car, and a Charlottesville Police car pulled out and turned left heading out onto the main highway.

"Hmm," I mumbled. "I wonder what they're doing here. I guess I'll just have to go see for myself."

I turned into Jonathan's driveway and drove the curvy path until I reached the end. There was no one in sight. I didn't even see Jonathan's Humvee or Lu Ann's Suburban. That's strange. The Fire Marshall's not even here. Where is everyone... and why isn't there any crime scene tape up? I guess they must be finished.

Before I could get out of the car, my cell phone rang. I looked at Caller ID and saw that it was a call from my house. I flipped open the phone and said, "Hello. You miss me already?"

"You know I do," Billy said. "Your mother called. She's on her way home. Robert also called to let us know that he'll be sending over some food from the restaurant."

"That's good. Is there anything else?"

"I'm going to get sad on you for a minute."

"That's okay, Billy. Go ahead."

"I just want to say that I never knew how much I could love someone until I met you. Don't get me wrong—I loved Ruth, and I still do, but you're going to be the love of my life. I love you, Jesse."

I sniffled as tears rolled down my cheeks.

"I'm sorry. I didn't mean to make you cry."

"They're tears of joy, Billy. I feel the same way. We will be together forever."

"I must go." Billy laughed. "I have big job waiting. I am warrior!"

His Cherokee accent is always a delight to me. "Yes, you are," I agreed.

I closed up the cell phone and slipped it in my coat pocket. I sat in the car and looked around. The house and sheds were nothing but a memory now—their shells were pieces of burnt timber blackened by an intense fire, and now covered with snow. The beautiful cedar trees that once surrounded the house were mere stalks devoid of bark and greenery. The whole circle looked like the aftermath of a nuclear explosion—only on a much, much smaller scale. Snow hid any traces of the sorrow that lay among the ashes. The scene was heartbreaking. I had to leave. There was nothing I could uncover. The snow was too deep, and not knowing where solid ground was, I figured that it was a waste of time, not to mention dangerous. I guess I just wanted to return to where it all happened. I needed my own form of closure. This would be the end of a time, but a new beginning would soon emerge from the ashes. Jonathan would rebuild his home, and hopefully, share it and his life with Lu Ann. Even though he would be laid to rest, Daniel's memory would live on. His killer would be brought to justice.

My cell phone rang again. I didn't bother to look at Caller ID, instead I flipped open the phone, and said, "Yes, dear."

"Mrs. Blackhawk? This is Sue Ellen."

"Oops, sorry. I thought you were Billy."

"That's all right," she said. "I've done the same thing myself. I called because I just checked the messages at the office, and there was a weird one on the machine. I called your house, but no one answered, so I called Mr. Blackhawk's cell phone. It was turned off. I didn't know what else to do except call you. I hope you don't mind."

"Of course, not," I replied. "That's okay. So, Billy didn't answer at the house, huh? That's odd. He should be there. He's taking care of the children."

"I'm sorry, but he didn't answer."

"He was probably busy and couldn't get to the phone in time. I'll call him in a minute, but for now, what about this message on the machine?"

"There was a call from someone who sounded like a teenager. He didn't leave a name, but he said he wanted to speak to you. He said it was urgent. I've been checking the machine every hour, so it couldn't have been too long since he called."

"What else did he say?"

"His message said that he would call back at 2:00."

I looked at the clock on the dashboard of the Toyota. The digital read-out said 1:45. I could make it if I hurried up.

"Sue Ellen, I'm going to head on over to the office and see if I can catch the caller. Thanks so much for calling me."

"What about Mr. Blackhawk? Should I try to call him again?"

"No, I'll call him. You just keep checking the messages every hour or so. Thanks again for calling me, Sue Ellen."

I hit the end button and then pressed the programmed number for our house. The phone rang several times before someone answered.

"Hello," the voice on the other end said. It sounded like a teenager. The first thing I thought of was that the teenager from the garage had broken into my house and was holding Billy and the children hostage.

"Who is this?" I demanded to know.

"Ah, this is Greg. Who is this?"

"Oh, Greg, this is Jesse. I'm sorry that I snapped at you, but... oh, never mind. Is Billy there?"

"He's in the den with your mother and her friend, Eddie. Do you want me to go get him?"

"No, that's not necessary. Just tell him I have an errand to run. If he needs me, he can reach me on my cell phone."

"I'll tell him."

"How are you doing, Greg?"

"I'm hanging in there. Poor Grandma isn't doing too well. She's been crying ever since Dad died. I'm worried that she's going to have a stroke or something."

"She's grieving, Greg. She'll probably cry for a long time. It'll get easier as time passes."

"That's exactly what Uncle Billy said. He said to be strong."

"He knows what he's talking about."

"Are you coming home? I'd like to see you before I go home."

"I'll be there shortly." I paused for a second. "Are you staying at your dad's house by yourself?"

"I've been living with Dad ever since he and Mom split up, so I'm used to being by myself. Except now he won't be coming home."

"I'm so sorry, Greg. You know you can stay with us until you're ready to go back home."

"I know, but if I don't go back now, I'll never be able to."

"I understand."

"Besides, my girlfriend is coming over to stay with me for a while. Grandma didn't even bat an eyelash when I told her. I guess she's in a world all her own. She's so hurt by this. I feel bad for her."

"I'm sure she is. She'll get better, Greg. Trust me."

"So, what are you doing? Billy said that you had a wild hair and wanted to go back over to Jonathan's house… well, I guess it's not a house anymore."

"We'll call it his place for the time being. How's that?"

"That sounds good to me. Where are you now?"

"Ah… I'd rather not say."

"Oh, Lord, you're out getting into trouble. Billy said you probably were. You should tell me where you are, so he can come and help… just in case you need him."

"Tell him that I'm going to run to the office to intercept a call and I'll be home soon."

"I'll tell him, but he's probably not going to like it. He's going to suspect something is up. Is it?"

"I'm not sure, but I'm fully armed, so don't worry. I'll be fine."

"Okay, Jesse. I'll tell Uncle Billy you called. If I'm not here when you get back, I'll see you later."

"Hang in there, buddy."

"I will."

I closed up the phone and tossed it on the seat. I turned around in the circle and headed down the driveway. I had fifteen minutes to make it to the office if I wanted to talk to the kid who left the message. I had to hurry. Time was flying by. I reached the end of Jonathan's driveway and looked around. The coast was clear, so I pulled out and drove until I came to the main road. I turned left and headed toward town. Five minutes down the road, I passed Crumpler's Market.

The store was shuttered up and had a sign on the door with the word CLOSED in big red letters on a piece of paper hanging from a string. A long, black cloth was draped over the top of the door—a symbol used to indicate a death in the family.

That confirmed what Sue Ellen had told me. The market owner was the father of the Greene County deputy, Ronnie Crumpler, and the woman who was killed in the Ruckersville fire. I would stop by once he reopened and offer my condolences. It was the neighborly... and right thing to do.

The snow was blinding. I could hardly see the road as I slowly crept into town. It was too dangerous to go any faster, but I needed to make it to the office in time to be there when the call came in.

Then it dawned on me that the boy might not call at the exact time he said he would. Why should I put my life in jeopardy for a call that might not come in until later? No, I would play it safe, and take my time.

"If it's important, they'll call back." That's what Mom always says.

I knew it had to be the same boy as the one in the hospital parking garage. Who else could it be? My question would be answered soon.

I pulled up in front of the office building and parked. I turned off the car, locked it up, and walked up to the front door. I could hear the phone ringing through the glass as I stood outside and tried to pick out the right key.

Finally, I found the key and slid it in the keyhole. I turned the key, shoved open the door, and ran to the front desk. The answering machine came on. I snatched up the phone and hit the stop button to turn off the message.

"Hello," I said, out of breath. "This is Jesse Watson Blackhawk. Who is this?"

"I'd rather not say, if you don't mind," the young fellow said.

"Look, I'm not in the mood for games. Tell me your name, or I'm hanging up."

I wasn't really going to hang up, but I decided to force his hand. If I didn't have a name, I had nothing.

"My name is Wayne Avery. I'm the guy you met in the hospital parking garage."

"Oh, yes, I remember you now. You're the one who shoved a gun in my face."

"It wasn't loaded," he said, softly. "I'm sorry. I've made such a mess. I didn't mean for all this to happen, and I didn't kill anyone."

"According to the police you did."

I looked up and saw two Charlottesville Police cars with sirens blaring and lights flashing pull up in the front of the building. The officers jumped out of their vehicles with their weapons drawn.

"Ah, Wayne, I'm going to have to put you on hold for a minute. Please don't hang up. I'll be right back. I have a problem on this end."

CHAPTER 11

Unsure of what to do, I raised my hands in the air and walked toward the front door. I had no idea what the police were doing here, but I was sure it didn't have anything to do with my caller. No one knew about the call from him except me and Sue Ellen, and I was sure she didn't suspect a thing.

"What's the problem, officers?" I asked as I approached them. I looked over at the security box by the foyer and realized that the silent alarm had gone off.

Last year, Billy replaced the alarm system that dinged twice when the door opened to one that didn't make a sound. He didn't want to draw attention to the alarm and possibly alert an intruder to its existence. I guess he didn't realize at the time that if one of us entered in a hurry and forgot about the alarm, the cops would show up. The ding, ding always helped to remind me to punch in the code. This time, I had forgotten to do so.

"I can explain," I said. "I'm Jesse Blackhawk and this is my husband's office. I was in a hurry and forgot to punch in the code."

They glanced at each other and then one of them said, "If that's the case, then reset the alarm." They were testing me.

I walked up to the keypad and punched in the code. The red light continued to blink. "I don't know what the problem is, officer." I tried the numbers again, but the red light didn't change to green. Then it came to me. Billy must've changed the pass code when he had the system changed and forgot to tell me. I tried to convey this to the policemen, but they weren't buying my story.

"Show me some identification or we're going to have to arrest you for breaking and entering," the red-headed officer said.

I looked at his nametag. "Ah... Officer Whalen," I said, trying to think for a minute. "My purse is in my car. I'll go get it."

"I don't think so," Officer Whalen said. He looked at the other officer. "Check it out, Spencer."

Officer Spencer turned and walked out the door, leaving just the two of us waiting in the foyer.

"I have someone waiting on the phone. Do you mind..."

"Yes, I do," he replied. "I guess you don't realize how serious this is."

"This is ridiculous!" I exclaimed. "My husband, Billy Blackhawk, owns this place and I have every right to be here!"

"Then why don't you know the code?"

"Because he must've changed it!"

"And he forgot to tell you."

"That's right!" I was getting irate. I had an arsonist on the phone waiting for me and I didn't know how long he would hold on. I had to get back to him before he hung up. "You don't understand, Officer Whalen. I have this guy on the line and I really need to talk with him. You see..."

Officer Spencer returned carrying my purse in one hand and my gun in the other. "I hope you have a permit to carry a concealed weapon."

"You went through my purse!" I accused him. "You can't do that. It's against the law!"

The two officers looked at each other and then gave me a sarcastic sneer. They'd obviously seen their share of liars and had been confronted by a weapon wielding psychotic, which is what they apparently thought I was. The officer carrying my purse tossed it to me and said, "It fell out of your purse. Now, produce your ID."

I reached inside my purse and pulled out my wallet. I opened it and showed him my private investigator's ID. "Here, see, I told you."

"Please take your ID out of the wallet."

"This is nuts." I pulled the plastic card from the slit and handed it to Officer Spencer, along with my concealed weapons permit card.

He took both cards, looked at Officer Whalen, turned and walked out to his patrol car. I could see that he was talking into his radio. A few seconds later he returned and handed me back my cards.

"Make sure that you get the code so you can punch it in next time. If we have to come out again on a false alarm our captain won't be too happy."

"And how is Captain Waverly doing?" I asked, trying to be smart. "Please give him my regards." I looked up and noticed that the green light was blinking. Then I realized that most alarms reset themselves after fifteen minutes... at least the one we have did. Then I saw Billy's pickup truck pulling up to the building. "Oh, me," I mumbled. "My husband's here."

"Good," Officer Whalen said. "Perhaps we should have a talk with him and explain that false alarms are a waste of our manpower. The force has its hands full as it is without adding useless calls to our job."

Officer Spencer handed my gun to me, butt first.

"Why don't you do that, Officer Whalen? I'm sure he'll appreciate your concerns. He's a law-biding citizen. He understands how difficult your jobs are. I'm sure it would make his day that he had to come out in the snow to rescue his wife."

The two officers turned and walked out the door. They stood outside and talked with Billy. I ran back to the phone and picked up the receiver.

"Hello," I said, but all I heard on the other end was a dial tone. "Crap!" I slammed the phone down in its cradle. He must've heard the sirens and hung up.

The officers got in their cars and pulled out of the parking lot, their lights no longer blinking, as Billy walked through the front door. He had a frown on his face.

"I know," I said as I walked up to him. "I can explain."

"Are you all right?" Billy asked.

I was surprised for a second. I thought for sure that he was going to give me a lecture about being so irresponsible, which I so rightfully deserved, but he didn't. His main concern was for my well-being. The first thing that came to mind was that he was a real keeper. Every woman should be as lucky as I am.

"I'm fine. I forgot about the silent alarm. The phone was ringing and I was trying to get to it before he hung up. Then the cops showed up... and I didn't have the new code... and then the officer found my handgun. It wasn't pleasant." I was rambling,

"Take a deep breath and then tell me what's going on."

"You changed the code. Why didn't you tell me?"

"I forgot to. You rarely come to the office anymore."

"I'm here now and I need the code."

"It's 1224."

"That's our anniversary! Why Billy, I think you're such a sweet, sentimental kind of guy."

"That's me. Now tell me about the phone call."

"First—you tell me what you're doing here. How did you know I'd be here?"

"I figured that you'd be here. Sue Ellen called and said she had tried to call earlier, but didn't get an answer."

"I told her not to call you. I said I would call the house and make sure everything was okay. I also told her that you were probably busy with the children and couldn't get to the phone. I called the house and Greg answered. It appeared that everything was under control, so I told him to tell you that I'd be back soon. I had an errand to run."

"I know about your errand. Sue Ellen told me about the message on the machine. She said a guy called and wanted to talk with you. She also said that he sounded like a teenager. I put two and two together and here I am. It's a good thing I showed up when I did. Officer Whalen said they were about to haul you in. He said that you were getting belligerent with them. Jesse, you know you can't do that. People get arrested for unruly behavior. It just gives the police an excuse to slap the cuffs on you and throw you in the slammer."

I had to laugh. "Your words are old-fashioned, Thunder Cloud."

"And so are my ways. I like it like that, and you like me for being that way. Admit it."

I hugged him and said, "I love you just the way you are. Would you like to go upstairs for a few minutes of intense lovemaking? We haven't had a chance to be alone in a while. I'll settle for a quickie."

"You're too romantic for me."

"How about this," I asked as I pressed my body to his and then ran my hand up and down his back. "I want to kiss you and lie in your arms… for at least ten minutes."

"We'll talk about the phone call later," he said, smiling. He picked me up in his arms and headed to the door leading up to the apartment where he was living when we first met. He reached the door, turned the knob, and then grunted. "It's locked. Let me fish out the keys." He put me down and reached into his coat pocket for them.

The phone rang.

"Hold that thought," I said. I ran over to the desk and picked up the receiver and answered. "Hello, this is Jesse."

"This is Wayne, again. I hung up when I heard the sirens. I waited a few minutes before calling you back. I was afraid you had called the police, but then I realized that they were at your door and not mine. What happened?"

"I forgot to punch in the access code and the silent alarm went off. Next thing I know the cops show up. That was a little spooky considering who I was talking with on the phone. We should meet and have a talk."

"I didn't set that fire in Ruckersville, and I didn't kill those people."

"That's a little hard to believe considering you gave me the impression that you weren't done. That you had other fish to fry."

"It wasn't me."

"I can only attest to the time you were at the parking garage. I have no idea what you did after you left me. By the way, you shouldn't go poking a gun in someone's face. It's not polite."

"I'm sorry. I don't know why I did that. The gun wasn't loaded."

"But next time it might be."

Billy walked over, stood beside me, and then hit the speaker button so he could listen in.

"What was that?" Wayne asked. "Is someone else listening?"

"Yes," I said. "My husband, Billy, is here."

"He's that guy's brother, isn't he?"

"Yes, he is."

There was a long silence, but Wayne didn't hang up. Finally, when he spoke, his voice broke up. "I'm... so sorry... I didn't mean for anyone... to get ... hurt."

"Well, someone did," Billy raised his voice. "My brother died because of you! Your actions killed him—be it accidental or intentional. You will have to pay!"

"I'm willing... to pay for... what I did." Wayne broke down and cried.

I looked at Billy, but didn't say anything. What could I say? He was talking on the phone with the person who was responsible for his brother's death. He had a right to be angry... and loud... and anything he wanted to be. I remained silent and let him have his say.

"You must turn yourself in to the police and suffer the consequences of your deed. You will be safe in custody... from me."

"I'm ready to... pay for my actions. I can't... live with... what I've done. All I wanted... was revenge. That bounty hunter... he killed my father. He sent... my father... back to jail... and my father... he hung himself while he... while he was locked up."

"That's not my brother's fault."

"But don't you see... it was. My father.... he never hurt a... soul in... his life. He was... a good man."

"So was my brother, Daniel. He was a good man. He had a family."

I nudged Billy and then said, "Wayne, why don't you come here and we'll go with you to the police station to turn yourself in."

"No... I can't do that. I just wanted to say... that I was sorry. You seemed like a nice person the other night." He sniffled once more and then stopped crying. "There's no one left but me. My mother is dead and now my father is, too. I killed someone and now I must pay. I just wanted to tell someone the truth. Did you know they said my father beat my mother?"

"No, I didn't. I'm real sorry about what happened."

"My mother was having an affair, and the guy beat her up real bad when she tried to break it off. She told my dad, and they had a big argument. A neighbor called the cops. My mom was angry and she accused my father of hitting her. The police took him away. Dad got out on bail, but by then it was too late. Mom had taken a bottle of sleeping pills and died before he got home. The day of my graduation from high school, I was at my mother's funeral. My dad had to go to court the following Monday."

"He jumped bail and Jonathan was the one who brought him in."

"That's right. My dad killed himself in jail. Can you understand why I was so mad? Shouldn't somebody be held accountable for what happened to my mother and father?"

"I don't know what to say, Wayne. What you did was wrong. Two wrongs don't make a right—that's what my mother would say at a time like this. Why don't you let me take you in? I promise I'll make sure that you get to tell your side of the story."

I looked up at Billy. I knew this was difficult for him to hear, but someone had to be rational.

"I just did, Jesse," Wayne replied. "I told you the truth and now I'm finished. Mr. Blackhawk, I want you to know that I never meant for your brother to die. I know you'll never forgive me for what I did, but I had to say I was sorry before it was too late. I know what it's like to lose the people you love, and I'm sorry your family has to go through that kind of pain."

"Wayne," Billy said. "You need to come in."

As if a light had gone off in my head, everything was coming together. Everything that Sue Ellen had told me now made sense. The guy from the Ruckersville fire was the one who had been having an affair with Wayne's mother. Did Wayne go over to Ruckersville and kill those two people? It had to have been him. He had a motive. The pieces of the puzzle had now fallen into place.

"I'm willing to pay for what I did to your brother, but I'm not going to jail for a crime I didn't commit. I didn't set that fire in Ruckersville, and I didn't kill those two people."

"That's for a judge to decide, Wayne," Billy said. "The two people who died in the fire in Ruckersville were shot before the fire was set. Do you own a gun?"

"Oh, God. That's awful. Yes, I have my Dad's gun, but I don't have any bullets."

I looked at Billy, stunned. This was a piece of the puzzle that I didn't know about.

"Then you need to turn yourself in and bring your gun. If you're innocent, ballistics on the gun will prove it."

"Mr. Blackhawk, please tell your family how sorry I am for making them suffer. And I want you to know how sorry I am. I never wanted that to happen. Jesse, I want you to promise me that the police know that I didn't mean for anyone to get hurt."

"You can tell them yourself when you turn yourself in."

"No, I've said my peace. I've done all I can. I said I'm sorry and now I will pay for my actions."

A weird feeling in the pit of my stomach made me take notice that something terrible was about to happen. "Wayne!" I called his name at the same moment we heard the shot. The line went silent. "Wayne," I yelled, tears flowing. "Oh, my God! Wayne!"

Billy and I stood there staring at each other.

I went to hang up the phone, but Billy stopped me. "Don't," he said. "They might be able to trace the call."

I lay the phone down on the desk and cried in Billy's arms. I would never forget this moment if I lived to be a hundred. A young life had ended too soon. Not only had a young life ended early, but that life had been filled with pain and anguish. I wept for his soul.

"I guess he lied about not having any bullets," I mumbled.

"Come on, Jesse," Billy said, tenderly. "We have to call the police and let them know what happened, and then we have to get you home."

Billy reached into his coat pocket for his cell phone. He dialed the Charlottesville Police Department, asked for Captain Waverly, and then waited.

"His name was Wayne Avery. I know you hate him for what he did to

Daniel, but he was just a kid. I don't know what to think. I hate it that Daniel died, but…"

"I know, Jesse. It's hard to separate right from wrong sometimes. It was wrong for him to seek revenge by burning down Jonathan's house, which led to Daniel's death, but I didn't want him to die for it… I don't think. I guess there is still a little forgiveness left in my soul."

"You've got more forgiveness in your little pinky than I do in my whole body. I probably would've hunted him down and killed him if it had been my brother."

"Not once you realized he was just a kid and he begged for forgiveness. I believe that he didn't mean for things to go so terribly wrong. I see that now."

"I was afraid of what you were going to do when you found him."

"I was, too. I had much hatred in me. I don't like that feeling."

"I feel sick." I let go of Billy, ran to the bathroom and heaved. What was left of breakfast was now a thing of the past. My nerves aren't what they used to be, I thought to myself. I flushed the toilet, wiped my face with a wet paper towel, and then returned to the front of the office. I stood by as Billy explained what had just happened.

"I don't know where he lives. Okay, I will. I'll hold on. Just let me know when I can hang up the phone. I need to take my wife home. She's a wreck."

We waited as the police and the telephone company did their jobs. It didn't take long. The captain must've said something to Billy, because he closed up his cell phone, and said, "They have an address for him. It won't take them long."

"Good," I replied, not knowing what else to say. "Can we go home now?"

"Will you be all right to drive? I know you're upset. We can leave your 4Runner here and then I'll get Jonathan to come back with me to get it."

"No, I'm going to be okay," I said as I watched Billy pick up the phone receiver and then place it back in its cradle. "I hate what just happened. Why does life have to be so hard sometimes?"

"I don't know, `ge ya. It just does. We can only live our lives and hope for the best."

We walked to the front door and peered out. The snow had stopped falling. "It looks as if it's going to clear up," I said. "Is that blue skies in the background?"

"If it is, it won't last long. I heard the weather forecast on the radio on my way over here, and they're calling for a foot of snow tonight."

Billy locked the door behind us. We got in our automobiles and I followed him out of the parking lot. It had been a long day and it wasn't over, yet. We hadn't gotten down the road very far when my cell phone rang. I dug in my purse, but couldn't find it. I felt around in the seat. "Ah, there you are." I flipped open the phone and said, "Hello."

"I did tell you that your mom and Eddie are at our house, didn't I?" Billy asked. "And Robert sent over food from his restaurant."

"I knew Mom was there, and I'm glad about the food. I'm sure we're going to have plenty of company, and I don't want my mother to spend all her time in the kitchen."

"Hold on a minute, Jesse. I have a call coming in."

I waited for what seemed like an eternity before Billy got back to me. We were almost home when he clicked back over. "You're not going to believe this," he said.

"Nowadays, I'll believe anything."

"Wayne Avery isn't dead."

"Good, he's still alive! How bad is it?"

"Not bad at all considering he wasn't even there when the police arrived, and there was no sign of a suicide as we assumed. There was, however, a bullet hole in the floor. So in other words, he either chickened out or he played us. It's all a game to him. He's jerking us around."

"That creep! How dare he get me all upset like that! Do the cops have any idea where he is?"

"I doubt it. Don't fret. He'll show himself eventually. Mark my words."

CHAPTER 12

AFTER FINDING OUT THAT WAYNE AVERY didn't shoot himself and was still alive, I was angry that he pulled one over on me, but glad he wasn't dead. It was obvious he had emotional problems that needed to be dealt with, and hopefully, one so young could be saved and put on the right path with a little help from a professional. I would help him get the help he needed.

Of course, he would do time even if he plea-bargained, but eventually he would get his life back—if he wanted it. For some reason, I wasn't convinced that he had anything to do with the killings in Ruckersville, but I could be wrong. He had lied about not having any bullets. It was one lie after another. All kinds of thoughts were racing through my mind as I pulled up behind Billy in the driveway.

He got out of his truck and walked up to my car. I hit the button to roll the window down. The cold air rushed in.

"You left your truck running, dear," I said, pointing in the direction of his truck and half-laughing. "Aren't you going to turn it off?"

"I'm going to park it in the garage, and I want you to do the same thing. With a foot of snow coming, the automobiles would be buried. Back your 4Runner into the garage."

"Ha! You must be kidding! Me—back my vehicle up into the garage? That's a joke."

"Oh, that's right. I've seen you in action. I'll take care of it."

Suddenly, I remembered that I was supposed to call the cleanup crew, but I hadn't. By now, the stench was probably unbearable.

"Ah... Billy," I said. "I forgot to..."

"... call the cleanup crew. Yes, I know. I took care of the mess when your mother got back. It only took me about fifteen minutes. It wasn't as bad as I thought."

"Yuck," I said, almost gagging at the idea of all that blood. "Are you sure it doesn't stink in there?"

"Nope. Not at all," Billy replied.

"I'm not going to see Bambi's mother's head hanging on the wall in the garage when you open the door, am I?"

"No. Don't be silly," Billy mumbled as he turned to go back to his truck. "It's hanging in the house." He chuckled as he walked away.

"What?" I yelled. "What did you say?" Did I hear him right? Did he say the deer head was hanging in the house? It had to be a joke! "Billy!"

"I'm just kidding, `ge ya," he said as he stood by his truck door. "Go on inside before you freeze."

I turned off the ignition, grabbed my purse, and pulled out my gloves. After slipping my hands into them, I stepped out of the vehicle onto slippery ground. The snow crunched under my feet as I made my way up to the porch. I held onto the handrails and steadied myself with each step.

Finally, I made it to the front door without falling. I turned and watched in amazement at how easily Billy maneuvered his truck into the garage. He backed it in with ease. Then he got out and walked over to my 4Runner. He got in, turned the vehicle around, and backed it into the garage. I waited for him to get to the porch.

"You make it look so easy," I said. "I just can't get the hang of it."

"I know," he said as he opened the front door. "That's why I did it for you. I didn't want to spend the next hour out here in the cold watching you spin around in circles."

"I'm not that bad."

"Yes, you are. I've never met anyone who has as much trouble as you do when it comes to backing up."

As soon as we walked in the house, Athena and Thor greeted us with their usual howling. I bent down and patted each one on the head to appease them. "Have you been good dogs while I was gone?"

They barked a couple of times and then turned and pranced down the hallway, going wherever it is they go when they've had enough petting.

"Where's that silly cat?" I looked around and saw Spice Cat staring down at us from the top of the refrigerator. "Ah, there you are." I looked back down the hall as I took off my coat. "Is anyone home?"

Mom came out from behind the stairs holding Ethan. She had been in the nursery. "We're here," she said as she and Eddie walked out into the hallway. "I was just changing Ethan's diaper. Maisy fell asleep on the sofa, so Eddie picked her up and put her in her crib."

"Hello, Jesse," Eddie said. "I know why your mother loves these kids so much. They're adorable."

"Thank you, Eddie," I said. "Billy and I think so."

I hung up my coat and then reached out for Ethan.

"How's my sweet baby?" Mom handed him to me. I held him close as I walked to the nursery to look in on Maisy. What a beautiful little girl, I thought to myself. Billy and I are truly blessed.

Billy walked up behind me and said, "We are blessed."

"I was just thinking the same thing. You have to stop reading my mind."

Billy must have felt the vibration of his cell phone, because he turned and walked out of the room before it had a chance to ring. I waited a second before following him.

Mom and Eddie walked with me to the den.

"Robert sent some food over from his restaurant," Mom said. "Everybody has had something to eat, except you. Are you hungry? I can fix you a plate."

"Maybe later, Mom. My stomach is all tied up in knots. I don't think I could handle anything right at the moment."

"Greg left. He wanted to wait and have a talk with you, but he had things to do. He said he'd see you later."

"How did he sound? I know he's depressed. I would be. I was so depressed when Dad died."

"I was, too."

"I know you were, Mom. I'm sorry you had to suffer through that."

"I'm sorry we all had to suffer through it, but dying is a part of life."

"It certainly is."

"Poor little Greg. He's so sad. It was all I could do to keep from crying when he talked about his dad."

Billy must have walked out back because he wasn't in the den when we walked in. Mom and Eddie sat down on the sofa beside each other.

"Why did Billy have to run out after you this time?" Mom asked. "He got a call from his secretary, and then he said that he had to go save you from yourself. Of course, I laughed. I thought he was joking."

"I set off the alarm at the office. I was trying to get there in time to catch a call…"

"From the kid who pulled a gun on you in the hospital parking garage. That's right, Missy. I know all about the kid and the gun and the call. When were you going to tell me about him?"

"Never, unless I had to. You know how you get when a kid's involved in anything. You blame the parents, and sometimes that's not the case. To make it easier on me, I don't tell you everything."

"I've learned a lot since those days, young lady. I read the papers and I watch the news on television. Criminals are getting younger every day. That's just the way it goes. Kids mature earlier than they did in my time, so it only stands to reason they would get into trouble at an earlier age."

"My mother is such a whiz," I said, looking over at Eddie. "She really knows how kids think, no matter what age they are."

"Any man would be lucky to have your mother as his wife," Eddie replied.

A red flag went up. Was he planning on asking my mother to marry him? He'd better think again. My mother isn't marrying anyone she's only known for a few short months. No way. I wouldn't stand for it. Oh, no… I've turned into my mother!

"Yes, he would," I agreed. "Mom is the absolute best." I looked down at Ethan who had fallen asleep in my arms. "I guess this little fellow needs his crib."

I got up and walked out of the room, leaving Mom to deal with Eddie's remarks. Whatever was going to happen between them was going to happen. I decided to keep my nose out of it... for now. As I turned to go into the nursery, I glanced back down the hallway and saw Eddie lean over and kiss Mom on the cheek. She smiled like a school girl. I laid Ethan down in his crib one second before the phone rang. I raced to the living room to answer it.

"Hello," I said.

"Jesse, this is Sarah."

"Hello, Sarah. How are you doing?"

"I'm doing a little better. Jenny and Beth helped us make the arrangements, but they've gone home now. Greg stopped by for a bit. He's so handsome... just like his father."

"Yes, he is." I could tell that Sarah needed someone to talk to, so I listened.

"Robert sent over some food, and it's a good thing he did, because people have been dropping by most of the day."

"I was going to come over as soon as I got home. Would it be all right if Mom and I came over for a few minutes?"

I assumed that Mom would want to go with me. Billy had already been over earlier, and Eddie hardly knew Sarah and the chief. He might feel uncomfortable. He could stay here and keep Billy company—not that Billy needed company. What he probably needed were a couple of days alone.

"It's time to cut down the trees."

"What trees?"

"Why, our Christmas trees, of course! Everyone goes go out into the woods about a week or so before Christmas and cuts down their own tree. Then they take it home to decorate. The next day we have a tree lighting ceremony here at our house. It's a family thing. You missed it last year, but you don't have to this time. I'm ready and I want to do it now. Daniel's service is in two days, and I want our tree to be up. Daniel loved Christmas more than any of my other kids. Oh, don't get me wrong, they all loved Christmas, but Daniel would get excited starting around Thanksgiving. By the time Christmas morning got here, he would be the first one banging on our bedroom door. He really loved the tree lights."

"I think I'd like that, but I'm going to have to leave Mom at home. I don't want her traipsing around in the snow through the woods. She can visit with you later," I said.

"I understand."

"It's so typical of the Blackhawk family to do something together. I'm so glad that I'm a part of it, Sarah. I couldn't have married a better man than Billy."

"Billy deserves a good woman, and he got one with you."

"Thanks, Sarah. I'm so glad you feel that way. Not to change the subject, but if you want to go cut down trees, I suggest we do it now. We're supposed to get a foot of snow tonight."

"That's what I hear. Beth won't be here because she's pregnant and doesn't need to be out in the woods stomping through snow, bushes, and thicket. Adam should be here any minute. He's going to cut down a tree for Jenny, too. Greg's coming back. He said he was going to have a big tree just like he and his dad had planned. Robert's going to cut down two trees. He usually puts one in his restaurant. His employees decorate it. They adore him."

"I can see why. He's a Blackhawk."

"I'm going to say something and I don't want you to think badly of me, okay?"

"I would never think badly of you. Why... you're like a mother to me. I love you."

She cried softly into the phone.

"Please don't cry. You're going to make me cry."

"Okay," she said. "I'll do my best."

"What did you want to say?"

"I really care a lot for Ruth, but you're the one Billy will spend the rest of his life with. His love for you is something very special. He told me that when you walked into his office that day, he knew the two of you would be together forever. He also said it didn't take him long to figure out that you were going to be a handful. I'm glad it worked out."

"I'm glad, too. Thank you for saying that. It means a lot to me. So, he really told you that?"

"He sure did. The day he brought you into the clinic, he told me that you were the one."

"Wow! I'm impressed."

"When can you and Billy come over? Is your mom at your house now? If she isn't, I'm sure that Geneva would be glad to baby-sit. I can promise you that she's not going out into the woods."

"Mom's here, so we're good."

"I'd like to do it soon, because I don't want to get too tired to join in the fun."

"How do you feel?"

"I feel fine. Why?"

"The chief said something about you being so tired all the time. I think he's worried about you. And now with…"

"He's a man. What do they know about how a woman feels? If she doesn't fix their breakfast they think she's sick. Well, I'm not sick. I'm fine."

"Then let's go get a Christmas tree."

"Speaking of being tired, the chief is taking a nap. Jonathan is with Lu Ann. I hope he doesn't mess things up with her this time. He'll be here soon. I told him we were going to chop down Christmas trees, and he knows he'd better be here for that. Adam, Greg, and Robert should be here soon. Eli wants to go, too."

"That sounds good to me. I'll have a talk with Mom, and then Billy and I will come over soon. Give us a couple of hours. That way we'll have time to tie up a few loose ends here. Is that okay?"

"That's fine. I'll see you in a couple of hours."

We said our good-byes, and then I hung up the phone. I turned to head down the hallway and met Billy in the process.

"Who was that on the phone?"

"It was your mother. She wants us all to get together and cut down some Christmas trees. It's a tradition! I'm ready. "

"Is she up to it? How did she sound?"

"She sounded fine to me. She was sad, but that's to be expected. It looks as if the whole crew will be at your folks' house in about two hours."

"Good. That gives us plenty of time. Captain Waverly just called me on my cell phone. He wanted you to come into the station to discuss your involvement in the case."

"What involvement in what case?"

"He knows about Wayne Avery confronting you in the parking garage and he wants a statement."

"Did you tell him that our family is suffering through a crisis right at the moment?"

"Yes, I did and he said that under the circumstances, he would interview you on the phone. He's going to call back in ten minutes. This could take a while, but it's better than going into Charlottesville to the police station."

"I'm surprised that he's going to talk with me over the phone. Normally, the cops get such joy out of dragging you out of your home especially if the weather is really bad, and hauling you downtown for questioning."

"They like to see the look on your face when they throw questions at you. They love to trip you up. I told him the young man wore a ski mask and dark clothing. I guess he figures there's not much else to tell, but he wants to talk with you anyway, especially now since…"

"Since what?"

"There's something weird going on with this guy, Wayne Avery."

"What do you mean?"

"The police traced the call to a house on Octonia Road in Stanardsville, but, as I said, when the police arrived, no one was there. They talked with the neighbors, and one claimed to have heard a gunshot, but failed to report it to the police. No one saw anything out of the ordinary. The house belongs to a couple who are out of town on vacation. There wasn't a break-in, so Wayne Avery had access to the house somehow. The receiver was still lying on the table. One round had been fired into the floor. He really pulled one over on us. I bet he thought it was funny, but I sure didn't. Anyway, the Crime Scene Technicians are just finishing up."

"Why would he try to make us think that he killed himself? Idiot. Didn't he realize we'd find out the truth?"

"He's young, Jesse. Sometimes kids don't think straight when they feel penned in. They come up with some elaborate scheme and think it's going to work. But it never does."

"I'm really mad about the whole thing. What's he trying to get me into? Why did he even bother to contact me?"

"It could've had something to do with what you said to him in the parking garage. He might have thought he could use you to get out of this mess if you believed that he was sorry."

"It's good to be remorseful, but he's still got to pay for his crime."

"When he said he was sorry, you began to have a little faith in him, didn't you?"

"I thought maybe he had a few redeeming qualities. I thought he wanted to make amends... that he wanted to pay for what he did to Daniel. Boy, was I ever wrong. Just wait until I see this kid face-to-face! And I will see him. Trust me. I'm going to get to the bottom of this if it's the last thing I ever do!"

"Don't say that," Mom said as she walked up to where we were standing in the hallway. "You never know what the last thing you'll ever do in life will be."

"That's true, but I can tell you that I won't rest until I have a few words with Wayne Avery!"

"I'm sure you won't, my dear. But for now, can we figure out what we're going to do next? It's almost time for dinner. Should I set out some food?"

I tried to get out of the blue funk I had fallen into. I hated it when someone lied to me or tried to use me. And that's what Wayne Avery had done. I heard the gunshot over the phone, but he didn't really shoot himself. He just made me think he had. But why? Did he think we wouldn't find him?

"Jesse," Mom said. "Did you hear me?"

"Yes," I replied. I wasn't really listening since I was lost in my own little world, planning my own form of revenge, but I pretended to be. "Sure."

"Do you want me to set out some food?"

"Thanks, Mom. That's a good idea. I have to talk with Captain Waverly, and then we're going to cut down Christmas trees. Do you want one for your house in Dogwood Valley? I know you're not there much, but I figured you'd still put up one."

"Yes, I would love a tree, but someone has to stay with the children."

"I'll be glad to cut one down for you," Billy said.

"I'll cut it down for her if you don't mind," Eddie said to Billy.

"Okay, that works for me."

"That sounds wonderful. Thanks, Eddie. I'm sure that my daughter wouldn't let me go out in the dark, dangerous woods to do it myself anyway."

"You can bank on it."

"Neither would I," Billy added. "It will be dark soon and you don't need to be out in the woods, Mother Elk. You have children to care for."

Eddie smiled at Mom. "Mother Elk, huh?" He looked over at Billy and then to me. "I like that name. It's so fitting. She is the head of the herd, isn't she? So, Mother Elk, I'll be glad to help you decorate your tree if you want me to."

"That sounds wonderful. Thanks, Eddie. We can do it tomorrow."

"Unfortunately, if you don't leave tonight, you might not get out of here at all," Billy said. "If we get the snow they're predicting, nobody's going anywhere."

The phone rang.

"Let's go to the kitchen and set out some food, Eddie," Mom said.

I walked back into the living room and picked up the receiver. I suspected that Captain Waverly was on the other end, and he was.

"How's everything in Charlottesville?" I asked him. "I thought the Albemarle Police or the Albemarle County Sheriff's Office would be handling this case."

"We're working together. We do that, you know. All surrounding law enforcement throws in together when we need more manpower, or when a criminal flees from one jurisdiction into another. That's the way it works everywhere. We want to catch our man, and we don't care who helps."

"Oh, I see. What do you want from me?"

"Did Wayne Avery confess to you that he was the one who set fire to Jonathan's house?"

"Yes, he did, but you know as well as I do that's hearsay."

"What else did he say? Maybe you forgot something."

"I didn't forget anything, because there's not much to tell. Look, Captain Waverly, I'm a little busy. I'm sure you can understand."

"Yes, I can," he responded. "When we catch Wayne Avery, I'll need you to come in and make an official statement."

"I'll be glad to, but until you catch him there's not much else I can do."

"If he contacts you again, please call me."

"I will, captain."

As soon as I hung up the phone, it rang again. This time it was Sheriff Wake Hudson from the Greene County Sheriff's Office.

"Why am I not surprised that it's you on the other end?"

"I don't know. Were you expecting me to call?"

"I'm always expecting to hear from you. Anytime something happens in this family, you're always there." I smiled. "Perhaps that's a good thing."

"I'm not going to beat around the bush, Jesse. I understand that Wayne Avery confronted you in the UVA hospital parking garage and confessed to setting the fire at Jonathan's house. Anytime we have someone who confesses to a crime, and then that same type of crime is committed a short distance away, we have to believe they're both connected."

"Wayne Avery needs to be arrested, Sheriff Hudson. He burned Jonathan's house to the ground and he needs to pay. He said that he wanted revenge against Jonathan, but he never expected anyone to die. A house can be replaced, but not people. He's frantic. I'm sure he doesn't want to go to jail."

"It's too late for that."

"It is ironic that the man who died in the Ruckersville fire is the same man who had an affair with this kid's mother. It kind of makes you wonder. These two fires have to be connected. I see that now."

"If he calls you again would you please let me know, or either call Captain Waverly? We need to get this guy off the street, and any help you can give us would be appreciated."

"You saved my mother's life, Sheriff Hudson. I'd do anything for you."

CHAPTER 13

GENEVA CAME OVER TO HELP MOM WATCH THE KIDS. After a quick bite to eat, we gathered at Chief Sam and Sarah's house to cut down trees for Christmas. Adam, Robert, Greg, Eli, and Jonathan were already there when Eddie, Billy, and I showed up.

I hugged everyone, and then asked Sarah and the chief if there was anything I could do for them.

"No," Sarah said. "I'm just so glad everyone showed up for the tree cutting ceremony. I love this part."

"What ceremony?" I asked as I looked at the chief and then back to Sarah, waiting for an explanation.

"I guess Billy didn't explain," she said. "When we go out and gather trees for Christmas, we say a prayer."

"I can handle that," I said, and then looked over at Jonathan. "Where's Lu Ann?"

"She had some work to do," he replied. "But I'll be seeing her to-night. I'm going to take a tree over and help her decorate it. I might even spend the night, so don't expect me back until tomorrow."

"From what I've heard, it's supposed to snow up to our eyeballs. You might get stuck at her house and not be able to get back for a while."

"Worse things could happen." He smiled. "I have a Humvee, Jesse. I can go pretty much any place I want to."

"You know, Uncle Jonathan," Greg said. "If you need a place to live for a while, you can always come stay with me."

"Thanks, Greg," Jonathan said. "I might just take you up on that."

I smiled at the thought. That would be perfect. At least, Greg wouldn't be alone.

"Saddle up, folks," the chief demanded. "We're ready to go."

Without many words spoken, everyone got into their vehicles and followed Chief Sam and Sarah's pickup truck into the woods.

I was surprised when the road led to a massive growth of real Christmas trees a mile into the back side of the Blackhawk property.

"Wow!" I said as I crawled out of the pickup truck. "There must be a hundred Christmas trees here!"

"Dad comes out and plants about twenty or so every spring to compensate for the ones we cut down," Billy said.

He walked up and put his arms around me.

"He's been doing it for years. He likes having this ceremony. He looks forward to it every year. It's his chance to have a brief prayer with his family to celebrate the start of the winter months."

"Your father likes to celebrate a lot of stuff."

"It's the way of the Cherokee. We are grateful for the land we live on and the air we breathe. We celebrate the many things God gave us, like fresh air, blue skies and much, much more."

"Yes, I've been a part of many of those celebrations."

"Saturday, we will celebrate Daniel's life. You might find it a little different than most funerals."

"Like how?"

"We dance and sing and eat lots of food."

"That doesn't sound too much different from some of the funerals I've been to."

"Then in a week we'll celebrate Christmas."

"So, the party's still on?"

"Of course," Sarah said. "We'll say a prayer for Daniel at the party."

"Come on," the chief yelled. "It'll be getting dark soon."

"That's one of the things I don't like about winter," I whispered to Billy as we followed the chief. "The days are too short."

"The short days don't give you enough time to get into much trouble," Jonathan said as he walked up next to me. "I heard about the police coming to the office today. I bet you freaked out."

"Yes, I almost did, considering I had Wayne Avery on the phone confessing that he burned your house down. He hung up when he heard the sirens in the background. He called back about the time Billy showed up, and then he pretended to shoot himself."

"I heard."

"That really irks me. He sounded so innocent, and then he goes and pulls a stunt like that. And he's such a liar! I've had enough sadness in my life for one day. Thank you, very much."

"I guess you know that the fire in Ruckersville was probably connected to the fire at my place."

"Yeah, I heard."

"Did you know that the two people who died in the fire in Ruckersville weren't found in the hallway trying to escape? Nope, they were shot in the head execution style before the fire was set."

"I heard," I said, looking at Billy.

We stopped in the middle of the path and waited for Chief Sam to say his prayer. Sarah put her arm around Greg when the chief began. The very last sentence was dedicated to his son, Daniel, and he spoke of the day we would all be together again. There wasn't a dry eye around.

Chain saws buzzed and it wasn't long before each truck was loaded with a tree or two. In our case, we had two. Billy wanted one for our house and one for the office. Eddie threw Mom's tree in the back of his pickup truck.

"I can't wait to help your mother decorate her tree," he said to me. "She's a wonderful person, and I enjoy her company so much. It gets mighty lonely when you don't have anyone in your life."

"I know something about that!" I said. "I'm glad my mother has such a nice person like you around, Eddie. I know she's been awfully lonely since my dad passed away. She has us, but it's not the same."

"It's a shame to have to be by yourself," Eddie said. "My wife died three years ago and I've missed her every day since."

"I hope that you and my mom will find comfort in each other. You both deserve to be happy."

I guess I had finally warmed up to Eddie. If he made my mother happy, that's all that mattered to me. I no longer tried to find things wrong with him, but instead, tried to see him for the good person that he is... and I quit comparing him to my father.

It was so cold outside you could see your breath. I shivered the whole time, and was so glad when we were ready to leave. I was chilled to the bone. We packed up and headed home. When we reached the fork in the road, we split off and each went their separate ways. Eddie stayed behind us.

"We need to hurry up, so Mom and Eddie can leave. I know she wants to go home and put up her tree. I'm just surprised that she went home this morning, came right back, and is going home again. She can't make up her mind what she wants to do."

"Sometimes a person has to get out and breathe. You do it. I do it. So, why can't your mother?"

"I guess you're right. How long do you think she'll stay away this time?"

"Not long," Billy said. "But she has to go home tonight because your sister, Claire, is coming tomorrow to stay with her until the funeral. I told your mom they could stay with us, but I think she wants to give us a little privacy."

"That's fine with me. Did Claire say whether she's bringing the kids with her?"

"No, she's not. They're going to stay with Carl."

"I thought he'd be dead by now."

"Now, `ge ya. Be nice."

"I can't help it. I despise that man."

"He is the father of her children."

"Regrettably."

We pulled up into the driveway, and then Billy backed the truck up into the garage. We got out and unloaded one of the trees, leaving the other one in the truck to be taken to the office. Billy carried the tree up on the front porch and leaned it against the wall.

Eddie parked his truck, and the three of us went inside. The minute I walked in, I heard the dogs barking and a child's cry.

"I hear someone calling my name," I said as Geneva walked up.

"Where's Eli?" she asked.

I looked at Billy and Eddie, and then said, "I guess he went home." I took off my coat and hung it on the rack by the door. I was tired and didn't feel like listening to her whine... which seemed to be something she did frequently.

"He was supposed to come back here and pick me up."

Athena and Thor came up to us and pranced around. I petted Thor on the head and then rubbed Athena's back. Seconds later they were out of sight. Spice Cat lay on the floor by the sofa, purring.

"I can take you home," Billy said. "You only live a minute away."

"I don't know what I'm going to do with that man," she said as she shook her head. "Sometimes I think he has Alzheimer's."

"Let's hope not," Mom said as she walked into the living room carrying Maisy." She handed her to me. "Maisy has a tummy ache."

"How do you know?"

"Because she told me."

"She doesn't talk, yet. All she says is ma-ma and da-da."

"That's right, she doesn't, but she points and makes noises. She pointed to her tummy and cried, so I gave her a drop of that stuff you have for babies. She's still a little weepy, but she's going to be all right." Mom leaned over and whispered in my ear, "She has gas."

"Don't we all?" Geneva asked. "Eli is the worst. He farts all the time."

Eddie and Billy burst out laughing. Mom was embarrassed.

I didn't think anything of her comment. It wasn't unusual for Geneva to spout out whatever comes to mind. I ignored her and kissed Maisy's cheek.

Maisy wrapped her arms around my neck and then laid her head on my shoulder. She was in the comfort of her mommy's arms. She was happy.

"Where's Ethan?"

"He's asleep," Mom said. "He's an infant. All they do is eat and sleep for the first few months."

"And poop," Geneva added.

It was all Billy and Eddie could do to keep from busting a gut. Billy excused himself by saying that he had to go check on Ethan, and Eddie grabbed Mom by the arm and led her down the hall to the den.

"Did I say something wrong?" Geneva asked. "I didn't mean to offend anyone."

Poor woman. I guess she just didn't realize that most folks don't like to have conversations about bodily functions in the presence of mixed company. I learned that from my mother. Yet, I tried to show compassion for the woman.

"Don't worry about it," I said, knowing there was no point in trying to change her. It was too late for that. "I'm starving. I didn't eat much earlier. I'm going to put Maisy to bed and look in on Ethan, and then I'm going to get something to eat."

I walked out of the living room. When I looked in the nursery, Billy was standing over Ethan's crib, looking down at him. I walked over to Maisy's crib and gently laid her down. I pulled her blanket over her and then turned and walked over next to Billy.

"He's fine, `ge ya. I've already checked. I put my hand on his back just like any mother would do. Fathers learn quickly."

"I'm going to fix a plate. Would you like something to eat before you take Geneva home?"

"I had something while you were out breaking into the office." He chuckled. "Then I had a bite before we went out to cut down trees. I'm stuffed."

I leaned over and kissed Ethan on the forehead, and then kissed Billy lightly on the lips.

"I'll be here when you get back. We'll have the house all to ourselves. I'm sure we can find something interesting to do with ourselves."

"Hmm, I'm sure we could," Billy said as he leaned over and kissed me on the neck, sending chills all over my body. "We'll pick up on this later... I hope. You never know, since there's usually always someone here other than us."

"Tonight it's just going to be you and me, kid... and the kids, the dogs, and the cat. That's okay. We have a lock on our bedroom door."

"Fortunately." Billy winked at me.

I turned and walked out of the room. I walked down the hall to the den and asked Mom and Eddie if they would like something to eat.

"We've already had something," Mom said.

"Then why don't you take some food home for later?"

"No, thank you. There's plenty of food at my house."

"I'm surprised," I said. "I would've thought that the cabinets would be bare since you're here most of the time."

"I have to keep some food in my house. You never know when I might actually stay there for a few days."

We both laughed.

"You can move in here permanently, if you want to."

"I don't think so, Missy. I like my privacy."

"I know, Mom," I said as I turned and headed to the kitchen. I passed Geneva on the way. She was standing outside the nursery looking in.

"She's such a beautiful child," she said. "Sometimes when I forget what my son looked like, I look at her. She's the spitting image of Brian."

"I didn't know Brian very well," I said. "But just by looking at Maisy, I'd say you're right."

"He was a wonderful son. I don't know what he saw in that woman. Vicki was mean and hateful. She tried to keep my son from me, and she did keep my granddaughter from me. God will punish her for being so evil."

I changed the subject. "Have you had something to eat?"

"Actually, I haven't."

"Then let's go raid the refrigerator."

We walked to the kitchen.

As I opened the refrigerator door, Geneva got a couple of plates from the cabinet. I stood there with the door opened. The refrigerator was filled to capacity. I took a plate from Geneva and started pilling food on top of it. I backed away and said, "It's all yours."

Geneva piled a little bit of everything on her plate, and then sat down at the table across from me. We ate in silence.

We had just about finished our meal when Billy walked in and said, "The kids are asleep for now, but I'm sure Ethan will be up again before the night is over. I'm just glad that Maisy sleeps through the night... most of the time."

I got up, walked over to the sink, and looked out the kitchen window.

"It's dark already," I said. "The days are too short for me. I love the long days of summer."

I was just making conversation since it was apparent that Geneva had very little to say. She's a strange woman... unlike her sister Sarah, I thought to myself. If you didn't know they were sisters, you'd never be able to tell by the way they act. They're so different. I loved Sarah, and tolerated Geneva.

Billy walked over to the kitchen window and stood beside me. He looked out and then turned to Geneva and said, "Let me know when you're ready for me to take you home."

"I'm finished," she said. "Just let me clean up my mess first."

"I can take care of it," I said as I walked over and picked up her plate.

I walked back to the sink, rinsed off the dish, and then opened the dishwasher door.

"It's almost full," I said as I tried to find a place to put the plate. "I'll run it later."

"Like you did with the garage? Oops, I'm sorry. That's none of my business. It's just that I'm the kind of person who does what I say I'm going to do."

I tried to remain calm. I wasn't going to let this woman get my goat. I guess she had finally found out that I wasn't too happy about her sudden return to the Blackhawk clan and her claim of wanting to be a part of Maisy's life.

If it was money she was after, which was my first thought, she was out of luck. Brian and Vicki's will emphatically states that Maisy was to receive everything, and that whoever was her guardian was to oversee the terms of the will. Since Maisy was now our adopted daughter, we were in control of her life and her money.

Geneva came on the scene a little too late to dispute that, plus, Sarah would never have permitted it. Crying foul would've made Geneva look like a gold-digger and not a caring grandmother. Sarah would've fought her tooth and nail over that. Maisy was now her grandchild, too.

"Would you like to take a plate of food home for Eli?" I asked, trying to be polite.

"No, he has plenty to eat. There're leftovers in the refrigerator, but thank you for asking."

I walked with Geneva to the door and watched as Billy helped her with her coat.

Mom and Eddie walked in the living room and got their coats off the rack and prepared to leave.

"I guess it's just me and the kids left," I said, frowning. "I'll have to manage all by myself, I guess."

"I'll stay, honey, if you want me to," Mom offered.

"I was just kidding, Mom. I'll be fine. Besides, Billy will be back in five minutes. Geneva only lives up the road."

"Are you sure?"

"Yes, Mom. I was just teasing. I'm a big girl. I can take care of myself."

Billy and Mom looked at each other and then Mom said, "We'll wait until Billy gets back."

"Don't be silly," I said. "I will be fine! Really. Just call me when you get home so I won't worry."

Billy opened the front door and then stepped back. "Wow! It's really coming down out there... again! We'd better hurry."

I looked at Mom and said, "Billy thinks this is the snowstorm the forecaster called for, so you'd better hurry if y'all are leaving."

"Don't worry about us," she replied. "I have that new SUV. Nothing can stop me. And Eddie has a truck, so we'll be okay if we get a little snow. Once the snow is over, I'll be able to plow right through any accumulation. I won't have a problem. That SUV practically drives itself."

"I don't think it's going to be just a little," Billy said. "It's supposed to get real nasty."

"Then we'd better hurry," Geneva said.

I hugged Mom and then to his surprise, I hugged Eddie. "Take care of my mother."

"We'll be fine."

The four of them walked out the front door and stood on the front porch. I stood by the door and watched. The snow was coming down so thick that it was hard to see off in the distance.

"I think you might be right, Billy," Geneva said as she buttoned up her coat. "When this storm hits, a lot of weird things might happen. It usually does. People get crazy when they're stuck inside for a long time."

"Speak for yourself," I said under my breath.

Geneva turned to face me. "Did you say something, my dear? It's hard to hear out here with the wind blowing so hard."

"Never mind. It wasn't important." I could see Billy giving me the eye as if to tell me to behave. He did that quite often.

They took off down the steps and out into the blinding snow. I got an eerie feeling just standing there watching them as they made their way to their vehicles.

I didn't like the idea of Mom driving in this mess, but I knew she had Eddie to watch over her, and that made me feel a little better. Once they were down the driveway and out of sight, I closed the door behind me.

Then an unexplainable feeling came over me. I was alone in the house with two children to care for. Where were those silly dogs? I called out to them, and they came running.

"Good pups," I said as I looked down at them and their wagging tails. "Sit by the door and protect us."

Athena and Thor flopped down by the door and stared up at me. Neither one moved as if they were glued to the floor. I smiled at the thought that they would be there to protect me and the kids.

"Demon killers!" I said, loudly. "Yeah… right."

I turned and headed to the back door in the den. I wanted to make sure that everything was locked up tighter than a drum. Nobody was getting into this house! I went to the utility room and checked that door, noticing that Billy's jacket was still hanging on the rack, and then I headed upstairs to make sure the windows were locked. I kept thinking about his jacket. I guess he can't bring himself to wear it so soon. Thank goodness, he has plenty of coats.

On my way down the stairs, I heard a loud thump on the porch as if someone had fallen trying to get to the door. Someone pushed on the door and jiggled the knob, but the door wouldn't open. There was a moment of silence just before the dogs sprang into action.

"Be quiet," I said to them as I walked to the front door. "It's probably just Billy. Geneva must've forgotten something."

The dogs refused to hush up. Their barking grew louder. Athena growled like she did that time she slowly crept down the stairs and then attacked an intruder that held Claire, Billy's mother, and me hostage. Her actions saved our lives by giving me the distraction I needed to get a shot off. Memories of that night came flooding back. Then fear struck me. When Athena and Thor behaved like this, something bad usually happened. I had to do something. Had I locked the front door? I saw the doorknob turn, but the door didn't open. Good! It must've been in the locked position when I closed it.

"Shh," I whispered, trying to calm the dogs.

But they wouldn't be silent. Athena jumped up on the door and let out a howl that sent my nerves over the edge. Cries coming from the nursery startled me.

The first thing I thought of was my gun. I ran to the bedroom and pulled out the .38 special from my dresser drawer and then headed back to the living room, trying to not let the children's cries distract me. In case there was something amiss, I wanted my wits intact.

I was afraid to look out the window; afraid of what I might see. Instead, I asked, "Who is it? Who's there?"

There was no answer.

The children's cries got louder, and I grew more frantic. I didn't know what to do. I hesitated for a moment and then all of a sudden, I heard a scuffle on the porch as if there was a fight going on.

"It's me, Jesse," Billy said. "Open the door."

I opened the door and there stood Billy, holding a boy by the scruff of the neck.

"Call the police," he commanded. "Before I kill this kid."

CHAPTER 14

B ILLY DRAGGED THE BOY OVER TO A CHAIR in the kitchen, shoved him down in it, and then looked over at me. "Is this the kid?" He looked back at the boy. "What's your name? Are you Wayne Avery?"

Billy took off his coat and threw it in a chair.

"Yes, I am," the boy replied. "I just wanted to talk to her." He pointed to me, his hand shaking. "She's the only one who believes me. She knows the truth."

"The truth is your actions caused my brother's death. I should kill you right now."

"It was an accident. I didn't mean to."

"I don't want to hear your lies." Billy looked at me and said, "Jesse, call the police."

I didn't move. I had been frightened beyond description and still hadn't calmed down. I shook all over. I was still holding the gun in my hand.

"Jesse, call the cops!" Billy demanded.

The dogs were howling, the children were crying, and I was glued to the floor as my heart pounded in my chest. I took a deep breath and tried to snap out of it. After a few more deep breaths, I said, "Just a minute, Billy. I'm going to go check on my children before I do anything. He isn't a threat to us." I laid the gun down on the kitchen counter and stared at him and Wayne, and then I looked in the direction of the dogs and said, sternly, "Quiet!"

The dogs stopped barking immediately and promptly left the room.

"All right," Billy said without arguing. "Go check on the children. He's not going anywhere. I'll see to that." The look on Billy's face was a testament to his words.

I turned and walked briskly down the hall. When I reached the nursery, Maisy was standing up in her crib holding onto the railing with tears rolling down her cheeks. Ethan cried as he lay in his bed. I reached over, stuck his pacifier in his mouth, and then gave him a pat. I pulled his blanket over him, and watched as he closed his eyes. I picked up Maisy and held her long enough to calm her down and then I lay her back in the crib.

She drifted off within a few seconds.

Satisfied that my children were okay, I turned and walked out of the room only to be met by the dogs sitting in the hallway. I gave them both a quick rub to let them know everything was all right.

They both wagged their tails, and then took their places on each side of the nursery door. When I got back to the kitchen, Billy was standing over Wayne, waiting for my return.

"Are the kids all right?"

"They're fine. They both went right back to sleep."

"Good. Now call the cops!"

"Okay," I said as I walked over to the wall phone and picked up the receiver. I waited momentarily and contemplated the situation. Then I hung up the phone.

"Let's think this over for a second," I said as I turned to look at Billy. "Let's find out exactly what this kid has been up to. How about it, Wayne? What's your story?"

"I know what he's been up to. I don't need to ask him anything. He's a liar. You know that. He's a danger and needs to be locked up."

Stunned, I asked, "Don't you want a chance to interrogate the kid... find out why he did this?"

"I'm not a kid!" Wayne yelled. "I'm eighteen!"

"Shut up before you wake up my children," I commanded. "You need to calm down right now."

"Jesse, just call the cops. Let them question him. I have all the answers I need. He's nothing but a scumbag killer. Sure, he might have had a hard life, but that doesn't give him a reason to do the horrible things he's done. That's all I need to know."

"Something's going on here, now what is it? Do you know this kid, Billy?"

Billy hesitated.

"Ah, ha!" Wayne butted in. "She doesn't know everything, does she, Billy Blackhawk?"

"Shut up, kid. You're a criminal and you're going to jail."

"You're the one who told my dad that my mother was having the affair! Why would you do that? Do you have any idea what you did? You ruined our lives!"

"What's he talking about, Billy?" I looked at the kid and then back to Billy. "Is he telling the truth? How do you know this kid?"

The look on Billy's face was a dead giveaway. He knew more about this case than he had told me.

"I was hired by his father to find out what his mother was up to. His dad suspected she was having an affair."

"What? Why didn't you tell me?"

"I didn't tell you about the case I was working on at the time because you were just about ready to have our baby, and I didn't want you getting involved. You were eight and a half months pregnant and you weren't in any condition to be running around town, or sitting out in a car in the wee hours of the morning. And you were busy getting the nursery ready. Jesse, it was a simple case that only took about two days. It wasn't important."

"It was important to me!" Wayne yelled. "Why did you tell my dad? You didn't have to. You could've lied! Why couldn't you just leave us alone?"

"Oh, my God!" I said, realizing for the first time that our lives could've been in danger. The scenario played out in my head as I spoke.

"Wayne Avery is knee-deep in the death of three people and he burned down two houses. Jonathan most likely had been targeted for death, but because he wasn't at home at the time, his life was spared. Then this kid comes here to do what? Kill us? Burn down our house?" I was furious. "We were probably next on his list. You should've told me, Billy."

"I didn't know. I'm just now putting it all together myself, Jesse. I had no idea that this kid was related to the case I worked on a couple of months back. The name didn't ring a bell."

"I bet it's ringing one now!"

"I didn't put it together until I was taking Geneva home. She asked me if Jonathan and I had worked on cases together, and I told her that we had... many times. She asked if you and I and the kids might also be in danger. Then I started thinking about that couple in Ruckersville. The man's name sounded familiar. I played it all out in my head and then I realized what was going on. I rushed back here and found him trying to break in."

"What would've happened if you had gotten here ten minutes later? He could've killed one of us... or all of us."

I looked over at Wayne Avery.

"Or... I could've killed him!"

"I swear, Jesse. I would've never put my family in harm's way if I had any idea that this was all related and that we could be in danger. Please believe me."

I had to believe Billy. He's my husband and he'd never let anything happen to us. I guess he must've had a lot on his mind and that's why he didn't put it together until now. His brother was dead. I'm sure that's consumed much of his thoughts.

"I believe you," I said as I walked over and hugged him. "You're not one to keep secrets."

"I can keep a secret when I have to, but not when my family's involved, especially if they could be in danger... never."

"It's time to call the police. You're right, Billy. This kid belongs in jail. It's probably the only safe place for him."

I looked at Wayne and asked, "How could you kill two people and then burn down their house? The man was the one who had the affair with your mother. His poor wife had nothing to do with it, but you killed her anyway. You disgust me! I can't believe that I almost felt sorry for you."

"You don't know the whole story," Wayne said with a hurt look on his face. "I can't lie anymore. I'm not the one who did all those terrible things. I'm not guilty. That's what I came here to tell you, but when I saw his face, I knew you'd never believe me. He's the one who belongs in jail—him, his bounty hunter brother, and all the rest of them."

"The rest of who?" I asked.

"It's whom," Wayne said, correcting me. "The rest of whom."

"BFD! So, you know your English. Who cares? You don't actually think I'm going to believe you're innocent, do you? How many times are you going to change your story? Now you say you're not the one who committed these crimes. Next thing you're going to tell me is that you weren't even there."

"I wasn't."

I looked at him and couldn't believe what I was hearing.

Billy stood there and didn't say anything. He was waiting for me to get it out of my system. He did that. If he thought that I was going to go on a tirade, he'd let me have the floor until I had exhausted myself.

"Are you now saying that you didn't do all those terrible things, that you didn't murder those two people or burn Jonathan's house down?"

"It wasn't me."

"Then who was it?"

"I can't tell you," Wayne replied. "He'll kill me if I do. I just want you to know that I'm innocent. I would never hurt anyone, let alone kill someone. I wouldn't do that. You have to believe me! I need your help. Nobody else is going to be on my side... and he's going to get away with it. Nobody can catch him."

I didn't know what to think, so I paced the floor contemplating his story. Was he innocent? Did he know who committed these crimes and was being forced to cover up for that person—or was he a lying killer? I just didn't want to believe that someone so young would be capable of such acts.

I looked down the hall and thought about my own children, and how they would be when they grew up. They have good parents, but does that mean anything? Could they grow up to be killers? No way! I had to get that idea out of my mind. My children would never be like that.

My thoughts were consumed with images of Wayne Avery as he laughingly doused Jonathan's house with gasoline, and then later shot two people to death. I closed my eyes for a second.

Billy grunted. He was fed up with the kid. He was ready for the police to throw him in jail and free us of this problem. He was convinced that Wayne Avery was a killer and a danger to society.

"I'm finished here. I'm calling the police," Billy said as he turned his back and walked over to the phone.

The minute he started punching in the numbers, Wayne jumped up from the chair and within a split-second, bolted out the front door.

He had caught us both off guard. He was out the door and into the snow-covered woods before we knew what hit us.

"I don't believe it!" Billy yelled as he slammed down the phone.

"Go after him, Billy! We can't let him escape."

Before Billy had a chance to get out the door and down the steps, flashing lights flooded the yard, followed by the sound of sirens. I looked up and saw a yard full of cop cars.

The police jumped out of their vehicles and several of them took off after the kid. Billy ran over to one of the cars and started talking to an officer.

The dogs walked up and sat together beside the door, waiting for a command, their eyes trained on me.

"Go get him!" I yelled to them. "Go eat that kid!"

They took off down the front steps and disappeared into the night. Their barking was so loud, I was sure they were going to wake the children, but they didn't. Their barking continued until they were so far off into the woods that they could no longer be heard over the wind and the blowing snow.

I kept thinking to myself that if Wayne harmed my dogs, I'd hunt him down and choke him to death. It was then that I realized how easy it was for Billy's mind to be in another place and not on the case at hand. I was sure that thoughts of Daniel had clouded his thoughts, keeping him from putting the pieces together. I never should've been so gruff with him. He was in mourning and I had been insensitive.

I heard a gunshot off in the distance and the faint sound of a dog's howl... a howl that conveyed pain. My heart skipped a beat. All I could think of was that Wayne had shot one of my dogs.

Where was my gun? *Where was my gun?* Then I remembered that I had laid it on the kitchen counter. I looked around, but the gun was gone. Did Wayne have time to grab my gun before he took off out the door? I didn't think so, but I wasn't sure. I had my back to him at the time.

The thought that he had shot one of my dogs with my own gun made me sick. I had a moment there where I actually imagined myself with my hands around his throat, choking the life out of him... for killing my dog. I had to go after Athena and Thor. If one of them had been shot, I couldn't leave them in the woods.

I grabbed my coat, slipped it on, and then ran over to the chair in the kitchen and snatched up Billy's. I checked first to make sure the door wasn't locked and then I closed it behind me.

When I got outside, I heard both my dogs barking! Both of them were alive! I knew their barks and I could tell the difference. Athena's bark sounded as if she could be hurt, but at least she was still alive... and barking. I was so elated to know they hadn't been killed. I don't think I could've stood it if one of them had died trying to capture that punk kid.

"We've been trying to find him," I heard one of the officers tell Billy as I walked up and handed him his coat. "We've been patrolling the area and when we saw that old pickup truck parked on the side of the road, we knew something was up. Bear Mountain Road's a private road and we knew that truck didn't belong there."

"I'm glad you were so close," Billy said.

I snuggled next to him as he put his arm around me.

"Well... it wasn't quite like that. We already had a unit on duty parked in the woods. We had a feeling that he might show up. They always come back to the scene of the crime. The patrol officer was parked on Jonathan's property. That's where we expected him to come. It was just luck that Officer Whalen saw him when he passed by, so he radioed in. Don't worry.

Our guys will catch him. They won't stop until they do. That kid can't outrun them. Not in this snow."

"That's right," Captain Waverly said as he walked up. "They'll get him." He greeted us with a pleasant smile even though he was being blasted in the face with falling snow and a stiff wind. "Is everyone all right? We should go inside, so you can tell us what happened here tonight."

"If you were already on the scene, what were you waiting for? Why didn't you come to the door?"

"Why don't we go inside, Mr. Blackhawk? Your wife looks as if she's going to freeze."

"Don't worry about me," I said. "Besides, I'm going after my dogs." I could still hear their barking, however faint. "I think one of them has been hurt. If that kid shot my dog, I'll… never mind. Y'all go on inside. I'll be back as soon as I find my dogs."

"Hold on a minute," Captain Waverly said. "Someone's coming out of the woods."

I could scarcely make out the figures, but when I did, I saw Thor trudge his way through the deep snow, shadowing the officer next to him. The officer was carrying Athena.

Thor continued to bark, but by now, Athena was silent… and limp. I ran toward them, my heart in my throat. Billy followed.

"Don't worry, ma'am," the officer said. "Her leg is hurt, but I think she's going to be all right. She just can't walk on it. She must've stepped in a hole or something."

"Thank you so much for bringing her back to me, officer," I said, crying.

I rubbed Athena's head and then kissed her. "You're going to be okay, girl." I cried while Thor barked.

"Please take her to my car," I told the officer. "We'll take her to the chief's house. He can fix her right up."

Billy and the officer followed me to my 4Runner and waited for me to open the door. I looked over at Billy and said, "Will you go get the keys to my car? I'm taking her to the chief."

He pulled a set of keys out of his coat pocket and handed them to me.

"I'll call Dad. You go on ahead." He pulled out his cell phone.

Once Athena was safely stretched out on the back seat, the officer closed the door.

"I'm surprised she didn't try to bite me," he said. "Usually, when dogs are injured, they can be aggressive."

"My dog's smart. She knew you weren't a threat and that you were trying to help. Thank you so much," I said. "You don't know how much these dogs mean to us."

"I think I do." The officer turned and walked over to his captain.

As soon as I opened my door, Thor jumped up in the seat ahead of me. "Okay, I guess you want to go, too." I jumped in the car, turned on the ignition, and waited while Billy finished his call.

"Dad said to take her to the office. Adam will be there when you get there. If her leg is broken, she'll need to have an x-ray before Adam can set it." Billy looked around at the policemen and then back to me. "I should take her. The roads are really bad. I don't want you out there by yourself." He leaned over and whispered, "Can you stay here with the kids and handle the police without incriminating either one of us?"

As soon as the words were out of his mouth, we saw the lights of a vehicle coming up the driveway. Jonathan pulled up alongside us and got out of his car. He walked over and asked, "What's going on here?" He looked around the yard. "What's with all the cops?"

"What are you doing here?" I asked. "I thought you were going over to Lu Ann's house."

"I did," Jonathan replied. "I dropped off the tree, and then she told me that her soon-to-be ex-boyfriend was coming over. She's going to break the engagement. I had to leave so she could do it in private. You know how that goes."

"The kid showed up."

"Where is he?"

"It's a long story. Would you go with Jesse to the clinic? Adam's meeting her there so he can examine Athena's leg. I don't want her driving in this mess by herself, yet I don't want to leave her alone here with the kids with that criminal running loose."

"Sure," Jonathan said. "I'd be glad to, but I think we should take my Humvee. It's ugly on the roads. Cars are in the ditch everywhere."

"My 4Runner can handle anything Mother Nature throws her way," I said. "I don't think we should move Athena if we don't have to."

Billy and Jonathan looked at each other and then back to me.

"Okay," Billy said. "Go ahead. Pull out of the garage."

I could tell that this was a test. Billy wanted to see how I handled the 4Runner with so many cars in the driveway. So, I put the car in gear and maneuvered it around the other cars and pointed the front end toward the road.

"I'm ready when you are, Jonathan," I said. "Come on. Let's go! Time waits for no man... or dog!"

Jonathan walked around to the other side and opened the door. Thor jumped to the floorboard as Jonathan crawled in. Then he grabbed the lever to let the seat back so Thor would have plenty of room.

Billy walked up to the vehicle and tapped on the window. "Wait a minute and I'll run in the house and get your purse. You'll need your gun... just in case."

We waited while he ran into the house. A second later he was back with my purse. "The 9MM is in there. Where's your .38? I thought you laid it on the kitchen counter."

"I think Wayne grabbed it before he ran out. I meant to say something, but..."

"Say it isn't so." Billy slapped his forehead. "What next?"

"I'm sorry, Billy. I never expected him to be so quick."

"I'll tell Captain Waverly that he's probably armed with your gun."

"I'm sure he's going to like that."

"Especially since the gunshot you heard off in the woods sounded like a .38. I hope he hasn't shot an officer."

"I hope not, either. I sure hope he doesn't kill someone with my gun."

"I don't know why he grabbed your gun. He already has one."

"He was probably out of bullets. Isn't that what he said just before he pretended to shoot himself? He had used his last one, so instead of stealing more bullets, he stole a gun. Who knows why he did what he did? He's confused and unbalanced… and a big, fat liar."

"He's dangerous. The cops need to catch him."

"We will," Captain Waverly said as he walked up to my car. "He just shot one of my guys. I got a distress call from Officer Whalen. He's down."

"Oh, no!" I said. "I hope he's going to be all right."

"He's not dead, but he's hurt real bad. If you're leaving you'd better go right now. There's an ambulance on its way here and you might get blocked in. My guys come first."

"I understand. We're leaving right now." I stuck my hand in my coat pocket and felt the bulge of my cell phone. I pulled it out and threw it up on the dash. I looked at Billy and said, "I'll call you as soon as we get there to let you know we arrived safely. Are you going to be okay?"

"Yes, we're going to be fine."

"Will you call Mom? She never called to let us know she got home okay." I looked at the clock on the dash. "She should've called by now."

"Go, `ge ya, while you can. I hear a siren."

I blew Billy a kiss and put the car in gear. By the time we got to the end of the driveway, an ambulance had just turned onto Bear Mountain Road.

"That was close," I said, pulling out onto the road and then pulling over to the side to let it pass. "Another minute and we'd…"

A vision went through my head and sent shivers all through my body when I saw the small, dark-colored pickup truck sitting on the side of the road. I was sure that this was the truck that Wayne Avery had been driving. I grabbed the cell phone and punched in the number for Billy's cell phone. It rang several times before he answered.

"I just had a terrible feeling about Wayne Avery. I saw him coming through our back door. Where are you?"

"I'm still in the yard, but I'm going inside as we speak. Hold on, and I'll check the house."

The silence was eerie and the waiting was worse. "Come on, Billy. Get back on the phone."

"There's no one here but me and the kids, and a room full of policemen, so you can relax. The house is locked up and he's not coming back here. If he does, he'll be in for a real shocker. Trust me."

"I always do, Billy."

I closed up the phone and laid it on the console. I had a really bad feeling I couldn't shake. Wayne might not be in my house, but I knew he was still close by. I could feel it in my bones.

CHAPTER 15

THE DRIVE TO THE VETERINARY CLINIC WAS PERILOUS. The roads were slippery and the visibility was poor at best, but after a long, white-knuckled ride, we finally made it there in a little over thirty minutes. The clinic is only six miles from our house.

Adam gave Athena a shot for the pain as soon as we got her up on the table. Thor barked and just about had a hissy fit when Athena let out a yelp. After a complete examination and x-rays, Adam told us that Athena's leg had a hairline fracture, but it would be all right. However, she would not be able to put her full weight on it for a while. He handed me a bottle of pain pills and said to give her one twice a day. There was very little else he could do for the fracture.

"Shouldn't you put a cast on her leg?" I asked as I stroked her.

"A cast isn't necessary. It's a tiny crack. It'll heal in no time. If I put a cast on her leg, she'll gnaw at it, and could make matters worse. Give her the pills and try to keep her calm."

"That's easier said than done. She's a feisty one."

"That leg will slow her down, and if it doesn't, the pills will. She'll be as good as new in a couple of weeks."

"Thanks, Adam. I appreciate your coming out on a night like this."

"Hey, we're family." He rubbed Athena's head, and then slipped his arms under her, picking her up. He turned and handed her to Jonathan, and then looked back at me. "Try to keep her off her feet as much as possible. That shot I gave her will make her sleep for several hours. When she wakes up, give her a pill. The pills will also make her sleep, so don't worry. She'll probably walk with a limp when she does walk, but that's okay, too. She's lucky it wasn't worse. I'm just glad I didn't have to put a cast on her leg. Animals hate that."

An hour later we were on our way back home. Athena was asleep on the back seat with Thor lying next to her. Thor whimpered the whole way.

"Thor, if you don't stop that whining, I'm going to pull my hair out," I said. "I can't concentrate."

"Do you want me to drive?" Jonathan asked as he held on tightly to his seat.

I chuckled when I looked over at him. His face was pale and the knuckles on his hands were as white as the snow. His right hand had a firm grip on the door handle.

"You look petrified. Would you feel better if you were driving?"

"Probably," he said. "But, then again, I'm used to being the one who is in control. I rarely ride with anyone. Usually, I'm the one driving."

"So, you have trust issues, huh?"

"Don't you start in on me, too."

"Ah, I know where that's coming from. Lu Ann has her doubts about your ability to commit."

"Somewhat."

"She loves you. That's all that matters, Jonathan. Don't let your fear keep you from what could be the best thing that ever happens to you. Take a chance. For Pete's sake! You have one of the most dangerous jobs in the world, yet you let something like making a commitment scare you. Please don't tell me you're having second thoughts."

"No, I'm not. I'm just…"

"Whatever you're thinking, get over it! Take that first step. You'll be so glad you did. I know. When I said yes to Billy, I had butterflies in my stomach for a week. I knew he was the one, but I was scared, too. We all are. You just have to let go of that single man mentality."

"What is that?"

"Men are so afraid that a woman is going to lasso him in, and then he's never going to have his freedom again. It's so ridiculous. Where do y'all come up with this crap? Don't you get it? You're never really free. There's always something that ties you down, whether it's your job or your family. There's a commitment there already, but you just don't see it like that."

"Now that you put it that way…"

I heard the sound of my cell phone vibrate on the dash board and then it rang its zippy little tune. I grabbed it, flipped it open, and said, "Hello."

"I was beginning to worry," Billy said.

"We're on our way home. We'll be there shortly. We've just passed Crumpler's Market."

"Tell Jonathan his cell phone is off. Lu Ann tried to call him."

I glanced over at Jonathan, and then said, "He's got the jitters."

"Oh, no. Say it isn't so."

"You should have a man-to-man talk with the guy. Tell him how happy you are with your wonderful wife."

"Let me talk to him," Jonathan said as he reached for the phone. "Jesse is full of herself tonight, brother. She seems to think she's the love doctor. She's been giving me advice."

Their conversation continued until I pulled into the driveway. The police cars were gone. The only one left was Jonathan's Humvee. I scanned the yard, and out of the corner of my eye I saw the glint of a shiny object off in the woods. For a second I thought I saw a person's figure, but realized that the falling snow must be playing tricks on me. My stomach churned, but I didn't say anything. Maybe I was hallucinating. It had been a scary evening and my emotions were still in high gear. I looked away, and when I looked back, I still didn't see anything. Yet, deep down, I had a feeling that someone was out there. I would tell Billy about my fear.

I grabbed the garage door opener from the console and opened the garage door. I pulled straight in, not bothering to even think about trying to back in.

Jonathan carried Athena inside as Thor followed his every move. I closed the door behind us and then shook off the snow. I looked over by the fireplace and noticed that Billy had a raging fire going and had put a blanket down on the floor in front of it.

"You're so sweet," I said to him as Jonathan walked over in that direction. The two of them gently laid Athena down on the blanket. Thor cuddled up next to her.

"How are the kids?" I whispered.

"They're asleep," Billy whispered.

Athena is not a small dog. She probably weighs close to eighty pounds, and anyone carrying her will attest to it. Jonathan was almost out of breath.

"That dog weighs a ton," he said as he took off his coat, hung it on the rack by the door, and then headed toward the kitchen. "I need a drink."

Once I was confident that Athena was comfortable, I turned and walked to the kitchen and joined the guys. They were seated at the table opposite each other with a bottle of bourbon and three shot glasses in front of them.

"I need one after a day like today," I said as I sat down at the end of the table and downed the vile liquid. "Whew! That was nasty. May I have another, please?"

"It gets better after the first one," Billy said, and let out a sigh of relief. "This has been one of the longest days. What else could possibly happen?" He looked up at Jonathan and said, "You need to call Lu Ann. She said she tried to call you, but your phone's been off. What gives?"

"Nothing," Jonathan replied. "I must have turned it off by mistake."

I coughed. "That's not likely."

He pulled his cell phone from his pocket and looked at it. He held it up for us to see. "I told you that I must have turned it off, and I did. See?" He pushed the on button and it came to life, ringing immediately. "Excuse me for a second." He got up from the table and walked down the hall toward the family room in the back of the house.

While he was gone, I used the opportunity to catch up on what I had missed and talk to Billy about my suspicions. "What happened while I was away?"

"Officer Whalen is in the hospital with a gunshot wound to the abdomen. They're not sure he's going to make it. Taking a bullet in the gut is not good. I've been there."

"I know you have," I said. "I'm glad I wasn't around." I hesitated, thinking about how horrible it must have been for Ruth when he got shot. I tried not to think about it further. "Was Wayne the one who shot him?"

"Yes, he was."

"Did they catch him?"

"No, they didn't, but they will."

"All their cars are gone. Where are they now?"

"Captain Waverly got a call from one of his guys and they all took off. He said something about the fugitive being spotted out by the road. They think the kid was trying to get back to his truck."

"Oh, Lord. He's still out there. I hate this."

"I know you do. I do, too. I can't believe we could be so inattentive. He never should've gotten away. We let our guard down."

"It was my fault. I'm the one who absentmindedly left my gun lying around. I didn't think he was a threat, and now someone paid for my mistake." Tears filled my eyes. I was upset by the fact that someone was hurt and might possibly die because of my stupidity.

"It wasn't your fault," Billy said as he got up from the table and walked over to me. "Wayne Avery is a killer." He put his arm around me. "I made a few calls while you were gone and then I did what I do best: investigate."

"I don't think investigating is what you do best... maybe second best." I winked at him. He kissed my tears away as I wrapped my arms around him and cried more. "What did you find out?" Then a thought struck me. "Hold that thought. Have you heard from my mother?"

"Yes," Billy replied. "And I have a story there to tell you, but that can wait. Let me tell you about this guy, Wayne, first."

"But..."

"Your mother is fine. They made it home safely and everything is okay. Now, I want to tell you what I learned about Wayne Avery."

Jonathan walked back in the room and said, "You found out that he's psychotic and he killed his mother."

"What?" I asked, stunned. I looked at Billy. "Is that true? Did he kill his own mother? I don't believe it. Why would he do that? From the way he acted, he loved his parents."

"They could never prove he was responsible, but the police believe he did it," Billy said. "He probably confessed to his psychiatrist, but we'll never know. Confidentiality—you know how that goes."

"How... I thought his mother took a bunch of sleeping pills."

"She did, but the medical examiner said she had bruising around her mouth which would lead one to believe that she might have been forced to take the pills, and since the father was in jail..."

"That's conjecture," I said. "She could've fallen on her face."

"And I'm the Pope. Face it, Jesse. You just don't want to believe he could do something so awful," Jonathan said.

"He's just a kid," I said. "Kids aren't supposed to kill their parents."

"You'd be surprised how often that happens. People do some pretty bad things to each other. The worst part is that most killers don't have any remorse about what they do. What I find so hard to believe is that a person can kill someone and then sit down at the dinner table and eat a meal as if nothing happened."

"He did that?"

"That's what they say. They think he was so distraught about his mother accusing his father of physical abuse and his father being arrested for it, that he flipped out and killed her. At least, that's what they say."

"Who said that?"

"I just talked with Cole."

"I thought you were talking to Lu Ann."

"I was, but then a call came in and it was Cole on the other end. He said he's been trying to reach Billy, but your line is dead and Billy's cell phone is off."

As soon as the words were out of Jonathan's mouth, my cell phone rang. I got up from the table and walked over to the coat rack to retrieve my phone. Cole James' name appeared on the Caller ID.

"It's Cole," I said as I flipped open the phone and then watched as Billy went to the wall phone and picked up the receiver.

"The line's dead," he said. He had a concerned look on his face. "I'll go outside and check it out."

"No, don't," I said. "Wait a minute before you do."

"Okay," Billy replied as he hung the phone back up. He looked at Jonathan and then back to me. "I'm in no hurry to go out in the freezing cold."

"Hello, Cole," I said. "I'm sorry to keep you waiting. It's a bit hectic over here."

"I guess it is," Cole replied. "I've been trying to call Billy. Is he there?"

"Yes, he is. Hold on a minute." I walked over to Billy and handed him the phone.

"What's going on, Cole?" Billy asked as he took the cell phone. He did all the listening, speaking only when he said thank you, and then closed up the phone. He handed it back to me.

"What is it? What did Cole have to say?"

"It's a long story."

"I have nothing but time." I looked at Jonathan and asked, "Is everything all right with you and Lu Ann?"

"She broke off the engagement with her boyfriend. She said she wanted to be alone, so I guess I'll be staying here for the night if you don't mind."

"Give her the space she needs and everything will work out. I'm sure. And until then, you can stay here as long as you like."

"I'll stay here tonight, but I think I might take Greg up on his offer to bunk in with him after his girlfriend leaves in a couple of days. She's going to stay until after Daniel's funeral."

Silence chilled the room. Billy got up, went over to the fireplace, and threw a couple of logs onto an already glowing bed of firewood.

"By then he'll need someone around to help him get through the tough times."

"What about Lu Ann?"

"She understands. Now that she has her claws dug in, she's not worried about losing me."

"You're awful, Jonathan. Why do you talk that way when you know this is what you want?"

"Because I'm a man and we're scumbags. It's our way."

"How true!" I snickered. "You finally see the light! All kidding aside. You and Lu Ann are going to be happy together. You just wait and see." I looked at Billy and asked, "What did Greene County's finest have to say?"

"More than I cared to hear." Billy tried to clear his throat, then had a coughing spasm.

"Are you all right, Billy?"

He held up his hand and waited for his coughing fit to pass.

I looked at Jonathan and then back to Billy. "How long has this been going on and how have you managed to hide it from me? Do you need to go back to the hospital?"

"I'm going to be fine." Billy poured himself another shot of whiskey and downed it in one gulp. "Ah-h-h," he said, dragging out his words. "That felt good." His voice was raspy.

My concern was lessened by his apparent recovery from the hacking spell. "One more of those and I'm calling Dr. Bryant."

"Doc said it would take a while, Jesse. You heard him. I'm going to be fine, as long as I don't cough up my insides out onto the table."

"That was just plain gross," I said, gagging.

"Here," Billy said as he poured another shot of whiskey and handed it to me. "This will wash down that nasty image."

"Or bring it back up in the form of fried buffalo meat, or whatever that was I ate earlier. What was that meat Robert sent over? Was it chicken... or dog?"

Athena barked when I said the word dog, but then went back to a restful nap.

"Never mind. I don't want to know. It tasted good. That's all I can say. What about Cole's phone call?"

Billy poured Jonathan another shot of whiskey.

"Are we going to get drunk tonight, or what?"

No one said anything as Billy poured more whiskey.

"I guess we are," I said as I took my shot glass and turned it upside down. I slammed the glass on the table and waited for Billy to pour another one.

"This is your last one," he said as he filled the tiny glass. "I know how you get when you drink. Next thing I know you'll be outside running around in the snow... naked."

"I want to see that!" Jonathan said.

"If I didn't know better, I'd think you were trying to get me drunk," I said to Billy, feeling like I was getting tipsy. "Am I slurring my words?"

"Not yet," Billy said. "But you're well on your way."

"I haven't had so much to drink that I don't know when you're trying to put me off. Now give. Tell me everything. Don't leave anything out, and make it quick. My eyelids are getting heavy."

"Wayne Avery lives in a new subdivision off Octonia Road in Stanardsville. His family moved there four years ago. When his parents died, he got the house, which is paid for."

"How nice for him."

"That explains why he called us from a house on Octonia Road. The house was close by, and he must have known the owners were on vacation," Billy said.

"That's typical of someone so young. What an idiot."

"He turned eighteen in April. He went to William Monroe High School, but dropped out. He never did graduate like he claimed, and he hasn't held a job or had contact with any of the few friends since then," Jonathan added. "He has emotional problems. He's been seeing a psychiatrist for over three years."

"After three years you'd think he would've made some progress."

"Not according to Cole. Sheriff Hudson has a file on the kid that is full of petty complaints. He's done things like throw rocks at the neighbor's kids, hurting one bad enough that the girl had to have stitches. Then he set a trash can on fire and almost burned down the woods behind another neighbor's house. He hit a dog with a hammer. He shot a cat with a BB gun, and then the cat died. He borrowed his father's car without permission one afternoon and used it to run over a family of ducks crossing the road. The first hit didn't kill all of them, so he backed up the car and finished the job. A neighbor saw him and called the police."

"He sounds like a real sicko. That's how serial killers start out. They torture small animals and beat up on other kids. Wait a second. Isn't Octonia Road over there by my mother?"

"Yes, it is," Billy said. "But don't get upset. He hasn't returned to his house. Sheriff Hudson's deputies are watching the place. The minute he returns, they'll catch him."

"Just like Captain Waverly and his men did a little while ago?"

"He won't be out there for long. Trust me, `ge ya. They will catch him."

"Let's just hope they get him before he kills again." I shook my head. "I just can't believe that he's a killer. He seems so..."

"Nice? Sweet?" Jonathan asked. "Serial killers prey on others' kindness and their belief that nothing bad will happen to them. That's their first mistake. Their second is that they let him in their house or car. That's usually their last mistake."

"He said he didn't kill anyone. Someone else is the guilty party, but he couldn't tell us, or that someone would kill him."

"I think it's a bunch of hogwash," Billy said. "Until the police apprehend him or until he crosses my path again, we'd better go on alert. I'm going outside to see if the phone line has been cut. If it hasn't, the storm must've knocked out the service, and it should be back up soon. Either way, I need to find out why the phone isn't working. Jonathan, I want you to get on your cell phone and start making the calls."

"But it's so late," I said. "Everyone's probably in bed by now."

"It's never too late to wake up the family if we need to go on alert."

Billy took me by the arm and said, "Come on, Sleeping Beauty. It's time for you to go to bed."

"I have to brush my teeth."

The alcohol had taken effect, and brushing my teeth was all I could do before falling into bed. I fell asleep as soon as my head hit the pillow... and I had forgotten to tell Billy about my suspicions of someone hiding in the woods. That was a mistake I would later regret.

CHAPTER 16

N O MATTER HOW TIRED YOU ARE, or how much alcohol you've consumed, you should never forget to tell someone something important, especially if it concerns the safety of your family. When I awoke at daybreak, the first thing on my mind was to tell Billy about my suspicions that someone was watching us. I rolled over in bed to see his side empty. As soon as I sat up, my head felt as if it was going to explode.

"I know better than to drink," I said to myself. "What's wrong with me?"

"You needed to chill out," Billy said as he walked into the room carrying a glass of orange juice. "Here, drink this. It will make you feel better."

"I think I'm going to need something more than a glass of juice to fix this headache."

He held out his hand and offered me two aspirins.

"That might do the trick." I took the aspirins, tossed them into my mouth and then gulped down the juice. "Ah, I'm already as good as new."

"Why don't you take a shower while I fix you some breakfast?"

I lifted the sheet and saw that I was naked. "I guess you undressed me last night. Thanks. I prefer not to sleep in my street clothes."

"It was all my pleasure." He smiled and then did that silly thing with his eyebrows as if he had been a bad, bad little boy.

"What am I going to do with you," I joked. "You're such a pervert."

"That's me," Billy said, and then leaned over to kiss me.

I put my hand to my mouth and said, "Not before I brush my teeth. My breath smells like a rotten egg."

"That's pleasant." He backed off. "I'll wait until later."

"What about the kids?" I asked. "Are they up? How's Athena?"

Billy chuckled, and replied, "The kids have been up for a while. Jonathan's in the kitchen watching them. He makes a good babysitter."

"He's hired."

"I put Athena's bowl of food and water by the fireplace so she wouldn't have to walk all the way to the utility room. After she ate, I gave her another pill, and she went back to sleep. Thor's by her side, but the cat's missing."

"What do you mean? Where's Spice Cat?"

"I don't know. I can't find him anywhere."

"Do you think he might've gotten outside last night when the door was open?"

"Who knows? But don't worry. I'll go looking for him if he doesn't come home soon."

"I have to get up and find my cat."

Billy sat down on the bed beside me and said, "Spice Cat will be okay. Cats have a way about them. If he was hurt, he'd meow loud enough for the whole world to hear. If he's out running around, he'll come back when he gets good and ready to. Don't worry. He'll come home. I'm sure he's okay."

"He better be."

"He is, `ge ya. He'll come home when he's ready. Trust me. You need to get in the shower. We have many things to discuss."

"Yes, we do. I think you have some explaining to do."

"I will answer your questions, but first know that whatever I do, I do for the sake of my family."

"You scare me when you talk like that," I said as I grabbed the sheet and crawled out of bed. I wrapped it around me, but not until I was sure that Billy got an eyeful. I might not have the best body in the world, but Billy likes it, so I don't hesitate to show it to him every chance I get. Maybe I'm the one who's a pervert. I smiled as I headed to the bathroom.

"I can tell the conversation is going to be one-sided, with you being the one who's doing all the talking," I continued. "Are you going to lecture me? Because if you are, I can tell you right now that since you're usually right, I'll agree with whatever you have to say. I think. I'll let you know when I get out of the shower." I handed him the empty glass. "If you'd like to join me..."

"I do, but I can't." He got up from the bed and walked to the bedroom door. "I have things that must be done."
Billy turned and left the room while I went in and turned on the shower.

Twenty minutes later, I was dressed in a clean pair of blue jeans with a T-shirt under my turtleneck sweater. My long hair was still wet, but I didn't feel like blow drying it. Instead, I ran a brush through it and put it in a ponytail. I was ready to start the day. My headache had disappeared and I was in a somewhat cheerful mood. I don't know why considering the past few days' events, but I was. Maybe things were going to get better and the bad guys were going to jail.

I made the bed and then went to the kitchen for breakfast and a chat session. Billy was putting food on the table when I walked in. I kissed him on the cheek, and then went over to Maisy.

"Good morning," I said to Jonathan, and then glanced out of the kitchen window. "And what a beautiful day it is. The snow has stopped and the sun is out. I guess we didn't have such a bad blizzard after all. It sure is beautiful out there. Everything is white."

"You haven't been outside," he replied. "There's at least eleven inches on the ground. We didn't get all they called for, but we got enough. We're snowed in."

"For the moment," Billy added. "But not for long. We're going to plow the driveways and Bear Mountain Road, so we can all get out. We have business to attend to."

"Oh, yeah," I said as I went over to Maisy and picked her up. She hugged me and tried to pull my ponytail. I snickered, and then walked over and kissed Ethan on the forehead before I sat down at the table close to him. I propped Maisy in my lap and waited.

Jonathan sat across from me at the table and was way too interested in his cup of coffee.

"Okay, I guess it's time to strategize. What's on the agenda for today? Is the phone working? Has my mother called?"

"Yes, the phone's back up. I don't know what happened to it, but the lines weren't cut and it's working now. The storm must've knocked it out."

"Good," I replied. "I don't like to be without a phone in the house." I paused and then looked at Billy and Jonathan. "I think I saw someone or something in the woods when we got home from the clinic."

"Why didn't you say anything?" Billy was visibly shaken.

"Because I'm not positive. I thought maybe I was being paranoid. I get like that when people try to kill off members of my family." I saw the surprised look on both of their faces. "I'm sorry. I didn't mean to sound…"

"That's okay, Jesse," Jonathan said. "We can't ignore the fact that someone in our family died, and occasionally we might say something that doesn't sound right. We're human. Our tongues slip."

"Mine has a tendency to do that frequently."

"And that's why we love you," Billy added. "Would you like a cup of coffee?"

"Okay, stop lollygagging and tell me what you did. I know you're going to tell me something I'm not going to be happy about, so just say it."

"First things first. I found Spice Cat. He was shut up in your mother's closet upstairs. I guess the door wasn't closed all the way, so he took advantage of the situation. Jonathan and I kept hearing a meow upstairs, so he went to investigate. Look on top of the refrigerator."

I looked up and saw a big, furry tail wagging back and forth. I smiled a relieved smile. "Welcome back, Nosey Cat. See what happens when you go places you're not supposed to go? You won't do that again."

"Don't bet on it," Jonathan said. "He's a cat who has a new place to hide. Next time he goes missing, that's where I'd look."

"That's one thing off my mind." I started dishing up eggs onto my plate. "Would you pass the grits, Jonathan?" I looked up at Billy and asked, "Aren't you going to eat?"

"I've already had breakfast." He leaned against the kitchen counter, holding a cup of coffee in one hand. "Eat up and enjoy."

Jonathan filled my plate for me as I held Maisy. I ate everything except a few small pieces of baked apples, which I cut up into smaller pieces and fed to her.

"Have you heard anything about the Greene County killer?" I asked. "Have they caught him?"

"Ha... that's a good name for him. Where did you come up with that?"

"I just made it up, but he does live in Greene County, so it only makes sense. That is, if Wayne Avery is the one."

"I think we can say for certain that he is our guy," Jonathan said. "We can call him whatever you like. It doesn't matter to me as long as he pays for his crimes. To answer your question—no, they haven't found him, yet. He managed to sneak past the police. The truck they saw last night is gone, too. That kid is one sly fellow. I can't believe the police didn't catch him last night. I was sure they would. However, there has been an interesting development."

"What is it?" I asked, eager to hear more.

"I have one more thing to tell you before we continue," Billy interrupted. "I don't know how you're going to take this, so I have to say it now before I lose my nerve."

"This must be serious."

Billy walked over and sat down at the table next to me. He sat his coffee cup down and then took my free hand into his. "I talked with your mother and she agreed that we need to hire a nanny."

"What?"

"Don't get mad, `ge ya. Your mother needs a life of her own that doesn't include watching our kids twenty-four hours a day. I want her to be here, but I don't want her to turn into our permanent babysitter. It's not fair to her."

"Is that what she said?"

"No, but after we talked, she agreed. This will free her up to spend more time with Eddie. Jesse, she needs her life back. She can stay with us all she wants, but I want her to have the freedom to come and go as she pleases. This is her time, too. Plus—I miss having you to work with."

"Wow! I can't believe it. I've been trying to figure out how I was going to broach the subject without hurting her feelings, or feeling bad about not staying home with the kids every minute of the day. I love them dearly, but I need to do something other than talk to the kids and the dogs all day. Am I awful for feeling that way?"

"No, you're not," Billy said, stunned. "I'm just surprised to hear you say that. I thought you'd have a hissy." He looked relieved. "Then it's settled."

"I suppose that you have someone in mind, and before you answer, don't even think about saying Geneva. She's not going to be my children's nanny. No way—no how!"

Billy looked at Jonathan and then back to me. "My cousin, Helene Sullivan. She's my age and she lives in that big house by herself over in Crozet. All her kids are grown and her husband died a few years back. She's all alone. She was thrilled when I called her. She can move in here with us and then rent out her house. Don't get huffy on me. I didn't say yes. I told her that I had to discuss it with you first. Your mother met her and she likes her."

"What... where..."

"The discussion came up one day while you were gone, and Mom mentioned Helene. You'd really like her. She's Cherokee. She looks just like one of us."

"Oh, I bet that's a pretty sight—a woman who looks like one of you guys."

"You know what I mean. You love our Cherokee people."

"That's true. I do love your family and just about all of your relatives—except... you know who."

"Geneva is not a bad person."

"I never said she was."

"I thought you liked Geneva," Jonathan stated.

"I like her okay, but I just don't feel as if I can trust her."

"Maybe one day you and I can sit down and discuss her. You'd be surprised at some of the things I could tell you about her that might change your opinion."

"I would welcome your input, Jonathan." I looked at Billy. "When do I get to meet your cousin?"

"I have to call her back, but I did mention that sometime around noon would be good. It'll take that long to plow the driveway. She drives an SUV and she isn't the least bit afraid to get out in the snow in it."

"That soon?" I scanned the room. "We have to straighten up before she gets here."

"The house looks fine, Jesse," Jonathan said. "After a while, Helene will see your house and you at your worst, and I'm sure she'll be able to handle it."

"I sure hope so," I mumbled as my mind drifted. Now that the opportunity had presented itself, I wasn't so sure that I wanted a stranger in my house, but if I liked her, I guess I'd get used to it. Who knows? It might work out just fine. And if it didn't... well... we'll just have to wait and see. "Now what else is there that you're afraid to tell me?"

"That was the main thing. I wanted to get that out of the way before we go on to the more serious stuff."

"I'd say that hiring a nanny is serious." I looked down at Maisy. "Why don't I put you in your playpen little one? Your brother needs some attention from his mother." I stood and walked over to the other side of the table. When I sat Maisy down in her playpen, she started playing with her toys and didn't fuss one bit when I walked away. I went over to Ethan's lounger and picked him up. He was such a tiny thing. He smiled up at me and melted my heart. I clutched him close and swayed back and forth. The next time I looked down, he was asleep. I held him for a moment longer, and then I walked over and laid him back down in his lounger. I tucked his blue animal print blanket around him and stood there, admiring his precious face. His olive skin and dark hair were the same as his father's. He would be a heartbreaker when he grew up. Isn't that what all mothers say about their children?

"I guess you'd better call Helene."

Billy pulled out his cell phone from his back pocket and dialed her number. The conversation was short. Billy told her to pack a few bags and come on. He told her to take it slowly, and if anything happened to call us.

I grabbed my cup and walked over to the kitchen counter for a refill. I looked over at Jonathan and asked, "What is this new development you were going to tell me about? I hope no one else has been murdered since I went to bed last night."

"Let Billy tell you. He's the one who talked with your mother."

"What does my mother have to do with anything?" I was beginning to get a little nervous. When my mother gets involved, I worry. I would prefer that she stay at home and never leave the house so I wouldn't have to worry about her, but as I can see now, that isn't going to happen. What can I say?

Billy came over to where I was standing and said, "I called your mother this morning to make sure she was all right, and she had a pretty bizarre tale to tell."

"I'm listening."

"Last night she met one of her neighbors. The woman lives right down the road, and her name is Savannah Kelley. She's an author who just happens to drive a green Mustang convertible."

"She's not the same one…"

"Yes, she is. She's the one whose car was stolen by Naomi Kent while she was out of town at a book signing. It was the same car that we encountered in the parking lot that time."

"It seems to me that she got her car back all in one piece. She was lucky."

"I gather from your mother that the woman has so much money that she wasn't upset about the car. However, she was concerned that someone could get that close to her."

"If she wants seclusion and security, she needs to have a tall, brick wall erected around her property."

"After that incident, she did. It wasn't a brick wall, but it was just as good. She had a gated, wrought iron fence put up around her house."

"I bet that cost a pretty penny."

"I'm sure it did," Jonathan chimed in. "Enough money can buy you just about anything."

"Except more time," I said.

"Last night, Ms. Kelley got stuck in the snow in front of your mother's house. She was driving her Mustang and it obviously doesn't do well in the snow. She slid off the road and when she tried to get out of the snowbank, she dug herself in. Your mom and Eddie saw her and went out to offer help."

"Knowing my mom as I do, she probably invited her in for coffee."

"She did. They got to know each other as they waited for the tow truck. Well, the tow truck didn't get out there for almost an hour and a half, so that gave them plenty of time to chat. It seems that Ms. Kelley was on her way to the Greene County Sheriff's Office. Her phone was out of service, so that's why she was out in the snow. She was extremely upset and had to get there immediately. She has a police scanner she listens to and she'd been following the case closely. She said she knew who the killer was going after next, because she had written about it in her latest fiction novel. She writes murder mysteries set in this area. Of course, it's all fiction, but she claims that everything that's happened so far was in her book. The parents of a teenager die, and so the teenager goes after everyone he thinks contributed to their deaths. The first victim dies in a house fire, then two other victims are shot to death, and then their house is burned down."

"I'm sure it's just a coincidence," I said. "And it's not exactly accurate. Jonathan didn't die in the fire."

"No, but I'm convinced that he was supposed to."

"Who, in their right mind, would commit crimes according to what's in a book?"

"It happens more often than you think," Jonathan added. "A nut case will read something in a book and then go out and do it. It's not the author's fault, but sometimes they actually get sued over it. If I hadn't gone hunting that day, I might've been in bed at the time of the fire."

Chills went up and down my spine. We were in the middle of a story that was unfolding as we spoke. Something had to be done. I looked back over at Billy and asked, "Why didn't Mom call us last night as soon as she found out about this?"

"She said she couldn't get through. Since Ms. Kelley's phone was out, she figured that's what was wrong with ours—which it was. And she said she tried our cell phones and got that message that comes on when the phone is off. I guess I had turned them off by then."

I let my mind absorb the news and then said, "If all of this is true, then who is the next victim?"

"The boy's psychiatrist."

"Wow! Maybe we should buy her book and find out how it ends," I said, half-joking.

"According to what she told your mother, it isn't pleasant. He kills six people before he's finally caught and killed. The title of her book is *Greene County Killer*."

Now Billy had my full attention. I was shocked. "This creeps me out," I said. "I just called him the Greene County killer, and now you're telling me that a woman who lives right down the road from my mother wrote a book with the same title, and we're reliving the story. We need to get a copy of her book, or better yet, we need to talk with her. It would save time." I stood and began pacing the floor. "Who else gets killed?"

"We didn't get that far. Ms. Kelley was alarmed when she found out that Jonathan was the first victim, and that your mother is related to him. She was rather upset—and so was your mother."

"I guess she is. I know I am. Aren't you?"

"I don't know what to think."

"I say we have an open mind and find out more about this author and her book. I need to call Mom."

"You might want to wait until a little later. Your mother and Eddie are probably still in bed."

I stared a hole through Billy when I asked, "Who's still in bed? Are you talking about my mother and Eddie? You must be joking!"

"Don't get all riled, `ge ya. I didn't mean it like that. I just meant…"

"Don't lie to me, Billy Blackhawk. What do you know?"

"I never lie. Lying is not in my nature. I am an honest person!"

"You skirt the truth, just like my mother tells me I do. I want to know if he's sleeping with my mother!"

"Jesse," Jonathan jumped in. "Listen to yourself. Your mother is a grown woman. She has a right to do whatever she wants, and knowing your mother, she doesn't take intimate relationships lightly. Cut her some slack."

I thought over what Jonathan said, and then calmed down. "Yeah, I guess you're right. It's none of my business what my mother does. At least, now I know the truth behind why she wants me to get a nanny. She wants to canoodle with her new boyfriend."

Billy and Jonathan broke out in laughter.

"Did you just say canoodle?" Jonathan asked. "And I thought I'd heard everything."

"It's a word my mother has said to me many times, usually in a different context. Normally, it's me who's doing it. Call your cousin back and tell her to get over here right now. I need my nanny so I can go over and have a chat with my mother about her social life."

"Jesse, please tell me that you're not serious about giving your mother a hard time."

I smiled and said, "Gotcha!"

The sound of heavy equipment coming up the driveway interrupted our conversation.

"What on earth is that?" I asked as I walked over to the living room window and looked out. "It's the chief! And look at the size of that thing. I didn't know he had one of those. If I'd known that, I would've gotten him to let me use it so I could've plowed a garden this past summer."

"Oh, that would've been a pretty sight," Billy said. "My extremely pregnant wife operating a backhoe... trying to dig a garden that she couldn't possibly work in. What would the neighbors think?"

"We are the neighbors," Jonathan said. "And we know her. We wouldn't laugh too hard."

"If you want a garden next summer, I'll get the tractor and till you one. I'll even help with the planting, but I don't want to hear you complain when you come across a snake. And believe me you will."

"There goes the garden. I'll buy my vegetables from the market."

The telephone rang and startled me out of my thoughts about snakes in my imaginary garden.

"I'll get it," I said. "It's probably my mother calling to tell me about her new roommate."

"Be nice, `ge ya. I know you're kidding, but you might hurt your mother's feelings if you joke about her relationship with Eddie."

"You know I'm not going to say anything to hurt my mother. I love her more than anything on this planet, right along with you, the kids, our family, and chocolate."

Athena raised her head just long enough to let out a tiny bark. Thor made a grunting noise. The cat jumped down from the refrigerator and took off down the hall.

Jonathan laughed. "I think I'm going to stick around for this conversation. There's no way you're going to let this pass without putting in your two cents' worth. I just know it." He looked over at Billy and said, "Go talk with Dad. He shouldn't be out in this cold weather clearing driveways. We can do it. In the meantime, I'll watch the children while your wife acts like one."

"Acts like one what?"

"A child."

"Bite your tongue. I'll behave myself." I walked over, picked up the receiver and said hello.

"Hi, Jesse. It's me, Claire."

"Hello! How are you doing?"

"I'm fine, but the question is, how are Billy and his family doing? I'm so sorry about Daniel."

A scratchy noise was interfering with our conversation. "I can barely hear you, Claire. Where are you?"

"Randy and I are on the road heading to Mom's house."

"You know you all can stay with us."

"Mom wants us to stay with her. You don't need us under foot while you're getting ready for the service tomorrow. I'm sure your house will be full of people. Abby and Isabel aren't going to be able to come. Izzy has a terrible cold and Abby didn't want to leave her. She sends her regrets. Abby says she'll come for a visit as soon as Izzy gets better."

"Izzy and Abby, huh? I see you're now on a more personal level with those two ladies. I'm glad to hear it."

Claire was a wee bit jealous when I bonded right off the bat with Abigail and Isabel. The first time I met those two, Abigail insisted I call her Abby, something she'd never done with Claire. For once, I felt more important than my sister. Of course, I was over that now. I no longer was jealous because my sister had everything. Now I was the one who had it all, and I was deliriously happy. The pettiness vanished when I met Billy.

"I'm sorry they won't be able to make it, but you'll be here."

"To be honest, I thought we'd stay at your house, but Mom says there are some pretty scary things going on. She said that they haven't caught the guy who burned down Jonathan's house. I'm glad he wasn't at home."

"We were, too."

"Look, I'm going to let you go. I'll call when we get to Mom's house. Randy says to say hi and he sends his regrets." The telephone cut out before she could finish. A minute later she called back. "I'm sorry, but the reception here is terrible. I'll call you later."

"Okay, Claire. Y'all be careful on the roads. We have eleven inches of snow."

"That's okay. We're driving my SUV. We'll be fine. See you later, Jesse."

"Love you."

"Same here."

I hit the receiver holder, waited for a dial tone, and then punched in the number for Mom's house. She picked up on the second ring.

"Hello, Jesse," she said. "It's about time you called. We need to talk."

"We certainly do. What's going on over there?"

"It was terrible out there last night, Jesse. The roads were nothing but a slick bed of ice. I was a nervous wreck. I stayed right on Eddie's bumper the whole way home. I almost ran into him once."

"I was worried about you staying by yourself." Mom seemed awfully secretive about something. I could tell it in her voice. "What aren't you telling me?"

"You don't have to know everything I do," she said.

"Yes, I do. You're my mother and I worry about you."

"I'm doing well."

"How's Eddie?"

"Go ahead and ask me. I know you're dying to know all the explicit details of our romantic relationship."

"It's none of my business."

"Since when?"

"You're a grown woman. If you want a boyfriend, who am I to butt in?"

"I'm glad you see it that way."

I grunted.

"How's Billy holding up?"

"He's hanging in there. He had a coughing fit and scared me half to death, but he recovered."

"I was talking about last night. He told me everything when we talked this morning. I'm surprised he didn't tie the kid to the chair. I can't believe he got away. Billy must've had his guard down."

"We both did."

"I was hoping that he'd let the police handle the capture of this guy, but I should know better. I remember when he rounded up his brothers and went after Claire's kids. He wasn't going to wait on the police. And he had the kids at home and in bed before they even got to Carl's house. What I'm saying is—Billy has his own way of doing things and he doesn't let anyone get in his way. And he's usually right."

"Billy will do what Billy wants to do, and I'll go along with it… no matter what."

"What if he decides he wants his own form of justice—the Cherokee way?"

"If he decides to scalp the guy, I guess I'll hand him the knife."

"Give him the butcher knife. It's just been sharpened."

CHAPTER 17

M Y MOTHER NEVER CEASES TO AMAZE ME. Just when I think she couldn't say anything that would surprise me, she usually does. I wanted to discuss her relationship with Eddie, but didn't know how to go about it without sounding childish. I didn't want her to be alone. After the scare I had last night, I'd never sleep knowing she was by herself. I didn't think she would let Eddie stay over, but I guess I was wrong. Normally, she didn't take kindly to people living together if they weren't married. At least, that's the way she used to be. When I started dating Cole James, she told me to call if I wasn't coming home at night. She said she knew times were different and that people lived together before they got married, and even had sex before marriage. Her attitude about life had obviously changed, so it should not have surprised me that she would let Eddie stay over. I couldn't wait another minute. I had to inquire.

"Okay, I have to ask."

"I knew you would."

"Did you let Eddie spend the night?" I asked, waiting for the fallout.

"Yes, I did, if it's any of your business, Missy," she said. "The roads were dangerous out there, and to tell the truth, I've discovered that I don't like to stay by myself anymore. I'm used to having someone around all the time. I get lonely by myself. I guess we'll just have to get married."

I almost choked on my own saliva. "What… what did you say?"

"That's what you get for being so nosey, young lady. You're not choking to death, are you?"

"No, I'm not. I just wasn't expecting you to say something like that. I
was going to say that you didn't have to have sex with him just because
you let him stay the night, but I can see now that's moot."

"There you go again with those words. Moot—who uses words like
that?"

"I guess I'm just too smart for my own good."

"Yes, you are very smart."

"Claire just called."

"I know. She also called me, but that's not what I want to talk about."

"I see you and my husband have been plotting behind my back."

"Don't say that, Jesse." She hesitated for a second and then said, "I
knew you'd get mad. I told him you weren't ready for a nanny."

"Stop, Mom. I was going to tease you, but we've been through too
much lately, and frankly, I'm just not in the mood. I don't have a joke left
in me right now."

"I find that hard to believe. I can always count on you to either say
something funny or something totally embarrassing. What's the matter?
Are you sick?"

"And I can always count on you to make me feel good, and no, I'm
not sick."

"I'm your mother. That's my job."

"I don't want you to feel guilty, so I'm going to let you off the hook
and tell you the truth. I've been joking about getting a nanny for a while.
You know how I'm always saying that, but the truth is, I've been giving it
some serious thought for some time. You need your life back. You can
come over anytime you want and you can stay as long as you want, but I
think it's time to hire a nanny to look after the kids. Besides, how can we
pull one of our stunts like we did that time we got caught hiding in the
woods watching Kansas Moon's house?"

"Speaking of which, Daisy called this morning. She and Gabe are coming to the funeral. They also send their regrets."

"I'm glad. I like her and Gabe. They've turned out to be good people."

"Eddie and I have gone to dinner with them several times. I like their company. They're very interesting people."

"All right. We've talked about everything except your new author friend. Tell me about her."

Jonathan walked over to me, holding a sleepy Maisy. "I hate to butt in, but I think she's ready for a nap."

I looked over at Ethan and saw that he was also asleep. "Hold on a minute, Mom. I'll be right back." I laid the phone down on the kitchen counter and pointed down the hall.

"Would you put her in her crib while I get Ethan?"

"Sure thing," Jonathan said as he turned and walked toward the hallway. I gently picked up Ethan and followed. Once the kids were down, I went back to the phone while Jonathan headed for the front door.

"I'm sure Billy has his cell phone, but in case he doesn't you can call me on mine," he said before walking out the door. "We're going to plow the driveways and the main road into the compound. It might take a while."

"That's okay. I'll be right here. Thanks for helping with the kids."

Jonathan waved as he left. He's such a good man, I thought to myself. Lu Ann will be lucky to have him as her husband. I walked back over and picked up the receiver.

"I'm sorry to keep you waiting, but the kids needed to go down for their morning nap. I guess it won't be long before Maisy stops taking one. She's at that age. Tell me about your new friend, the author."

"She's very nice. I guess Billy told you everything."

"He said she thinks a killer is acting out the murders in her book. I guess we have a copycat killer living in Greene County. That's a little scary, if it's true."

"She believes it is. She carries a few of her books in her car, so she gave me a copy of her latest one. Jesse, I'm telling you—it's strange. I started reading it this morning."

"And..."

"She's a very good writer. I can't figure out where she comes up with all this stuff. She says she just sits down at her computer and it just flows out. You have to have a creative mind to think up some of this stuff."

"Not to change the subject, but where's Eddie?"

"He went home, but he'll be back soon."

"Are your doors locked?"

"After reading some of this book, you can bet on it. I'm glad I didn't start reading it last night. I would've never gotten to sleep."

"Billy said that six people died in her book, and that the psychiatrist is next. Did you know that Wayne Avery was in therapy for three years?"

"That's what Billy said. If I were him, I'd find out who his psychiatrist is and go warn him."

"As soon as my new nanny gets here, maybe we will."

"You'll love her, Jesse. She's so nice, and she knows a lot about kids."

"We'll see," I said. "Do you know what happened when the author got to the Sheriff's Office?"

"She didn't go. While we waited for the tow truck, we talked about the book. Eddie told us about a movie he once saw that was just like what was happening here. He said the police blamed the author. All the evidence pointed to him. They thought he was the killer, because he came forth with all the details. They thought he wrote the book and then went out and did everything he wrote about."

"That's crazy."

"Yes, it is, but you know how the police rationalize things. They get a briar in their claw and they don't stop. Anyway, what Eddie said was a wake-up call for Savannah. She got scared and decided that she would think it over before putting herself in that situation. She doesn't want to be a suspect. She made up everything in her book. It's not her fault that someone is playing it out in real life. After the tow truck towed her car, Eddie took her home."

"Does she live alone? I mean… she was out by herself in a snowstorm. If she had a husband you'd think he'd be with her."

"They're apart, not separated. That's all she would say, and I didn't ask for more details. His name is McCoy. He's an attorney and lives in their house in Fancy Gap, Virginia."

"Wow, that's an odd name. Is that his first name?"

"That's what she called him… McCoy."

"I've never heard of Fancy Gap. Where's that?"

"Savannah said it's in the southwestern part of the state, down in the left-hand corner. That's how she explained it to me. She says it's a lovely place."

"How on earth did she end up here?"

"She said they vacationed at Massanutten Ski Resort about ten years ago and fell in love with the area, and that's how it all started. They found a piece of land and built a house on it. They were going to use this place as a mountain getaway, but it turned out that she got away and never went back. I think that's when their problems started. She wanted to live here all the time, but he didn't. She lives here now and he lives in Fancy Gap. We really hit it off, so I'm sure she'll tell me more when we get to know each other better."

"Maybe she should've talked with her husband before she went out last night."

"That's exactly what she said! She's going to call him today and see what he has to say about the situation. She's hoping that he'll come to his senses and move here. They've been apart for two years."

"Two years! I'd think that if he was going to change his mind, he would've done it by now."

"He still comes to visit."

"They have strange living arrangements."

Mom is a trusting soul. I was worried about her friendship with Savannah Kelley. She barely knew this woman, yet she believed her story about her book and the killings, and most likely had told her everything about our family. I was leery. I didn't know this woman. She could be a kook. I had to meet Savannah Kelley.

"She said she would be interested in talking with you and Billy after I told her that you guys are private investigators. I have her number. Why don't you call her and talk to her about her book?"

"That's a good idea."

"It would be quicker. If what she says has any merit, I would think that the sooner you find out what's going to happen next, the better your chances are of stopping it. I would hope so, anyway."

"What makes you think we're going to do anything? That's what the cops are for."

"Don't try to fool me, Jesse," Mom said. "I know you want to meet her in person, so you can tell if she's lying. But I don't think she is. It's all in her book. If you'd read it, you'd see. I'm at the part where he just killed his psychiatrist and is stalking his next victim. You know he stalks them before he kills them."

"That's creepy, Mom," I replied. "Let's just say, for the sake of argument, that what she says about her book is true. That means the killer has been lurking around our house. Jonathan comes here all the time, and the killer would know that. And Billy just told me that he investigated Avery's mother for the father a while back. That puts him on Avery's kill list."

"No! Oh, Heavens! That also means he probably knows where I live, too. I'm your mother and you're married to one of the men he wants dead."

"I can tell from the way you're talking that you've been thinking a lot about that murder mystery of hers."

"It's really good, but scary considering we're involved."

"I want to tell you something, but I don't want you to freak out. The bad guy, Wayne Avery, lives off Octonia Road in that new housing development."

"That's right up the road!"

"That's why I want you to make sure you keep your house locked up, and keep your eyes open. If you hear something outside, don't open your door without your gun. I'm serious."

"Okay. I'll go get my gun right now and leave it on the kitchen counter. After reading that book and then listening to you, I'm not going to ignore anything. I'll have my guard up. Claire and Randy should be here soon, so I won't be alone for long. And Eddie's coming back before dinner."

"Why don't you give me your friend's phone number and I'll give her a call."

"All right. It's right here on the counter. I put it in my bill basket. Just a minute."

I heard Mom rustling papers as she hunted for the number. When she found it, she read it out loud to me as I wrote it down.

"I'll give her a call in a little while. I want to talk with Billy first, but right now he's outside plowing the driveway. I need to call Sarah as soon as I get off the phone with you."

"I'm sure she'd be glad to have a distraction, however short-lived. Oops! I didn't mean it like that."

"I know you didn't. I'll call her right now. We'll talk later. Okay?"

"Let's check in with each other frequently. That guy is still on the loose. Who knows what he's going to do next?"

"You will, if you keep reading her book."

We said our good-byes and hung up the phone. I was worried about Mom being alone, but hopefully, she wouldn't be for long. Eddie was coming back, and Claire would be there soon. I would call her again in a couple of hours, but now, I had to call Sarah. I dialed the number for their house. Chief Sam picked up on the third ring.

"Hello," he said.

"Hello, Chief Sam," I said. "What are you doing home? I thought you were out plowing the road?"

"The boys made me come home. They said I shouldn't be out there in the cold. What's wrong with them? I plowed these roads for the last forty some years. I don't know why they expect me to stop now."

"I can't say a word. If it was my father, I wouldn't want him out there either."

"I must admit it's a lot nicer sitting inside by the fireplace."

"How's Sarah holding up?"

"When she's not crying, she's sleeping. It's her way of dealing with Daniel's death. She can hardly talk. She's so distraught."

"How are you doing?"

"I'll be better when they catch my son's killer. I just can't believe a teenager did this to our family. It's hard to hate one so young."

"I felt the same way at first. You know he confronted me at the hospital and swore that he didn't mean to kill Daniel. He said it was an accident. I almost felt sorry for him. Can you believe that? It didn't take long for me to realize that even someone so young could be dangerous. It seems that killers get younger every day. It's a crying shame!"

"I've been saying that for years. Some of the stuff that I see on television and read in the newspaper makes me sick. I say we stop blaming the parents and make these kids pay for what they do."

"I totally agree. A parent can only do so much. You raise your kids the best you can, and how they turn out is up to them."

"Ah, Sarah's up. Would you like to talk to her, Jesse?"

"Yes, I would. And Chief Sam, if there's anything you want me to do, you just say so... anything at all."

"You're a good squaw." He handed the phone to Sarah.

"How are you doing?" Sarah asked, speaking softly. "I'm sorry that I haven't called you."

"No, Sarah. It's me who should be apologizing. I should've called, but I thought you might need some time to yourself. I knew you'd call if you needed anything."

"I need my son back, but that's not going to happen." She started to cry.

"I wish I could fix this, but I can't. I hate to see you hurt like this."

"We can't control what happens to our children," she said, sniffling. "We give them life and that's all we can do."

"That's what the chief just said."

"He's a good man... stubborn... but good."

"Have you talked with Billy this morning?"

"No, I haven't. He called, but I was still in bed. Sam talked to him. Why? What's going on? Have they caught the kid who killed my boy?"

As soon as the words were out of her mouth, I started to cry. Unable to talk, the two us cried over the phone.

"We're going to catch this kid and put him behind bars for a long time."

"Jail is too good for that criminal!" she shouted into my ear. "I want him dead!"

"You don't mean that, Sarah. You're upset."

"I do mean it, Jesse. He killed my son. I want him to pay!" Her sobbing became uncontrollable. "And I want my son back!"

Chief Sam took the phone from her and I could hear him trying to calm her down.

"Jesse, she can't talk anymore. This has been too much for her to handle. She's falling apart. It's going to take some time for her to come to terms with Daniel's death."

"I understand. Please tell her that I love her and all she has to do is call if she wants me to come over. I can sit with her, if you want me to. Maybe talking would help."

"She'll be okay," he said. "Jenny is here with us."

"Good."

"The doctor gave me some pills to help calm her down, and it's about time for another one. She'll be asleep before you know it. When the soul is shaken to its core, rest is the only thing that will help."

"Call us if you need anything."

"Thank you, Jesse."

"Thank you for being my family. I love you all so much."

"We will see you tomorrow." The chief hung up the phone without saying good-bye, but that didn't bother me. That's his way.

I hung up the phone, walked over to the front window, and looked outside.

Snow covered everything except the driveway. It looked so cold. I went to the front door and opened it. The cold air rushed in.

Athena got up from the fireplace and limped over to me. She let out a sad bark as if she was begging me to close the door.

"What's the matter, girl?" I asked as I bent down and rubbed her coat. "Are you cold? I am, too."

Without as much as a word, or in her case, a bark, she limped her way out on to the porch and stood there, her nose pointed in the direction of the woods.

Thor lazily pulled himself to his feet, stretched, and then abandoned his warm spot by the fire. He ambled over to where Athena was standing, circled her, and then sat down beside her.

I heard a meow and looked down to see that Spice Cat had joined them. "Hail, hail! The gang's all here!"

A second later, Spice Cat took off down the steps heading in the direction of the woods. His fluffy coat was barely visible in the snow

"Spice Cat, get back here!" I screamed. "You're going to drive me nuts!" I looked down at Athena and asked, "Where's he going, girl?"

I could hear Spice Cat's meow and see his long tail wagging as he continued his trek to the woods. I worried that he too would get hurt, but I wasn't about to leave my kids alone to go after him.

"I don't know what the three of you have cooking, but I'm staying right here. You better get back here, you crazy cat!" I yelled one last time.

Between the blowing wind and the roar of the bulldozer, I was sure that my voice had gotten lost. Spice Cat probably couldn't hear me, but even if he could, he was not coming back until he had accomplished his mission, whatever that was.

This I was sure of because Athena and Thor had acted the same way on a few other occasions—like the time Thor snatched a plastic bag containing Billy's bloody shirt from a cop's hand and sprinted out of the house, not to be seen for several hours. That was funny.

But what was Spice Cat up to? Was he out in the woods searching for something incriminating?

Mom always said that the two dogs were pretty smart, so what about Spice Cat? Did he have an uncanny knack for digging up something like my two canines, or was he just on a jaunt through the woods?

Most cats don't like to get their paws wet, but not Spice Cat. He proved early on that he liked the snow and all the playful things he could do in it as long as he could come back inside when he finished playing, and dry his coat by the fire.

My pets know the difference between good people and bad. They also know where the bodies are buried—at least Athena and Thor do. That was Mom's little joke after Thor dragged up a severed hand onto her front porch.

Oh, Lord! Is that what Spice Cat's going to do? Is there a body out there somewhere in our woods? I sure hope not. One incident of a dead body in the backyard was enough for me.

I ushered Athena and Thor back inside, against their wishes. They wanted to wait for Spice Cat's return, but I wouldn't let them.

Actually, I was afraid they would take off after him and then I'd have to go out hunting for them all. As long as one was alone, I was sure that one would come back. If all three of them were together, I'd be knee-deep in the frigid snow looking for them.

"Not today," I said as I closed the door. "I'm not going out there. If you want to freeze to death, help yourself!"

Athena and Thor sat by the door and wouldn't move. They both whimpered as if they expected me to run right out in the snow and look for that cat. Silly dogs.

"Suit yourself," I said. "But I am not going after him. I mean it."

I walked to the kitchen to get a cup of coffee and saw the piece of paper with Savannah Kelley's phone number on it lying on the counter.

I was going to call her as soon as Billy got back, but that could take a while. Maybe I should call her now and find out for myself if she's genuine. I had my doubts.

Even if she had written a book that a copycat killer was using as a guide for his killings, things never do go as planned.

He has to trip up somewhere. Isn't that what they all do? They think they're never going to get caught, but as the saying goes, no one commits the perfect murder. It's just not possible.

Killers always leave something behind, however small.

That's it! The killer left something behind, and Spice Cat has gone after it! Yeah—right.

"I must be losing my mind," I said, looking over at the dogs. "You might as well go lay by the fire where it's warm. There's no telling when he'll drag his butt home."

Ten minutes later, I heard a loud meow outside the front door. I walked to the door and opened it to see Spice Cat standing there, covered with snow. The flakes flew as he shook them from his coat.

I heard a jingle and looked down to see something shiny caught up in his collar. I reached down and untangled a set of keys.

"How did you get these stuck in there, silly cat?"

Spice Cat sprinted past me to the fireplace.

"Good boy," I said as I held the cold set of keys. "Who do you think these belong to?"

CHAPTER 18

I WALKED OVER TO THE KITCHEN COUNTER and lay the set of keys on it. I wondered about the pickup truck I saw last night parked on the side of the road. Was it still there? Was one of these keys a key to that truck? I fixed a cup of coffee and headed to the kids' room to have a look at them. I peeked in and saw that they were still napping, so I headed to the family room to sit down and rest while I still could. When I walked into the room, I saw the tree that Billy had cut down standing in the corner. It had been put in a stand. I looked closer and noticed that it had water in it. Billy must've put up the tree this morning while I was still asleep. I had forgotten about it until now. Maybe this afternoon we could decorate it if Billy was in the mood, but then I realized that we didn't have any decorations. We got married on Christmas Eve last year, so having a real Christmas tree at the time was the last thing on my mind. This year, we were going to have one. As soon as Billy got back, we'd discuss what to do about the decorations.

Another thought crossed my mind. Tomorrow was Daniel's funeral. It would be hard to enjoy decorating a Christmas tree tonight knowing that in the morning, Billy's brother would be laid to rest. A tear slid down my cheeks. When I went to wipe it away, I caught a glimpse of something outside the window. I turned quickly, walked over, and stared out. Nothing was there. It must be my imagination. I must be seeing things. Then I heard a thump by the back door. I spun around and saw Billy standing in the doorway.

"God, you scared me half to death! What are you doing out back?"

"I'm sorry, `ge ya. I didn't mean to scare you. I was checking the perimeter." He took off his coat, laid it in a chair, and then kissed me on the cheek. "You've been crying. Don't you like the tree?"

"I love the tree," I said, sniffling. "It's beautiful, but we don't have any decorations."

"No problem," he replied. "When Helene gets here she can stay with the kids while you and I go shopping for ornaments. Speaking of shopping, do you have something to wear tomorrow?"

"I have a nice pair of black wool slacks and a sweater to match. Will that be okay?"

"I remember that outfit. It'll be perfect."

"What about you? Do you have something to wear?"

"I thought I'd wear the suit I wore to our wedding. Do you think that's all right?"

I smiled and then kissed him on the cheek. I put my arm around his waist and said, "I think that would be nice. You look so handsome in that suit. You took my breath away when I saw you in it standing by the altar. You were the best looking man in the room. I was so glad I was marrying you."

"Don't get all mushy on me, `ge ya, or I'll be crying right along with you."

We stood there and held each other as we stared at the tree. The scent of pine filled the air and for me it brought back pleasant childhood memories. However, the moment was brief. The phone rang and Billy scrambled over to the table in the corner of the room to answer it before it woke the kids. He picked up the receiver after the first ring.

"It's your sister," he said as he handed the phone to me. "I'm going to get a cup of hot apple cider. I'm chilled to the bone." He turned, grabbed his coat from the chair, and walked out of the room.

I talked with Claire for a few minutes before excusing myself. "I have to go. Billy and I are going to buy decorations for the tree after my nanny gets here."

"Mom says she's real smart when it comes to kids," Claire responded. "Mom likes her, so she has to be a nice person."

"We'll see," was all I said before I ended the call. I put the phone back in the cradle and headed to the kitchen.

When I walked into the room, Billy was standing by the sink examining the set of keys. "Whose keys are these?"

"You're never going to believe this, but the cat dragged them up."

Billy chucked and said, "Why does this not surprise me? Now our cat has turned into a detective."

"He does come by it naturally. I guess he's been hanging out with Athena and Thor too long."

We both got a good laugh out of that one.

"They haven't been out there for long," Billy said as he looked at the keys. "They don't have any rust on them, and look at this." He held the keys out for me to see. "It has a keyless remote on it. I wonder if it got wet inside."

"I though that maybe one of those keys might belong to that truck out by the road."

"That truck's gone."

"Did the police tow it away?"

"I don't know, but it was gone when I went out this morning. I just assumed the cops towed it to the impound lot. They probably wanted to go through it to check for evidence."

"Can you find out?"

"I can do anything, dear."

"I know you can, heap big warrior."

"Ah, you say the nicest things."

"When Helene gets here, we could take a ride over to Octonia Road and look for Wayne Avery's house. I think these might be his keys. Who else could they belong to? I mean, how many people have been wandering around in our woods lately?"

"You have a point, Jesse. It won't take us a minute to find out if these are his keys. The remote will give him away."

"Call and see if Helene has left yet."

"She has. I already called."

I smiled. "You're getting excited about having a nanny aren't you?"

"I think it would be good for our family."

"Are you going back out to help with the plowing?"

"Yes, but I wanted to check on you before I did."

"If you're worried about me, don't. I can take care of myself."

"Yeah, I know. You've proven that many times. And when it comes to our children, you're like a psychopath. You'd shoot first and ask questions later if anyone threatened them. I count on you to be the other half of Blackhawk & Blackhawk. That's what being partners is all about. You have to be able to count on your partner."

"You sound like my mother."

"I just have this nagging feeling that he's still out there watching us."

"I do, too. I thought I was just being crazy!"

"Trust your instincts, Jesse. They've worked for you before. While I'm outside, I want you to keep a gun close by at all times, and keep the doors locked. Nobody is getting through these doors, if they're locked. That way I can leave without fear that someone will break in."

"You know I'm not going to let anyone near our children. They'll have to go through me first."

"Oh, I called Cole on my cell phone while you were talking to your sister. He said they have a deputy watching Wayne Avery's house, but so far, he's been a no-show. It's as if he's disappeared off the face of the planet. Even Captain Waverly's men lost him. Now how slippery can one kid be?"

"He's not a kid, Billy. I see that now. I had to get past the fact that just because he looked like a kid, he isn't. If he's eighteen, he's an adult."

"And when they catch him, he'll be tried as one. Sheriff Hudson says the D.A. will seek the death penalty once they can get enough concrete evidence to prosecute. They're convinced he's the killer. That kid's pretty sly. They haven't found a thing that proves he's guilty, except his confession to you concerning the arson, which won't hold water in a court of law, and there's nothing linking him to the murders in Ruckersville. No, they need something substantial. They need fingerprints or some sort of forensic evidence that proves he was at the scene of both crimes. Finding the gun he used to kill those two people in Ruckersville would cinch his fate."

"All they have to go on is his confession to me. I guess that's not enough to make an arrest. Are they looking for anyone else?"

"Right now, he's their only suspect, but I'm sure they're not ruling out others. This is an ongoing investigation."

"They could arrest Avery for shooting Officer Whalen."

"They have to catch him first."

"That's so sad. How could one's life go so terribly wrong at such a young age? Do you think there's any truth to what he said about someone else being the killer? He did say that he didn't do it, but he knows who did. That makes me wonder. Is he a cold-bloodied killer, or is he in the middle of something that he can't get out of? If he's innocent, then who's the guilty one? And if he is guilty, I'm curious to know what triggered his rampage. Did he snap and then turn into a killer? He has a history of trouble. Some kids grow out of that stage after a while."

"His parents moved around a lot, staying in one place for only a few years at a time because his father kept changing jobs. Their last address was in Bumpass, Virginia, and before that it was Niceville, Florida, and before that it was Round Rock, Texas, where Wayne was born. Sheriff Hudson had one of his men do a thorough background check on the entire family. His family moved to their new home in Stanardsville, and then everything went sour."

"He probably had a hard time adjusting to his surroundings, or his new school. You know how mean kids can be to the new kid in school. It doesn't matter where you live. It happens everywhere."

"I'm curious to know why they selected Stanardsville."

"They could have family here."

"We can speculate all day long. What we need to do is get out and find the kid."

"Before he kills someone else. Mom said that he's going after his shrink next according to Savannah Kelley's book."

"I don't think I'd put too much stock in a murder mystery book. Besides, if Savannah Kelley really believes someone is committing crimes according to her book, why hasn't she gone to the police?"

"She was going, but she got scared when Eddie told her that the cops might turn on her and believe she was the one behind the killings."

"That wouldn't surprise me."

"Why don't we talk about this when you finish your plowing? Do you want me to fix you a sandwich before you go? There is still a lot of food in the refrigerator from Robert's restaurant."

"No, I'll get something when I'm done. The day will be gone before you know it. Helene should be here soon." Billy looked over at the dogs lying buy the fire. "Do you want me to let the dogs out before I leave?"

"That might not be a bad idea."

Athena and Thor rose to their feet and walked over to the door to answer nature's call. I noticed that Athena's limp was less noticeable. Spice Cat stood as if he planned to go with them, but I immediately told him to lie back down and forget it. He already had his fun for the day.

"The litter box is in the laundry room, pal."

Billy grabbed his coat, opened the door, and the three of them went outside. I heard their footsteps as they descended down the steps, and then they were out of earshot.

Spice Cat meowed as if he wasn't too happy, but he lay back down by the fire anyway. He licked his coat and a minute later I'm sure that I was nowhere in his thoughts.

I snatched the keys off the counter and walked over to the desk to put them in my purse. I wanted to make sure that we had them when we left for our shopping and snooping excursion. I picked up the phone with the intention of calling Savannah Kelley, but was distracted by a noise upstairs. Spice Cat must've been bored, because he arose from his crouching position and followed me as I stealthily climbed the stairs. I tiptoed through each room, opening closet doors and checking bathrooms.

"I guess I'm turning into a nutcase, Spice Cat. I keep hearing things."

Spice Cat hissed and then backed up.

A crushing blow to my head sent me to the floor. I tried to open my eyes, but when I did all I could see was a blurry figure leaning over me. I could smell the putrid smell of his breath as if he hadn't brushed his teeth in a while. He bent down closer and whispered, "I killed the psychiatrist this morning while he slept in his bed. Aren't we having fun?"

He laughed a sinister laugh. "Heed my warning. I'm not finished, and you'd do well to stay out of my way. If you don't, the next ones to die will be your precious kids."

I tried to scream, but the words wouldn't come. I felt as if I was having a terrible nightmare, and as hard as I tried, I couldn't make myself wake up. I felt a warm flow of blood run down the back of my neck as I turned my head to follow the image of the person who had done this to me. I caught a glimpse of his brown boots and the word, *Leatherneck*, imprinted on the side just before I passed out.

I don't know how long I lay on the floor, but when I came to, I was on a stretcher being shoved into an ambulance. I shivered from the cold as I opened my eyes.

"Where's my husband?" I asked, my voice harsh.

"I'm right here, Jesse," Billy said as he held onto my hand.

"The kids... he said he'd kill our kids."

"The kids are fine. No one is going to hurt them."

I tried to sit up, but the pain in my head was horrendous. "Who's watching the children?"

"Don't worry about the children," he replied. "They're being taken care of. Just lay back and rest."

"I can't rest!" I screamed. "He's going to kill our children! He said so!"

Billy leaned in close to me and said, "Relax, Jesse. You have my word that nothing is going to happen to them. I promise."

I closed my eyes. When I opened them again, I was in the emergency room.

"Hello, Mrs. Blackhawk," a man said. "I'm Dr. Staton, and you're at Martha Jefferson Hospital. I'm going to fix you right up. You took a terrible blow to the head. We're going to put in a few stitches."

"Make it fast, Doc. I have to get home."

"We need to run some tests…"

"Stitch me up, give me something for this headache, and then I'm going home." I looked around the room. "Where's my husband?"

"He said he had to make a call. He'll be back shortly, but for now, we need to get started on you. You're going to feel a little sting."

I felt a sting to the back of my head, and then I closed my eyes while the good doctor did his job. When he was finished, he asked, "Would you like to see my handiwork?"

"Thanks, but I'll pass, Dr. Staton. Put a Band-Aid on my cut and let me go home."

"I think we're going to need more than a Band-Aid, Mrs. Blackhawk. I had to put six stitches in your scalp. You're going to have a headache to go with that wound."

"Okay, but put the smallest bandage you can on my head. I have a funeral to go to tomorrow, and I'm not going with a big bandage wrapped around my head."

"I'll tell you what. I'll fix you up, and you can wear a scarf tomorrow. It's going to be cold anyway."

"That sounds good to me."

At the time, I would've agreed to anything just to get out of the hospital. My vision was beginning to clear up, but I had a terrible headache. "May I have an aspirin?"

"I have something here for your headache. Don't take aspirin." He handed me a small paper cup containing two pills. I downed the pills, and then took the paper cup filled with water and gulped it down. I sat the cups down on the metal tray next to the bed.

Billy walked into the room and said, "How's she doing, doctor?"

"She'll be fine. Don't let her take aspirin. Aspirin thins the blood. She needs to take Tylenol."

"Sounds good to me," I said. "Are we done here?"

The doctor looked at Billy and said, "We really need to do a CAT scan when there's a…"

"No! I want to go home."

I slowly sat up and inched my way off the bed. "See, I'm fine." I felt a little dizzy for a second, so I moved slowly. I looked at Billy and said, "Let's go home."

"I can't make you stay, Mrs. Blackhawk, but it would be in your best interest to let us do a CAT scan before you leave. You have a head injury and you..."

"Okay. You can do your CAT scan, but only if you do it right this minute and don't make me wait. If I have to wait, I'm leaving. I mean it. I'll leave if you put me in a room and tell me you'll be right back."

Billy looked at the doctor and threw up his hands. "She has a mind of her own. I can't make her do anything."

The doctor motioned to a woman dressed in scrubs and said, "Take Mrs. Blackhawk down for a CAT scan STAT."

The woman retrieved a wheelchair, and within ten minutes, I was having a CAT scan. After the scan, I was wheeled into the hallway where the doctor was waiting. "Give me ten minutes and then you can leave."

"Ten minutes, and that's all."

Dr. Staton turned and walked down the hall to another room. Ten minutes later he returned with the results. "You have a concussion and you'll need to take it easy. This injury isn't something to take lightly. I would suggest bed rest, but I know that's out of the question."

"Then I can go home now, right?"

"Yes, you can. I have an information sheet here for you. Read it, and if any of the symptoms appear that are listed on this paper, call 9-1-1. Your life could depend on it. Sign here. I'll have someone get you a wheelchair." He motioned to the woman next to him. He held out his clipboard and pen.

"No wheelchair."

He pulled the clipboard back and said, "No wheelchair, no pen."

I smiled. I knew that I could just turn and walk away, but I also knew that if I didn't sign the form and leave in a wheelchair, his butt could be on the line. I signed on the dotted line, and then handed the pen and clipboard back to him. "Thanks, Dr. Staton." I grabbed the piece of paper he held out to me, folded it, and stuffed it into my jeans pocket. I flopped down in the wheelchair and started wheeling myself down the hallway, leaving the two of them standing there.

Billy caught up with me, grabbed the back of the wheelchair and said, "Slow down, Jesse. You're acting insane. You have no idea how bad your head injury is. You could pass out anywhere, or have a stroke."

The word *stroke* stopped me in my tracks. "What do you mean, I could have a stroke?"

"You need to read that paper and then if you want to go off half-cocked, help yourself. I won't try to stop you." He walked around and stood tall in front of the wheelchair with his arms crossed across his chest. He looked like one of those big Indian chiefs you see on television. He stooped down to my level and said, "But I won't be a part of your killing yourself."

"Okay," I said, winding down. I took a deep breath before speaking again. "Listen to me carefully. I don't think it was Wayne Avery who struck me on the head. I didn't see his face, but I heard his voice, and I'm telling you that it wasn't him. That's what really scares me. When I thought Wayne was the killer, I wasn't so scared. I don't know why, but I just wasn't. I know that sounds crazy, but there was something familiar about Wayne, and it wasn't intimidating. Now that I know there's someone else in the picture, I'm terrified. Push me out of here, Billy."

"People disguise their voices, or when they're nervous they sound differently." Billy got behind the wheelchair and pushed me down the hall to the entrance.

I looked around, but didn't see anyone from the family. "Where is everyone? How are we going to get home?"

"Cole is waiting for us. Here he comes now."

I looked up to see Cole getting out of his Jeep and heading to the front entrance. "What is he doing here?"

"Your mother called him as soon as she heard what happened."

"Who told my mother?"

"I did. I had to. Your mother would have a fit if I didn't call her. If she found out about it from someone else, I would be in big trouble."

"Who's watching the kids?"

Billy didn't say anything.

I got up out of the wheelchair when Cole walked through the door.

"Are you ready to go?" he asked as he handed me a coat. "You might need this."

I looked at the two of them stand there with a guilty-as-sin look on their faces. I knew they were plotting something. I took the coat from Cole, slipped into it, and then the three of us walked out to the car and crawled in. As soon as Cole pulled out into traffic, I turned to Billy in the back seat and asked, "Is Geneva watching the kids?"

"Yes, but it's only temporary until Helene arrives. I didn't want to ask my mother, so I called Geneva."

"I understand." I didn't have the energy to argue.

"She rushed right over. She even got there before the ambulance arrived."

I looked at Cole. "What are you doing here? I know you must have something up your sleeve. Did Sheriff Hudson send you to spy on me? I hate it when you keep things from me—and stop looking at my head like that!"

"I think that bump on your head has made you crazy," he replied. "Actually, I was at the hospital when they brought you in. My mother took a nasty fall."

"I hope she's going to be all right."

"She broke her hip, so they admitted her. She's been sedated, and won't be awake for several hours. For now, I'm all yours."

"How did that happen?" I asked, trying to sound concerned.

Truth be told, I wasn't any fonder of his mother, Elsie, than I was of Geneva. Both women had left a sour taste in my mouth for one reason or another.

I'll never forget the time Elsie had the audacity to call my mother and tell her to keep her girls away from her son. Cole and I had a relationship, and when it was over, he started seeing my sister, Claire. He was on the rebound and out to make me jealous, but I knew that relationship was as ill-fated as the Titanic, so I didn't say or do anything. I just let it play out.

Elsie was jealous of anyone who dated her son, and when Cole dated two different women from the same family, she went crazy. She blamed us for trying to break her son's heart.

"It's not enough that one of you used my son. Now the other one's after him, too. Can't you just leave him alone?" she had said.

It was all I could do to keep my mouth shut about it, but Mom said the old biddy didn't bother her, and there was nothing Elsie could say that would make a difference about anything. People are who they are. Mom found Elsie to be a sad, lonely woman who tried to keep her son from having any kind of relationship with a woman. She wanted him all for herself. She didn't think there was a woman on Earth who was good enough for her son.

I thought she was sad. Fortunately, Cole knew how she was and refused to let her interfere with his love live.

"I saw Billy," Cole said, breaking my train of thought. "He explained what happened. I told him not to call anyone; I'd give you a ride home. And I'm not staring at that huge bandage on your head."

Cole snickered. Billy was in the back seat doing everything he could to keep from laughing out loud at Cole's remark.

"Okay, I'm sorry for being so hateful," I pouted. "I guess I was a little suspicious of you two, and acting a bit crazy."

"That's all right," Billy said, chuckling. "We know you're nuts."

"You can't help it," Cole agreed as he laughed right along with Billy.

They both stopped laughing when I said, "He killed the psychiatrist."

CHAPTER 19

NOTHING CLEARS OUT A ROOM OR SILENCES IT QUICKER than announcing that someone has been murdered. Billy and Cole were speechless when I blurted out the news. Cole pulled his Jeep off to the side of the road and asked, "What did you say?"

"You heard me. After the guy hit me on the head, he took great pleasure in telling me that he had killed the psychiatrist. I can only assume that he meant the one who treated Wayne Avery. I think there are two killers out there and they're working together."

Cole pulled the Jeep back out onto the road. He was silent and it appeared that he was deep in thought.

I glanced in the back seat at Billy and then looked back at Cole. "Why do I feel as if I'm the only one here who is in total darkness?"

Billy reached up, put his hand on my shoulder and said, "Why don't we save this until we get home? You just got hit on the head and you're not thinking straight."

I knew Billy had something bad to tell me, but didn't want to do it in a confined space. I pace when I'm upset and he probably figured I would need room to let off steam. We were only minutes from the house. I could wait until then.

Even though there was plenty of snow on the ground, the main roads had been plowed and were almost back to normal. The ride wasn't as treacherous as I had expected. I relaxed and laid my head back on the seat. I closed my eyes for a second, and before I knew it, we were pulling up in front of the house. A white Dodge Durango was parked next to the garage. I figured that must belong to my new nanny, Helene.

The walk up the porch steps proved to be more difficult than the ride. I slipped my way up them and was relieved when the front door opened. I was greeted by a woman who had to be Billy's cousin. She had the same Cherokee features: long, black hair pulled back in a braid down her back, dark olive skin and deep brown eyes. She was my height, but weighed twenty or thirty pounds more than me. She had a kind face, and when she smiled, her manner was infectious. She reminded me of my mother.

"Hello, Jesse," she said. "I'm Helene. I'm so glad to meet you." She gave me a big hug, and then closed the door behind us. "It's so cold outside. Come on in by the fire and warm up." She looked up at Billy and Cole and said, "I've made coffee if anyone's interested. I thought I'd fix a snack once everyone's had a chance to warm up." She put her hand on my shoulder and walked me over to the fire. "I hope you don't mind, but I made myself at home. Jonathan introduced me to your beautiful children. They're in the den with Geneva. How's your head?"

They say that you only have one chance to make a good first impression on someone, and Helene had done that. I took a liking to her right off the bat, and knew that she would be a welcomed addition to our family.

Billy and Cole took off their coats and made their way to the kitchen. I couldn't hear what they were talking about, but that was okay. For now, I wanted to get to know Helene.

"I guess I'll make it. Is that your Durango out there?"

"Yes, it is. I just love that car."

"It's cool." I looked around. "Where are the dogs and the cat?"

"They're in the den, too. Geneva's been telling stories to the kids and it seems that the dogs and the cat have taken an interest. You'd think they'd get bored after a while, but they've been hard at it."

"I appreciate your coming here, and I hope you'll like living with us."

She laughed. "After what happened this morning, I guess I need to ask for hazard pay."

I laughed at her comment, but she was right on the mark. "Anyone who lives with us has to be tough, considering the type of work we do."

"Oh, honey, I know all about this family," she said. "I know what to expect. You can't do what these guys do and not be tough." She looked over at Billy and then back at me. "He says that you're as tough as they come, too." She looked at the bandage on my head. "If you want me to, I can have a look at your head and maybe we can downsize that bandage. I know you must hate it."

"I do!" I said. "Do you think you can do something about it? I can't walk around with this monster on the back of my head."

"Follow me and I'll see what I can do."

I followed her to the bathroom beside the nursery and watched as she removed the bandage, examined the wound and then said, "This isn't too bad. I think I can fix you right up. I need a pair of scissors."

I opened the cabinet door, pulled out a pair, and handed them to her.

She grabbed a small gauze pad and a roll of gauze tape, and then closed the cabinet.

"They shaved your head a wee bit. That's good." She cut two small pieces of tape and stuck them to the countertop, and then took a small gauze pad and cut it in half. She pressed the pad to my head and then applied the tape.

"Ah, that's much better," she said.

"You're hired."

"We're going to get along just fine. I don't know why Billy was worried."

"I have my moments and he knows it," I replied. "I need to go see my babies."

The two of us walked out of the bathroom and headed down the hall to the den. Geneva was holding Maisy in her lap, reading from a children's book, and Ethan was sitting in his lounger on the floor by the dogs. The cat was lying on the sofa with all four feet up in the air. Nobody moved or said a word when we walked in. I smiled and waved as Geneva continued with her story. I bent down and kissed Maisy and Ethan and then whispered my thanks to Geneva. She nodded her head in agreement, yet didn't miss a beat with her tale.

"Everything seems to be fine," I said as we turned and walked out of the room.

"Geneva is real good with the kids," Helene said. "I've already settled in. I took the room upstairs across from your mother's room; the one next to Jonathan. You sure have a full house."

"We still have empty bedrooms upstairs."

"Yeah, but for how long?"

"You never know around here."

"I just want to mention that I cleaned the blood up off the floor in the hallway upstairs."

"Thanks so much, Helene. I never thought there might be some of my blood on the floor. Yuck. I'm sure that was a nasty job."

"It wasn't so bad. I've seen worse."

Helene and I walked to the kitchen and meandered over to the coffee pot. She poured us both a cup, and then the two of us sat down at the table and listened to Cole and Billy.

"We have to do something," Billy said. He looked at me. "My mind hasn't been on my job. I'm supposed to protect my family, but instead I've been too consumed with grief over Daniel's death."

"Don't be silly," I said as I touched his hand. "Your brother just died. No one expects you to be in control every minute of the day."

After the words came out of my mouth, a thought came to me—our house just got broken into, I was hit on the head, yet not one cop showed up to take a report. Did Billy call the police to report the break-in and my attack? And if he did, where were they? They were nowhere in sight when the ambulance took me away, and they never showed up at the hospital to question me. What was going on?

"Billy," I said, looking from him to Cole and back. "Why haven't I seen any police? Why didn't they come and take a report after that man attacked me?"

"I didn't call them."

"Why?" I asked, stunned.

"They aren't going to find anything, and I didn't want to deal with them." He looked at Cole. "No offense, but sometimes the police just get in the way."

"None taken," Cole replied. He didn't seem to be surprised at Billy's remark.

I looked at Cole and asked, "But don't you have to make a report now that you know a crime has been committed? That man broke into my house and attacked me."

"I wasn't present and I don't know that a crime has been committed until you tell me so. Do you want to file a report? I can see to it that the proper authorities are notified… since this really isn't my jurisdiction."

I looked at Billy and realized that he was right. Why bring the police into this and have them take up our time with their useless questions? They weren't going to find anything that we couldn't find ourselves. I would match Billy's ability to catch the bad guy against the police any day.

"What crime? I don't know what you're talking about. I fell and hit my head."

"Yeah, that's what Billy said," Cole replied. "But we've been friends too long for him to fool me. I finally pried the truth out of him. But, like I said, there's nothing I can do if you don't want to make an official police report. If he claims that you fell and hit your head, who am I to doubt him?"

"I see," I said, and then let the matter drop. It was apparent to me that Cole knew he'd be wasting his time trying to get us to make a police report. In our business, we handle everything in-house… if we can.

Helene had been sitting there quietly listening to us, until she finally spoke up and said, "Geneva thinks he got in through the upstairs fire escape. Before the ambulance got here, Billy got her to go around and make sure all the doors were locked. She didn't tell him about the unlocked door upstairs because by the time she made the discovery, the ambulance had already arrived. Once Jonathan and I got here, she told us about it. When we checked it out, we could see that there had been footprints on the land-

ing and on the steps. Someone had tried to cover them up by swishing the
snow back and forth like we used to do as kids when we played out in it.
Of the few prints he could find, Jonathan said the tread was deep and the
pattern fit that of a hunting boot."

"That doesn't tell us much," I said. "Virginia is for lovers and hunters."

Helene chuckled. "How true," she agreed. "I've always heard that if
you go into Charlottesville, you'll find an artist or a writer on every corner. Well, if you go to Greene County you'll find a hunter on every corner."

"Ah," I said. "Speaking of writers, have you heard about the one in
Greene County?" I looked at Cole.

"Yes, I have," he replied. "Your mother filled me in about her latest
book, and according to her—the writer—she seems to think that we have
a copycat killer on the loose, and he or she is using her book as a guideline. I don't put much stock into what a writer says in a book of fiction."

"And why not?" I asked. "Have you seen the book? Have you read
any of it? Let me tell you something. Mom thinks there's a connection,
and I have a tendency to pay attention to what my mother says. I think we
need to check out this book."

"That's a waste of time," Cole said. "Things like this happen in the
movies, not in real life."

"Don't be so sure," Geneva said as she walked into the kitchen with
an entourage of dogs and a cat following her. She was holding Ethan in
one arm and Maisy in the other.

I almost fell out of my chair. I jumped up and grabbed Ethan from her.

"Here, let me help you. These kids are too heavy for you to be hauling
both of them around at the same time." The truth of the matter was that I
was afraid she might drop one of them.

"Thanks," she said in a kind manner. "They were getting restless, so I
figured we'd come in here and see what all the fuss was about. Have you
figured out who broke into your house?"

"Not yet, Geneva," Billy said as he got up and pulled out a chair for
her to sit down in. "I hear that you're the one who discovered the unlocked
door. Good work. We might make a detective out of you after all."

She giggled like a school girl. "After Jonathan left, Helene and I had a closer look at that lock. I don't think the door was unlocked. I think the lock had been picked. Eli knows how to pick a lock. I've seen him do it many times. He likes to do stuff like that. Anyway, there were scratches around the keyhole—that's why I think it was picked. And why don't you have a deadbolt on that door like you do all the rest?"

"I wanted to make it easy to open, so I only put one lock on it. The whole purpose was to have an easy egress if we had to get out in a hurry... you know... in case of a fire. Until I did the remodeling, there was no way to exit the second floor unless you crawled out of a window, and if you had to crawl out of one of the windows there was nothing for you to stand on. You would've fallen two stories to the ground."

"And if the fire didn't kill you, the fall would," Geneva added. "I see your point. I guess you weren't expecting someone would use that door to break into your house, since you saw it as a means of escape. But now..."

"But now it's time to put a deadbolt on that door."

Billy looked as if he had the weight of the world on his shoulders.

"It's not your fault, so don't blame yourself, Billy," I said. "The door did have a lock on it. It's just that the intruder broke in anyway. It won't happen again. There are still a couple of deadbolts in the garage. I saw them sitting on a shelf the evening I went out to check on you guys and your deer-skinning party."

The room was quiet. The silence was deafening. We were all obviously thinking back to that day with sadness.

"Forget it," I said. "It's over and done with. We need to concentrate on the killers. I know there are two of them working together. Wayne Avery and this guy are connected, and we have to find out how. What do they have in common?" I looked at Cole. "What can you tell us about the case?"

"There's nothing I can say that you haven't already heard on the news."

"That's a load of crap," Billy said as he slammed his fist down on the table. His outburst took us all by surprise. Helene jumped back in her seat as if someone had taken a swing at her, and Geneva flinched. Both children started crying. The dogs and the cat immediately dispersed... gone to hide in their favorite hiding places, wherever that was.

Billy got up from the table and walked over to the front window. He hung his head and uttered, "I'm sorry." He looked back over at Cole and repeated his words. "I'm sorry, Cole. I know you're just trying to help as best as you can."

I handed Ethan to Helene, got up from the table, and walked over to him. I put my arms around his waist from behind and whispered, "It's okay, Billy. Come on back to the table. We need to figure out what we're going to do next."

Helene and Geneva managed to calm the children, and then Helene said, "We're going to the den, if you don't mind. You don't need us around."

"I tell you what," I said. "Let's all eat something. Food usually seems to help." I looked around at everyone. "Is anyone hungry?"

"I'll fix something for us," Helene said. "I'll put Maisy in her playpen and get started right now. Why don't you guys take your discussion to the den, and when I have something thrown together, I'll give you a holler."

"I could definitely eat a sandwich," Billy said, looking at me. "I was going to eat one earlier, but had to run to the hospital when my wife got conked on the head. How about you, Cole?"

"I wouldn't mind a sandwich," Cole replied.

"Say no more," Geneva said. "I'll help. Could you bring Ethan's lounger in here for me?"

"Sure," Billy said as he headed to the den.

Cole and I followed. After he took the lounger back to the kitchen and then returned, the three of us sat down and discussed our next move.

"What *can* you tell us about the case?" Billy asked Cole as he leaned forward in his chair, his elbows on his knees and his hands clasped together in front of them. "And, please, don't insult my intelligence by saying there's nothing you can tell me. My brother is dead, Cole. I need your help."

Before Cole had a chance to say anything, his cell phone rang. He got up to excuse himself and walked over to the corner of the room. His call was lengthy. Finally, he closed up his phone, turned around and said, "That was Sheriff Hudson. Dr. David Wellsworth has been murdered. He was killed in his sleep in the middle of the night. He lives over in Syria in

Madison County. He is—was a psychiatrist."

Cole had a forlorn look on his face.

"What is it, Cole?" I asked. "You have a strange look on your face."

"I almost slipped and told my boss about what you said. One of these days I'm going to lose my job because of you two."

"Why do you say that?"

"I should've called Sheriff Hudson the minute you said the psychiatrist had been killed."

"But you didn't know he was telling me the truth. They were words spoken by a madman. He could've been lying, but even if he was telling the truth, it was already too late. Besides, you just found out."

He looked at his watch. "About an hour ago."

"It was still too late."

"What did the sheriff have to say?" Billy asked. "Do you have to leave?"

"No. Actually, I took some personal time because of my mother's accident. Sheriff Hudson just wanted to keep me abreast of the situation. All of us are still on the lookout for Wayne Avery even when we're off-duty. Anything that happens that might be connected to him is important, so that's why the sheriff called me."

"I guess the sheriff already knew that Wayne Avery had been in therapy."

"Oh, yes," Cole replied. "He surmised that the doctor could be in jeopardy, so he alerted the Madison County Sheriff's Office. I assume they contacted the doctor and warned him."

"You guys still don't have anything on the kid, do you?" I asked. "I mean, you don't have any prints, or…"

"All we have so far is a name, thanks to you. Otherwise, we'd still be looking for clues. At least, we had somewhere to start. Once the kid called you and gave you his name, we had a lead to follow. From the way it looks, Wayne Avery is our killer."

"He has an accomplice. The guy who knocked me out didn't sound like Wayne. His voice was deep and husky."

"Like Billy said, he could've been scared. That could've been why his voice sounded different. I think we're looking for one person."

"I know this may sound silly, but I think we need to get our hands on that book, or at least go talk with that author."

"Okay," Billy agreed. "Let's go pay her a visit."

"And we'll ride by Wayne Avery's house."

"I don't know what you think you're going to accomplish by that," Cole said. "The sheriff has a deputy watching the place, and so far, Avery hasn't returned home. I'm sure he will eventually. It's only a matter of time."

"Ah, you just never know what you'll find until you look," Billy replied and then winked at me. "We have something we want to check out."

I could only assume that Billy was talking about the set of keys that Spice Cat had dragged up.

Cole's cell phone rang again. When his conversation was over, he smiled and looked at the two of us and said, "The thing about not having any proof—that's not the case anymore. We now have concrete evidence linking Wayne Avery to the murders in Ruckersville. After the fire, a neighbor discovered a discarded gas can in his backyard that didn't belong to him, so he called the Sheriff's Office. They found one print, and it belongs to our bad guy, Wayne Avery. That puts him at the scene of the crime, and pretty much nails his coffin shut."

"Could we not use that word?" I asked. "It makes me think of Daniel. I'm sad enough as it is."

"Yeah, I guess that was a bad choice of words. Sorry."

Helene walked into the room and announced, "Lunch, however late it is, is now being served in the main dining room."

The three of us got up and headed back to the kitchen. While Billy and Cole ate, I nibbled on cheese and crackers. Food wasn't appealing to me at the moment. Actually, I felt a little sick to my stomach and I had a terrible headache—but I wasn't about to say anything.

Billy's cell phone rang, so he excused himself to answer it. He walked out of the room, but returned within minutes. He said that the call was from Jonathan and that the medal he found in his yard had Wayne Avery's fingerprint on it.

"I guess we now have our killer. All we have to do is find him before he kills again."

"That's my job," Cole said with a strange look on his face. He stood up and excused himself from the table. "I need to go. Thanks for the lunch, ladies. Jesse, Billy, I'll call you if we come up with anything else. Just keep your eyes open and watch out for this kid. He's a killer, and so far he's been true to his word." Cole looked directly at me. "Remember what he said to you about your kids? Keep that in mind when you leave the house. Make sure there's plenty of protection handy for whoever's staying here with them. He could come back and you won't know when, until he's here. I'm going to ask Sheriff Hudson to contact Captain Waverly and see if they'll post an officer on the premises out of sight."

"Would you check to see if Officer Whalen is okay?"

"I already know the answer to that. He's going to recover and should be back on duty in a couple of weeks... maybe a month. Is there anything else you want me to check out?"

I thought for a minute and said, "Yes. Could you find out if the CPD towed that pickup truck that was sitting out by the road to the impound lot?"

"I can answer that for you, too. No, they didn't. It vanished. They have no idea what happened to it, but they do have an APB out on it."

"Thanks for being so helpful, Cole," Billy said as he walked him to the front door. "If we come across anything, we'll let you know."

"Sure you will." Cole said, and rolled his eyes as he waved good-bye to the rest of us.

Billy walked outside with Cole and when he returned, Jonathan was with him.

"I didn't hear your Humvee pull up," I said as I kissed him on the cheek. "Let me take your coat."

"I should stay away more often," Jonathan said. "I get a kiss from a beautiful lady and lunch waiting for me on the table. What more could I ask for?"

"Come have a seat," Helene said. "I'll get you a plate."

"What have I missed so far, other than Jesse's big bang on the head?"

"They found a print on a gas can that belongs to Wayne Avery," I said. "And Cole wants to help us out on the case of the Greene County Killer."

"He wants to help, or is he just digging?" Jonathan replied. "No offense, but Cole is a cop and he's always in cop mode. You should know that by now giving your past history with the guy."

I was a little surprised at Jonathan's bluntness, but not angry. He was stating a fact. "Just say what's on your mind, why don't you?" I laughed.

Helene put a plate on the table for Jonathan, looked over at me and said, "As I said before, there are no secrets in this family."

"If that's the case, then why haven't I met you before?"

"You have, Jesse," she replied. "I was at your wedding, but you were so elated about becoming Billy's wife that you just don't remember. I was the one dressed in red."

"I remember now! I loved it. When I saw you I told Mom that you really looked snazzy. You were definitely dressed for the occasion—a Christmas wedding. That was so sassy."

Jonathan sat down at the table and started digging into the food.

"The police know about the medal," Billy said.

"Yes, I know. I told them when I got the results from Caroline. It seems we're always doing their job for them."

"Is that the same Caroline that you know, Billy?"

"Yes. She's an old friend of the family. Jonathan used to date her."

I laughed out loud. "Is there anyone in Charlottesville that you haven't dated? Or Greene County... Albemarle... Orange... Madison?" I asked.

"Ah... yes, but we're not going there."

"You're such a... what's the word I'm looking for?"

"Not one you should say in mixed company," Helene intervened. She grunted and then went to the refrigerator. "Would anyone like something to drink?"

"I'll have another glass of tea, if you don't mind," Geneva said.

"I have something in my truck for you guys," Jonathan said to Billy. He looked over at me. "I hope you don't mind, but I took the liberty of shopping for Christmas tree decorations while I waited to hear from Lu Ann. Billy said that the two of you were going to go shopping later, but I figured if I waited for that to happen, your tree would go undecorated until the very last minute. I know my brother wants to keep with tradition, so I handled it. I hope you don't mind. I knew that the first thing the two of you were going to do is go out looking for that criminal, and that the decorations would have to wait. Now they don't have to. Besides, I had to go buy some new clothes and a suit for the funeral."

"Thank you, Jonathan," I said as I walked over, leaned down and gave him a big hug. "You're so thoughtful!"

Jonathan wolfed down his food, and then stood to take his plate to the sink.

"I'll take that," Helene said. "You all have unfinished business and time is slipping away."

"You're wonderful," Jonathan said as he leaned over and kissed her on the cheek. "I'm so glad you're here. I've missed your smiling face."

"Don't try to lay that bull on me, young man. I got your number. You're just trying to butter me up so I won't give you grief about being single. Don't you think it's time you settled down and got married? Aren't you tired of chasing after low-lifes and criminals? You should be married with a house full of children."

"I will be soon."

Helene had a stunned look on her face. "Tell me more!"

"Jesse can fill you in when I leave, but for now, I have to go out and catch low-lifes and criminals."

"You are such a bad boy!"

"And you love me for it."

Helene smiled a sheepish smile and I could tell that she adored Jonathan as she probably did the rest of the Blackhawk brothers.

Jonathan turned to Billy and said, "Come help me bring in the packages from the car, and then I'm going to be leaving, brother. Take care of this little filly." He pointed to me. "She's a spry one. I half expected her to hit you over the head with a frying pan when you let that kid slip through your fingers."

"She doesn't know what one is," Billy replied, laughing it off.

"I heard that, pal. You can sleep with the dogs tonight."

Athena and Thor appeared and took notice.

"That's right. I was talking about you guys. Go bite your daddy."

They both had a confused look on their face. Athena twisted her head and Thor howled.

"They know who the boss is in this house, `ge ya," Billy smirked. "I'm the chief of this teepee!"

"Yeah, you're right. You are the head honcho, and they know it. Right, guys?" I snapped my fingers.

Athena, even with her limp, walked over and sat down by my feet, and Thor couldn't get to me fast enough. He slid across the hardwood floor and landed on top of Athena. I laughed. "See what I mean?"

Jonathan walked over and gave me a hug before leaving. "Please don't hurt my brother. He means well, but we know who is in charge here." He winked at me.

Billy walked with him to the door, and then the two of them walked outside. They seemed to be gone far too long, so I went to the door and opened it. They were standing there, packages in hand, talking about something they obviously didn't want me to hear. They stopped talking when they saw me. I asked them if they were plotting something that I should be privy to.

"Not today, `ge ya," Billy replied.

"I know when you're hiding something, Billy Blackhawk, so you might as well tell me what it is. I'm going to find out anyway."

"Jonathan thinks he knows where Wayne Avery is hiding out, and we're going to go looking for him."

"I'll get my coat," I said. "Don't think you're going without me, Tonto."

CHAPTER 20

THE DECORATIONS FOR THE CHRISTMAS TREE were piled, still in their bags, on top of each other by the tree waiting to be hung, and the bags of new clothes Jonathan had purchased were stacked on top of the bed in the room he would use for a while. His new suit was hung in the closet.

Mom called, but I told her we were on our way over and that I was in a hurry. I didn't mention the morning's events, and she didn't ask. I guess she was waiting until she saw me in person so she could read me the riot act. I asked her to please call her friend, Savannah Kelley, to see if we could have a few words with her at her convenience—hopefully before the day was over, and that it was a matter of great importance. Mom wanted to tell me more about the book, but ended her monologue when I told her that Billy was standing at the door waiting for me. I did manage to tell her how much I liked Helene before I hung up the phone—and I could've sworn that I heard a sigh on the other end of the line.

Geneva packed up some food at my request and took it home to Eli. She insisted on returning so that Helene wouldn't be by herself under such dangerous conditions. A killer was still out there, and might possibly return. The kids, the dogs, and the cat would be under the watchful eye of their new nanny, Helene and her helper, Geneva. I felt secure knowing this, even the part about Geneva.

Billy called his dad before we left to see how everything was going and to check on Sarah. Apparently, all was about as good as it could be. Several relatives were there lending their support, and Sarah was up and about. That was everyone's main concern—that Sarah wouldn't fall into a state of depression and not find her way back. The death of a loved one can do that to a person.

We followed Jonathan's Humvee in Billy's Dodge pickup truck, knowing that it was always better to have more than one means of transportation while on a mission, or in this case, another means of escape. We had no idea what we were going to encounter, so as they say, we came prepared. Jonathan had a cache of weapons that he kept stored in his Humvee, which was a good thing since most of his guns and grenades had been destroyed in the fire. Billy and I came with our own small arsenal. We were ready for anything.

It was cold outside, but at least it wasn't snowing right at the moment. I looked around at the passing scenery and wondered what the rest of the day would have in store for us. We didn't need another blinding snowfall while we searched for a killer. The temperature was supposed to drop into the single digits tonight, so whatever it was we were going to do, we needed to do it before it got too late. I didn't want to be hiding out in the woods behind someone's house in the freezing cold.

Billy pulled out his cell phone, punched a number on the pad, and then laid the phone in its holder on the dashboard. I could hear the numbers being dialed.

"I want to be able to talk with Jonathan while we're on the road," he said. "I have it on speaker, so watch what you say."

I smiled and replied, "Are you afraid I might cuss out loud?"

"I never know what to expect from you."

"Hello," we heard Jonathan say.

"What's the guy's address?" Billy asked.

"I'm not sure about the number, but he lives two doors down on the right."

"What are you talking about? What guy?" I asked.

"Hold on a minute, Jonathan, while I fill Jesse in."

Billy explained everything to me as we rode down Rt. 29. "All the information the police have on Wayne Avery is only part of his criminal background. They implied that his trouble really started when he moved here, but that's not true. He was always getting into something everywhere he moved to. It was his grandfather who saved him every time and cleaned up after the kid. His grandfather was a judge in Texas until he died a couple of years ago. The judge made sure that his grandson didn't have a criminal record. Once he passed away, there was no one to cover for the kid. That's why he has a record in Greene County. He doesn't have anyone to fix things for him, nobody to wipe his slate clean."

"Where did you get the dirt on Avery?"

"Jonathan has a friend on the force in Texas where the kid was born, so he made a call. Need I say more?"

"Why am I not surprised? Jonathan has connections everywhere. Who's this guy you're talking about who lives two doors down?"

"He's the only living relative we could find in this area," Jonathan said. "The rest live in Texas. The guy's name is Eric Webster, and he lives two doors down from the murdered couple in Ruckersville."

"Webster—huh. Was he related to the mother? I mean, if he was related to the father, you'd think his last name would be the same."

"That's just it," Billy said as he made a left turn onto Rt. 33 at the Ruckersville intersection following Jonathan's Humvee. "He was the stepbrother of the daddy—same father, different mother."

"Yeah," Jonathan broke in. "My contact in Texas tells me that there was a big stink about that situation. It seems the wealthy judge had planted his seed where he shouldn't have and it came back to haunt him. He refused to marry her and then paid her off. When her son got older, he made it a point to make contact with his father. The old man wanted nothing to do with the boy, so he paid him off, too. The only problem was that the boy found out he had a stepbrother and then hunted him down. What happened after that is anybody's guess. All we know is that after the grandfather died, Eric wound up in Greene County, living close to Peter and his wife Judy, and their son, Wayne."

"Are you telling me that Eric Webster is Peter Avery's stepbrother, and that he lived two doors down from the murder victims in Ruckersville?"

"That's right," Jonathan replied.

"That makes him Wayne Avery's uncle."

"Step uncle," Jonathan replied. "That sounds weird."

"I'll tell you what sounds weird," I said, my mind going as fast as it could. "Could it be possible that Eric... oh, forget it. That's a crazy thought."

"What, Jesse?" Jonathan asked. "Say what you're thinking."

"Is it possible that Eric could be the one Wayne talked about, the one he said would kill him if he told anybody about him? Isn't it a little ironic that Eric lives close to the murdered couple? This is too much of a coincidence. I told you that I thought Wayne had an accomplice, and the man who assaulted me this morning was an adult, not a teenager. I'm pretty sure of it."

"How can you be so sure?" Jonathan asked. "You said he came up from behind..."

"I'm telling you that the man who conked me on the head was a grown man. He was bigger than Wayne and his boots were huge. *Leatherneck—* that was the name printed on the side of his boots. They were the last thing I saw before I passed out. I remember the boots and that he had bad breath. It just about made me gag."

"That's good to know," Jonathan said. "We're looking for a big guy with *Leatherneck* boots and bad breath." He chuckled.

"I heard that," I said. "Laugh if you want, but killers have been captured by far less evidence than bad breath. Look at... ah... it doesn't matter. If Eric Webster is the man who assaulted me, I'll know."

My cell phone rang.

"What was that?" Jonathan asked. "Is that your cell phone, Jesse?"

"Yes, it is," I said as I pulled it out of my coat pocket. "It's just my mother. She was supposed to call me as soon as she talked to that author."

"Fix her phone, Billy," Jonathan demanded. "All we need is for it to go off while we're breaking into someone's house."

"I'll take care of it as soon as she finishes talking with her mother."

Our conversation lasted for about one minute. Mom wanted to tell me that Savannah Kelley said to come by her house as soon as we could, and that she lives up the road on the left. We were to look for a house surrounded by a wrought iron fence. A double gate marked the entrance to her property. Everything was electronic, so she would know when we arrived.

When I closed up the phone, Billy told me to push the button on the side and hold it down until the word *vibrate* appeared on the display screen. I did as he said.

"You're so smart," I said as I shoved the phone back into my coat pocket. I leaned over and kissed his cheek, and when I did, I suffered a dizzy spell. It was all I could do to maintain my balance and not fall over in the seat. I was suddenly afraid. What would happen if I was with Billy and Jonathan and things got a little hairy? Would I be a burden to them and get one of them killed? As much as I wanted to keep silent about it, I had to say something. I surely didn't want to jeopardize their lives, or mine.

"Wow," I said. "I just had a terrible dizzy spell."

"I knew it!" Billy said. "You should've stayed home. You're not well enough to be out on a dangerous job like this."

"We can't take her home," Jonathan said. "We're almost there."

"All right," Billy agreed as we pulled off the road and into a gas station parking lot behind Jonathan. "You'll have to stay in the truck."

"But..."

Jonathan made a U-turn in the parking lot and pulled up alongside Billy's truck, their driver's side adjacent to each other, and then rolled down his window. "Are you okay, Jesse?"

"I'm fine. I just had a dizzy spell."

"This puts a kink in everything," Jonathan said. "We can't let you go with us. What happens if you pass out right in the middle of everything?" He looked back at Billy. "We can't take that chance, brother."

"I told her the same thing."

"She'll have to wait in the truck."

"Okay," I said. "I'll stay in the truck, and be your lookout."

After a few seconds, Jonathan said, "Jesse, we have to be able to count on you to do what you say. One of us could get killed if you don't have all your faculties together. If you faint, we could all die."

"I understand, Jonathan. I promise you I'll stay in the truck until you tell me differently."

"Follow me and when we turn onto Little Creek Road, look for a blue house on the right. Don't stop. Just keep following me until we come to the end of the road."

"I'm with you," Billy said.

"Okay, brother. Let's get this party started!"

Jonathan pulled back out onto Rt. 33 and headed down the road. We were right on his bumper until we came to Little Creek Road. He turned right; we followed. About a mile down the road we passed a section of houses on the right. I touched Billy's arm when we passed the blue house. He glanced over at it for a second and it was then that we both saw the old pickup truck — it was an old, black, Ford Ranger — the same one that had been parked out on Bear Mountain Road when Billy caught Wayne trying to break into our house. We followed the road until we came around a bend where the road abruptly stopped. After turning around, Billy and Jonathan sat, parked side by side, and talked on their cell phones. No one could see us because of all the trees, and it helped that the road curved before it ended.

"Here's what we're going to do," Billy said. "We'll park right up by the bend out of sight, but close enough for Jesse to be able to see what's happening. You and I will go through the woods and come up on the back-side of his house."

"I think we should storm the house."

"I agree. We need to catch him by surprise." Billy turned to me and said, "If you see anything suspicious, call me on my cell phone. It's set on vibrate, and I won't say anything when I answer, so don't be surprised. Just tell me what you saw. Okay?"

"If something happens and you can't get through to Billy, call me."

"What do mean? What's going to happen that I won't be able to reach Billy?"

"Jesse, anything could happen. Just keep your eyes open."

Billy pulled his truck in front of Jonathan's and then the two of them inched their way up to the bend in the road. We were just close enough for me to see the houses, but not close enough for anyone to notice us. We hoped.

Billy kissed me on the lips and said, "I'm leaving the keys, so if this breaks loose, I want you to drive this truck right through the front door."

"What do you mean, breaks loose?"

"If you hear gunshots, call the sheriff and then come after us."

"Okay," I said, weakly. "Are you sure you don't want me to go? I could..."

"I need to be able to count on you, 'ge ya. Promise you'll do as I ask."

"I promise," I whispered.

Billy and Jonathan crawled out of their trucks and had disappeared into the woods before I even had time to slip over into the driver's seat. I looked around and scanned the area. All the houses were average single-family ranchers—starter homes designed especially for just that—starting a family. Yet, the killer who lived in the blue house had no intention of starting a family. He was on a killing rampage that I was sure would leave him dead... eventually. At least, that's how I summed up his life and his future. He obviously had a death wish. He probably was so unhappy with the way his life had turned out, and the fact that his own father had rejected him, that he just didn't care anymore. Or did he? What was his story? I had this nagging feeling that he felt he not only had a reason to kill, but enjoyed it. It was a game to him. He quietly broke into our house, knocked me out, and then left without taking anything or killing anyone. What was that all about, if not a game? The message he whispered when he bent down close to my ear convinced me the man could be capable of anything.

Being left alone in the truck and not being with Billy gave me the willies. I didn't like the idea of him going into a dangerous situation without me. We are a pair and needed to be together. What was I thinking when I agreed to his demands? I have a keen sense and can tell when there's danger lurking about. I could be a big help. I should be with my husband.

I forced myself to stop thinking like that. I had made a promise to Billy and I was going to keep it. If he needed me, I would know. I made up my mind that I would sit here and do nothing, except keep watch. As much as I didn't like it, I did it anyway.

I had been sitting in the truck for about ten minutes and was beginning to get cold. It was just a few degrees below freezing outside, so it didn't take long for the truck to lose the warmth inside the cab. I thought of turning on the ignition long enough to heat it up inside, but then decided against it. The exhaust from the tailpipe might be seen. No, I would stay here and freeze to death before I would give us away.

Then... I heard a gunshot. I looked up just in time to see someone limp out the front door and down the walkway to the black pickup truck. The man jumped into the truck and backed out of the driveway onto the road. His tires spun as he fishtailed up the road and out of sight. This happened in less than a minute, but long enough for him to get away.

I was so stunned and caught off-guard, it took a few seconds for me to get it together. When I did, instead of calling the police, I started the truck and punched the gas pedal. The truck skidded into the driveway and managed to come to a stop intact, without running into anything. I shoved the gear into park, reached down into my purse on the floor, and pulled out my 9MM. Then I pushed the door open. I slid out, holding onto the door handle as I did, and then slammed the door shut. I took off running, slipping and sliding as I went, gun in hand as I followed the trail of blood droplets up the porch steps. I kicked open the front door like a madman and stood poised, my gun pointing straight out in front of me. My hands were trembling, and my heart raced. I had no idea what to expect... and it didn't matter. I was here to save Jonathan and Billy.

Jonathan ran up to me and said, "Everything's okay, Jesse. You can put the gun down. We have the situation under control."

"Where's Billy?" I asked, looking around the room. I hung my head for a brief minute and closed my eyes. My head hurt and I felt as if I was going to faint. The room got dark, but I held on and managed to stay with it. When I raised my head, I saw Billy walk out of a bedroom with his huge arm wrapped tightly around Wayne Avery's neck. He dragged the young man along with him as he walked toward me.

"Thank God, you're all right," I raved, jumping around like a chicken with its head chopped off. "I heard the gunshot and saw a man run out of the house."

I wanted to run up to Billy and throw my arms around his neck, but under the circumstances, I decided that I'd better wait until he had Wayne Avery handcuffed to a chair.

"That man's my uncle," Wayne Avery shouted. "Your Injun buddy here shot him."

"That Injun is my husband and you had better not call him that," I hissed at him. "I'm the only one allowed to call him that. You... you don't deserve to even say his name... you killer!"

Billy smiled at me and held onto Wayne as Jonathan walked over and slapped the handcuffs on the young man. He grabbed the handcuffs in the middle and dragged Avery over to a chair by the window. He shoved him down in it, and then pulled out his cell phone. He called the Greene County Sheriff's Office and made an anonymous call, telling them where they could find their fugitive.

"One down and one to go," Jonathan said as he closed up his cell phone.

The boy was angry and began to yell. "He had me in a chokehold. He almost broke my neck. He tried to kill me."

"I doubt that very seriously," I said, looking at him. "If that had been the case, trust me, son, you'd be dead. Gee, wouldn't that make our job easier?"

"I want a lawyer," the kid screamed. "I know my rights."

"You're lucky you're going to jail and not have to suffer the wrath of the Blackhawk brothers. That's not something you want to have to deal with. I've seen their ire. It's not a pretty sight."

I taunted the kid. I walked over to him and just stared at him.

"I'll be right back," Jonathan said. "I'm going to get my tie-wraps, so I won't have to leave a perfectly good set of handcuffs behind. Once I get my Humvee, we're getting out of here."

I backed my way over to Billy. I wasn't about to let Avery out of my sight. I grabbed Billy's hand and held onto it as Jonathan walked out the front door. We listened to Wayne Avery spew forth his lies.

"I'm innocent," he swore. "Eric made me go with him when he burned down your brother's house and when he killed those two people down the road. I didn't want to go, but he forced me. He said I should help him avenge my father."

"And I guess he made you go with him when he killed your psychiatrist, huh? Did he make you watch him murder the man who had tried to help you?"

"He did. Finally, someone knows the truth! You believe me, don't you?"

I walked back over to him, leaned over and got right up in his face. "Sure, I believe you, kid. I believe every word you say."

I got a whiff of his breath, stepped back and stared at him in shock.

"Liar!" he screamed. "All of you are liars. I should've killed you this morning when I had the chance."

It was then I realized that I had been wrong about there being two killers. Wayne was the one, but where did Eric fit into this scenario?

"That's right, `ge ya! Isn't that what your half-breed hubby calls you?" He looked up at Billy and asked, "Hey, Injun, what does that mean? Tell me something. Is she good in bed? I mean, she isn't much to look at. She's way too skinny. I don't know what you see in her."

My anger was beginning to get the best of me. He could call me all the names in the world that he wanted to, but I refused to stand by and let him talk down to Billy, calling him hurtful names. He was nothing but a punk kid with bad manners. I could see that now.

"How's your head? I bet it hurts like a big dog." He laughed out loud in a menacing way. His eyes bored a hole in me. He smiled when he saw the surprised look on my face. "That's right. I was in your house this morning. I wanted to slit your throat to finish you off, but I decided to save that for later. You got lucky this time, but you won't be so lucky next time. Next time, I'll kill you and your snot-nosed little brats."

"You'll never get a chance." I smirked. "You and your loser uncle are going to spend the rest of your lives behind bars, unless you get the death penalty, which is highly likely since you murdered someone in the commission of a felony... and it was premeditated."

"You don't know what you're talking about. I've never been in trouble until I moved to this God-forsaken dump."

"That's a big, fat lie and you know it. Liar!"

"Shut up!"

"We know all about your past and your grandfather, the judge. He's the one who cleaned up after you every time you got into trouble with the law. He's the one who kept you out of jail. But he's dead now. He can't help you anymore. You're going to have to stand accountable for your crimes. You're going to do some serious time, if you don't get the death penalty." I looked over at Billy and then back to the kid. "I hear the D.A. is hot to see you have a needle stuck in your arm, and then watch you die!

"Even if I made it to court, the judge would let me off with a stiff warning. They don't give people my age the death penalty. You wait and see. You're just trying to scare me."

"Who's been telling you that—your precious uncle who just ran out on you? Boy, are you in for a rude awakening. You're such an idiot. Don't you keep up with the news? The courts have sent kids a lot younger than you to prison for life. Don't think they'd hesitate to give you the needle."

"All I did was watch. I didn't kill anyone, and I'm not the one who struck the match to the fire... either time."

"Liar! God, you're such a liar! I can't believe that I actually thought you might be innocent. Liar! Liar!"

"Don't call me that!"

I could tell that Wayne Avery hated to be called a liar. I could see it in his face. This gave me something to use against him. I figured that if I called him a liar long enough, he'd get mad and spill his guts. I was willing to give it a try.

"I bet you're the one who killed your own mother. What did she do to deserve having a bunch of sleeping pills stuffed down her throat? The medical examiner found bruising around her mouth consistent with just such an act. How could you do that to your own mother?" I looked at Billy and asked, "What kind of person does that?" I looked back at the kid.

"You deserve to die, you creep. You're a killer… and a liar! Liar, liar, pants on fire!"

"She's the one who deserved to die! She ruined our lives. She cheated on my father and broke his heart. He killed himself because of her!"

"Oh, well. Then by all means, she had to pay for what she did. She had to die."

"Don't patronize me. If you're so smart, then why don't you know she wasn't my real mother?"

The look on our faces said it all. He had caught us off-guard. Obviously, the judge must've kept a lot of secrets since this was the first Billy and I had heard about a stepmother. No one else had said anything either.

"Ah, ha! I see that I know something you don't! That's right. My real mother died when I was little. My mother was good. Judy could never take her place! Judy was nothing but a lying, cheating whore. I hated her. She made a terrible mistake when she lied to the cops about my father. He never hit her. I should've killed her a long time ago."

"I bet you killed your real mother, too. Did you stuff pills down her throat just like you did to Judy?"

"Shut up about my mother!"

I must've been pushing the right buttons, because his face was blood red and the veins in his neck were popping out. Another minute and he would tell all. I could feel it. I pushed on.

"Judy probably was having an affair with your uncle, too! That's it! She was cheating on your father with your uncle!" I had no idea where I was going with this line of accusations, but it appeared to be working.

"You're sick! My uncle would never do that to my father."

"Why not? It's not as if they were real brothers. They had different mothers. Your grandfather liked to sleep around. I bet you got more aunts and uncles out there that you don't even know about. What a family! You know what they say: The apple doesn't fall far from the tree. Do you have any brothers and sisters hiding out in the wood pile? Oh, that's right. You wouldn't know if you did."

"I see what you're trying to do, but it won't work."

"Oh… you didn't know. My, my… the plot does thicken. You know, if you didn't spend so much time being a liar, you might actually find out a few things. If you weren't so busy sucking up to your no-good uncle, you might see the truth, and the truth is that he was sleeping with your mother right under your father's nose. He lied to him and he lied to you. I guess it runs in the family. Your father was probably a liar, too."

"Watch your mouth, you hateful…"

"Be nice to me, liar, or you're going to regret it."

"I know where your mother lives, and when I get loose, I'm going after her first."

That hit a nerve. I started making up lies to goad Wayne.

"Your father was gay. Did you know that? That's why he couldn't keep a wife. That's the real reason he killed himself. He didn't want to see his son grow up to be like him. That's right. He was so deep in the closet, it would've taken a backhoe to get him out."

Wayne was beginning to drool like a mad dog. As cool as it was in the house, he was starting to sweat, and on the verge of losing it. My ploy was working. Dogging his father was too much for him to handle. Suddenly, he went off the deep end.

"I'll do terrible things to your children before I kill them. You won't even recognize them when I'm finished. I'll torture your dogs and that pesky cat, and then I'll finish them off by smashing in their skulls with a baseball bat. I'll kill everyone in your family and leave their mangled bodies for you to see. I want you to suffer unimaginable anguish before I put you out of your misery."

"I have news for you, punk-liar. I'm not the one here who's miserable. To tell the truth, I'm kind of happy right now. We have you handcuffed, and pretty soon the cops will be here to take you away. Then you'll fry." I should've stopped there. Wayne Avery had told the whole story in front of Billy, and I was no longer the only one who had heard his confession. We had him dead to right.

"I'm going to kill your mother. I will get free. Then when you least expect it, you'll get a phone call in the middle of the night saying that your mother was found tortured and murdered. I'll plunge a knife so deep into her heart, it'll come out on the backside."

That was it. The vivid picture he painted in my head sent me into a tailspin. I was so full of rage that I hated Wayne Avery more than anyone or anything on Earth. I wanted to hurt him. No, I wanted him to die for what he said he'd do to my family.

I had spent so much time trying to set him off, that I didn't see it coming. He hit a nerve when he explained in gory detail how he would kill Mom. That was the last straw. He would never pull off his threats if I had my say-so about it. Without hesitating, I walked over, grabbed him by the shirt, pulled him up out of his chair, and then slapped him hard across the face.

He fell to the floor. Blood ran down the corner of his mouth. He tried to stand, but only managed to pull himself back up in the chair.

I glanced down and caught a glimpse of his boots. *Leatherneck* was imprinted on the side.

Furious, I screamed, "You won't live long enough for that, punk-liar!"

I pulled the gun from my coat pocket, aimed it directly at his chest, and squeezed the trigger.

CHAPTER 21

LUCKILY, BILLY GRABBED THE GUN FROM MY HAND before I had time to get off a round. I had to sit down and catch my breath. An anxiety attack was on its way and this one was going to be a big one. When I thought about what I almost did, I started to hyperventilate. As I was trying to catch my breath, Jonathan ran in and went right over to the kid.

"What happened in here?" he asked as he picked the kid up off the floor and proceeded to take off the handcuffs.

"What are you doing?" I yelled. "Stop! He's a killer! Don't let him go!"

"I'm not letting him go." Jonathan pulled out two long, plastic tie-wraps and bound the kid's hands together. He dragged the kid to the kitchen, opened the bottom cabinet door under the sink, and tied him to the drain pipe with another tie-wrap. He dug into his pocket, pulled out something and tossed it to the floor by the kid. "Here," he said. "You might want this medal back. You'll need something to keep you company where you're going." He turned quickly and commanded, "Let's get out of here before the sheriff arrives."

Wayne Avery's sinister laugh was unnerving. He yelled at us as we ran out the door. "My dad was a hero! He was better than all of you put together! You better watch out or that woman will write you out of the story altogether." He laughed uncontrollably. "I'll sneak up on you like I did with the psychiatrist. He didn't see it coming when I put a bullet in his head."

I turned and looked at him one final time. All I could think of was how could he be such a horrible person. If he was this bad at eighteen, what kind of maniac would he be when he reached thirty… if he lived that long? He gave a new meaning to the term—natural born killer.

The three of us high-tailed it out of the house, jumped into our vehicles, and hauled butt down the road just in time to pass the parade of deputies heading to the blue house on Little Creek Road.

"Where are we going now?" I asked, still shaky from the ordeal.

Billy got on his cell phone with Jonathan. I just listened. I was too freaked out about the fact that I almost killed that lying, murderous punk. I was still in shock. I could barely catch my breath.

"Don't let it do you in, `ge ya," Billy said after explaining what had just gone down to Jonathan. "It was a natural instinct to try to put an end to the danger he posed. However…"

"You just can't go around killing people you don't like, Jesse," Jonathan said, trying to make light of the situation. "That's my job!"

"I know you're trying to make me feel better by joking about it, but it's not working."

"Okay, then, how about this? How would you feel if that kid had killed you this morning?"

I had to laugh. "Gee, I don't know. I'll have to think about that for a minute. Ah, let's see. I don't know. I wouldn't be around anymore."

"It's over, Jesse. Forget about it. Like Billy said, don't let it get to you. Put it behind you and let's move on. We have other things to do."

I looked at Billy and asked, "Are we going to Savannah Kelley's house? You heard what he said about her, didn't you?"

"That's our next stop."

"They know about her. Do you think she's in danger? I mean, Wayne Avery will be in jail soon, and Eric Webster won't make it far. He's been shot."

"He's not dead," Jonathan said. "As long as he's on the loose, everyone's still in danger. He's only wounded and he's not finished. From the way it looks, he won't stop until someone kills him."

"And I'm not going to let him kill anyone else if I can help it," Billy added. "We'll be on the lookout for his truck. If he's got any sense, he'll ditch it and find a new means of transportation."

"We should call the house to warn Helene, and then call my mother."

"I put out the alert when I went to the Humvee to get the tie-wraps. Dad will make the calls. I didn't have a number for the author to give him. Sorry."

"I'll call my mother and have her call Savannah Kelley after I catch my breath."

"I'm sure Dad probably called your mother."

"I want to make sure." I sat there for a moment and took long, deep breaths, trying to relax, and then I pulled out my cell phone to call Mom. I didn't need to explain anything to her, because the chief had already called her and told her the situation. She immediately called Savannah. Sad to say, there was no answer at Savannah's house. I warned Mom to keep her doors locked and her gun close.

According to Wayne Avery's last words to us, he and his cohort knew about Savannah Kelley's book. Obviously, she had been right all along. If they knew about her book, it only stood to reason that they were using it as a guide for murder. Why else would they even know about her? Wayne Avery and Eric Webster didn't appear to be the kind of men who would spend a leisurely afternoon enjoying a good mystery novel. Under the circumstances, it was apparent that she could be in danger. Given the fact that she wasn't answering her phone when she should've been at home waiting to share her knowledge of the crimes committed in her book with us, we made a mad dash to get to her before Eric Webster. She didn't stand a chance against someone as ruthless and unfeeling as the killer she had written about in her fictional tale.

Copycats, as they say, are just that. They take someone else's ideas and make them their own. They aren't smart enough to figure out how to commit their crimes without the help of others. That's what Eric Webster had done, and he had enlisted the help of his nephew—a troubled young person who himself needed psychological help. Given the age of Wayne Avery, it was my guess that he had been led astray by his uncle. At least, that's what I had thought of when we first found out about their connection, but after listening to Avery rant and rave about killing my family, I came to the conclusion that he hadn't been led astray, but was a willing participant in the murder of three people and the attempted murder of another. Both men were dangerous and had to be taken out, whether they were killed or locked up forever—it no longer mattered to me.

And… today I had learned something about myself. When push came to shove, I could have pulled the trigger. If it hadn't been for Billy grabbing the gun from my hand, I, too, could've turned into a killer. Scary as it may seem, the fear for my family's safety and my anger toward someone who threatened their lives, could have turned me into *one of them*. How easy it would've been for me to cross over into their dark world. These thoughts went through my head as we raced down Rt. 33 and headed to Stanardsville.

Twenty minutes ago I almost killed an eighteen year old boy. That was a lot for me to take in. I needed to relax, and get myself focused. I lay my head back against the headrest and closed my eyes. I had an uneasy feeling about what we would find when we reached the author's house. A grisly scene played out in my head. I could hear her screams as she ran from room to room trying to escape the killer she had portrayed in her writings. She was alone—with no one to protect her from a homicidal maniac. Later, after her demise, her husband, many miles away and unaware of the dangers his wife faced, would receive a call from Sheriff Wake Hudson of the Greene County Sheriff's Office informing him of the brutal crime his wife had suffered through. If he loved his wife, he would suffer many years of self-doubt and self-hatred for not being there to protect her. Not only would Eric Webster have destroyed her life, and added her to his list of accomplished crimes, he would ruin the life of Savannah Kelley's husband.

"Whoa!" I heard Jonathan say through the cell phone on the dashboard. "I almost lost it there for a second, buddy."

"Yeah, I saw you," Billy responded. "You have to watch those curves. South River Road is no picnic in this weather. It looks like snow on the road, but actually, it's snow-covered ice. Even your Humvee can't handle the ice, buddy."

My mind was in that place I usually go to when I need to think, but the minute Billy mentioned South River Road, I snapped out of it, raised my head up from the headrest and looked around. The scenery was so familiar. I had traveled this road many times since I had moved to the beautiful mountains of Virginia. That seemed like a lifetime ago.

South River Road is a secondary road, and alas, one of the last ones to be plowed after a snowfall—if at all. The Virginia Department of Transportation has its hands full during the winter, and it's all they can do to keep the main roads plowed, let alone secondary or back roads. Usually, by the time they do get around to it, traffic has already done the job for them—in most cases—but not this time. Today, the shade from the overhanging tree branches had kept the rays of the sun from melting any of the snow, and the road was like a sheet of ice, making traveling on it a hazard. If you aren't careful, and even if you are, you could end up in the South River—which is exactly what happened to Billy a while back. He had gone to get Mom and was bringing her to stay with us when he lost control of his truck in the middle of the curve by the church at Turkey Ridge Road. His truck had to be pulled out of the stream with a winch, and I'm glad to say that no one was hurt. Later, when I asked my mom if she was scared, she said no and went on to tell me what an exciting time she had. That's when I realized there was, indeed, an adventurous side to her.

Once we had passed the church, I felt more confident that we wouldn't land in a ditch or in the river—or up against that big tree across the road from the church. A lot of folks had not been able to maneuver that curve, as was evident from the scars on the tree's trunk. Large pieces of bark had been skinned off over the years, yet the tree still remained intact. Amazing as it is, so far, none of the vehicles that have struck the tree have been able to uproot it or take it down. The tree was a landmark. Everyone knew about that curve on South River Road by the church… and the tree.

As we turned off South River Road onto the road to Mom's house, I started getting jittery. I sensed that we might be too late, and hated the idea that Eric Webster might have killed another innocent person. He didn't care. His goal in life was to kill as many people as he could before he was stopped. He had no conscience. It takes a different kind of person to kill someone for the joy of it and not feel a thing. He was one of those people— and so was Wayne Avery. The line runs deep.

Billy tooted the horn when we passed Mom's house. I saw her standing at the window looking out, waiting for us to pass. My cell phone vibrated.

"Hello, Mom," I said. "Is everyone all right?"

"We're fine," Mom answered. "Jesse, I'm worried about Savannah. I've been trying to call her ever since I got the call from Chief Sam. I even tried her cell phone. I just know something bad has happened."

"Have you seen a small, black pickup truck go by?"

"Yes, I did. I saw the truck about ten minutes ago. He drove past and then came back by a few minutes later. Why?"

"He's the one we're after. He's the killer."

"Oh, no! He's after Savannah now, isn't he?"

"We think so, Mom. We're on our way to her house."

As we rounded the curve, we came upon a scary sight. There, in the middle of the road, was the green Mustang. The car door was standing open as if someone had gotten out in a hurry, but there was no one in sight.

"Mom, I have to go. I'll call you right back." I closed up the cell phone before she had a chance to speak, and then slid it in my coat pocket.

"Oh, my God!" I cried. "He's been here already. We're too late."

Billy slowly pulled up beside Jonathan's Humvee and turned off the ignition. Both of us jumped out of the truck and ran over to the car.

Jonathan reached over and touched the hood of the car. "The hood's still slightly warm, and in this cold weather, that means we just missed her... probably less than two minutes ago."

"Is that blood in the snow?" I pointed to a couple specks of red.

Jonathan squatted down and touched it with his finger and then brought his finger to his nose and sniffed. "It's blood, all right."

"It couldn't be too bad," I said. "There's not much blood."

I scanned the area looking for any clues that might tell us what happened. I cupped my hands over my mouth and yelled out, "Savannah! Savannah Kelley! Where are you?" The silence was eerie. The only sound to be heard was that of the wind blowing through the snow-covered trees. I made one last effort to attract her attention. "Savannah! Savannah!"

"She's gone, Jesse," Jonathan said. "You can stop yelling."

Off in the distance, a dog's bark was the only answer to my call.

"Mom said she saw the black pickup truck pass by a little while ago and then the same truck went by again shortly thereafter. How could we have missed him?"

"It only takes a minute."

Jonathan walked up to the wrought iron gate and looked for a call button.

"There's not one," I said. "It's all electronic. If anyone's home, they'd know we were here. Forget it. Let's get out of here

"He's got her."

Just then, we heard the sound of a car coming in the opposite direction around the bend in the road. The three of us turned, looked up, and saw Cole's olive green Jeep approaching. He pulled up behind the Mustang and got out of his vehicle. He was dressed in street clothes, and considering the fact that his mother was in the hospital, I figured he was probably on his way to see her.

"What's going on here?" he asked as he looked around.

"He's got the author," I blurted out before Billy or Jonathan had a chance to say anything. I was shaking all over and nervous as a hen in a chicken coop with a fox. I couldn't stop myself. "Billy shot him in the leg, but he got away. He came here and abducted the author. He's going to kill her. He used her book as a manual to murder all those people and now he has abducted her. See, look here. There's blood. We have to catch him!"

"Sheriff Hudson just called and said he got an anonymous tip on the whereabouts of Wayne Avery. I don't guess either one of you know anything about that, do you?"

None of us said a word.

Cole looked at me and asked, "Got anything else in that box, Pandora?"

I laughed nervously at his joke, and then turned to Jonathan and Billy.

"We might as well tell him. You know he's going to find out in the end. Besides, he's our friend. How do you think he's going to feel if he finds out that we kept him in the dark after all the times he's helped us?"

"I got a tip—and I'm not telling you where I got it—about Wayne Avery," Jonathan offered. "I was told where I could find him, so we went looking. We snuck around to the back of the house and then busted the door down when the opportunity presented itself. I used tie-wraps to tie up Wayne Avery and then made the call to the Sheriff's Office."

"Tell me about shooting the guy in the leg."

"He pulled a gun on me, but I shot him first in self-defense," Billy replied and then looked at me. "It was your .38. I saw the initials on the butt."

When I first got the .38, I used an electric etcher to inscribe my initials on the butt of it. Since then, I've done the same thing with my other guns. I guess it was a rite of passage. They say if you name your gun it becomes your friend for life. Me, I go one step further. I etch my initials on the butt of the gun, that way it makes me feel connected. Call me crazy, but that's just me.

"I bet Wayne Avery used my gun to kill the psychiatrist. He said he shot him in the head."

"He confessed to the murder?" Cole asked.

"Oh, he did more than confess. He went as far as to describe in detail his plans for murdering my children, my family, and then finally me. He's a psycho, Cole. He has no remorse. He kills for the fun of it. He enjoys discussing it too much for him to have done his dirty deeds on impulse. His crimes are planned. He's sick, and I don't mean in a way that can be rehabilitated. I think he's too far gone to be fixed. He needs to be put away… or killed. I say we go for the latter."

The shocked look on all three of their faces was enough for me to realize that I might have gone a step too far, but I didn't care. I didn't want to have to look over my shoulder every day and wonder if Wayne Avery was going to show up. I didn't even know Eric Webster, yet he wasn't the one who really scared me. Wayne Avery was the one who frightened me.

Anyone with such a sadistic personality was a danger to everyone he came in contact with. He was truly a danger to society. He needed to be eradicated.

"I'm going to pretend that I didn't hear you say that, and I don't want to ever hear those words come out of your mouth again in that context," Cole said. "Are we clear on that?"

"Yes, we are."

"We have to find Savannah Kelley," Billy said. "I'm afraid we don't have much time."

"How could he get away without our seeing him?" I asked. "We didn't pass him on the road, but Mom said he drove past her house coming and going."

"He could've made a left turn at the bridge on South River Road," Cole replied. "If that's the route he took, you would've missed him when you came in from the opposite direction."

"Let's split up," Jonathan said. "Cole, you go left, and I'll go right. I'll take Teel Mountain Road and we'll meet up on Middle River Road."

"I'll alert Sheriff Hudson," Cole replied. "I'll tell him everything you all told me, except what Jesse said about killing Wayne Avery. I still can't believe you said that." He looked over at me. "He must've really ticked you off."

"You know how I am when it comes to my family."

"Jesse and I will stop at her mother's house and see if she might have any information we can use."

"And we'll get her to lend us her copy of the book," I added. I looked at Cole. "Stop looking at me like that. If you had seen the look in that kid's eyes, you'd understand why I feel the way I do. His demeanor was scary. He'd kill either one of us and not blink an eye. At first, when I found out about Avery having an uncle who might be involved in the killings, I though the uncle was the one who led the kid astray. But once I talked with Avery, I realized that he's the one with the screwed up mind." I looked at Billy and added, "I'm surprised you didn't stop me from badgering the kid. You let me go on and on."

"Yes, I did, and it worked. You got the truth out of him."

"What are we going to do about her car?" I asked. "We need to at least close the car door."

"The keys aren't in it," Jonathan said. "If they were, we'd be hearing that annoying ring or beep they do when you leave them in the car."

A wild thought occurred to me as I shivered from the cold, mountain air. "Hold on a moment," I said. I ran over to Billy's truck, fished around in my purse until I found the set of keys, and then ran back over to where everyone was standing. I knew it was most likely an improbability that they were hers, but I wanted to see for myself... out of curiosity. I aimed the remote on the key chain toward the Mustang and pressed the panic button. The alarm instantly went off.

The four of us stood there as the horn beeped away. I hit the button again and the horn stopped. I slipped the keys into my coat pocket and said, "Now, how do you like that? They know each other."

"This has really been a strange day," Cole said. "But I think it's about to get stranger."

"I think you're right," Billy said. "After this, nothing would surprise me."

"Me, either," Jonathan added.

"I knew it all along," I boasted.

"Liar!" Billy said and then laughed. "I'm going to have to start calling you Wayne the Liar."

"That's just too creepy. I don't think I'll ever be able to hear that name again and not think of him."

"Hey," Jonathan said. "Time is fleeing and so is our killer."

With that said, we jumped into our vehicles and headed down the road. Jonathan and Cole went chasing after the bad guy, while Billy and I headed to my mother's house to see what we could find in Savannah Kelley's book. I had no idea how much worse it was going to get, but I was about to find out.

CHAPTER 22

A FTER PULLING UP INTO MOM'S DRIVEWAY, I was surprised to see that it had been plowed. Snowbanks lined each side. The front yard had two pairs of round depressions going across it and into the woods. Billy said they were the prints of a deer. A lone yellow iris in full bloom seated in a cluster of green, spiny shoots attracted my attention.

"Look at that, Billy," I said as I crawled out of the truck. "I've never seen an iris bloom in the winter. Have you?"

"Sometimes that happens," he replied as he crawled out of the truck and walked over to me. He pointed to the opposite side of the yard. "There's another one."

"That's so cool. It's so exciting to be living in the mountains. There's no place like it. I'm constantly seeing deer and other animals that you'd never see living in Tidewater. Newport News used to be farm land until developers took over. Now it's nothing but a concrete jungle." I took a deep breath. "It smells so good out here even in the cold."

Mom opened the front door and yelled out to us, "Come on inside before you freeze to death. I have a pot of coffee brewing. Hurry up. I have a lot to tell you."

Mom's two-story Cape Cod is such a lovely house. The fireplace with

its woodstove insert in the living room makes everything so cozy. I especially like the way the living room, dining room and kitchen is in one big
open space separated only by a pass-through bar. I adore her bedroom off
to the left. It's huge. It has a fireplace, and the walk-in closet is bigger than
the bedroom I had in my Newport News duplex. The two large bedrooms
upstairs which are separated by a full bath aren't like what one would
normally encounter. Usually, builders would cram four small rooms in
that amount of space. I like fewer rooms and more space in each room.
Mom was so thrilled when she and Dad found the place. The move was
well worth it even if their time together here was brief. Dad died shortly
after they moved to Stanardsville.

After taking a last look around to admire our beautiful surroundings,
we headed inside. Claire greeted us with a smile and a big hug. "I'm so
glad to see you guys," she said. She looked at Billy. "I'm so sorry about
Daniel. Nothing will make the pain go away, but at least we can be thankful for the time we had with him."

"Words are not necessary," Billy replied. "We will miss him, that's
for sure."

"He flirted with me every time I saw him," she continued. "Did you
know that?"

"I'm sure he did," I butted in. "He flirted with every woman."

Billy looked over at Randy and said, "Nice to see you again. How was
the trip?"

Randy walked over and shook Billy's hand and then hugged me. "It
was a little hairy. At one point I was afraid I might not be able to keep the
SUV on the road, but we managed to make it here in one piece." He looked
at me. "Mom said to tell you hello and that she's sorry she couldn't make
it. Izzy's been sick for a few weeks and Mom's really worried about her. I
suggested that she get a nurse to come in, but she wouldn't hear of it."

"I don't blame her. I sure hope Isabel is going to be all right," I said as
Billy and I took off our coats and laid them on the sofa. I turned to Mom
and said, "Savannah Kelley is missing. Her Mustang was sitting out in
front of her closed gate with the car door open, and there was blood on the
ground."

"Oh, my word!" Mom exclaimed. "She was afraid something like this would happen. She gave me the phone number for her husband. She said that if anything happened to her to please call him and let him know."

"You might want to do that now," Billy said. "She's disappeared, and if she's been abducted as we suspect, her life could be in serious danger."

"We're looking for a small, black pickup truck like Dad's."

"I saw it fly by. I remember telling Claire that whoever was driving was headed for trouble. You can't drive that fast on these roads. They're so slick when it snows." Mom turned and headed for the kitchen. "I made a fresh pot of coffee. Who wants a cup of coffee?"

"I could sure use one," Billy said. "I need something to warm me up."

I walked over to the kitchen counter and stood next to Mom. "I noticed that your driveway has been plowed. Did Eddie do that for you?"

"Yes, he did, if it's any of your business. He helps me with other chores sometimes, too. What do you have to say about that?"

"I'm glad. I like Eddie. Can I call him Daddy?"

"You're being silly." Mom fixed a cup of coffee, walked over to the table and placed it in front of Billy. "You might as well sit down. We have much to discuss."

Claire and Randy took their seat at the table, a cup of coffee already in front of them. I poured coffee for myself, added milk, and then walked over and sat down in the chair next to Billy.

"This Webster guy is a bad dude. Put him together with his freaky nephew, Wayne Avery, and we've got a real dangerous pair."

"Are they together?" Mom asked.

"No, Avery is probably in jail right about now," Billy replied. "Jonathan got a tip on their whereabouts, and when we left, he had Avery handcuffed with tie-wraps to the pipe under the kitchen sink, and the police were on their way. Webster got away from us."

"That Jonathan is something else," Mom said. "He has a lot of nerve to do what he does... just like the two of you. I never thought I'd see the day when one of my daughters would be carrying a gun, hunting for killers. Sometimes it scares me."

"It scares me most of the time, Mom, especially when we come across a cold-blooded killer like Wayne Avery. As for Eric Webster—I can't say anything about him, because he's not the one who confessed to me."

"It all makes sense," Mom said. "Savannah's book is so close to what's going on in real life, it's scary. In it, there's a killer who has an accomplice, but the accomplice isn't the one who does the actual killing. His job is to supply the transportation and the can of gasoline to start the fire. He's more like a gofer."

"We're not sure who the actual killer is right now," Billy added. "All we have to go on is what Avery says, and he says he's the one who killed the couple in Ruckersville and the psychiatrist over in Syria in Madison County. At first, he denied his involvement to Jesse, but now he claims to have done it all. He says that Jonathan was supposed to die in the fire, but fortunately for us, he wasn't home when the fire was started. One thing we're certain of is that if we don't find Savannah soon, there won't be any hurry to keep looking. Eric Webster is on the edge. We got his partner, and he knows it's only a matter of time before we get to him. Edgy people panic, and when they panic, people die."

"Where's that book, Mom? I want to borrow it if you don't mind." I glanced over to the front window and saw a newly decorated Christmas tree. "Your tree is beautiful! Don't you just love a real tree?" I walked over and smelled the fresh needles and then looked at the many decorations—some were familiar and some were not. "I see you bought some new ornaments."

"Yes, I did. I bought them when they went on sale right after Christmas last year." She looked over at me. "You know how much I love Christmas."

"You always loved seeing us open our presents as kids, and then as we got older, you said that at least you could still count on all of us being together at Christmas. Your children knew better than to not show their faces on Christmas Day." I walked back over to Mom and put my arm around her. "We're going to have a good Christmas, Mom. It might be a little different this year, but at least we'll all be together."

"I do love having my children around," Mom replied. She paused for a second as if her mind had wandered off, and then she said, "I love the smell of pine." She looked at Billy. "Please thank your folks for me. That was so nice of them."

"You're quite welcome. Hey, you're family."

During Mom's brief pause, my mind drifted to thoughts of the many wonderful times we had spent with my father at Christmas. I was sure that's where her mind had traveled, but I didn't say anything. Instead, I said, "I think we should go home and decorate ours, don't you, Billy? We want it done before tomorrow... before the funeral."

"I'd like that. We can't do anything else except wait to hear from Jonathan or Cole. The Greene County Sheriff's Office has been notified of Savannah's abduction. We were there when Cole reported her missing. I'm sure that the cops are looking for her as we speak..." His voice trailed off as the sound of oncoming sirens grew louder. All of us turned our heads to the front window and saw a rush of police cars with flashing lights go by.

"There they go," I said. "It sure took them long enough."

Billy looked at his watch and said, "We've only been here for five minutes or so. I'd say they've made good time." He remained calm and changed the subject. "Let's go home, decorate the tree and read some of that book while we wait."

"Don't you want to follow those deputies?"

"I don't see why," he responded. "I have better things to do than get tied up with them."

"Let me just say this before you leave," Mom said. "In Savannah's book, the woman who gets abducted was held at the home of the killer— not his accomplice. So, when you determine who the real killer is, you'll know where to look."

"In the book, does the woman escape?"

"No," Mom said softly. "She dies."

"Just because the woman dies in the book doesn't mean that Savannah will," Claire chimed in. "For Pete's sake—it's just a book. It doesn't mean a thing."

"It does when someone is using it as a guideline for murder," Randy said as he looked at her. "This should be taken seriously, Claire."

"I believe that's what has happened here," I agreed. "Mom read the book and she says that everything in it has come true—to some degree. However insane it is, people are dying."

"You can't blame Savannah," Mom said, defending the woman. "It's not her fault."

"No one said it was, Mom, and it really doesn't matter. The fact is that she wrote a book and now someone is playing out the scenario. I don't want to see your friend get bumped off because she wrote about it in a book."

"I don't want her to get killed at all."

"You know what I mean, Mom."

"All right," Billy jumped in. "Let's be rational. The sheriff and his men are on the case and I'm sure that by now they realize the necessity of finding Savannah Kelley as quickly as possible. If there's anything we can do to help, the time is now." Billy looked over at Mom. "I realize that you haven't known this woman long, but is there anything you can tell us that might help?"

"I don't know," Mom replied. "Is there?"

"Tell us about the woman in the book," Billy said.

"The only thing I can tell you is that she knew the killer, because she had hired him to fix a leaky faucet. That's how he got into her house the first time. He stole a set of keys while he was there, and later he came back and let himself in."

Billy and I looked at each other and then back to Mom. I walked into the living room, searched my coat pocket and pulled out the set of car keys. "Spice Cat dragged these into the house," I said as I walked back to the kitchen and showed them to everyone. "They belong to Savannah."

"How do you know that?" Mom asked.

"Because when we found her abandoned car, I pulled out the keys, pressed the panic button, and the car horn went off."

"How…"

"I didn't know they were her keys. I just tried them to satisfy my curiosity. After the keys were proven to belong to her, the rest was el-ementary. Avery or Webster must have dropped them in the woods when they were skulking around our house. They've been on our property and in our home."

"It all makes sense!" Mom said. "You know the story about her green mustang. She was out of town on a book signing event and the thief helped himself to her car. She got the car back and it wasn't even damaged. She was lucky on that count, but it scared her that someone could get that close to her. She had a wrought iron fence erected around her house—not all of her property, just the house and an acre of land. She also had a security gate installed. I think it operates on a beam. Break the beam and the alarm goes off in the house. That was a few weeks ago. She also said something about a missing second set of car keys. She was rather distraught over it, because the killer in her book had stolen keys from his victim. That's how he got into her house."

"Do you know who installed the fence?"

"No," Mom replied. "Far be it for me to accuse anybody, but I'm willing to bet that the person who put up her fence also stole her keys. Who else would've had the opportunity?"

"Doesn't she have a housekeeper?" Claire asked.

"Yes," Mom said. "The housekeeper isn't involved. From the way Savannah talked about Vera, they're close friends."

"I better call Jonathan and see if he's found out anything," Billy said. He got up from the table, walked to the living room, and dug his cell phone from his coat. He spoke briefly on the phone, closed it up, and walked back to the kitchen.

"You have a strange look on your face," I said.

"Jonathan tried to call me, but because I had my phone on vibrate, it didn't ring. I missed his call."

"What did he say when you got to talk to him?"

"There's been an accident," Billy replied. "Jonathan found Webster's pickup truck over in Madison. The truck had been wrecked and there was blood on the seat, and the passenger side of the windshield was busted. Jonathan thinks that most of the blood came from the passenger since that side of the windshield was where the most concentrated amount was."

Mom gasped. "Oh, no! Is Savannah hurt?"

"It looks that way," Billy said. "There's more. Webster crashed the truck in front of someone's house right on Main Street. The folks in the house heard the crash and went to investigate. Webster shot the man in the leg and then demanded the keys to his SUV. The guy's going to be all right, but his wife said she feared for the woman who was with the shooter. She said the woman had a bloody nose and was bleeding from a gash on her head. She thought the woman was being forced to go with the man, because he dragged her to the SUV and then took off down the road."

"Did the man say which way they were headed?"

"No. He was too shaken up to notice and his wife was busy trying to help him. She ran inside and called the police just as Webster was leaving. Neither one saw anything."

"That's not much help."

"Jonathan asked if we had heard from Cole. He said they were supposed to meet up on Middle River Road, but that Cole didn't show, so he kept on going."

"Where do you think Cole is?" Randy asked. "Could he have encountered Webster?"

"I don't like the sound of this."

"Me, either," Mom agreed. "I sure hope he's all right."

Just as we were beginning to get concerned about Cole's whereabouts, Billy's cell phone vibrated. He looked at it, smiled, and then said, "It's Cole." Billy walked away, one hand over his ear as he listened with the other. The conversation seemed to go on forever before he finally closed up the phone, and said, "He's safe, so you all can relax. He came up on the wreck just as the police were getting there, but by then, Webster and Savannah were gone. The cops put out an APB on the white, SUV, but so far, nothing. We'll keep our eyes out for it on our way home."

"We're going home?"

"That's all we can do for now, unless you want to ride around looking for them. I think we need to regroup and rethink the situation before we spend our night on the road. There're plenty of cops out looking for her, Jesse."

I was surprised that Billy was giving up so quickly until I thought about the situation. His brother was being buried tomorrow. He had a lot on his mind.

"I want her to be found as much as anyone, but they could be anywhere, Jesse," Mom agreed. "You need to go home to your family and get ready for tomorrow. Pray for her safe return and let the police do their job. You can't save the world. Sometimes you just have to step back and realize that there's a higher power at work."

"Then tell your higher power to get the lead out."

"I can't believe you said that!" Claire gasped. She looked at Mom. "Don't listen to her, Mom. You know she's a heathen!"

I had to laugh at her remark. "That's me," I said.

Mom smiled. "I know all about you, Missy, and you're no heathen. You just act like one sometimes."

"Okay," Billy interrupted our banter. "It's time to go home. Don't forget to call Savannah's husband."

Mom's smile turned into a frown as she wrung her hands. "I don't know what to say to him."

"Just tell him the truth, Mom. Tell him his wife has been abducted by a killer, and that he might want to show his face."

"That sure was ugly, Missy. I won't tell him that."

"Don't you think it's a little strange that he's married to this woman, yet he lives at the other end of the state?"

"That's his business… and it doesn't make him a bad man."

"I'm sorry, Mom. You're right. I don't know what got into me. I guess I'm just a little upset about this whole abduction thing. Savannah's in danger, and we can't do anything about it. That scumbag will probably kill her and get away with it."

"Don't say that!" Mom cried. "She has to be all right."

"She will be," Claire said, trying to console her. "I have faith in Billy and Jesse. If anyone can find her, they can."

"You give us too much credit."

"I know you two," Claire went on. "You say you're going home, but the next thing we know, you'll be calling to tell us that you found Savannah Kelley, and that she's okay."

"I'd really like that, but I don't think it's going to happen," Billy said. He looked at Mom. "We'll call you if we find out anything. Otherwise, we'll see you tomorrow at ten o'clock."

"Please do call," Mom begged. "I won't be able to sleep a wink tonight. I'm so afraid Savannah's going to meet the same fate as the woman in her book."

"Where is that book?" I asked. "I'd like to read it."

"Sure. I'll go get it." Mom walked out of the kitchen and then returned a few seconds later. "Here it is. Please take care of it, because I'd like to have it back. She signed it just for me."

"I will," I said as I took the book, opened it, and read the inscription. *"I hope you enjoy my book. My best, Savannah Kelley."* I closed it up and smiled at Mom. "I'll take good care of it, and see to it that you get it back in one piece."

Billy and I grabbed our coats, said good-bye, and headed out. Claire stood at the door beside Randy and waved to us just as we were walking to the truck.

"Please be careful," she said. "Call us when you get home so Mom won't worry."

"We will," I said. "Y'all call us if you should hear something. I don't care how late it is."

Billy and I jumped into the truck and pulled out of the driveway. By the time we got to the bridge at South River Road, I was on the second page of Savannah's book.

"My gosh," I said. "She's good. She grabs you right from the beginning. Usually, you have to wade through a couple of chapters before you get to the good stuff. This one is good. I can't wait to read the rest of it."

"Pay close attention to what you read," Billy said. "You might find the one clue that can help us. Sometimes people read so fast that they miss some little detail that could bring the whole thing into perspective."

"I'm not that fast of a reader. Besides, I like to savor what I read. I'm not one to skim through the pages. If I'm going to spend my time reading, I want to remember what I read."

I just couldn't stop reading! Savannah's descriptive writing was so good that her words formed incredible pictures in my head. I was determined to find time to finish her book even if I couldn't do it right away.

Billy's cell phone must have vibrated, because he pulled it out and flipped it open as we rode along. I was so ensconced in the book that I wasn't paying attention to his conversation until he said. "That was Jonathan. He said that Eric Webster works for Jenkins Fencing in Charlottesville—the company that installed Savannah's fence. He's going to check it out."

"We were right about him! He did steal Savannah's car keys, and he probably stole one of her books while he was at it—read it, and then decided to play it out in real life. Maybe he has a crush on her. Perhaps they had a fling."

"We know he abducted her. All we have to do is figure out where he's holding her. Read faster!"

"I probably should just go right to the last chapter."

"You might want to put that book down for a second."

I did as he said. I lay the book on the seat, and then looked up. Since we'd been on the road only a few minutes, I realized that the houses I was looking at must be the ones in the new subdivision off Octonia Road—and that one of these houses was the home of Wayne Avery. "I knew you had something up your sleeve."

Billy was slowly driving past a large, gray, two-story house that was situated on approximately a half acre of land, partially surrounded by evergreens. I looked around and saw more houses of similar design, equally spaced. They were obviously high-dollar homes.

"I didn't think it would hurt to have a look around before we headed home. We might ride by Eric's house, too. I doubt we'll find anything, but it won't hurt to look. It's right on our way."

There were no police cars in sight.

"Pull over in front of the house for a minute. I want to check out something." Billy pulled over and put the gear in park. I reached into my coat pocket, pulled out the set of keys and said, "Let's just see if one of these keys fits the door."

"That might not be such a bad…"

Before Billy could finish his sentence, I had opened the truck door, slid out and was making my way up the front walk. I almost lost my footing a couple of times because of the snow, and it made me think of how sad it was that there was no one to plow the walkway. The parents were dead, and the son was in jail, or would soon be. As I fidgeted, Billy came up behind me, gently took the keys from my cold hands, and said, "Let me help you, dear."

"Why, thank you, sweetheart."

He tried each key, but none would open the front door.

"Nice try," I said. "I guess this was a waste of time."

Billy stood still for a moment and tilted his head. "Did you hear that?" he asked. "I though I heard someone groan."

The two of us stood there and listened. The cold air made things creak, and it was hard to tell what we were hearing... until we both heard a moan and then the sound of an object being banged up against the wall.

"There's someone in the basement!" I yelled.

"There sure is!" Billy replied as he handed me the set of keys. He stepped back, got his momentum going, and then slammed the full weight of his body up against the front door. The door splintered off its hinges and landed in the foyer.

"They just don't make them like they used to," he said, smiling. "Let's go see who's in the basement."

CHAPTER 23

B EFORE WE STEPPED INTO THE FOYER, I looked at Billy and asked, "Do you have your gun strapped to your ankle? You're not wearing your shoulder holster, and my gun is in the truck. I don't want to enter this house without a gun. I'm going to run back to the truck and get mine." I turned and ran to the truck before he had a chance to reply. I pulled out my 9MM, and was back in the foyer within seconds.

Billy lifted his leg, raised his pants, and showed me the gun that was strapped to his ankle. "I never go anywhere without being armed. You should know that by now." He snatched the gun from the ankle holster and said, "I guess I'm going to have to buy you one like mine, so you can always be armed without your weapon being visible."

"That might not be a bad idea."

We heard another groan. Billy and I took off running, listening for another sound. Looking for the basement, we opened every closed door in the house, but couldn't find it.

The house was so clean and everything was so in order that it didn't look as if anyone had lived in it for a while. The only sign that someone had been in the house was the wet, muddy footprints on the hallway carpet. The prints were damp and hadn't had time to dry and become crusty.

"Whoever is here hasn't been here long."

"Yes, I see the wet footprints," Billy agreed as he turned around in circles. "Where is the basement?"

"They must not have one. I though for sure the groans were coming from a lower level."

Billy stopped for a second and thought. He looked around and then as if a light bulb had gone off in his head, he said, "I think I know where the door to the basement is. Follow me."

I followed him down the hall, through the kitchen, and into a large laundry room.

"Wow!" I murmured, scanning the room. "This is wonderful. Look at the size of this place. This is every woman's dream." I pointed to the shelves that held the neatly lined-up detergents and other laundry essentials, and then to the racks used to hang clean clothes. Up against a back wall were a state-of-the-art washer and dryer, a laundry tub, and a large table for folding clothes. "This is almost as big as our bedroom!"

"I will buy you anything you want."

"I know you would, Billy. I don't need all this stuff."

Billy tilted his head as if he needed to be reassured.

I walked over to him and kissed him on the cheek. "I love my home. There's nothing I need that you haven't given me."

A moan came from behind a door to the left beside a rack of clothes.

"Ah, that's where the door is," I said looking at Billy. "I always thought a basement door was usually in the hallway."

"That's the way it used to be, but not anymore," Billy whispered. He put his finger to his lips as if to silence me as he held his gun out in front of himself. "Stay behind me." He grabbed the doorknob and jerked opened the door. The two of us hustled down the steps like soldiers on a charge, not knowing what we'd encounter.

The room was very dim, but not completely dark. When we got to the foot of the stairs we could see a woman tied to a wooden chair sitting next to the wall in the corner of the room. Her face was dirty, her nose had been bleeding, and blood had caked along the side of her head. Someone had wrapped a T-shirt around her head to staunch the flow. Her blouse was bloody and her pants were torn at the knee. She was gagged. Tears streamed down her face.

I ran over and untied the gag from her mouth. "I'm Jesse, and this is Billy. We're here to help you, Savannah. Don't worry. You're safe now."

The look on her face was one of sheer relief. She was so glad that someone had come to rescue her.

"You must be Minnie's daughter. She's told me so much about you in the little time that I've known her."

"We can talk about this later," I whispered. "Right now, we have to get you out of here."

"He's coming back," she cried as Billy untied the rope from her wrists. "I've been making noise ever since he left hoping someone would hear me. I even banged the chair against the wall. I thought it was hopeless! I just knew he was going to kill me." She coughed. Her body shook uncontrollably.

"We need to get you to a hospital," Billy said.

All of a sudden, we heard a noise on the floor above us. We froze and looked at each other, silencing our words. Savannah tried to stand up, but was too weak. I grabbed her arm as Billy grabbed the other.

"Try to stand up," he whispered to Savannah. He looked at me. "Hold onto her, Jesse. We're going to hide and wait for him to come down here. I want to catch him by surprise."

Billy and I managed to help Savannah limp over to a spot behind the stairs where we could crouch down and hide. We would wait for the killer, and then Billy would jump out and surprise him, and hopefully, save us all from a psycho. I shook almost as hard as Savannah as the seconds ticked away. It was all I could do to keep from coming out of my skin. The two of us huddled together like two little lost kittens shivering in the rain, with me holding a gun in my shaky hand. My teeth chattered—not from the chill in the air—but in fear.

Billy got up and inched his way over to the foot of the stairs just out of sight.

The stairs creaked as the killer's footsteps grew closer... closer... until finally, the killer was standing at the foot of the steps. Billy, with his gun pointed straight out in front of him, snuck up behind the culprit, and said, "Stop, or I'll shoot you dead."

A familiar voice responded, "I sure hope not, brother."

Billy lowered his gun. "What are you doing here?" he asked.

"Probably the same thing you are. I decided to check out a few places before heading to Charlottesville. I saw your truck and figured that you must've had the same idea. My next stop was going to be Eric Webster's house."

Jonathan's face came into view when Savannah and I crawled out of our hiding place.

"I see that you've found the missing author," he said. Jonathan quickly introduced himself to her and then added, "It's nice to meet you, ma'am, but we need to get out of here now! I'll go upstairs and put the door back up and then prop something against it. That way it'll be hard to tell that we were even here. When Webster comes back he won't know she's gone until he tries to open the door. By then the police should be lying in wait."

"I'll help Savannah to the truck," Billy said as he handed me his gun, and then picked her up. He headed for the stairs.

Jonathan pulled out his cell phone and made the call to the Greene County Sheriff's Office as we climbed the stairs. He explained the situation and told Sheriff Hudson that we were transporting Savannah Kelley to the hospital. The sheriff must've suggested calling an ambulance, because Jonathan responded that it would draw too much attention, and that her injuries weren't life-threatening. If they wanted to catch Eric Webster, they would need to get over here before he came back. Once Webster discovered the author missing, he would hightail it out of here and be gone forever.

I brought up the rear as we exited the back of the house. I was silent and also disturbed by the fact that the one thing on my mind at the time was the intense twinge of jealousy I felt when I saw my husband with his arms around another woman. Was I still a little insecure after all this time? I told myself that I was just being ridiculous, but I still couldn't shake that feeling. I guess that when a woman finally finds the man she wants, there's always that idea in the back of her mind that one day she's going to lose him, silly as it may seem. Does anyone ever become totally secure in a relationship? I didn't know the answer to that question, but I wasn't about to let it get the best of me. I shook off my insecure feelings and replaced them with the warm smile Billy gave me when he helped me up into the truck.

I shoved my gun in my coat pocket and then slid in next to Savannah, waiting for him.

Billy made his conversation with Jonathan brief and then jumped in the truck and started it up. He turned the heat on full blast.

"I bet you ladies are cold," he said as he adjusted the controls. "Jonathan's going to hang around and wait for Cole and the sheriff. He says he wants to be around when they catch Webster." He looked over at Savannah and added, "We'll get you to the hospital as fast as this truck will take us."

"I'm in no hurry," she whispered. "After what I've been through, I'm just glad to be alive. I'm so thankful that I'm safe. I don't know how I'll ever be able to repay you for saving my life."

"Thank you will do," Billy replied as he pulled out onto Octonia Road, heading to Rt. 230.

"Thank you both," she replied looking back and forth at each of us. She hesitated for a moment and then said, "I never realized that Eric was so…"

Ah, ha… I thought to myself. She does know him! The silly notion I had earlier that they might have something going, or at least that he had a crush on her, might not be so silly after all.

"Were you seeing him?" I asked. "I don't want you to think I'm being nosey, but you can bet the police will ask the same kind of questions. They'll want to know if and how you made his acquaintance."

She began to cry. "If McCoy finds out, he'll never forgive me. He'll divorce me for sure. It's just that we've been apart for so long, and I was lonely. I made a foolish mistake one time and now I'm going to pay for it the rest of my life."

"Your situation seems a little odd to me," I said. "I understand that you've been living here for a couple of years and your husband lives somewhere else, yet you two aren't divorced. What's the deal?"

"Our house in Dogwood Valley was supposed to be a getaway for us, but once I stayed here for a while, I just couldn't bring myself to go back to Fancy Gap. Oh, don't get me wrong. I love my home there, but I love it here more. At least, I did, until this happened."

"Don't let what happened ruin it for you here. Greene County is a terrific place to live. The scenery is beautiful and the people are so friendly. And you never know what kind of wildlife you're going to come upon. I wouldn't want to live anywhere else."

"Where do you two live?"

"Charlottesville, in Albemarle County. About thirty minutes from here."

"It is beautiful," she remarked. "I would love to raise kids here, but McCoy's job is in our hometown. I've tried to talk him into living here, but he says he can't leave his work."

Savannah Kelley is a pretty woman. Even under all the blood and dirty clothes, her beauty was visible. She's thirty-five or so, approximately five feet tall and looks as if she weighs about a hundred and five pounds — kind of like me with the exception of a few pounds and the color of her hair. Mine is a washed out, poorly-dyed red color, and I wear it in a long ponytail most of the time. After looking at her silky, blond locks, I realized that it was time for a trim or a complete restyling. To top off everything, she has the figure of a model. I hated her already! No, I didn't really hate her, but I sure could take some beauty tips from her. And how could someone who is so gorgeous be so nice? It's just not right. I guess that jealous side of me is still hiding in there somewhere.

"I thought Mom said that your husband is a lawyer. Why can't he move his practice here? I can assure you that he'd be as busy here as he would be in Fancy Gap."

"That's what I told him, but he insists that he can't leave his clients."

"It sounds like muck to me."

Savannah laughed a dainty, yet hardy laugh. "Your mother was right about you. She said that you wouldn't hesitate to say what's on your mind. Maybe that's my problem. I've never been able to stand up to my husband. The only time I demanded anything was when I insisted on staying here."

"Well, after this, lady, you shouldn't have any problem. A near death experience can bring the life back into you. Trust me. I've been there, and I've learned that if you want something, you'd better go after it. Nobody's going to give it to you. Life is what you make it."

Savannah panicked. She tried to duck down in the seat. "It's him!" she shouted. "Don't let him see me with you, or he'll come after us!"

Billy and I looked around and saw Webster, driving a white SUV, pull up to the stop light across from us at the Ruckersville intersection. He was heading west, probably going back to the house where he had stashed Savannah, and we were heading as far away from him as we could get. Savannah stayed crouched down as we turned right at the light.

"You can get up now," I said. "He doesn't know Billy's truck, so I doubt that he even saw you."

"Call Jonathan," Billy said. "Tell him that Webster is on his way. Oh, and call your mother and tell her we found Savannah. I don't want her to worry needlessly. I guess Claire hit the nail on the head when she said that we'd be calling to tell them we found the author." Billy chuckled.

"You two must be really good if your family thought you'd find me."

"We are." I smiled.

"We got lucky," Billy said. "But sometimes that's all you need."

"And we sure do get our fair share of luck."

As I opened up my cell phone, Savannah's stomach growled.

"Excuse me, but I haven't had anything to eat since breakfast."

I looked over at Billy and said, "I'm starving, too. Do you think we could stop at one of these fast food places and pick up a burger?"

"We could eat it on the way," Savannah added. "Of course, I don't have my purse with me, so you'll have to buy mine."

All three of us laughed.

"You were abducted and almost killed," Billy said to Savannah. "We're on our way to the hospital to get your head sewn up. You look rough. Yet, the two of you want to stop at Burger King."

"It doesn't have to be Burger King," Savannah said. "I'll eat anything right about now."

"I agree," I added. "Besides, aren't you hungry?"

"Fast food it is," he replied. "We'll stop at the next burger joint."

Savannah and I relaxed a bit as I made my calls. First, I called Jonathan and warned him about Eric Webster, and then, to be on the safe side, I placed a call to Sheriff Hudson.

"It's freaky to know that you have the sheriff's number on your speed dial," Savannah said to me.

"Well, we do have a lot of dealings with the sheriff in our line of work," I explained. "Sheriff Hudson isn't the only law enforcement officer who is one of our Fav-5."

"I bet not," she agreed. "I bet you two have a pretty exciting life together."

"You could say that." Billy looked at me and winked.

I pressed the number for Mom's house and she answered immediately. "Hello, Jesse. Do you have any news on Savannah?"

"I sure do," I replied. 'She's sitting right next to me in Billy's truck. We're headed to Burger King before we go to the hospital. She's hungry."

"Stop pulling my leg," Mom demanded. "That's not a bit funny, Missy."

"I'm not joking, Mom. She's hurt, but she's going to be fine. She has a bloody nose and a head wound, but the bleeding has stopped."

Mom screeched on the other end. I could hear her and my sister, Claire, rejoicing at the good news. Mom sounded as if she was crying when she said, "I'm so glad to hear that she's safe. Claire said she thought that the two of you were up to something. She said it was unusual for Billy to give up so easily. I told her that he probably had a lot on his mind with the funeral coming up tomorrow. I had no idea that… I thought… oh, never mind. I'm so glad things worked out well. Have they caught that guy?"

"Not yet, but it's only a matter of time."

"Where did you find her?"

"He had her tied up in Wayne Avery's house over in that new development off Octonia Road."

"Can you believe that she was so close and no one knew? I'm telling you, Jesse, you and Billy sure do make a good team."

"We sure do, Mom. He's my soul mate."

"I'm so glad you have him for a husband. He's such a wonderful man.

I just love him so much."

"Me, too!" Claire yelled in the background.

"Ditto!" Randy hollered. "I love him, too!"

I could hear the cries of joy in the background. It was, indeed, a monumental occasion. We would have much to celebrate — a life had been saved. Yet, lives had been lost, too. But I wasn't going to let the sadness set in just yet, if I could help it. I didn't say anything to Billy about this being a happy occasion. He had too much sadness to bear as it was, and as his loved one, I would help him get through the loss of his brother in the days to come. For now, all I could do was pray for this to come to an end. When Wayne Avery and Eric Webster were locked up, I would relax.

"I could hear your mom and sister in the background," Billy said as I punched in the number for our house.

"They're happy we found Savannah. According to Claire, she was sure we'd find Savannah."

"We got lucky."

"It doesn't matter. What matters is that she's safe from that killer," I replied as I waited for someone to pick up the phone on the other end. But no one did. I let the phone ring several times before I closed up my cell phone.

"What's the matter?" Billy asked.

"I just called the house and no one answered. Billy, I'm worried. What's going on over there?"

"I'm sure everything's all right. Try again."

I opened the phone and tried the number again. On the second ring, Helene answered the phone.

"Hello," she said.

"Helene, this is Jesse. How are the kids? I just called and you didn't answer. I was beginning to worry. Is everything okay?"

"We're fine," she replied.

Her voice sounded funny. I could tell there was something amiss. I felt that she wasn't alone and that whoever was there shouldn't be. Just in case, I thought I would play a little name game with her. She's a smart woman, I thought to myself. She'll pick up on it right away. "How are the dogs? Are they okay?"

"Oh, they're just fine, but your cat, Duke, gave me a fit until I put him outside."

"Okay, then," I said, my stomach churning. "Tell that darn cat to behave himself, and we'll be home in a couple of hours." I said good-bye and closed up the phone.

"What was that all about?" Billy asked with a concerned look on his face. "Who is Duke?"

"There is no Duke," I said, my hands trembling. "I knew something was wrong by the tone in her voice, so I played the name game."

"What's the name game?" Billy asked.

"I can't believe you don't know about the name game," Savannah said. "You being a P.I. and all. You see it happen all the time on television on some of those detective shows. It's a trick to see if someone's there that shouldn't be, or a way to cover up something."

Ah—she watches television—a woman I could appreciate! She understood right away what was going on.

"I told Helene that we'd be home in a couple of hours just in case someone was listening in. That should buy us some time to figure out what we're going to do before we get there." I looked at Savannah and said, "I'm sorry, but..."

"You don't have to say a word. I won't bleed to death, or starve. Do what you have to do. I can hang in there as long as I have to."

"Head home, Billy! There's trouble brewing!"

Billy put the pedal to the metal and sped down Rt. 29. By the time we got to Charlottesville, we had put a plan together. Whatever was wrong, I knew I could count on Billy to save the day—he always does.

CHAPTER 24

T HE CLOSER WE GOT TO HOME, the more concerned I became. I knew
something was going on, but I didn't know what. Not knowing was
the worst. As Billy drove along the dirt path on the backside of our property, Savannah and I had to hold onto each other to keep from bouncing
off the seat. The ride was rough. The path was filled with potholes.

"This sure is a rugged ride," I said. "Perhaps one day we should consider filling in some of these holes."

"No," Billy replied. "That's the whole point of having a back way to
our house. No one knows about it and if they do, they sure will have a hard
time negotiating the holes and the trees."

"O-o-h!" I said, closing my eyes and praying we wouldn't hit that big
tree we were heading into. When I opened them, we had passed the tree.
"That was close!" I looked at Savannah. "You can open your eyes now."

"I think I'll just keep them closed until we get to where we're going."
She snickered.

"I understand."

We made it to the end of the path. The back of our house came into
view. Nothing seemed out of the ordinary except the car parked behind it.

"Whose car is that, and why is it parked behind our house?"

"If I didn't know better, I'd think it was my housekeeper's vehicle," Savannah said, surprised. She sat up straight, unbuckling her seatbelt, and then pulling herself up closer to the dashboard. "She drives a car just like that one."

"Now that I think of it," I said. "I was wondering where your house-keeper was the whole time you were being snatched from your car... right in front of your house. Did she not see you out there? Didn't you toot your horn?"

"It all happened so quickly that I didn't have time to make it to the security beam or toot the horn. I was terrified. Having someone block you in and then jerk you out of your car is a little unsettling. I banged my nose on the car window."

"Ah, that's why you have a bloody nose."

"Stupid, huh?"

"Not considering what you've been through." I handed her my cell phone. "Here, call your housekeeper and see if she's at home."

Savannah punched in the numbers for her house and waited for some-one to answer. After several seconds, she closed up the phone and handed it back to me. "All I got was the answering machine."

"I guess that settles it," Billy said. "Why would your housekeeper be parked in our backyard? Tell me something about her." He turned and looked at Savannah.

"She's worked for me for about a year. Her husband died just before the time my car was stolen. She was alone, and I was frightened, so we teamed up. I can't believe that she's involved in this mess. She's always been so loyal. She takes care of my house and anything else I ask of her. She even screens my calls and picks up my mail."

"I'm wondering how she knows us," I said. "You only met my mother the other day. It's not as if you've been friends with her for a long time."

"I told my housekeeper about you guys," Savannah said. "When I got back home that night, I told Vera that I had run into a snowbank and that your mother and her friend rescued me. I told her all about Minnie and her family. Your mother can be an open book sometimes. Pardon the pun."

"She is friendly. Once she likes someone, she doesn't hold much back."

"Why didn't you call Vera for help when you ran off the road?"

"She refuses to own a cell phone. She was out Christmas shopping. She didn't get home until after I did. It's kind of funny," Savannah went on. "I was scared about what was going on with the murders, so Vera and I sat up late drinking hot chocolate and talking about it. I thought she was my friend."

The look on Savannah's face was so sad. She had put her trust and friendship in someone who had turned against her, someone who had obviously lied to her and who wasn't really her friend at all. I knew it must've hurt, so I tried to comfort her.

"Don't worry about her anymore. You have us for friends now. You don't need her kind, but you might have to hire a new housekeeper."

A smile came to her face. "Your mother was so right about you. You have a way of turning a situation around and making it not seem so bad. No wonder she adores you."

"I'm her daughter—she has to."

"Wait a minute," Billy said. "We don't know that she's part of this. She might be an innocent bystander. Suppose that she saw what happened, couldn't do anything about it, and then decided to come to us for help."

"Why didn't she just call the police?"

"She might have and we just don't know about it. I think we should give her a chance to explain."

"Billy, you always look on the bright side," I said. "I, for one, think we should storm the house, break down the door, and then hogtie her."

Billy looked at me as if I'd lost my mind. When he realized that I wasn't serious, he replied, "I really don't feel like repairing another door. Before I go in and put a bullet in her head, I'd like to hear her side of the story. She might have come here for help."

His statement about putting a bullet in her head really got our attention. We both gasped at his words. I looked at Savannah and said, "He's not serious... about the bullet." I looked at Billy. "Are you?"

"Change of plans," he said, ignoring my question. "Jesse, I want you to turn this truck around and go home as if nothing is wrong. I'll get out and slip in through the back door."

I looked at him with raised eyebrows, and said, "You want me to back up this truck? You can't be serious. Ha, ha. You made a joke, big buddy."

"Oh, that's right. I forgot that your ability to back up an automobile is as bad as your..."

"Don't go there, pal."

"What's he talking about?" Savannah asked. "Is there something I missed?"

"Let's just say that I'm backing-up-challenged as well as being cooking-challenged."

"To say the least." Billy snickered.

I gave him the evil-eye, a look that wasn't missed by Savannah. "Hmm," she remarked. "I've seen that look before. I can back up the truck and turn it around if you want me to... I think. This is a pretty big truck."

"Never mind," Billy said. "I'll do it. If I let you do it, Jesse will be mad at me for a week."

"That's not true." I grunted. "It'll be a lot longer than that."

In three swift maneuvers, Billy turned the truck around in the small pathway and had it heading in the opposite direction. He put the truck in park, and left it running while I got out and walked over to his side. He opened the door, got out and then hoisted me up into the driver's seat. He kissed me and then said, "You know I love you, 'ge ya. Be sure to put your gun in your coat pocket and be careful. I'll be your backup, so don't do anything rash. Okay?"

"My gun's in my pocket. You can count on me."

"I know I can," he said and then disappeared into the woods.

"I hope you know how to use that gun," Savannah said. "I've always been afraid of guns. I wouldn't allow one in my house, but you can bet that's going to change. After this is over, the next thing I'm going to do is buy one."

"That's a good idea. If you'd like, I could help you pick out one and then we could go up to Chief Sam's target range to practice."

"Would you really?"

"Sure," I said as I buckled my seatbelt and waited for her.

Once she was buckled in, the two of us bumped and tossed our way down the path, discussing Chief Sam's shooting range on the backside of his property and the gun she was going to purchase.

"I don't need anything fancy," she said.

"I say, go big—or go home."

"What do you mean?"

"If you're going to own a gun, you need one that takes as little effort as possible to use, because if you hesitate or miss, you could die. If there ever comes a time when you have to shoot someone, make your shot count. Always keep in mind that you never point a gun at someone unless you intend to shoot. Pretending could get you killed, and so could a small caliber gun. A 9MM or a .38 will do the job just fine." I quickly glanced at her. "For you, I would suggest a revolver, something simple."

"You sure do know your guns."

"No, not really. All I know is that I want one on me in case I ever need it. Other than target practice, I've only shot at someone once." I thought for a minute. "Maybe twice. I can't remember."

"Have you ever killed anyone?" She stopped, and then said, "I'm sorry. That's none of my business."

"It's okay," I replied as I continued to drive down the small path. "A while back, Billy and I were working on a case. The couple we were in-vestigating broke into my house with the intention of killing anyone who was there at the time. Thank goodness, my dog, Athena, surprised the man and woman, giving me the opportunity to get off a shot."

"And you killed one of them?" she surmised.

"No, actually, I killed both of them."

"With just one shot? How did you do that?"

"The bullet hit the man at an angle in the side of his neck, severing an artery, then passed through and hit his wife square in the forehead. It was a lucky shot."

"I'd say! Wow! That's one for the books."

I chuckled and asked, "Am I going to read about something like this in your next book?"

"You might," she replied. "It's a good kill. I'm always looking for a way to bump off a character." She laughed and then asked, "Have you read any of my books? I noticed that you had one stuffed in your purse. I'm flattered."

"That's my mom's book. I started reading it, but I haven't gotten far. I liked what I read, and when I get a chance, I plan to finish it. I have to give it back to my mother. You signed it for her, and she really liked that."

"Your mother is a very nice person."

"Thank you. I love her."

I pulled out onto the main highway and headed back toward our house. The truck handled beautifully. I was a little leery of driving such a big truck considering there were still patches of ice on the road, but it was smooth going all the way... until I turned onto Bear Mountain Road. The truck fishtailed, shattering my confidence. I tried to do as Billy had told me many times. I turned into the skid and regained control. I slowed to a stop and just sat there, my hands trembling.

"Whew! That was freaky. I thought for a minute you were going to lose it."

"I did, too." I held out my hands so she could see them. "I'm still trembling."

"Take your time and get it together. It's hard to drive after almost losing it. Just take a deep breath."

I did as she suggested, and it helped. I let off the brake and we continued our journey. I turned off Bear Mountain Road onto our driveway and made the trek to our house.

"The sign said that Bear Mountain Road is a private road."

"It is. It's the road leading into the Blackhawk compound."

"You call this a compound?"

"It's just a name. That's what the Blackhawks call it, but actually, it's just another word for family. Most of Billy's family lives here, except his two sisters. They live in the city. It's too rural for them out here. Why?"

"It's just that every time I hear the word compound, I think of Waco."

"That's creepy. I don't think of it like that. I see a loving family who guards their privacy."

"That's nice."

I parked the truck and turned off the ignition. I removed the keys and stuck them in my coat pocket opposite the one holding my gun. Without even asking, Savannah reached down, grabbed my purse and handed it to me. She was shivering.

"Next time you leave the house you might want to wear a heavier coat. The winters here can be rather harsh. Luckily, the basement in that house was heated, or you would've frozen to death before you ever died from blood loss."

"You say the nicest things, Missy," she responded, nervously.

"Oh, no. You're been around my mother too long. You're starting to talk like her. Next thing I know, you'll be picking up her bad habits."

"I doubt very seriously that your mother has any bad habits."

I looked Savannah in the eyes and said, "We've stalled long enough. Are we ready?"

"I guess it's now, or never."

"Let's just play it cool," I said as I climbed out of the truck. "Keep your fingers crossed that everything is going to go smoothly. I'd hate to shoot someone this late in the day."

The two of us giggled, huddled together, and then made our way up the steps to the front porch. I turned the doorknob, but it was locked. I tapped on the door lightly as if nothing was wrong, and waited for someone to answer.

The door opened and we were greeted by Helene and Geneva.

"I'm so glad you're back," Helene said. "We have company." She turned and looked at a woman who was standing in the kitchen holding a cup of coffee in one hand and a gun in the other. From the looks of her puffy eyes, we could tell she had been crying for a long time.

"Are you all right?" Savannah asked her as she approached the upset woman. "Vera, where did you get that gun?"

She laid the gun on the counter along with the cup of coffee. "I'm so sorry," she said, looking at Geneva and Helene and then back to Savannah and me. "I know I must have scared them half to death coming here in such a state, but as I explained to them, I wasn't trying to intimidate them. I was trying to protect us all. I didn't know what else to do after I drove past the house and saw all those cops. I knew something bad had happened. I told you that man was no good. I tried to warn you. He was after your money all along. I tried to tell you, but you were so…"

"Everything is okay, Vera," Savannah said as she walked up to the woman, gave her a hug and tried to soothe her. "You were frightened. I'm sure you didn't do anything to these ladies, did you?"

Helene stepped forward and said, "We weren't afraid of her until she showed us the gun. That scared the life out of me, but just for a second. You see, I didn't really think she was a threat. I'm pretty good at sizing up people. I knew she was scared and from what she had told us, and she had good reason to be. She brought the gun with her for protection from that killer. Besides, I had everything under control."

Helene walked over to the cabinet above the sink and opened the door on the left. She pulled out a 9MM handgun just like mine. "Billy left this for me… just in case. He hid it in the cabinet behind the coffee container, and explained that even criminals can be soothed by the offer of a cup of coffee if they're waiting for someone. And if that didn't work, I could always use this one. Helene pulled up her long skirt, unbuttoned a pocket in her pantaloons and pulled out a Derringer. She showed it to everyone and then replaced it, buttoning the pocket to keep it from falling out.

"Why did you let me think something was wrong?" I asked, locking the door behind me and not bothering to take off my coat. "I was worried sick."

"I'm sorry, Jesse, but I couldn't take any chances." She looked over at Vera. "I don't know this woman from Adam, as the saying goes. Sorry, Vera. And I wasn't about to be flippant about the situation. Always suspect the unexpected. Isn't that what Billy says?"

"Okay," I said loudly. "You can come out now."

Billy stepped out from behind the stairs with his gun drawn. Everyone froze at the sight of him, even me. I'm his wife, and I'm the one he loves. I know he's not going to shoot me. But after seeing the spooky look in his eyes, I decided not to move. Who knows? He could've gone off the deep end. He's been under a lot of stress since his brother died. I almost killed a teenager today in cold blood and hot temper — murder is what the police call it. When you cross that line — whether it is only in your mind, or in your actions — there's no turning back. At this stage, I have come to realize that I, too, could become a killer. Now isn't that a pretty thought? What have I turned into?

Billy, kind as he is, wasn't taking any chances or taking anything for granted. He walked over to Vera, picked up her gun from the counter and handed it to me. He lowered his gun, pulled up his pant leg and then holstered it.

"I can see that everyone is all right and I'm not going to have to shoot anyone at the moment, so you ladies can relax. I'm going to take care of everything."

"I have never seen so many guns in one place," Savannah said. "Am I the only one who isn't armed?"

All of us let out a sigh of relief, including me. I was a little concerned there for a minute... not for my safety, but for the safety of our uninvited visitor. As I said, Billy is on the edge. I've never seen him quite this emotionally intense. It's as if he has a bomb ticking inside of him that could explode any minute and take everyone with him. I know this because I feel the same way.

He looked over at Savannah and said, "We're going to see to it that you get to the hospital soon. Jesse will take you while I stay here and hold down the fort. I think Vera should also go with you. I think we can round up enough guns so that all three of you will have one. Helene and Geneva can fix dinner, and watch the kids while I bring out the cannons."

We all looked at Billy as if he'd lost his mind, and then I asked, "What's the matter with you? Are you taking drugs?"

He chuckled and said, "I was just trying to lighten the mood."

The ladies remained quiet.

I looked at them and said, "He doesn't normally act insane like this. I think he needs more vitamin C in his diet."

Everyone laughed, and the room's temperature went up a few degrees. I wondered if our new acquaintances thought this could possibly be a nut house.

"I guess I'm not very good at making jokes," Billy said, and then changed the subject. "We should get a move on it. I think our first priority should be to get Savannah to the hospital." All of a sudden, Billy had a coughing spasm.

"Are you all right?" I asked, concerned.

When he finished coughing, he responded, "I will be. I guess my lungs haven't cleared up just yet. Don't worry about me, `ge ya. I'm okay."

I pretended to be okay with his coughing fit, but I was worried. Yet, I tried not to show it. "I'm going to go see my children before I do anything." I looked over at Helene. "Where are they? It's late in the day for them to be down for a nap before bedtime. And where are the dogs and that silly cat?"

Helene had a guilty look on her face. "I guess we played too hard. The kids are asleep. They've been fed and bathed, and the dogs are in the nursery with them, asleep on the floor. The cat is in the house somewhere."

"I thought you said you put Duke outside," Vera stated.

"I lied," Helene replied. "And his name isn't Duke. It's Spice Cat. Although..." She looked at me. "I kind of like the name Duke."

"I need an aspirin and a shot of whiskey," I whined. "After I go see my babies."

"May I come with you?" Savannah asked.

"Sure," I said. "You can all come if you'd like."

They all did.

The children lay in their beds, content and oblivious to the outside world. Athena raised her head to look at me for a brief moment, but Thor only rolled over on his back, and never bothered to open his eyes.

"This is a lazy crew," Billy announced.

"I say let sleeping babies lie," Helene remarked.

"I thought that was supposed to be sleeping dogs," Geneva corrected.

A thunderous bang on the front door startled all of us. The kids woke up immediately and started wailing. Thor jumped up and took off for the door, nearly knocking down everyone in his path. Athena limped behind him. I grabbed up Ethan, Helene snatched up Maisy, and all the ladies huddled to together waiting for Billy to do something.

He pulled the gun out of its ankle holster and said, "Don't anybody leave this room until I say so."

The pounding continued until Billy got to the door and yelled, "I'm coming! Give me a minute!"

Taking orders has always been my downfall. I wasn't good at it when I was a child and I haven't gotten any better with age. I passed my screaming child to the closest lady next to me without even looking to see who she was, and grabbed my gun from my coat pocket. I snuck out of the nursery and edged my way out to the staircase. I stood there, hiding behind the stairs, waiting to see what was going to happen. I was determined to provide backup for my husband, or die trying.

Billy snapped his fingers at the dogs, and both of them turned and ran back behind the staircase. They crouched down beside me. He then motioned for me to get back as he grabbed the doorknob and opened the door, stepping back behind it as the door swung open.

A stranger stood in the doorway with his gun raised. "Time to die!" the man yelled. He scanned the room, stunned that there was no one there to confront.

Athena and Thor starting barking like two crazy dogs, and then took off for the front door again. I tried to stop them, but it was no use.

The commotion of the dogs must've startled the man, because he fired off one shot that hit the floor, fortunately missing both dogs. Their barking continued as they ran around in circles, distracting the intruder. At the time, the only thing I could think of was why didn't they attack him?

Billy stepped out from behind the door, stuck his gun up to the back of the man's head, and said, "Drop the gun and put your hands up in the air, or die right here on my living room floor."

Suddenly, Billy's coughing spasm returned, giving the man time to raise his gun in one swift motion up under his arm. Without hesitation, he fired his weapon. From the shocked look on Billy's face, I could tell that he had been hit. He stumbled backward, still pointing his gun at the man.

Thor backed up, snarled, and then attacked, sinking his teeth into the man's leg, while Athena viciously chomped down on the other. The man screamed out in pain, and tried to shake them loose.

I had an instant rush of adrenalin and all sane thoughts left me. I ran out from behind the staircase and fired my gun repeatedly with each step, until I had emptied the magazine. I couldn't seem to stop. I had no fear. My gun clicked several times before I realized that it was empty. Oddly enough, even with all the shots I fired, only three bullets hit their mark: one in the arm, one in the shoulder, and the third one in his thigh. The man fell to the floor in agony. I reached down and snatched up his gun and looked at it. When I realized that it was my .38, I kicked him in the stomach as hard as I could. I was really angry.

"How dare you try to use my own gun on one of us? Are you crazy, or just a bloodthirsty killer? You dirt bag!"

I called off the dogs. "Athena! Thor! That's enough! Back off!"

The two of them released their grip, stepped back, and stood there with their teeth bared, ready to attack again at my command. "Good work!" I praised them.

I knew I had startled the intruder when I came barreling out from behind the staircase like a banshee, but I was petrified and my emotions had taken over. My stomach was in knots and my ears were still ringing as I rushed over to Billy.

He had one arm held against his chest as blood dripped from the fingertips of his other arm. I had to see how badly he had been hurt, so I gently moved his arm and pulled back his jacket, all the while praying that the bullet hadn't hit him in the chest. I knew that a .38 square to the chest was a death sentence. I should've known better because he was still standing, but, at the time, I was in a state of shock and my mind wasn't being rational. When I saw that he had been hit in the upper arm I was so relieved, even though it was a nasty wound. I cried as I tried to get the words out.

"I'm sorry it took me so long. I was scared. I didn't know what to do." I turned my head and yelled down the hallway, "Helene! Geneva! Someone call 9-1-1!"

CHAPTER 25

T HE DOOR WAS STILL OPEN, CAUSING the temperature in the room to drop drastically. I grabbed a chair for Billy so he could sit down, and then went over to close the door. I had to shove the man out of the way to do so. He cried out in pain.

"Oh, did that hurt?" I asked him in a most patronizing tone. "Too bad. You're lucky you're not dead. If I were a better shot, you would be."

"You're crazy!" He coughed, and whimpered in pain. "I need a doctor," he moaned before curling up into the fetal position. Blood ran from his wounds and soaked the floor. His boots caught my attention. I didn't see the word *Leatherneck* on the side. He wasn't the one who attacked me!

Athena and Thor stood guard over the man while we waited for the ambulance to arrive.

I offered him no aide. I had to attend to my husband.

Savannah, with her housekeeper by her side, had made the call for help explaining that we had three people with injuries and that we might need more than one ambulance. She proceeded to describe the extent of the injuries, while Helene and Geneva made sure that the children were taken to another part of the house, out of sight of the bloody mess in the living room. That was something they didn't need to see.

I ran to the laundry room to grab a clean towel and then to the bedroom for one of Billy's belts. When I returned, I wrapped the towel around Billy's arm, coat and all, and then secured it with the belt. I pulled the belt tight, hoping to staunch the flow of blood. He looked pale, but I knew he was going to be all right.

Before the ambulances had a chance to arrive, three vehicles pulled up into the yard—Jonathan's Humvee, Robert's pickup, and the chief's new Dodge truck. Jonathan didn't even bother to knock; instead he opened the door with his gun drawn, followed by Robert and his gun. Both men almost fell onto the man lying in the floor. Chief Sam and Sarah were right behind them. The chief was carrying a shotgun.

"What happened here?" Jonathan demanded as he looked around at the carnage.

"Don't mind the man lying on the floor," I said. "Come in and close the door. I see everybody came prepared." I looked at their weapons. "That's just one of the many things I love about this family."

Sarah, after seeing Billy sitting in a chair with a blood-soaked rag wrapped around his arm, ran up to him and started to cry. She stooped down to his level and managed to get out, "We heard the shots all the way up at the house. Are you all right, son? You don't look so good." She looked at me.

"Billy's lost a bit of blood, so he's weak, but he's going to be okay. That scumbag on the floor shot him."

Jonathan walked over and hugged me, as did Robert, and then the chief.

"This looks bad," Jonathan said. He looked at Billy. "What you got going on there, brother?"

"Just a flesh wound," Billy replied, and then had another coughing attack.

I looked up at Jonathan and said, "He started coughing again."

"He never stopped," he replied. "He just never did it in front of you if he could help it. I told him I was going to tell you if he didn't go to the doctor."

"Then why didn't you tell me?"

"I..."

"Savannah!" the man called out in a raspy voice.

All of us turned our attention to the man lying on the floor.

"We should help him," Sarah announced. She looked at her two sons standing close to her.

Jonathan and Robert obeyed her without question. They both walked over and bent down to check the man out.

"Get away from me!" the intruder screamed. "I don't need your help!"

Jonathan looked at Robert and nodded his head. Robert walked over to me and asked if we had any rags. After telling him to look on the shelf in the laundry room, he left and then returned with a stack of clean, white rags. He and Jonathan proceeded to apply the cloths to the man's injuries and tried to stop the bleeding. The man cried out in pain several times. All we could do was stand by and watch. To be honest, I would've let him lie there and die after what he did to Billy if it hadn't been for their intervention. Maybe after I was sure that Billy was taken care of, I might've gone over and tried to help him—I do have some compassion—but I can't say for sure. I guess I will never know what I would've done next, because I put it out of my mind.

"Savannah," he called out to her.

Savannah slowly walked over, bent down and whispered, "I'm so sorry for my part in all of this."

"It's not your fault," he murmured. "I love you."

"Don't say that!" she insisted. "I told you I was married. What happened with us was a mistake. It should've never happened."

"That's it. You don't care about me. I know your kind. Get away from me."

Hurt by his words, she stood up and walked over to the kitchen. Her housekeeper walked over, put her arms around her friend, and said, "I told you he was nothing but trouble. What happened here was not your fault. He's a loser... and a killer."

"I'm not a killer!" Eric Webster screamed out. "I've never killed anyone in my life. All I did... was love her."

"You kidnapped me, you psycho!" she yelled. "Look what you did to me. Look at my face. You see this?" She pointed to the bloody T-shirt that was still wrapped around her head. "I'll probably have an awful scar the rest of my life. You almost killed me. I told you to leave me alone, and then you came after me. You forced me into your truck, and then you crashed it. I was hurt, but you didn't care."

"I never meant to hurt you." His voice sounded weak.

"You tied me to a chair and left me. Is that what you do to someone you love? I don't think so. Don't you get it?" she asked him. "I made a mistake in a moment of weakness. I told you so, but you wouldn't let it go. You hounded me like someone stalking its prey."

"I never meant..." his voice trailed off... and then he was silent.

Jonathan walked over and pressed his fingers to Eric's neck, turned back to us and said, "He's still alive, but barely."

In the background we could hear the endless sound of sirens. A minute later, Captain Waverly and several of his officers were on the scene. Two EMTs followed them into the room, and then after assessing the situation, motioned to others outside. Within minutes, Billy, Savannah, and Eric Webster were strapped down onto gurneys and then put in separate ambulances with the most critical in the lead.

Billy had refused to let his parents go to the hospital. He told them that his injury was nothing more than a mosquito bite, and that he'd call them as soon as he got back home. He asked Robert to make sure they got home safely, which was just his way of soliciting his brother's help.

Sarah relented even though she didn't like it, but after the chief told her she needed to listen to her son, she got in the car with him and left.

Captain Waverly stayed to take a statement from Helene and Geneva since they were at the scene of the crime, and he assured us that he would be in touch with us later for ours. I took that to mean that he would be at the hospital before we had a chance to get in and get out.

I was tired, hungry, and dirty. I desperately needed some rest, but nothing was going to stop me from being with my husband.

Helene and Geneva talked it over and offered not only to clean up the blood on the floor, but said they would also patch up the bullet holes with duct tape. Of course, that was after they got the kids settled down, and had let the dogs out for the night. I accepted their generosity, and told them that they made a good team. They seemed to like that.

Vera rode in the ambulance with her friend to the hospital, and after quickly kissing the kids, I jumped in and rode with Billy. Eric Webster had only the company of two EMTs for his journey.

As usual, the hospital was busy. Orders were being barked, hospital records were being passed around, and people filled the seats in the emergency room waiting area.

Billy, Savannah, and Eric were rushed through a set of doors that Vera and I weren't allowed to pass through. I started to go off on one of my tangents, but decided against it. I told myself that I'd give them a few minutes and if nobody came out to tell us anything, I'd find a way to get in. Vera and I found a couple of chairs by the window and went over to sit down.

About fifteen minutes later, Jonathan and Robert walked into the emergency waiting room.

I jumped up and went to them. Vera followed.

"I'm so glad you're here," I said. "This waiting is agony. They must be really busy, because they won't let me go back there to see Billy."

"Have the cops shown up?" Robert asked.

"No, not yet. Why?"

"I figured they'd be here by now. You know how they are."

"Yes, I do."

"I'm going to nose around," Robert said. "Why don't you stay here with them?"

"I'll be glad to," Jonathan agreed. "You ladies don't mind, do you?"

"You know better," I said and then hooked my arm in his.

He waited for Vera to do the same, and then the three of us went back to the window and sat down.

Ten minutes later, Robert returned with a tidbit of news. He sat down in a chair facing us and said, "Eric Webster was rushed into emergency surgery. They expect him to live. Two Charlottesville Police officers have been stationed in the hallway leading to the operating rooms to make sure he doesn't escape—not that he is physically able to."

"What else did you find out?"

"That's it… for now. If you're not in need of medical attention, they won't let you go back there. It seems there was a six car pile up on Interstate 64, and they need all the room they can get. They're still bringing in the injured."

"You didn't…"

All of us jumped up when Dr. Bryant came out of the double doors and walked over to us.

He told us that after a quick examination, Billy was to be cleaned up, stitched up, and would be released soon. The shot had been a through-and-through, and it wasn't expected to amount to much except a lot of pain. The doctor assured us that Billy would be fine. He'd clean up the wound, take a couple of x-rays, and then if nothing was found, he'd stitch him up, give him a prescription for antibiotics, and then turn him loose. Dr. Bryant knew he couldn't keep Billy for long. He'd had many dealings with him before and he knew there was to be a funeral tomorrow.

"Don't you worry," he said to me. "I'll have him fixed up in no time. He'll be as good as new in an hour… maybe two. We're really busy tonight. I'm sorry that you can't be with him, but we need to keep everyone out. We still have people coming in from the pileup on the interstate."

"Just fix him up, Doc. That's all I ask."

Dr. Bryant turned to walk away, but I called to him before he had a chance to leave. "How's our friend, Savannah Kelley? She had a nasty gash on her forehead from a… car accident." I looked at Vera who remained silent.

"She's doing well. She's being stitched up right now. She should be out soon." Dr. Bryant smiled. "You know the drill. You might as well have a seat."

"Thanks a lot, Doc. Where else would we go?"

The good doctor turned and walked down the hallway.

We waited for an hour before Jonathan finally said he'd had enough. "I'm going to find my brother. This is ridiculous."

"Look around, Jonathan," Robert said. "This place is packed. People are lined up against the wall. Many of them are just like us. They're waiting to hear about their loved ones, too. I'm sure the doctors are doing the best they can do. Let's give them a few more minutes."

After waiting another twenty minutes, I said, "That's it. I'm going to see what's taking so long. Something bad has happened. I just know it." I stood up and looked around as if trying to decide where to go.

Jonathan stood up and said, "You stay here, Jesse. I'll go find out what's going on with Billy."

"No, I'm going with you."

Just then, Savannah appeared. Her head was bandaged, and she was carrying some paperwork.

"I've been sprung," she joked. "And I'm ready for a large slice of pizza. I'm so hungry, I could..." She looked at each one of our faces. "What is it? What's the matter?"

"We haven't heard anything about Billy," I said, tears finding their way down my cheeks. "Jonathan and I are going to look for him. I have to know that he's all right."

"Well, then I'm not leaving," Savannah said. "I can't leave unless I know he's going to be okay. You two saved my life. I owe you..."

"You don't owe us a thing," I said. "But if you want to wait, have a seat."

"I heard that Eric is going to be all right," Savannah said as she joined us. "I talked to him for a second while they had us waiting in the hallway. He says that Wayne Avery killed those people and when you found them together, he was trying to talk some sense into him. He took the .38 from him. That's why he had your gun. When he banged on your door, he was scared. All he wanted was to find me. He wasn't going to hurt anyone, but it didn't turn out that way. I think I kind of believe him."

"I'm sure he'd say..."

"I think I might believe him, too, to some degree," I said. "He wasn't wearing *Leatherneck* boots."

Jonathan looked at me, and said, "You might be right. Evidence says it all. But the bit about him coming to your house wielding a gun is unacceptable. Shooting my brother is unforgivable."

"I agree. Now let's go find my husband."

"Follow me."

Jonathan and I took off down the hallway.

"Where should we go?" I asked. "You know we're not going to get far, so we'd better make every move count."

"Hey, I know this woman," Jonathan said, looking at a tall, dark-haired woman who had just walked out of the double doors. "She was back there. She might be able to help us out." He walked up to her, and said, "Hi, Holly. How have you been?"

"Jonathan," she greeted him with a surprised look on her face. She was pushing a wheelchair carrying an elderly woman. "It's been a while."

"Yes, it has. You look good."

"You do, too." She looked over at me and smiled. "I'm Holly Dante."

"I'm Jesse Blackhawk," I replied.

She looked back at Jonathan and said, "I didn't know you got married." Before Jonathan had a chance to tell the woman that I wasn't his wife, she introduced the woman in the wheelchair. "This is my mother, Roberta. I think you remember her. What are you doing here? Oh... that's right. I'm so sorry about your brother."

"Thank you," Jonathan said. "It's been hard on the family. Daniel was a good man."

She seemed genuinely shocked. "I didn't know about Daniel. Oh, my! I wasn't talking about Daniel. I was talking about Billy."

Jonathan's eyes grew wide as he turned and looked at me. He turned back to the woman and asked, "What about Billy?"

"I heard them talking about him. They said they couldn't stop the bleeding, and then his heart stopped. They couldn't revive him. I'm so sorry. I really have to go." She looked at us sadly and appeared quite uncomfortable. "I'm so sorry." She quickly excused herself and hurried away.

Jonathan and I just stood there and stared at each other. I couldn't catch my breath. I felt as if someone had their hands around my neck and was choking the life out of me. Tears filled Jonathan's eyes as he stepped back and leaned up against the wall.

"I can't tell my mother that she's lost another one of her sons. I just can't do it. Oh, Lord. Daniel is going to be buried tomorrow. This is going to kill her."

"No, Jonathan! Billy is fine. He can't be dead!"

"No, Jesse. He's not fine. You heard what she said."

The world around me ceased to exist and life came to a screeching halt. I felt as if I were going to die right there in the hallway. This can't be happening, I told myself. I don't believe it.

"No!" I screamed. "No! He can't be dead!" I collapsed to the floor, crying. "Don't leave me, Billy! Please don't leave me. I'll die without you!"

Jonathan bent down, grabbed me by the arm, and tried to help me stand. "Come on, Jesse. You need to sit down. Let's go back to the waiting room, and then I'm going to find Billy even if I have to knock a few heads together to do it."

"No! I want to see my husband! I don't believe her. She's lying! I know she is! My God, Jonathan! He came in with a simple through-and-through wound. What did they do to him? I want to talk to the doctor."

"Come on, Jesse."

"Let me go!" I looked at him and screamed, "She's lying, Jonathan! Billy is not dead! It's a joke! A sick, twisted joke! I'm going to find my husband!"

"No, Jesse," Jonathan said as his tears streamed down the sides of his face. "She wouldn't lie to me. We've been friends for a long time."

As much as I wanted to believe that Billy wasn't dead, my gut told me differently. My Billy had died and left me alone. I would never get over this. I wanted to die with him. If he was going to leave, I want to go, too. I couldn't live this life without him. I just couldn't.

"What's all the commotion?" Robert asked as he approached. "I could hear her screaming all the way down the..." Robert stopped. He looked at Jonathan and then looked at me. "Oh, no... say it isn't so."

When I looked up and saw the tears flowing down Robert's face, I cried harder.

"I'm going to be sick!" I mumbled.

Jonathan held onto me as he led me to a bathroom down the hall. I went in and closed the door, locking it behind me. I sat down on the floor and cried. I cried for so long, I felt as if my insides were coming apart. What was I going to do with myself? I couldn't go on without him. Billy was my world.

Jonathan tapped on the bathroom door and said, "Are you all right, Jesse?"

I stood up, looked at myself in the mirror, and quietly said, "No, I'm not all right. I'll never be all right again." I opened the door and stepped out into the hallway.

Savannah, Vera, Jonathan, and Robert were standing there waiting for me. All of them had tears in their eyes. It was one of the saddest moments in my entire life.

"Please tell me this is a bad dream and that I'm going to wake up and find out it isn't real. I'll wake up and see Billy standing in front of me with that charming smile of his. He'll ask me if I had a bad dream and I'll tell him that it was a whopper, but things are all right now."

The look on their faces said it all. My Billy was gone.

Savannah hugged me and cried right along with me. The rest of them joined in, bringing back the sad memories of when we had found out that Daniel had died.

A lot can happen in four days, I told myself as I wept.

When I looked up and saw Mom's face at the end of the hallway, I fell apart. She rushed up to me and held me as we both cried.

"Billy died, Mama."

"I know, honey."

CHAPTER 26

Jonathan and Robert helped me back to the waiting room. I was inconsolable and Mom wasn't in much better shape. Our tears wouldn't stop.

"Just sit down for a minute," Jonathan said to me. "I'm going to find the doctor." He seemed as if he was in a daze, too. He stormed down the hall.

I held onto Mom's hand as I sat down in the chair by the window. I couldn't speak. I wanted to curl up in a ball and die.

"I got a call from Helene," Mom said, her tears sliding down her cheeks. "She told me about what happened at the house. She figured that I'd want to know, and she knew you'd be too busy to call. She said you were like Rambo." Mom laughed and cried at the same time. "She said you went running out from behind the stairs and fired your gun until it was empty."

"A lot of good it did."

"I didn't know about Billy until just now."

I looked into her sad eyes.

"When I got here, I saw Savannah, and then I heard you screaming. They all jumped up and went after you, but I couldn't follow them. I've heard my baby cry many times, but never like this. I knew Billy was gone.

I just had that feeling. Nobody had to tell me anything."

I looked outside and thought about the times Billy and I had shared.

"I'll never forget the first time I met him," I reminisced. "He seemed so nice during the job interview, but then as I was leaving, the first thing that came to mind was that I hoped he wasn't a psycho. Isn't that funny? Can you picture Billy as a psycho? That was a joke. He was so kind... and charming. And then when he took me on my first stakeout, I was so excited. I knew it could be dangerous, but I didn't care. I was hooked. I loved being with him. I never would've thought that the two of us would get together, but when we did, I knew he was the one for me. And now... now... he's gone. Oh, Mom." I cried as she wrapped her arms around me and held me close.

"I just can't believe he's gone," Mom said. "Maybe it's a mistake. Did the doctor say what happened in there? Helene said that Billy's wound wasn't bad. She joked and said that he's had worse injuries before. She told me about the time some guy shot him in the gut. Now that was bad, she said. She told me not to worry, but I had to come find out for myself."

I closed my eyes and held onto Mom. The pain was so deep; I knew that my life would never be the same. I would be lost without Billy. I sat and cried in that chair for what seemed like an eternity. Then my heart skipped a beat when I heard the voices in the hallway coming our way. I tried to stop crying and sit up straight when Dr. Bryant and Jonathan approached us. I didn't want to hear what the doctor had to say. All I wanted was to have my husband back, but I knew I had to listen to him tell me how my beloved husband had died and how sorry he was for my loss. I'd heard that one many times being told to someone else. Now, I was going to be the one getting the bad news.

Then I looked up and saw Billy!

I jumped up from the chair, ran up to him, and threw my arms around his broad shoulders.

"Oh, God, Billy. They said you were dead."

Mom followed. She hugged Billy... and continued to cry.

"Easy ladies," he said. "The old arm is a little tender."

His coat was folded over one arm and the other arm was in a sling.

Billy looked around the room and saw all the tears flowing and then looked back at me.

"Jonathan said Holly told him that I had died. He forgets that he left this woman at the altar. No wonder she lied. The opportunity to hurt him presented itself, and she took it." Billy glanced over at Jonathan. "I'm sure she's never forgiven you for jilting her. What woman would? And what better way to get back at you?"

"I did not leave her at the altar."

"You might as well have. You broke up with her two days before the wedding."

"How did she know we were waiting for you?" I asked. "When she came through those doors and saw Jonathan, the first thing she said was how sorry she was that you had died. And she was quite descriptive about how you died."

"She saw me. She even said hello," Billy said. "We talked for a brief moment while I waited for the doctor to return."

I looked at Jonathan and said, "I'll kill her! No, better yet, I'll make her wish she was dead!"

"Don't bother, `ge ya," Billy said. "She has enough problems. She has much pain. Her father had a heart attack and died a month ago, and her mother has cancer. Leave her be. I'm alive… and I'm fine. I'm starving, but otherwise, I'm okay."

"Is that true, Dr. Bryant? Is Billy going to be all right?"

"He's as healthy as a horse," Dr. Bryant said. He handed me a sheet of paper, one similar to the many others I've seen over a period of time. "You know what this is, but I'm going to tell you anyway." He went on to explain about Billy's wound. The fact that the bullet was a through-and-through and hadn't hit any bone was a good thing. "He'll be in considerable pain for a while, but I've written a prescription to manage that, and he'll need to be on antibiotics. If he starts running a fever, or…"

"I know the drill, Dr. Bryant," I said. "I'll check the wound for redness or signs of infection when we change the dressing and if he starts running a fever, I'll make sure he comes back to the hospital. I'm just so glad my husband is alive!" I jumped up and down until my head felt as if it was going to explode. "I think I need to sit down."

"I'll hold you up, `ge ya," Billy said as he grabbed me by the waist with the arm holding his coat.

"Just don't ever let me go!" I demanded as I kissed him about the face several times. "I'm so glad you're okay!"

Dr. Bryant smiled and said he had to get back to work. "I have children in college, so I have to go earn a living. You folks take it easy, and by all means, stay safe." He turned and walked away.

All of us gathered together and were about ready to leave when we saw Holly pass by. She smiled and waved as she pushed the wheelchair holding her mother through a set of double doors.

"I could hate her if I didn't know she had so much on her plate," I said. "The heck with her. You're alive and that's all that matters." I hugged him again.

"Let's get something to eat. I'm starving," Billy said. "Somebody call the house and tell Helene to throw something on the table. We're coming home."

"I hope that invitation applies to us as well," Savannah said. "We need a ride back to Vera's car."

"I'm going to head home," Robert said as he gave Billy a hug. "I have a lot to do before tomorrow. I'm glad you're all right, brother."

"I am, too," Billy replied. "Are you sure you don't want to follow us home and get something to eat?"

"No, I'm good," Robert said. "I'm going to stop by the restaurant to make sure everything's running smoothly. I might get something while I'm there. I'll see you tomorrow."

"Now that I know Billy's all right, I'm going to head back home, too," Mom said. She looked at me. "Unless you want me to go home with you."

"No, I'll be okay, Mom. Claire and Randy are waiting for you. You go on home. Just call me as soon as you get there. Okay? I'll worry the whole time. Or… maybe you should…"

"I'll be okay," Mom said. "Eddie's been waiting in the cafeteria. He didn't want me to come by myself, so he rode with me."

"Why didn't you …"

"Because this was very personal, and I wanted my time with my baby."
She hugged me, tears rolling down her cheeks. "Look at me. I'm such a
mess. Eddie will…"

"He'll love you, Mama. It takes a good man to sit in a hospital cafeteria waiting for his woman, not knowing how long he'll have to sit there.
But he did it for you. I'd say you got yourself a fine catch. Daddy would be
happy for you. I know I am."

"Stop!" Savannah said. "I just can't cry anymore."

Mom sniffled and said, "He is a pretty decent feller, isn't he?"

"Yes, he is," I answered. I looked over at Robert and asked, "Would
you mind walking my mother to the cafeteria? I don't want her to be alone."

"It would be my honor," Robert said. He held out his hand to her, and
the two of them headed down the hallway.

Mom glanced back one last time and blew a kiss our way.

"Let's hit the road, folks," Billy said. "I've had enough of this hospital to last a lifetime."

All of us turned and headed for the hospital exit. The day was coming
to an end and so was the pain I had suffered through a little while ago. I
had my husband back, and that's all that mattered. My anger toward a
woman who had tried to bring pain to my family was also gone. We walked
out into the cold night air.

"Whew!" Savannah said. "It sure is cold out here."

I looked up at the sky and watched as a snowflake fell on my face.
Another flake fell… and then another. I held out my hand as if I were
trying to catch the falling flakes. I smiled as I said, "I love the snow. I love
the way it falls to the ground and then accumulates, covering everything
in sight."

The ride home seemed short. I clung to Billy the whole way. We pulled
up into the driveway and then got out of the Humvee.

"You don't have to hold onto me," he said as we walked up to the
porch. "I'm not going anywhere."

"I'm not taking any chances," I replied. "I'm not letting you out of my
sight for the next ten years. Never. Nada. No way!"

"That ought to be fun," Billy joked, giving me the eye.

We laughed… and it felt so good.

Helene greeted us as we all filed inside, one by one. Athena and Thor stood quietly by her side. She closed the door and remarked about the weather. "They're calling for six inches of snow by the morning. It's going to be a long day tomorrow."

"It's already been a long day," Billy said.

I took off my coat and hung it on the coat rack, and then took Billy's coat from around his shoulders.

"I guess I'll need to wash this one along with the one in the laundry room."

"I guess so," Billy said, and smiled a faint smile as if to say everything was really going to be all right.

I kissed him on the cheek and then looked down at the dogs. "What's the matter with them?" I asked Helene. "They didn't even bark."

"I've trained them to be quiet when the children are asleep. They barked when you arrived, but now they're silent. I explained to them that there was no need for such a fuss when one bark would do."

"Hmm," I uttered. "That's scary. I've never seen them so quiet. I think I like it!"

As soon as I said that, Athena and Thor starting barking and ran up to me. They jumped around until I reached down and rubbed their heads. They both immediately calmed down, walked over by the fireplace, and laid down.

"Well, that didn't last long," Billy joked. "Where's the cat?"

"Last time I saw him he was asleep on Minnie's bed. I know she's going to like that."

Everyone took off their coats and huddled by the fireplace. Billy and I joined them. We needed instant relief from the cold outside—and we needed the closeness of each other.

"So, the kids are asleep, huh?" I said. "I bet they're wondering what their mommy looks like. I haven't seen them in hours."

"They're children," Helene said. "They don't forget their mommy."

"You know just the right thing to say," I said. "Billy was right about you. You're a terrific person."

"That's me," she chuckled. "I made a pot of stew. We had all that food, so I tossed most of it in a pot. Anyone hungry?"

"You bet," Billy answered.

"I'm starving," I agreed. "I haven't been able to eat much. If I keep this up, I'll blow away." I looked at Jonathan, Savannah, and Vera. "How 'bout it, guys? Anyone want a nice, hot bowl of stew?"

Jonathan made a remark about my thin frame, but pretended he didn't say anything when I called him on it.

"Some women would die to look like me," I said, teasing him.

"Some actually do," Savannah said. "A character in one of my books literally starved herself to death. I was trying to make a statement about eating disorders."

"Do you always do that in your books? I mean, make some kind of statement?"

"Of course, I do. I think all authors find a way to plug something or inject their opinions on a subject they're writing about."

"I'd like to talk more about your books, but first, I have to go see my little ones."

"I'm coming with you," Billy said. "I don't want them to forget me, either." He chuckled.

Everyone gathered at the table while Billy and I went to the children's nursery. After a quick look, we headed straight to the kitchen table. We sat down and joined the others.

"Oh, I forgot to tell you," Helene said as she served up the bowls of soup. "Savannah, your husband called. He said he'd get here as fast as he could."

"How did he know where to find me?"

"Minnie called him and told him what happened, and then she gave him every number she could think of just in case he couldn't reach you. She even gave him the number of the Greene County Sheriff's Office."

As soon as the words were out of her mouth, the phone rang.

I jumped up to answer it and was surprised to see Sheriff Hudson's number on Caller ID. "Hello, Sheriff Hudson. What can I do for you?"

"I just thought you'd like to know that we got a full confession out of

Wayne Avery. It seems that he was the one who did it all. He set fire to Jonathan's house. He killed those two people in Ruckersville and then set their house on fire to cover up the murders. He also killed the psychiatrist in Syria."

"Do you believe him? He's told so many lies."

"Oh, I believe him. You had to be there, Jesse. That kid's got mental problems."

"Sheriff, sometimes kids are just born bad. That's what my mother says. She seems to think that it's in their genes."

"You have a pretty smart mother. Regrettably, I think this kid turned bad not because of a gene, but because of the events in his life. As a young child, he was sexually abused by his grandfather's friend."

"How sad."

"When the grandfather found out that his friend had abused his grandson, the man disappeared and has never been found. The man's wife filed a police report claiming that the grandfather had something to do with her husband's disappearance, but nothing was ever proved. That was over twelve years ago, and when the grandfather died, the case died with him."

"Are you serious?" I gasped.

"Oh, it just keeps getting better and better. I think that the only thing that kept Avery semi-sane was his father, and when his stepmother confessed to having an affair, it triggered something in him. He confessed to forcing pills down her throat—the same pills that killed her. In essence, her confession started a chain of events that led to arson and murder."

"That's terrible."

"Did you know about the stepmother?" Sheriff Hudson asked, sheepishly.

"I just found out."

"Wayne said the night the police were called to his house—the same night that his stepmother's lover beat her, and she then pointed the finger at his father—the deputy pulled out of the driveway and ran over his dog. That deputy was Ronnie Crumpler, the same deputy whose sister was married to the guy who had the affair with Avery's stepmother. So, as you can see, Wayne Avery had a lot of people he wanted to make pay. But he didn't know how until his uncle let him read Savannah Kelley's book. That's where he got the idea to rid himself of those who had caused him pain."

"Wow! This story sounds like something out of a soap opera."

"Listen to this," Sheriff Hudson continued. "Avery was furious that the deputy didn't even apologize for killing his dog. Deputy Ronnie Crumpler was the next one on his list, after the psychiatrist."

"I bet Deputy Crumpler is glad that Wayne Avery is in custody."

"The weird thing is that Deputy Crumpler didn't run over Avery's dog. Avery didn't have a dog."

"Why would he say that if it wasn't true?"

"He laughed and said that he made it up. He planned to kill my deputy because Deputy Crumpler was the one who arrested his father. See what I mean? The kid's not right in the head. Look, I know you're busy, so I won't keep you. We can talk about this at another time."

"What about Eric Webster?"

"That's still to be determined. Wayne Avery incriminated Webster at first, and then he recanted, laying claim to all the murders. But we're still going to arrest Webster for the abduction of Savannah Kelley, and I'm sure there will be other charges related to the shooting of Billy."

"Thanks for calling, sheriff. I'm glad the killer has been caught."

"He's going to be locked up for a long time," the sheriff added. "Oh, tell Billy that I'm glad he's all right. I heard about the incident at the hospital. I'm surprised you didn't attack Holly Dante."

"Believe me, I gave it some serious consideration. Hey, how do you know all this stuff? Isn't there anything we can do that you won't find out about?"

"Like you told me recently, we're friends. I keep track of my friends."

"I'm glad you do. It's nice to have someone looking out for us."

"Just don't cross the line, or I'll throw your butt in jail just like I would anyone else."

"I know you would."

"My thoughts are with you and your family. I know it's going to be a tough day tomorrow."

"Thanks, sheriff." I said good-bye, hung up the phone, and then went back to the table.

"That was a long conversation," Billy said. "So, Wayne Avery confessed to everything."

"Yes, and it's a good thing he got caught when he did. His next victim was going to be one of Sheriff Hudson's deputies. But that's another story."

"A story you can bet that I won't write about," Savannah said.

"According to what Avery told the sheriff, you already did. You told his story, only in real life it turned out a little differently."

"I just can't believe someone would use my book as a guideline for killing people."

"The similarities are rather eerie," Billy said. "The only difference is that the villain got caught before he managed to carry out the other murders."

"Have you read my book?"

"No, I haven't, but I think I might after Jesse finishes it. I'm just going by what I've been told. Your book sounds like something I'd be interested in, now that I've actually lived part of it."

"I don't mean to butt in," Helene said, looking at me. "But did Captain Waverly talk to you at the hospital?"

"No, he didn't," I said. "I didn't see him there."

"He said he was going to the hospital to follow up on what happened here."

"I talked to him," Billy said. "He agreed with me that the killer has been caught, and there will be various charges against Eric Webster."

"Life is good," I said, and then my thoughts turned to Daniel. "Except when it's bad."

"Where is Geneva?" Billy asked. "I thought she'd still be here."

"She got a call from Sarah and then left. I got so busy looking after the kids and making the stew that I forgot to call her."

I'm sure everything is fine, but maybe we should give your mother a call," I said to Billy.

"I called her on my cell phone from the hospital. I wanted her to know that I was all right. I didn't want her to worry."

"They let you use your phone in the hospital?"

"They didn't have much choice. I told them that if they didn't let me call my mother, I'd sue them. I think that scares them more than anything. Just threaten to sue. You can get anything you want. Well... almost. Besides, the lady who examined me had the hots for me. I could see it in her eyes."

"You liar! Billy the Liar!" Jonathan said, making fun of what Billy had said to me earlier.

A cell phone played musical notes. Everyone looked around the table at each other.

"It's your cell phone," Vera said to Savannah. "I don't know how it got in my purse. I guess I'm going to have to break down and buy one for myself. Although, I really hate these things." She reached into her purse, pulled out the phone and looked at the display. "It's your husband." She handed the phone to her.

Savannah flipped the phone open and said, "Hello, McCoy."

She got up from the table and walked out of the room. When she returned, she handed the phone back to Vera and said, "He's at the airport. I guess we should go get him."

"He's not going anywhere," Vera replied. "Let's eat first."

"That's a good idea," Savannah said. "I've waited for him long enough. It wouldn't hurt for him to wait for me for a change."

"I love it when women take charge and stand up for themselves," I said.

"I don't know how in charge I'm going to be when this incident hits the papers. McCoy's going to find out about my relationship with Eric Webster. My marriage will be over."

"I hate to say this, but I think your marriage was in trouble the minute your husband refused to relocate here with you," I said to Savannah, and then turned to Helene and said, "This stew is delicious."

"I agree," Savannah replied. "On both."

We finished our stew, and then went about putting our lives back on track. Now that the Greene County killer had been arrested, he would no longer be a threat to anyone.

Savannah and Vera left to go pick up McCoy at the airport with a promise to let me know how things turned out.

Mom called to say they had made it home safely, and she was so glad that Billy hadn't died. She said that Claire and Randy were on pins and needles until she called them from the car.

Helene, Jonathan, Billy, and I decorated the Christmas tree and then had a late night glass or two of eggnog. I didn't care for the egg, but I sure liked the nog.

Athena tried to eat an ornament, while Thor tried to eat the ornament boxes.

Spice Cat lay under the tree the whole time.

Later, we all sat back and admired our handiwork as we discussed the last four days.

"Now that you're not dead, Billy, I think we should take a vacation. How about a cruise?"

"Oh, Lord," he replied. "Bullets and boats—I'm not so sure I like that idea."

"You will, heap big warrior," I said. "Trust me."

EPILOGUE

S ATURDAY MORNING WE AWOKE TO A LANDSCAPE of white. As predicted, six inches of snow had fallen and covered the leftover dirty snow from the previous snowfall. It was a beautiful sight. Daniel would have approved of this day. He, too, loved the snow. He once told me that everything seemed tranquil when it snowed. The world was at peace. This would be a perfect day to lay him to rest. His final journey would be that of a pristine, white landscape leading to a site he loved, attended by all who loved him. The cemetery on the hill overlooked the entire family property. Daniel would be there to watch over us. This gave me comfort as I dressed for the funeral of a beloved family member… and friend.

When I asked Billy about the road up to the cemetery, he said that the minute the snow had stopped, the chief had a crew come in to plow the road. It must have been awfully early, because I never heard a sound.

The service was held at Chief Sam and Sarah's home. They balked at the idea of having their son laid out at a funeral home. There was no visitation the night before like there usually would be. This was a Cherokee funeral and things were done differently. At first, there was only going to be a graveside service, but Sarah decided she wanted everyone to have a chance to say their good-byes in the comfort of the Blackhawk home. The open casket was set in the large living room with Chief Sam paying homage to his departed son, and anyone who wished to speak was invited to do so. There wasn't a dry eye in the house when Billy got up and spoke. I stood beside him and held his hand as he told of stories that made us laugh and then of times that made us cry. Some of his words were spoken in Cherokee, but that didn't matter. We all understood.

I looked across the room at the friends and family members who attended. Folks were scattered everywhere, some sitting while others stood side by side, shoulder to shoulder.

I smiled when I saw Frank Trainum and his fiancé, Alexandra, Isabel, Abby and Pete Morgan, Cole, Sheriff Hudson, Deputy Ronnie Crumpler—according to the name on his uniform—and two other Greene County deputies, Captain Waverly and two of his men, Savannah and McCoy, Vera, Daisy and Gabe Clark, Lu Ann Knots, and the many other friends and family members—some of whom I didn't know their names.

The drive to the cemetery was sad. I held onto Billy's hand the whole way… and cried.

"Don't cry, `ge ya," Billy said. "Daniel will always be with us."

After a brief prayer at the grave site, we gathered together to console each other and talk about Daniel. Mom never left my side. Her strength and the love of my husband kept me going. I like to think that I gave the same strength to Billy. Before we were to depart, snow started to fall.

"My son would approve," Chief Sam said to the crowd. "As a child, I couldn't keep him inside when it snowed. Now we will celebrate his life. Please join his mother and me back at the house for a feast prepared by Robert's restaurant." The chief looked at Robert and said, "Thank you, son. Your brother would be honored."

"It is my pleasure to be able to do this last thing for my brother," he replied, a tear in his eye. "I will miss him every day of my life."

Greg came up to me, hugged me, and told me that his father adored me. He said that this family needed a rebel like me. I laughed and said, "Thanks. I think."

He rejoined his mother, but not before he had a chance to tell me about his girlfriend. He was in love. I smiled at him as he walked away.

I shivered as I crawled back into the car. The trek back to Sarah and the chief's home was an emotional ride… as if the end of an era had come. I told Billy about my feelings and he agreed.

"When you lose a loved one, you are changed forever. You must accept it and move on."

"I'll do my best." I continued to cry.

He laughed at me and said, "You have a kind heart."

"I'm such a crybaby, but I can't help it."

"Your feelings run deep. That is why you cry."

"Promise you will never die on me."

"I'll do my best."

I looked down and said, "This is the first funeral I've been to that I had to wear snow boots."

Billy only smiled.

As everyone gathered together for a toast, Chief Sam thanked his family and friends for their devotion to his son. "Let the celebration begin," he said as he raised his glass. "This is for you, Daniel."

The festivities continued for most of the afternoon. People gathered to talk about Daniel or whatever was on their mind. Finally, I asked Sheriff Hudson about Eric Webster.

"He's going to make it," the sheriff said. "Unfortunately, he's going to spend a lot of his life behind bars. Wayne Avery might not be so lucky."

"I told him he was going to get the death penalty."

"You might be right. You always seem to be one step ahead of me."

"Not so. I would've used the old death penalty threat on anyone if I wanted to get a confession."

"You surprise me, Jesse. Here's one for you. Your mother wants me to perform the wedding ceremony for her and Eddie at her house. She asked me about it a little while ago."

"What?" I gasped. I looked over at Mom and then back to the sheriff. "She never said a word to me."

"I know. Gee, it's so nice to know more than you."

"Not so, pal," I smiled. "Here's one for you. Vera has a crush on you."

"That's just not true!" He looked over at Vera.

She smiled back at him.

"She's a very nice person. She'd make you a good wife."

"She's got ten years on me."

"What does that matter when true love is involved? Look at me and Billy. He's got more than ten years on me, and we're great together. Besides, you need a woman in your life. Your job can't be that rewarding."

"I know, but she's old enough to be my mother. Don't you know anyone close to my own age?"

"I'll keep my eyes open for you."

"Never mind. I don't think I want your help." He smiled and walked away.

"What did you do to him?" Savannah asked. "He looked as if he was afraid you were going to shoot him." She chuckled. "Jesse, I want you to meet my husband, McCoy." She looked at him and said, "This is Jesse, the one I told you about."

"It's nice to meet you," he said as he held out his hand. "Savannah speaks highly of you."

"That's because she doesn't know me well." I winked at her.

"You saved her life and for that I would like to extend my heartfelt thanks."

"Savannah is a wonderful person. You're lucky to have such a loving wife. If you want to keep her, I suggest that you move your butt here."

He laughed and said, "She said you were up-front, and she was right. I wish someone had been that frank with me a while back."

"Some wives have a tendency to be non-confrontational. I'm not one of them. I would've told you to be with me, or get out of my life. Either you love your wife or you don't. Which is it?"

"But you don't understand. I have a law practice back home."

"And you don't think we have enough criminals for you to sustain a practice here. Boy, have I got news for you. No, I think you're afraid your wife's success will overshadow yours."

"Wow! That was hard."

"But true," Savannah agreed with me. "I've felt that all along, but could never bring myself to say it."

I smiled and stepped closer to McCoy. "I know you must think I'm terrible, but the truth is, there is no excuse to be separated from your wife unless you no longer want to be in the marriage. She deserves better."

"You're absolutely right," he said. "I love my wife. There's no reason for us to be apart."

"Now that I've overstepped my bounds, I have other fish to fry. It's been nice meeting you, McCoy, and I hope you will move here."

"Thanks, Jesse," Savannah whispered as I walked away.

I went in search of my mother. At first, I thought I was imagining it, but now I was certain that my mother was avoiding me. I was also beginning to wonder if she had sent Sheriff Hudson over to break the news of her impending nuptials. I was about to find out. I saw Mom standing over by the buffet table talking to Billy. When I approached her, she looked up and stepped closer to my husband.

"He can't help you, woman!" I said.

"Behave yourself, `ge ya," Billy said, defending my mother. "She was going to tell you, but never found the right time." He looked at Mom and said, "I guess now would be the right time."

"Yes, I guess you're right, Billy. There's no time like the present."

"I'm so happy for you, Mom," I said, hugging her. "Dad would approve. Eddie's a nice man. If you love him, that's all that counts."

"Does that mean that you don't?"

"I don't what?"

"Love him?"

"I hardly know him, but if I did know him better, I'm sure I would."

"You would what?" Claire asked as she walked up with Randy by her side.

"Love Eddie."

"He is a wonderful man, isn't he?" Sarah asked as she peeked out from behind Claire. "Isn't it wonderful news?"

"What news," Chief Sam asked.

"The news about Eddie and Minnie," Daisy Clark added.

"Yes," Gabe stated. "We were so glad to hear about the baby."

"What baby?" Mom asked.

"Claire and Randy's."

All of us turned to look at my sister.

"What else is going on that I don't know about?" I demanded.

"Alexandra and I got married last week at the Justice of the Peace," Detective Frank Trainum stepped forward and said. "We'll be moving here in a couple of weeks. She got a job at UVA Hospital, and I'm taking a job with the Charlottesville Police Department. I'll be working for Captain Waverly."

My mouth dropped open. "That's it!" I said, holding up my hand. "Stop! I can't handle any more news!"

"Then I guess you don't want to know about..."

Everyone turned to look at Jonathan.

"Your news is old news to me, but I'm sure everyone here would like the details." I smiled.

"I'm going to marry Lu Ann."

Chief Sam looked over at his wife. I saw a concerned look on his face and I didn't think it was about the soon-to-be wedding. No, he had something else on his mind. I was determined to find out.

Sarah was thrilled at the news that her son was going to get married. "Grandchildren!" she said. "I want lots of grandchildren!"

I quietly walked over to the chief and whispered in his ear, "What's the matter, Chief Sam?"

"I worry about Sarah. She has not been feeling well, but she won't go to a doctor. I do not have the medicine to fix her."

"I'll take her to the doctor."

The chief looked at me and smiled. "I believe you will. If anyone can get her to go, it will be you."

"Excuse me, Chief Sam, but I have someone I need to talk to."

He kissed me on the cheek and said, "You are a good woman. My son made the right choice."

"Who said that he was the one who made the choice?" I winked at the chief and walked off.

I walked over to Captain Waverly and asked, "How is Officer Whalen? I've been very concerned about him."

"He's doing very well. He should be back on active duty soon."

"Please give him my best."

"I will," the captain responded. "I talked with him this morning, and he asked about you. He wanted to know if you were still alive. He told me to tell you that." The captain smiled.

"I bet you guys get a good laugh at my expense, don't you?"

"It's just that you're so predictable, Mrs. Blackhawk."

"Oh, I think you can call me, Jesse, Captain Waverly. If you're going to make fun of me, we might as well be on a first name basis."

"Okay," he said. "And you can call me, Captain."

"I usually do," I said, walking away.

I chuckled to myself as I walked back over to the buffet table to be with my husband.

"I see you've made the rounds and you haven't been locked up, yet."

"The day is still young," I replied. "Anything can happen. About that vacation. I really do need one."

"I didn't think you were serious."

"That's what you hoped. Nope. We're going to take a vacation... and soon... and we're not taking the children."

"Taking the children where?" Helene asked, walking up. "I think I'd better head back to the house. I don't like the idea of our children being watched by a babysitter."

"The kids will be fine," I insisted. "Joshlyn is quiet capable. She's the daughter of one of Daisy Clark's friends. You stay right here with us."

Helene leaned over and whispered in my ear, "But isn't she the one who was in that club, the one with all those snobby women who got killed off?"

I had to laugh out loud.

"You kill me, Helene!"

"I sure hope not!" she exclaimed.

Someone caught my attention out of the corner of my eye. An elderly man was standing off to the side by himself holding a soda in his hand. Our eyes locked. I excused myself and walked over to him.

"Hello. I'm Jesse Watson Blackhawk. You must be Mr. Crumpler. I saw you standing by your son at the service and it has just now dawned on me who you are. I'm glad you came. We've all been touched by this tragedy in one way or another."

"You are an insightful woman, Mrs. Blackhawk."

I chuckled and said, "You can call me, Jesse."

"I owe you a debt of gratitude—you and your husband. I understand you're the ones who caught that criminal who killed my daughter. Thank you so very, very much."

"Actually, Jonathan was the one who found out where the guy was. He's a bounty hunter, you know."

"You don't give yourself enough credit, Jesse."

"I give myself plenty of credit, Mr. Crumpler, when I deserve it. I'm just glad the guy was caught before he had a chance to kill anyone else."

"Sheriff Hudson said he was going after my son next."

"I'm afraid so."

"Be sure to drop by my market sometime. I have fresh vegetables and good beef... and I'd like to meet your children."

"I've stopped at your market a few times."

"I remember. There's not much I miss these days."

"I bet there isn't."

Mom walked up and said, "I see that you've met my daughter, Mr. Crumpler. She's a handful. I can tell you that."

"Did my mother tell you that she's getting married soon?"

"No, she didn't. Congratulations."

"She didn't tell me, either."

He smiled and said, "I think I'll go get something to eat. It sounds as if you two have a lot to talk about." He shook my hand, tipped his head at my mother, and then walked away.

"You ran the poor guy off," Mom fussed. "He's such a nice man. It's a shame about his daughter. If that happened to one of my kids, I'd go crazy."

"Who's going crazy?" Sarah asked.

"I am," I replied.

The celebration wound down to a close, and Billy and I headed home after saying our good-byes. I was worn out. From the look on Billy's face, I could tell that he was, too.

Daisy and Gabe Clark followed us home to pick up Joshlyn.

We thanked her for babysitting, and Billy gave her a very generous tip along with her pay.

"Anytime you need me, Mrs. Blackhawk, all you have to do is call. I have my own car, but since Mr. and Mrs. Clark were coming, they gave me a ride. I'm available at a moment's notice."

"I'm glad to hear that, because everything we do is at a moment's notice."

They waved as the three of them left. Helene passed them on their way out.

"I hope that we won't need her services for a while," she said as she closed the door behind her.

Billy and I looked at each other and smiled.

"If I didn't know better, Helene, I'd think you were jealous."

"I am new here."

"But you're family. No one's going to take your place."

"I knew that. I was just..."

I hugged her and said, "Let's go have a look at the children. We want to make sure that she didn't slap them around, or anything."

Helene gasped.

"Don't listen to her, Helene. She's pulling your leg."

"That Mr. Crumpler was right about you."

"Oh, yeah? What did he say about me?"

"He said that I needed to keep an eye on you. And then he told me that he's surprised you're not in jail. It seems that the sheriff in Greene County has some strong words to say about you."

"Sheriff Hudson loves me," I said. "He has right from the start."

"Liar Jesse!" Billy grunted. "Heaven help us all!"

"I need a nap!" Helene sighed.

We all managed to get through Daniel's funeral. It was a day we will never forget, and hope not to have to go through again for a very long time.

Two days after the service, I called Sarah and insisted that she go shopping with me. She was hesitant at first, but I told her that I wouldn't take no for an answer. When I picked her up, all she talked about was the upcoming holiday. She was so excited until she mentioned that she would miss seeing Daniel's smiling face sitting across from her at Christmas dinner. I told her that we all would.

"Let's not talk about that today," I said as I pulled into the doctor's parking lot. "I have to make a quick stop first."

"Oh, Jesse! Are you pregnant again?"

"No, I'm not. This visit isn't for me, Sarah."

She glared at me.

"Don't go getting all huffy on me. I told the chief that I would get you to a doctor, and I keep my promises. When's the last time you saw Dr. Joe?"

"It's been a while. I've been busy."

"Well, you're not busy today." I smiled at her. "I promise he won't hurt you. If he does, I'll shoot him."

Sarah laughed at my silliness, and opened the car door. "If we're going to do this, let's do it now before I change my mind. Come on."

Sarah's doctor was certain from her symptoms that she had diabetes, but to confirm his suspicions, he did a blood workup. She wasn't happy about that, but she agreed to the tests. Dr. Joe gave her a diet plan and said that if that didn't work, she would most likely have to go on insulin.

"I've never had to take medication before, and I'm not taking any now," she ranted as we left the doctor's office. "He's crazy if he thinks…"

"God, you sound just like my mother. Face it, Sarah. As you get older, your body changes. Just do what he says, or I'll tell Billy."

"You would not!"

"Don't test me on this one, Sarah."

"Okay, you win. I'll make a deal with you. I'll watch my diet and if that doesn't work, I'll take the insulin… if… you promise to have a house full of kids."

"I see that my mother's been talking to you."

We both laughed all the way to the mall. We shopped until we were about ready to drop, and then we had a late lunch at Robert's restaurant, The Rising Sun. All things considered, we had a nice time.

Sarah called me the next day and said that her tests had confirmed that she had diabetes. She thanked me for forcing her to go for a check-up. I told her that I would go with her anytime she wanted me to. She seemed relieved.

Billy and I managed to survive our first-year wedding anniversary on Christmas Eve. We are now so familiar with each other and know what the other one thinks, one might think we'd been married for thirty years.

We celebrated by spending our time at home with Helene, our children, the dogs, and the cat. Neither one of us wanted to go out and be away from them on Christmas Eve.

As an anniversary present, Billy presented me with a beautiful diamond bracelet. He said he knew that I didn't care much for fancy jewelry, but he fell in love with the bracelet the minute he saw it.

I handed him a card, and as he was opening it, I said, "This bracelet will look lovely on my wrist when we dine at the Captain's table on our cruise to Alaska."

The airline tickets fell out from the card.

He held them up and said, "My thoughts exactly!"

To be continued…

ACKNOWLEDGEMENTS

T O MY READERS: Thank you for spending your time with my books. I enjoy bringing a smile to your face and, hopefully, a tear to your eye.

A special thanks to Kelley Cleaton—Graphic Artist, and Elaine Barnett—Photographer.

Thank you so much Billie Kerfoot, Norman Slezak, and Cora Chlebnikow for your help in proof/editing this book.

Thanks, Mom. You're always in my heart.

This book is dedicated to my dear aunt, *Elsie Joyner*, and her daughter, my red-headed, feisty cousin, *Joyce Hayes*. I love you both.

"Life is too short to be in a bad mood."
---Ann Mullen

LOOK FOR ANN MULLEN'S NEXT BOOK:
Death on the Bella Constance

VISIT THE WEB:
www.aftonridge.com

SEE WHAT'S HAPPENING IN JESSE'S
NECK OF THE WOODS.
VISIT:
www.vgreene.com

EMAIL THE AUTHOR:
amullen@aftonridge.com
aftonridge@aol.com

AFTON RIDGE PUBLISHING
434-985-1957